VAMPYRRHIC

SIMON CLARK

LEISURE BOOKS NEW YORK CITY

For Janet, Alex and Helen, and who could forget Sam?
And a special "Thank you" to Chris Reed for his patient advice,
indefatigable support for new writers—and for publishing
my first book!

A LEISURE BOOK®

July 2002

Published by

Dorchester Publishing Co., Inc.
276 Fifth Avenue
New York, NY 10001

ISBN 0-8439-5031-5

Visit us on the web at www.dorchesterpub.com.

VAMPYRRHIC

It Begins in Darkness

1. The Hotel Room. Midnight.

She was twenty-three years old; fair-haired, dark-eyed.

She couldn't sleep, even though she'd been in bed for more than an hour.

The reason for this sleeplessness?

She was frightened. So frightened it felt as if her heart had become frozen into a great ball of blue ice. It chilled her blood from head to toe.

The conviction that someone was pacing the hotel corridor outside her door had lodged itself deep within her brain. Pacing up and down, up and down. She heard nothing, that was true, but she sensed it. If she closed her eyes she could feel, as if they were her own, those silently pacing feet, pressing down against the dull red carpet beyond her hotel room door. The feet, in her imagination, were always bare.

She pulled the sheet up as far as her nose and closed her eyes.

But the feet continued to pace silently outside her door. Bare toes sank into what remained of the pile of the thirty-year-old hotel carpet.

I could open the door and see who's there.

The same thought always occurred to her.

But to open the door she would have to drag aside the heavy chest of drawers that barricaded it.

Also, lately, she had begun to imagine who it might be on the other side of the door, pacing relentlessly hour after hour, night after night. Her imagination always wickedly conjured up pictures of a fat man with blood-red holes in his face where the eyes should have been.

The first lord of mischief is Imagination. It was always eager to slip into her mind's eye those images that are calculated so accurately to frighten.

1

Bernice, before you switch off the light, look under the bed for the lurking psychopath—and is that a severed hand in the bottom of the wardrobe? And don't forget the hungry rat lurking in the S-bend of the lavatory as you sit on the toilet seat. Can you imagine the pain of such a bite?

She looked at the door again, the massive chest of drawers that she lugged across the floor each night jammed tight against it. Now barricading the door was as much part and parcel of the bedtime ritual as brushing her teeth, kicking off her slippers and—

Yes, yes, admit it, Bernice: checking under the bed for that wild-eyed psychopath, who'd slither out the moment you were asleep.

Needless to say there was never anything under the bed— only clots of fluff and (the first time she'd nervously peeked there) a balled pair of grey socks left by some long-departed hotel guest. These she'd poked out with a coathanger and carried at arm's length to a bin on the landing as if they were radioactive or something.

And now her imagination, with exquisitely sadistic glee, was telling her that someone paced the landing.

—someone without eyes, Bernice; someone with only holes, big, blood-red holes, where the eyes should be; and he's got a big, fat, bloated body, and big, fat fingers; and he grins as he snaps on latex gloves stained with the body fluids of sweet young—

With an irritated sigh she sat up and switched on the bedside light. No, Bernice, she told herself firmly, there is no one pacing up and down outside the door. It is your imagination. Your stinking, lousy, rotten imagination.

But deep down she knew if she opened the door that would be that. The same fate waited for her as awaited the man in the video.

2. Video Diary. Half-past Midnight.

She thought: Alcoholics must do exactly the same thing. They see the bottle of vodka. They know they shouldn't reach out for it, unscrew the cap, drink. But they can't stop themselves. The bottle has this power over them. It can make them do anything. The suitcase in the bottom of her wardrobe exerted the same kind of influence. She meant to throw it out—let it take the same one-way trip as the dust-infested socks to the municipal dump!—but she couldn't.

It was as if that tan imitation leather suitcase called her name; told her to flick open the silvered clasps, lift the lid, gaze in wonderment at the contents—clean clothes in bags, reporter's notebooks held together by a rubber band, a pair of white trainers, the soles messed with a black tarry substance. Then the camcorder. And the videos. Those bloody, stupid, awful videos. She should burn them, she really should.

But like the alcoholic's bottle of Smirnoff, lying there snugly amid bags of frozen peas and sausages in the freezer or wherever the lush had hidden it, those videos—those bloody, stupid, awful, *terrifying* videos called her name. In her mind's eye she could imagine—just as she could imagine the bloated alive/dead man, eyeless and monstrous, pacing beyond her door—she could imagine the camcorder video cassettes. There was one she always found herself watching (it chooses me, I don't choose it, she'd tell herself with a fatalistic sigh). It bore the handwritten label VIDEO DIARY—ROUGH EDIT.

Watching it was the last thing she wanted to do.

For a full minute she stared at the wardrobe, picturing the tan suitcase, the videos inside, cushioned by the carrier bags stuffed with clean clothes . . . *it chooses me, I don't choose it . . .*

Then with the defeated sigh of an alcoholic who'd promised there'd never be another bender—never, ever, *EVER!*—she went to the wardrobe.

Bernice, this is the last time. Do you hear?

Shivering, scared, yet strangely eager, she got ready to watch the damned thing.

3. The Dead Box. Seven Days Ago.

All hotels—great and small—have a Dead Box. OK, so they give it different names: Lost Property Office, Deadman's Dump, Junk Room, Dross Hole, Abandoned Belongings Store, Shit Pit, and many more epithets.

3

Anyway, in the Station Hotel it was referred to as the Dead Box by the hotel's proprietress. She said it easily, with the kind of smile that hinted the name Dead Box had a hidden meaning; something more than a little salacious. Bernice had smiled, too, unsure whether Dead Box was supposed to be some deliciously funny double entendre.

How she had come to find herself mooching through the contents of the Station Hotel's Dead Box she hadn't a clue. It might have been that on her day off from the Farm she was at a loose end, that it was raining, that she was bored with the town's single shopping street, that . . . oh, what the heck. She'd found herself in the room under the stairs and that was that.

Looking back now, she could believe forces beyond her understanding had guided her into that room with the sloping ceiling that followed the forty-five-degree angle of the stairs, illuminated by a single light bulb hanging by its flex from the ceiling.

For various reasons hotel guests sometimes leave without checking out. The obvious one is that they don't want to—or can't—pay their bill. To avoid arousing the hotel receptionist's suspicions, they saunter out without suitcases as if just going for a stroll round town. They don't return. The suitcases—usually themselves worthless, containing clothes certainly worthless—are packed away into the Dead Box. The Station Hotel's abandoned suitcases dated back more than a hundred years, and contained a range of clothes that Bernice found astonishing.

Some caused a lump in her throat. A tin trunk contained a Victorian bride-to-be's trousseau, consisting of crisp cotton underwear, and a still neatly folded nightdress for the honeymoon that never was. This stimulated Bernice's imagination. Had lovers eloped? But why had they never married? Perhaps the groom had got cold feet the day before the wedding and left his fiancée at the hotel with the unpaid bills and the precious trousseau bought with what little money the girl had been able to salt away from her work as a parlour maid.

Some of the older suitcases were grimly fascinating. A hundred years ago, those hell-bent on suicide would book into hotels where they'd carry out the deed. It was a common enough practice. A man wants to die, but he doesn't want his wife or children to experience the shock of finding his body. So he takes

4

a room in a hotel. He stuffs towels where the door meets the floor and walls to seal the flow of fresh air as best as he can. Then he turns up the gas lanterns without lighting them; he lies down on the bed, fingers knitted together across his chest, where he listens to the whisper of coal gas flooding the room, then his lungs. In the Dead Box Bernice had held up a note written in ornate copperplate . . . *I end this life gladly. There is no one else to blame but me.*

There is no one else to blame but me.

Victorian suicides were courteous and thoughtful even on the eve of their deaths. They went to the trouble of making sure that no one blamed themselves for their suicide. Invariably they ended the note the same way: *There is no one else to blame but me.*

Bernice wondered why the next of kin hadn't collected the suicide's belongings. Not that there was anything of real value. And who would really want a dead man's socks and underpants, after all?

She looked at the firm, decisive signature in black pencil: William R. Morrow. I wonder which room you died in, Mr. Morrow?

She tried to stop the little voice in her head that rushed to supply the answer. Supply it eagerly and with pictures—Mr. Morrow choking his eyes out on the coal gas.

So: in which room did you die, Mr. Morrow?

Mine. The little voice had said. *He died in my room, number 406. Choked his dead eyes out.* Shut up, she'd told it; you're only trying to frighten me. Besides, no one really chokes their eyes out. Savvy?

Later, Bernice had felt compelled to ask the question: "How many people have killed themselves in the hotel?"

The proprietress gave her usual mischievous grin. "Not telling. You'll only sprag to the other guests and frighten them away. Now, if you find any treasures buried in there, you'll share them with me, won't you?"

Then Bernice struck gold. She found the suitcase containing the camcorder and the videos. The pang she felt in her stomach was a mixture of surprise, delight, curiosity—but, underpinning it all, dismay.

The sense of dismay intensified.

5

Now, in her hotel room at half-past midnight, she knew why she was dismayed.

"Because I knew you were there all along," she said to the video tape that she held in her hand. "You were waiting for me to find you. And to uncover your secret."

Feet on carpet. Feet on carpet. The sensation of someone pacing beyond the door barricaded by the chest of drawers came strongly again. Bare feet on that worn red carpet. *Oh no, Mr. Morrow, eyeless and hungry and as dead as dead can be, you're not coming in here to share my bed. Don't you get tired, Mr. Morrow, with that endless pacing? And that endless staring at my bedroom door with those two blood-red holes where your eyes should be? What if I was to open the door and see if there really was—*

There was only one way to gag the wheedling voice. She pushed the tape into the video machine. Shivers shot up her spine as the loading mechanism pulled the cassette from her hands and swallowed it whole into the guts of the machine—a weird sensation that she could never get used to. The way it seems to grab the tape from your fingers as if you'd change your mind and do something else instead.

Change'd be a fine thing.

No; there were no options in that lonely hotel room at midnight, with the rain falling silently on Leppington's deserted streets.

It was either the video.

Or move the chest of drawers, open the door, see what paced the landing.

Oh, good evening, Mr. Morrow. Grown bloated, green-lipped and eyeless in our grave, haven't we? Come to bed and cuddle up close; I have a lovely bare throat; veins as thick as bananas—

She shivered a deep, cold shiver that went to the roots of her heart. That damned voice in her head. Wittering nonsense all the time. She had to shut it up.

There was only the video. It disturbed her and it frightened her. But what choice did she have?

She switched on the TV, turned it low so as not to wake the other guests who were no doubt sweetly and wonderfully asleep,

6

and pressed the "Play" button on the video machine.

Then, as if she'd lit the blue touch paper of a particularly dangerous firework, she ran back to bed, huddled up tight, knees pulled up to her chest and watched the screen, the blankets shielding her body as far as the tip of her nose.

The title came up on the screen:

A VIDEO DIARY.

It wasn't a video diary. It was a horror story.

4. Late-Night Television

The girl watched the TV screen from the safety of her bed. There was no introductory music. And once the title VIDEO DIARY had melted from the screen it was replaced with a static shot of the front of the Station Hotel: a four-storeyed red-brick building with a pointed tower at each corner. (The proprietress always referred to it as the Dracula Castle look. "Spooky or what, my dear?" she'd murmur through a haze of cigarette smoke.)

Bernice guessed the video was a low-budget travelogue intended for some overseas broadcaster. In these days of accountant-driven TV, more and more programmes were being made by just one guy or gal with a camcorder and the chutzpah to say: Look, I can make a great programme all on my own. Sod what the public and critics thought, the accountants at the TV stations loved those low, low budgets.

Bernice pulled the sheet a little higher. The bed was warm, and it did feel safe. As if an impenetrable force field surrounded it.

Her eyes locked on the screen with a morbid intensity she'd only experienced once before, when she'd come upon the aftermath of a car smash walking home from school—

Mum! Mum! Did you see all that blood? It was all dark red and black and there were white bits in it, like lumps of lard . . .

Now the screen held that same sort of dreadful fascination.

She watched as a man of about twenty-five appeared on screen to talk into the camera with the hotel in the background.

(*My room's that one on the top floor,* she thought. *Is that a face at the window? Pale, bloated, eyeless.*)

She focused on the man's voice (American: words softly spoken, cultured, well educated; a good-looking man with neat blond hair and glasses). He spoke in a friendly way (*I would have liked to meet him—not like dead old Mr. Morrow dragging his bloated graveyard feet up and down outside my door*).

She concentrated on the young man's words and the tormenting voice in the back of her head, at last—thankfully—faded.

"Hello," the man on TV said. "This is day six of my journey around haunted Britain—an old country occupied not only by the men, women and children of a modern industrialized nation, but by the demons, dragons and monsters of folklore. Here I am in the market town of Leppington, little more than ten miles north-west of the seaside town of Whitby. The same fabled Whitby where Count Dracula made landfall in Bram Stoker's 1897 novel.

"Leppington, population three thousand, built its prosperity on death. For more than a hundred years its biggest employer was the slaughterhouse and cannery, lying just across there behind the railway station. In 1881 Major Harding Leppington, patriarch of the Leppingtons, a family so inextricably linked to the town that they share the same name, won a contract to supply the British Navy with canned meat: back then the latest newfangled invention. Farmers out in the surrounding hills would drive their sheep and cattle right through the centre of the town, up the main street, past the church and the hotel behind me, across the market square, and funnel them through the big wrought-iron gates of the slaughterhouse. The beasts came in their thousands to be killed—in those days sheep, even cows, were hung alive by the back legs; then their throats were cut. After being left to hang for several hours to allow the blood to drain from their bodies into specially cut stone channels in the floor, the dead animals were moved through into the butchery hall where hundreds of furiously busy men cut them into small enough chunks to be cooked in what were basically cauldrons, fired by half a ton of coal at a time. These cooking vessels were so big that they would comfortably accommodate a small truck. Then the cooked meat went into the tin cans—which in those

8

days *were* made of pure tin—and was sealed, cooled and then dispatched to Her Majesty's ships where it could be safely eaten anything up to two years after the doomed animals last trotted across these cobblestones where I'm now standing. Colonel Leppington's Clinical and Nutritional Meat and Gravy, as the product was snappily known, could be found in ships' galleys anywhere from Alaska to Zanzibar.

"So this is Leppington: the town built on blood. Long before communism the workers from Leppington's meat factory were known as Reds. They could be seen walking home at night, red from head to clogged feet with the blood of the animals butchered that day."

Now there came a sequence of postcard-view shots of the town—the post office and minimart (formerly a leper hospital), the church, Saint Colman's (founded AD 670, originally Celtic, then Roman, then Anglican, destroyed by lightning AD 681 and by earthquake in AD 1200 and damaged in the South Transept by Nazi doodlebug in AD 1945), with ancient gravestones depicting swordsmen fighting, riding or even mating with she-monsters—historians still argued over those etchings.

Following the gravestones came shots of a river. "The River Lepping," ran the narrative, "believed to have been named in prehistory after a goddess, as is customary in Britain. In Scotland the Clyde is named after the goddess Clota, which is interpreted as "the Divine Cleanser'; the River Dee comes from Deva, meaning Goddess." There were more scenes of the Lepping: fast-flowing water creaming white around car-sized boulders; a boy fishing optimistically for salmon.

The narrator continued in his softly-spoken accents: "The name Leppington, a name of Norse origin, first appears in the writings of the Abbess of Whitby Abbey, one Saint Hilda, who lived around six hundred years after Christ. She'd already risen to fame by driving all the local snakes over the cliff, then finishing the job by cutting off their heads with her whip.

"A whip-wielding nun, beheading the phallus-shaped snake? If that doesn't leave you with one humdinger of a Freudian S&M image nothing else will. Anyway, in AD 657 she sent a letter to the local ruler, King Oswy of Northumbria. In it she wrote: 'Leppingsvalt (as it was known then) is a nest of demons who prick the navel and sup the blood of God's children. They have grown fat on the blood of innocents and prey on travellers, merchants and pilgrims alike. They are night-seers and necromantic in their arts.' She goes on in these outraged tones, even accusing the demon folk of Leppington of acting as cobbler and quartermaster to the Devil. She ends with a plea that Leppington, or rather Leppingsvalt be burnt to the very foundations and the earth seeded with salt. That is the old tried and tested way of destroying haunted houses. However—there's always a big 'however,' " isn't there?" continued the good-natured voice-over while showing shots of Leppington's Eatwell Cafe—*Pork-'n'-cider pies our speciality*. "However, Leppingsvalt was home to more than two hundred tin miners—tin mining was a filthy, dangerous, and highly specialized job—and tin was vital to the King's treasury. If he killed the miners—even though they were raving pagans with antisocial habits—he put a God Almighty hole in his own income. Therefore, shrewd old soul that he was, he suggested to St. Hilda that, instead of massacring the townsfolk in the name of Christ, she should preside over the forcible baptism and Christianizing of the pagan inhabitants of Leppingsvalt, then oversee the construction of a handsome church and that would be that. So the mass baptisms went ahead in the River Lepping—which claimed the lives of three monks from Whitby Abbey during the process: the old gods weren't going to give up without a fight. The church got built and, as I've mentioned before, quickly got itself struck by lightning. And amongst the God-fearing folk outside Leppinsvalt, now renamed Leppington, there were whisperings that the worship of the old gods continued in the tin miners' tunnels. Those tunnels themselves have turned the rock under the town into something resembling a vast sponge that's probably today more holes than rock. Which has led more than one surveyor to speculate that the whole town will tumble into one almighty great crater one day."

The head and shoulders of the blond narrator appeared on the screen again. He was smiling. "So, there you have it: this is Leppington. Built on blood. Last bastion of pagan worship."

The narration continued, showing local places of interest—a motte-and-bailey castle, the local museum (built and funded by the Leppington family with a floor devoted to exhibiting Colonel Leppington's mummified animals), the site of the local gibbet where many a rustler and highwayman had dangled . . .

Bernice lay drowsy now, comfortably warm, relaxed to the point where she allowed her head to rest on the pillow so the TV appeared to lie on its side as she watched. The light from the bedside lamp seemed muted, leaving the shadows in the corner of the room to grow yet darker. Maybe the voltage had dipped again. It happened frequently enough in this out-of-the-way town tucked up in the hills of North Yorkshire. The rain fell gently with a rhythmic whispering sound that came and went like the relaxed breathing of a sleeping child. She allowed herself to relax with it.

Safe and warm in my bed . . . safe and warm . . .

Sleepily, she let her eyes take in the room: wardrobe, mirror, shadows—softening and deepening yet more as the voltage diminished. The yellow pool of light from the lamp. Blue curtains. On the wall over the bed, the portrait of a white-robed girl ankle-deep in a river. The spider-shaped crack in the glass panel above the bathroom door—funny place for a window: *To admit daylight, I suppose; not for seeing through*; her shoes lined up against a wall, the black patent-leather ankle-boots she had bought yesterday with the pointed toes and a high heel, deliciously high, almost a stiletto; a good buy, she thought, quietly pleased; a very good buy.

Safe and warm in my bed . . . everything's all right now. I'll sleep soon. She yawned luxuriously, then snuggled deeper in the warm bed. The voice of the narrator on TV, butter-soft, soothing—the words stroked her ears all the way deep inside. A nice voice. Comforting, warm, friendly . . .

After a while, the scene dissolved from views of the town to an interior scene. The man sat on a bed in a gloomy room. She guessed he'd filmed this himself, simply by leaving the camcorder running on something the height of the chest of drawers she'd pulled in front of the door; then the man had walked into the camera's field of vision, sat on the bed and begun to talk. He talked even more softly, yet the sense of wonder shone through his voice.

"You know, I've never ever believed in the supernatural," he said in a whisper. "Not until now. The time's a little after three in the morning; outside it's pitch black. In here, it's . . . it's as if the whole building, the whole hotel, is charged with an electricity of some kind. I have the strangest dreams at night. I

11

know . . ." He smiled into the camera, the lenses of his glasses filling with gold when they caught the light of the bedside lamp. (*A lamp like this one*, thought Bernice, drowsily lifting an eye to it; *funny, I never noticed it before*.) "I know dreams aren't evidence of the supernatural . . . but, Jeez, this is so exciting I don't know where to begin. I've covered alien abductions in Arkansas, werewolves in Russia, spooks from New York to Timbuctoo—all poppycock, balderdash, cockamamie nonsense. I heard it all, but I never believed, never felt anything, never had that creature gut feeling here"—he pushed his two fists against his stomach—"that it, or any part of it, was true. Until I came here, to a little English town called Leppington. Now . . . now, just watch this."

The scene cut from the room to darkness. "This is just raw footage," the narrator continued. "No fancy cutaways, no dissolves or tripod work—just honest-to-goodness raw footage as it went into the can."

5. Ghosts on Film

Bernice watched the screen. She saw a tilting image of the hotel room door as whoever held the camera hurried towards it. A hand appeared in shot, grabbed the handle, twisted, then yanked open the door. The soundtrack consisted of excited breathing. Then the camera was out in the corridor (of this hotel, she thought, dreamily; he was staying in my hotel).

"I saw it. I saw it. Hell, stay focused, Mike. It's two in the morning. I saw it just twenty minutes ago," panted the man's voice off camera. "I sensed there was someone outside my door. Opened the door and there it was. Nothing more than a shadow of a man. A tall figure, moving along this corridor like a cat. That's not just a . . . a simile. The sensation bowled me over; took my breath away—but I had the impression this was part man, part animal—lithe, fast, very fast. My God, I was scared, physically terrified like I'd tripped and fallen flat on my face in front of a speeding truck. The logic side of me said: OK, Mike. You've seen it. Now lock yourself in the room. Believe me, what I saw is bad; it is one *bad* son of a bitch. But there's part of me that said: *Follow. Go on, follow, follow, follow!* I couldn't stop myself. I had to follow it as it . . . watch it, Mike, here's the stairs." Scenes of a grand staircase descending to the hotel lobby and reception desk. Now deserted. "My God, it's got so cold in here. This is July, for crying out loud. But it's cold as ice. Just look at that." The camera turned so the cameraman—Mike—could film his own face. The face was out of focus and round as a full-moon. He blew his breath out. Vapour streamed from his mouth. "Cold or what, eh, folks? Now, Mike, watch the stairs, watch the stairs. Last thing I want to do is trip and break my fool neck. Now, where'd he go? *Where'd he go?*" The picture jiggled less crazily now that he was walking. "Upstairs, downstairs, in my lady's chamber . . . wee willie winkie. Where'd you go?" More shots of the dining room, the bar with the shutters down, the door to the Dead Box beneath the stairs. "Where'd you go? Oh, and for pity's sake don't jump out and shout 'Boo' at me." The man was trying to be humorous but Bernice heard the tremor of fear wobble the voice.

"Oh, man . . . oh, man . . . damn. He—it—has gone. Vanished. Damnit, damnit. But you'll notice all the doors to the outside are shut and locked. Did he run through the wall? Or just dematerialize there in the middle of the pool room? Or maybe he shrunk himself down and ran into the jukebox. Probably filed himself away between Kula Shaker and REM . . . good heavens, I'm rambling. I'm rambling because this has—as the English say—knocked me for six; I'm shaking like the proverbial leaf."

Cut to: The hotel room. Mike sitting on the bed, calmly talking to camera. "What you saw on the videotape just then was me, Mike Stroud, chasing the figure. Now, I need to backtrack a little here so I can explain what happened. First time I was aware of someone, or something, moving up and down outside my room door, I went out into the corridor, looked, saw this huge shadowy man-shaped figure slip like a cat down the corridor. Scared the hell out of me. But the strange thing is I wanted to run after it. Something inside of me yelled: *Run, run, run! Chase it! Don't let it get away!* I felt enormous excitement. Like I was part of this wild race, and I was caught up by the enthusiasm and the sheer, sheer exhilaration. I followed, then lost it. A moment later I went back to my room for the camcorder . . ."

(On the television, behind Mike, I can see the spider-crack in

13

the glass pane above the bathroom door. And there's the por-trait of the girl, ankle-deep in the river, Bernice thought lazily. *The room is mine.*)

The narrator continued, "All fired up, I raced back to my room, grabbed the camcorder, then waited. It'll never come again, I thought. Jesus, my first experience of the paranormal and I've blown it. Why don't you keep the camcorder ready, just in case? Now you've probably lost that once-in-a-lifetime chance to film a supernatural event. But, listen to this, folks, it *did* come again. Within half an hour or so. You've seen the results." The man spoke in quiet awe, not quite believing what he'd seen. "It was as if there was a sixth sense kicking in inside here." The man pressed the flat of his hand against his chest. "I didn't see it completely—a huge shadowy figure. It's what I felt so strongly, as if I knew absolutely it was part man, part animal. There was something almost familiar about it. If I close my eyes I can see its bare feet on the carpet; I can *feel* its bare feet on the carpet, too, as if they are *my* bare feet. But at least you can see it on tape. I've captured something there, haven't I?"

Bernice remembered what she'd seen on TV: the walls of the corridor speeding by, swinging shots of the carpet, the doors of the other rooms on that floor, the landing, the stairs, reception-ist's desk, dining-room tables laid for breakfast with white cot-ton table cloths. And always just ahead of the light, in the shadows, something fleeting. A sense of movement—quick and feline and oh-so-dark.

6. 1:15 A.M.

The rain sighed outside. She felt sleepy. The man talked on screen. She heard his rising excitement as he made plans to stay awake at night, camcorder charged and ready. As soon as he sensed the thing pacing outside in the corridor, he'd swing open the door—

—and then he'd have the figure on tape.

And this time it would be filmed properly; viewers would see it standing there, slap in the centre of the screen; they'd marvel at whatever face it possessed; Joe Public would look into the eyes of a supernatural being; they would shiver, they might re-

14

coil in horror, but they would behold that face in nothing less than awe. And he, Mike Stroud, one-man TV crew, would have brought that unique piece of tape to the world. Proof of the paranormal.

What would he do then? There'd be documentaries and books aplenty to flow from that kind of material; talk shows; Larry King on CNN; worldwide syndication rights.

Bernice listened to his plans with a kind of cosy collusiveness, as if he was speaking to her—only her. Nobody else. I, Bernice Mochardi, am his special friend and confidante. That pleased her; the feeling in her stomach was the same as when she knew she was falling in love with a man.

Her eyelids grew heavy. She was so deliciously sleepy.

". . . the magazine syndication rights alone would be enormous. A creature of English folklore captured on film to—wait, wait." He jumped up from the bed, lenses of his glasses flashing, as he looked from side to side. "It's here. It's back. I can feel it . . . sense it; it's outside. Right-oh, people. Here goes." He hurried towards the camera, then behind it, moving out of the field of vision. The picture jerked as the camera was lifted— jolting shots of the portrait of the girl in the river, the blue curtains, the spider-legged crack in the pane above the bathroom door.

(He stayed in my bedroom, slept in my bed, warm skin against cool, cotton sheet.)

She watched the TV as the picture showed her the closed door expanding to fill the screen as he approached it with the camera. Then he must have paused.

Was he unsure what to do next? Did he wonder just what in Heaven's name stood on the other side of the door? Was he afraid? Yes, he must have been. Any normal human being fears the unknown.

The picture juddered, then became rock-steady as he placed the camera on—what? A tripod? The chest of drawers?

In any event the picture of the door filling the screen was steady, perfectly focused. She saw him approach the door.

He opened it.

There was a blur of movement.

No sound.

He tossed one look back at the camera.

15

The movement so violent his glasses flew from his face.

The expression on his face went beyond the knowable. A kind of wide-eyed snarl of terror.

A split second later he vanished through the door as if yanked through on the end of a rope of elastic. The door slammed shut with tremendous force.

Yet, oddly, the microphone picked up no sound.

Bernice lifted her head a little, looking at the screen in drowsy wonder. How could that be? The scene, although full of fury and savage movement, was eerily silent.

She'd seen this video so many times before that it no longer scared her. If anything, it had a soporific effect, inducing even greater drowsiness.

She even blotted out what she saw in the darkened corridor beyond the man.

Yawning, she climbed out of bed, ready to switch off the TV and video. She'd sleep now.

As always the picture of the closed door would remain for a few moments. Seconds later it would switch to black as the tape ended. Then there would only be the electronic snowstorm of the dead channel.

She walked towards the TV. (Why don't all hotels trust their clients with remotes?) The screen blacked. Snowstormed.

Just as it always did.

Then the picture returned. She stopped and watched in surprise.

It showed the corridor, the stairs, the lobby. The camera moved with fantastic speed, yet with equally fantastic fluidity—and oh-so-smoothly—as if running on oiled wheels.

A door loomed. The little door next to the Dead Box.

Stairs descending.

Down into the basement. The walls were raw brick. Brick archways flashed by at incredible speed.

In the basement, there was a figure, standing at the join of two walls—one brick, one stone.

She saw the white shirt, blond hair. She recognized the man as Mike Stroud, the man in the video. But the composed, cheerful expression had long gone. His face was a snarl of horror. There were grazes round the eyes and mouth. He was screaming.

Yes, she was sure he was screaming and fighting something she could not see.

Then he was crying as if something was hurting him and wouldn't stop hurting—she thought of a child being bullied at school, the bully twisting the child's arm—

Stop it! Stop it!

—the more the child cries, the harder the bully twists the arm.

At last Mike Stroud was pulled sobbing into darkness; a second later he'd vanished, as if dragged through a hole in the basement wall.

Now the camera moved again.

(*But who is filming?* Bernice thought, frightened. *Who can hold the camera so steadily while running so quickly? Who?*)

On the TV screen she saw this: the brick walls blurring; the basement stairs filling the screen, the camera rushing up them, to the lobby, to the carpeted stairs. Up, up, up.

To the top floor.

Rushing along the corridor,

Hotel room doors flicking by one after another. The camera flying straight at a door.

My door; it's my door!

Room 406.

Now she heard the thump of bare feet hard against the floor.

The door—*My door, my door!*—filled the TV screen

She held her breath.

The door burst open.

Cracked window above the bathroom door. Girl-in-the-river portrait, dressed in white.

Thunder rumbled as if the hotel was falling into a pit.

The door swung open and out of sight.

There was a figure in the bed.

It's me, Bernice thought, heart pounding.

My eyes are wide. I'm rising to my knees, blankets held in front of my body like a shield.

A shield of cotton and wool?

No good at all, Bernice.

Whoever holds the camera runs into the room, then rushes at the bed to bounce onto it. On screen the camera looks down at the girl who falls back, fair hair splayed out across the pillow, mouth opening in a terrified scream.

And all the time the thunder pounds on and on and on as the floor splits open, the bed tips; she slides from its once warm and cosy safety to fall down into a pit where bloated figures wait with arms raised to catch her. A thousand faces look up. Hungry.

They have no eyes.

7

The sizzling sound was overlaid by a thunderous pounding.

She opened her eyes and thought she could smell bacon, just a faint whiff, but bacon nonetheless. Yawning, she climbed out of bed. Killed the TV with a jab of her index finger. The sizzle of static from the speaker stopped. The thunder continued.

Bernice Mochardi looked out of the window into the sunlit market square. Dumpster day. The municipal truck hoisted the market-place rubbish skips to upend them into the back, before the mechanical grabs pounded the big metal bins against a steel spar. Overripe tomatoes, bruised apples, squashed bananas and old boxes would soon be on their way to the big hole in the ground outside town where they'd lie forever with the grotty pair of stranger's socks she'd thrown out all those weeks ago.

Across the market square lay the single-storey station building; beyond that, the red-brick monstrosity of the slaughterhouse rose above the town. The blue-black slate roof still glistened after the night's rain.

A great jaw-cracking yawn came as she stared out, hanging tightly onto the normality of another day in a small town.

She didn't know when she had fallen asleep and when the reality of watching the video had given way to nightmare. She should watch the video in daylight. Maybe it wouldn't be so bad after all. But then again, it might show worse things. It was the same cassette, but it never showed exactly the same programme twice. Or so it seemed to her.

The church clock struck seven. A mere twelve hours until it grew dark once more. Already the spectre of another night—a night that would seem to last forever—was approaching fast.

Bernice Mochardi shivered and turned her back on the window.

Chapter One

1

The train journey to Leppington was a picturesque one. Dr. David Leppington stretched out his long legs as far as the seat in front would allow, relaxed to the rhythm of the wheels on the track, and watched the flow of fields, woods and hills pass the carriage window.

He'd recognized nothing yet. The river running alongside the track was, he guessed, the Lepping that tumbled down from the hills to cut the town in half before flowing on down the valley to join the River Esk for the rest of the journey to the sea at Whitby.

Would he recognize anything? Six-year-olds are more likely to remember incidents than places. He had vivid memories of the day his dog, Skipper, ran into the sea in Whitby and promptly got washed back up the beach again by a huge wave. After that, the dog flatly refused to have any truck with the beach, never mind the sea. He remembered when the chimney caught fire—he must have been about five—and being carried outside by his uncle to watch the sparks shooting from the chimney pot into the night sky like some great wonderful firework. But as for Leppington itself—the town from which his family took its name, or was it vice versa?—he'd not seen it in more than twenty years. There were fragments of images like clips of patched-together film. He remembered sitting on the kitchen table as his mother laced up his shoes—the wallpaper bore a pattern of plump black grapes. And he remembered sitting in what seemed a huge palace of a building where he'd eaten a ham sandwich. A film on television had scared him witless—his elder sister had smuggled a horror video into the house, he supposed. But had his family owned a video player twenty years ago?

Perhaps she'd surreptitiously switched channels to watch a horror film?

The train clattered over a level crossing.

The hills were steeper and higher now; the tops crowned with purple heather. Here and there, even though it was late March, he glimpsed white streaks where snow still clung to the hollows or was shaded by walls.

Perhaps returning to Leppington wasn't such a brilliant idea after all. It would be awkward meeting the sole family member remaining in the town after so long. Well, he'd cross that bridge when he got to it; it shouldn't be so bad.

Also, he had a letter in his pocket containing an invitation that had seemed almost irresistibly tempting. Actually, there were two letters in his pocket; but for the time being he'd prefer not to think about the second one. The time would come to open it, then eventually read it. But the time wasn't now. He'd postpone it as long as possible.

The train began to climb more steeply into the hills. Ahead black clouds tinged with green that made him think of severe bruising hung over the hills. (Bruises, properly known as contusions, require no treatment: his professional medical persona had clicked into gear—bruising is caused by a blow resulting in damage to blood vessels beneath the skin allowing seepage of blood; the later yellow colouration is due to the accumulation of stomach bile in the affected tissues . . .) Relax. He smiled to himself. You're on holiday. Once more he turned his attention to the passing countryside that looked so incredibly peaceful.

2

The relaxation was short-lived. Trouble had been simmering all the way from Whitby. The young man sitting in the seat across the aisle had lit a cigarette as the train had pulled out of Whitby for its thirty-minute run up into the sticks where Leppington had hunched itself in the valley for the last two thousand years or so.

The young man, early twenties, shaved head, with so many tattoos there was more blue than skin tone on his pelt, blew smoke in clouds above the grey head of the old man in front.

A scar that was a vivid red ran from the corner of the young man's eye to the top of his ear, making it look as if someone had tried to draw a spectacle arm in red felt-tip there.

"You must put that cigarette out," the old man had said, turning round.

"I've bought my ticket." The youth grunted rather than spoke.

"It's a no-smoking carriage."

No reply.

"Look at the sign. No smoking."

No reply.

"Can you read?"

"I've bought my ticket." The youth's voice turned hard.

"But you can't smoke."

"You're going to stop me?"

The old man paused, realizing this was someone who wasn't going to fold up and do as he was told. Maybe the old man had been a tough nut in his youth, or perhaps he'd occupied a position of authority in working life. In any event he didn't want to lose face.

"I'll stop you, young man. I'll tell the conductor."

"Tell your fairy godmother for all I care!"

"Put out the cigarette."

"No."

"It really is antisocial."

"I don't like your face."

David Leppington saw the danger signal in the young man's face. If someone's complexion flushes red they might get angry, shout, but when it turns white that's when the warning light should flash on. A suddenly white, bloodless face spells danger. The adrenalin's kicked in. The man's going into fight-or-flight mode. And from the look of that tattooed thug, David thought, he wasn't going to run.

David Leppington looked round the carriage. A group of old women sitting at a table seat had been chatting away until the raised voices told them there was trouble brewing. Now they lifted their heads to watch. In the seat in front of him sat a young woman with a toddler on her knee. She determinedly told the toddler to "See the horsey. See the trees." She wanted no part of the trouble.

If the young man took a swing at the old man David Leppington would have to step in quick.

"You're going to take this off me, then?" The young man held up the cigarette, his eyes locked onto those of the old man (who'd stood up so he could look back at the youth). "You just do that. You just try."

"You're being ridiculous now; I think—"

"You think what?"

"I think—"

"Come on. Take it off me. Stuff it down my throat. Why don't you try it?"

"Smoking in a non-smoking carriage is antisocial."

"I bought my bastard ticket, didn't I?"

"But that doesn't give you the right to—"

"What are you waiting for? Take it off me." Finger and thumb pinching the filter end of the cigarette he held it in front of the old man's face. The challenge was there. The man could either back down (and lose face) or he could try taking the cigarette.

David knew what would happen then.

A flurry of fists and the old man would go down like a sack of coal. The shock would probably be lethal to a man of his age.

"Take . . . the . . . bastard . . . cigarette . . . OK?"

The skin of the youth's face was so white now the tattooed teardrops on his cheek seemed to stand proud of the skin like blue pebbles.

David Leppington twisted sideways so he could push himself out of his seat. He'd got no enthusiasm for what he might have to do next, but he couldn't sit back and watch the old man become a punch ball.

"Take it." The thug held the cigarette up to the old man. David Leppington could see the muscles bulging under the youth's fists; tattooed daggers dripped blood.

"Tickets from Whitby . . . Your tickets from Whitby, please."

It broke the spell; the old man looked round at the conductor—a solid-looking man of around forty-five.

"I'd asked this young man if he'd stop smoking," the old man said in reasonable tones.

"No-smoking carriage, sonny," the conductor said breezily.

"I've bought my ticket," grunted the youth.

"I once bought a picture of the Eiffel Tower, but it doesn't give me the right to go and live there." The conductor spoke in a disinterested way; this was all run of the mill.

"I want a smoke."

"Next carriage is the smoker."

The conductor had handled it well. He wasn't being provocative, he was just being helpful. The young man stood up, pulled his holdall from the overhead luggage rack and stomped through into the next carriage.

After he had gone, and the conductor had moved on, the old man said cheerfully to the old ladies, "Sorry about that. He had to be told." Then, with a self-satisfied smile, he sat down and beamed out through the window.

3

The hills rose. The sky grew darker. The train rattled along more slowly as if reluctant to go further. The river Lepping contained flashes of white where it rushed over rapids.

On two occasions the youth had walked up the carriage to the old man and spoken to him: "Your face is giving me grief," the youth had said. Then he'd gone, only to return five minutes later. "I'm going to remember your face. I've got it locked up in here." The youth had jabbed a finger at his own shaved temple. Then he'd returned to the smoker's carriage again.

The third time he comes back he's going to bop the old man, David had thought. What now? Warn the conductor?

Before he could come up with an answer, suddenly there were old brick houses alongside the track, the train braked, and David realized, with a huge sense of relief, that they'd arrived in Leppington. Deliberately, he allowed the old man to leave his seat first. He followed, so that now at least he formed an obstacle between the old man and the youth if the young thug should come tearing down the walkway between the seats intent on beating the old boy to a pulp.

He needn't have worried. Through the window, he saw the youth walking at a furious pace along the platform and out of the station.

David pulled his own holdall down from the overhead shelf

23

and stepped out of the train into Leppington, the town that bore his name. For a moment he paused to look at the station sign.

Leppington

The sign was of the free-standing sort, being simply a board fixed to a post that had been set in concrete where the platform met a perimeter fence. If David had expected any sense of awe at standing in the land of his ancestors, he was going to be disappointed here, he realised. Leppington station was a dowdy red-brick affair. As he shouldered the holdall, ready to head for the exit, he saw a large crow swoop down over the roof tops. As black as if it had been carved from coal, it landed on the station sign, directly above the word LEPPINGTON. For a second it perched there, long, curving claws gripping the top of the sign, yet still flapping its wings before it found its balance.

As it stood there, huge wings outstretched, it fixed its gem-bright eyes on David, staring hard at his face. For all the world it could have dropped down from the sky to take a second look at him, as if to confirm his identity. Then the yellow beak opened to release a surprisingly loud cry. Almost instantly the wings beat hard, hard enough to flutter scraps of paper away across the platform, and then the bird rose slowly to flap above the roof tops, its long black wings pushing the air in a muscular yet unhurried way.

Well, I guess that some old reincarnated ancestor's come to welcome me back, David told himself with a smile. It was a flippant thought. At least, he meant it to be. But as he headed for the exit he saw the huge black bird circling, high above the station, and he couldn't escape the notion it was keeping watch on him. That it was curious as to why this last son of the Leppingtons had returned to the town of his ancestors—and what would he do next?

Chapter Two

1

David Leppington stood outside the station. Above him the crow glided in great circles, its beady eyes no doubt watching his every move.

He thought: *This is your kingdom, David. LEPPINGTON. The town is in your blood.*

Oh no, it isn't, he thought more light-heartedly. I haven't clapped eyes on Leppington in twenty years.

Leppington is your kingdom. Rule wisely and well.

But if you see the bloody great dragon run like hell. He'd added the second rhyming line flippantly but the voice he heard in his head sounded like that of an old man. As if he was remembering words someone had once told him with great seriousness: as if it was vitally important he should remember.

Oh well, I'm home, he thought, definitely being flippant now. Where are my subjects to greet me?

He stood at the entrance of the station and looked out across the market square. If these were his subjects they weren't taking a blind bit of notice of the return of their king. Shoppers mooched among the dozen or so stalls set out at one end of the market square—most of the people seemed well past middle age. At the far side of the square were a row of Victorian buildings—library, half a dozen shops, something called The Bath House. Dominating them all was the Station Hotel, a four-storey monstrosity with pointed towers at each corner in some kind of mock Gothic style. Perched above that was that great lump of bruised-looking sky filled with black and green cloud. And gliding across the face of the cloud, the crow that had risen so high it looked little more than a black speck.

David let his gaze roam over the motley collection of buildings. Colonel Leppington might have brought prosperity to the town in the shape of the abattoir and cannery; he hadn't brought style.

The abattoir itself backed onto the station. In fact the tracks ended at the vast brick wall of the abattoir building, which was big enough to cast a permanent shadow over the station and a good-sized chunk of the town, too. Before the rail track reached the station a spur line ran off behind the station buildings and disappeared through a vast set of doors in the looming exterior wall of the abattoir. No doubt goods trains would be backed into there to be loaded with tens of thousands of crates of canned mutton and beef ready for dispatch throughout the country. How many thousands of cows and sheep had gone into the mincing machine in there?

"Never a taxi when you want one, is there?"

It was the same old man who'd nearly had his face mashed by the thug on the train.

"You know," the old man continued, "when you don't need a taxi, you'll see them queuing up round the square. Today? None. None at all. No buses to speak of. Grubby things. Driven by impudent ignoramuses."

Dear God, David Leppington thought, heart sinking. Button-holed by the town bore. He was liking the town less and less by the minute.

"Going far?" the old man inquired, looking David up and down.

"No. Just to the hotel across there."

"Ah, the Station Hotel? Not bad. Not bad. Though not as good as the old days when Bill Charnwood had the place. His daughter's done her best since . . . but you know what young girls are like these days. Young people don't want to work. They don't know about graft and sweat. Don't recollect your face, young man. Are you visiting?"

"Ah . . . yes." *Don't tell him anything. He'll stand here all day interrogating you.* "Short trip," David added.

"Family?"

"Yes." David picked up his suitcase, ready to push on to the hotel. It looked like rain. Nice one, he thought, seizing on the notion. "Ah, it looks like rain." He hoped the old man would agree and go in search of a taxi.

"Oh, that old bruiser?" The man nodded up at the cloud. "This time of year it always bubbles up like that from the tops. Never brings rain, though."

Damn. That's one escape route closed.

"You know, you remind me of someone." The old man nipped his bottom lip between thumb and forefinger. "Let me see."

Arnold Schwarzenegger? Denzel Washington? Sharon Stone? The temptation to be flippant to the point of rudeness strained to surface.

The old man looked at him closely. "Yes . . . yes. You've got a very familiar face, young man. Think it must be around the eyes. And your height. Very distinguished you look for a young man. Police force?"

"No . . . a doctor."

"A doctor? Damn good profession."

Oh God, damn and hellfire. David maintained a polite smile. The man was going to stay there all day and winkle out every detail of his personal life.

(I wet-shave using Bic razors, my favourite films are *Flight of the Phoenix* (Jimmy Stewart is the bee's knees), *Lust For Life* and Tim Burton's *Ed Wood*; no, I hate soap operas set in hospitals—the doctors look phony. I love food that is bad for me—cheesecake, Indian takeaways, chocolate, and for bed I wear nothing but rubber, furs and a lecherous smile . . . Uh oh, stop the flippant comments, Doc.)

David held the false smile, but he realized he'd missed a question. "My name?"

"Yes, I didn't quite catch it." The old man pried.

"Leppington."

The old man gave a sudden blink of surprise. For the first time he was speechless. He'd not even been rendered speechless when it looked as if the young thug would batter him bloody and senseless.

Now the old man stepped back, his mouth open; he gave that surprised blink again.

David thought: *Oh, hell, that's torn it; maybe I did let something flippant out. Maybe that bit about sleeping in rubber and furs . . . that'll teach you, my boy . . .*

"Ahm . . . sorry, I don't think I heard you right. I thought you said . . . ahm . . . Leppington?"

27

"Yes," David said brightly. "Leppington. The same as the town. I suppose it's—"

He didn't have time to finish. The old man mumbled some words—one might have been "Taxi"—and walked quickly towards the town. Every so often he shot a look back at David that seemed nothing short of hostile.

Are you sure you didn't let something flippant slip, David?

At least it did the trick. The man was gone.

Up above, the great black crow gave a piercing cry. It floated directly overhead, wings outstretched, now unflapping. Again, David had the strongest feeling he was being watched.

2

With the time nudging midday, the old man gone, David Leppington realized he was hungry. When he'd booked into the hotel he'd been told the earliest check-in time was one in the afternoon, so with an hour to kill he headed for a door in the station that bore the sign STATION TEA ROOM.

The idea of scaring off the old man by simply giving his name amused him.

Go on, he thought, walk into the tea room and announce: My name is Leppington. See if the same trick works twice. Smiling, he headed for the door, imagining the mention of his name would have the old ladies in the tea room squealing for fear as they ran for the door.

Lock up your daughters, Leppington's back in town!

Grinning now, he walked into the empty cafe. Killed the grin with an effort, ordered a cheese salad sandwich, Bakewell tart and coffee and sat down to eat.

Chapter Three

Sky bruised all brown and green. Cruddy buildings. Big one with pointed towers like a castle. The town meant nothing to him. He hated it. He hated the stupid old git on the train who had complained like shit. All he'd done was grab a well-earned smoke.

No one told him what to do.

No one told him what to say.

No one told him what to eat.

He'd had a gutful of that in jail. Twelve months for sticking some weasel who'd grassed him up. They'd treated the guy in the outpatients'; he never even got his runty little arse on a hospital bed. But the cops were waiting for him to put a foot wrong, lying bastards. He wished some little rubber-necked cop would just walk out of the cafe there in the station. He'd wade in—wap! wap! wap! The cop would crash back into the wall, blood spewing out of his rubber lips.

Hasta la vista, baby.

He thought about waiting for the old faggot who'd whined about the smoke. Wait for him outside the station.

Wap! Wap! Wap!

He'd love to see the old guy fall croaking on the floor, bits of false teeth coming out onto the floor like broken biscuits. Then WA-RRPP! Plant a kick in his soft-as-shit stomach.

Over and out, grandad.

Got your wings, got your harp. Goodnight, sweetheart.

What was he doing in this tossing town, anyway? Leppington. He'd never even heard of it until last week. He'd been drifting ever since prison. Pulled a few wallets from drunks in some public shithouse. Walked out of a supermarket or two, cool as a cuke, with a bottle of vodka in each hand—had to wap the store detective in Hull with one. Wap. Smash. Tinkle. Left the bastard in a pool of blood and vodka.

Then he'd heard the name Leppington. It stuck in his mind.

Leppington. Leppington. Leppington. Leppington. Leppington.

Fucking name went round and around, like it was a fly stuck inside his skull or something . . . Leppington. Leppington. Leppington.

Couldn't sleep.

Leppington. Leppington.

He'd seen a mouse in a pissoir in Goole. He'd stamped on the little fucker. "Leppington! Leppington! Lepp—" it'd squealed before his big boot came crunching down to flatten its head.

So why Leppington?

Why had the name stuck?

Why was he here?

Fuck knew.

It was just a place. And he had to be in some place, right? You can't just jump out of the fucking universe and leave a fucking hole, for Chrissakes. Leppington was a place, so he might as well cool his heels here for a while.

He walked away from the station, through the market stalls, brushing aside biddies like they were moths. But he didn't so much walk as strut. When he walked that way he believed he could walk at a wall and bust right through, like he was a tank; bricks, mortar dust blasting aside, and he'd go right on through—unstoppable, a machine. He was big, he was glorious, he had muscles in his spit; his hair was shaved down to the skin, displaying to the world the scars he'd collected for twenty-two years. The first one he'd got—the one that ran from his left eye to his ear lobe, looking like it had been drawn there in red felt-tip—had come his way when he was a week old, just a fucking little baby—that was his best; that made people look twice at him—he was the fucking Frankenstein monster: scarred and beautiful and terrible; so get out of my fucking way or I'll crush you to shit.

OK . . . this is Leppington.

He was going to make a start. He'd make this shit town his own. It would be like a big fat tit to suck on. He'd suck the thing dry of milk, then . . .

Then, like he'd done before, he'd move on, leaving the tit dry, empty.

"Tit!" He spat the word at an old man in a cap. The man looked startled.

"Tit!"

Was it the same old sod who'd grumbled at him on the train?

Maybe a quick wap! wap! Leave him puking and pissing his baggy old-bloke trousers in the street.

Nah!

He'd work to do. He started at the pubs, looking for some people. He didn't mince in all timid. He strutted into the bars. Looked round—looked people dead in the eye. When he realized they weren't who he was looking for he walked—no, strutted—out—

—One day I won't use the fucking door; I'll go through the fucking wall—

—He tried the cafes; street corners. He wasn't looking for individuals he knew, only a type he knew. When he found them, he'd know; like alligators know their own kind.

He found them on a piece of wasteland behind the church. Four losers were kicking a can at each other. They were well traced up—probably glue or solvents—they were hooting in stupid voices.

—Like the faggots in C block. He'd got one in the showers one day. Faggot's eyes had lit up. Mebbe kissy-kissy with tattooed gorilla with muscles like spuds beneath his skin.

Mebbe you reckon wrong, fag-boy. He'd bounced the faggot off the wall so hard he'd cracked a dozen tiles. Water hissed from the showers, diluting the blood on the floor, so the clots looked like red roses that gave off this beautiful, beautiful smoky pink. Then, slowly, the wonderful reds had blossomed there around his bare feet, leaving him standing in a pool of water that misted with pinks and scarlets and crimsons: they looked fantastic; like something from a dream.

Today, in Leppington, he stared at the kids kicking the can. They were maybe late teens.

"Who the fuck are you looking at?"

They'd said that, or words to that effect as he'd walked forward. The first went down holding his busted nose, the second

31

hit the ground like he was dead—the uppercut all but broke his neck—the third tried to throw a punch.

... but he moved in slow motion; why do people move in slow motion?

Wap! Wap!

Blubbing his heart out, the third one folded up.

The fourth pulled a knife; shit, even a machine-gun wouldn't have saved him. The headbutt floored the kid.

Tempting to follow through with a kick in the face, but he hadn't come all this way to Leppington to kill.

No. He was here to teach.

Chapter Four

1

Bernice Mochardi took her lunch break in the farmhouse kitchen where she worked. Although lunch today was nothing more than a slice of toast and a cup of Earl Grey Tea.

She pretended to herself that too many meals at the Peking Garden, Leppington's only Chinese restaurant, were leaving their mark on her waistline. But the real reason was that she had little appetite these days; in fact, her figure was equal to that of any catwalk model.

And the real reason for that is the videos, she told herself. They prey on your mind, don't they, Bernice?

She put the kettle smartly down on the hob and lit the gas.

You can't get the man from the video out of your mind, can you? He has (had?) such a nice face; the voice turned her skin to gooseflesh. What had happened to him in the basement?

Bernice dropped a tea bag into her mug.

He was grazed; he was screaming even though no sound came from his mouth. His face was horrible, a leer of fright.

I should take that video, drop it in one of those market-place dumpsters. Squirt lighter fuel over it and burn the stupid thing.

That tape is taking possession of your soul. And then forget the name Mike Stroud. Forget it completely. It's not as if you'd ever met him in person.

"Don't frown at the milk like that, luvvie, you'll sour it."

"Oh, Mavis. I was just making tea." Bernice snapped free of her morbid thoughts. "Like one?"

"Only if you haven't turned the milk with that face of yours," Mavis said good-naturedly. She was around sixty, with a plump face and pink-rimmed glasses. "I'll put the milk in the cups, you raid the biscuit tin."

"I'm having a slice of lemon. Don't worry, I'll cut it."

"A slice of lemon in your tea? Oh, you and your fancy city ways."

Mavis was only gently teasing. She liked to play the country bumpkin with Bernice, goggling at her clothes before she donned the overalls that made all the workers in the farm look like hospital theatre staff. "Ooh," she'd coo, "that blouse is real silk, isn't it? And blue nail varnish. Mr. Thomas won't be able to keep his hands off of you."

"I painted them specially for Mr. Thomas." Bernice had grinned wickedly. "I want to ravish his senses."

They'd both broken off into peals of laughter. Mr. Thomas, the owner, was seventy if he was a day, and a dour Methodist at that. Once he'd sent one of the packers home after dryly proclaiming he could smell beer on the man's breath, and would swear the truth of the statement to Heaven on the Book itself.

Now they moved about the farmhouse kitchen—a clinical-looking place that gleamed with white tiles and silvery stainless steel—making their lunches; Mavis pulled a microwave hot-pot from its box.

When Bernice Mochardi had told her friends that she had found work on a farm they'd been amazed.

As they'd sat in a pizzeria on Canal Street in Manchester they had fired questions at her, clearly imagining her slopping through the farmhouse muck all day, wearing a checked shirt, with a piece of straw jammed in her mouth, and perhaps occasionally slapping some chubby sow on the rump while announcing, "Now which little piggy's going to market, then?"

When she told them what kind of farm they couldn't believe their ears.

"Leeches?"

"Yes, a farm that produces leeches."

"But what on Earth do they grow leeches for?" Bernice's friends had asked, horrified.

"Well, what do you think those black things are on your pizza?"

They'd shrieked. Rita had spat her mouthful into a serviette. Ariel had swallowed half a glass of beer in one go.

Bernice had laughed. "Those are black olives, you nitwits. Leeches are the latest big thing in medicine. They're used to prevent wounds becoming infected, help circulation, that kind of thing."

"But *leeches?*"

"But leeches," she mimicked. "Well, it's better than working for peanuts in that cafe. If I cook one more all-day breakfast I'll go nuts."

The conversation had turned to boys but Ariel and Rita said they were full and moved quickly on to the ice cream.

Bernice had been at the leech farm for two months. She liked it. Her job mainly involved packing the leeches up into their moist little travel boxes for dispatch to hospitals throughout the country. If a patient had crappy circulation in a finger or a toe or some other extremity, particularly after an operation, the leech, which is a close cousin to the common earthworm, would be applied to the affected area. There it would use its three tiny jaws to chew—painlessly, thank God—through the skin; then it would happily suck out the sluggish blood and quicken the blood flow, and so bring an influx of fresh, oxygen-rich blood to the flagging tissues. Best of all she liked the big Amazonian leeches. They looked like giant caterpillars and enjoyed having their softly flabby backs stroked. She was surprised to find she wasn't squeamish at all.

And she liked Mavis, who today was happily chatting about a trip to the travel agent. "I've booked Pete and myself on that Florida tour—we're doing the works: Disneyland, Orlando, Space Centre, Miami."

As she talked, Bernice found herself being drawn back to the video tape. What had happened to the man? What had he seen in the hotel corridor?

Mr. Morrow with no eyes and graveyard lips . . .

She closed off that train of thought. No, he'd seen something; it had snatched him from the room. She'd seen him on television struggling frantically with . . . with what?

And who had filmed the fight?

Then a surprising thought struck her.

After work tonight, I'm going back to the hotel and I'm going to go down into the basement and see what's really there.

2

Jesus encountered two demoniacs when He travelled through Gadarene. They were so fierce no one could pass. The demoniacs cried out, "What have you to do with us, O Son of God? Have you come here to torment us before the time?" Nearby, a herd of swine grazed. Jesus cast the spirits of the demoniacs into the pigs. Immediately, the swine rushed down a steep bank into the sea and were drowned.

Jason Morrow knew the story well enough. He would often think of it as the pigs were herded into the slaughterhouse, where their squeals echoed from the white-tiled walls. Jason Morrow no longer even noticed the sound, but he smiled when he saw visitors screw up their faces at the sheer volume and intensity of the pigs" squealing. It made an electric drill boring into brick sound as pleasant as a garden waterfall.

Pigs came trotting onto the killing floor, their pink bodies nicely plumped up from weeks of porking out on pig swill. Jason Morrow ticked off the relevant boxes of his inventory as the men moved forward with the electric paddles that they clamped to either side of the pigs" heads. There were no sparks or smoke or fuss. The jolt of electricity snapped from the metal contacts of the paddles, blasting the brain to buggery; piggy went down kicking, then lay unconscious, all ready for the *coup de grace*.

Jason Morrow moved efficiently from pig to pig as they fell, nodding to the men with razor-sharp axes when he'd satisfied himself the pig was stunned. He wouldn't claim to enjoy the job—"I work to live, not live to work" was what he'd tell his wife when she complained he didn't work more overtime—only on pig days he walked with a spring in his step, hummed pop

35

songs under his breath, while he watched the electrical contacts of the stunner being clamped to another meaty porcine head.

Slap. Another pig went down, its muddy trotters kicking; its piggy eyes, black as olives, bulged glassily. Jason nodded to Jacob who planted one bloody boot on the pig's head and raised his axe above the pig's neck.

Would axes have killed the demoniac-infested pigs Jesus had dispatched so efficiently? He liked to think they would. The axes glittered in the fluorescent lights; they were sharp as damned scalpels. One stroke severed the windpipe and major arteries. Blood gushed into specially cut stone channels in the floor, then poured on out of sight into the drains with a gurgling, sucking sound as if the drains were thirsty mouths sucking at that blood for all they were worth. Where the blood went then he didn't know; but it didn't take much imagination to picture it surging through the Victorian sewer system beneath Leppington's streets, a mini-tidal wave of blood sending a pink curling wave ahead of it to God knew where.

The pigs came in like . . . ('like lambs to the slaughter," Jason smiled to himself); axes glinted as they rose and fell; pigs still awaiting oblivion in the form of a squirt of electricity across the frontal lobes squealed their hearts out; the sound beating back from the walls was deafening.

Jason Morrow checked the tally of pigs. One hundred and twenty-one. That was a lot of bacon. His stomach rumbled with hunger. In ten minutes he could grab a mug of tea and—yeah, why not?—a bacon sandwich. He ticked yet another box and signed his name at the bottom of the form.

As he moved on from pig to pig, giving a nod to men waiting with the axes raised, he mentally replayed the story of Jesus's encounter with the demoniacs. He pictured the hot dusty hillside. The tombs that the demoniacs occupied would be deep tunnels cut into a cliff face. He saw the pigs run squealing into the sea where they thrashed at the water with their stumpy trotters as they drowned, taking the demoniacs with them. Hasta la vista, baby.

He didn't know why he found the story so satisfying; endless variations would work their way through his mind. Sometimes, when the demoniacs entered the bodies of the pigs, the pigs" heads would morph into those of human beings with tormented

36

faces all pig-snouted and drooling with bulging eyes . . .

He nodded at Ben Starkey who raised the axe. Down it came. Jason Morrow felt the heat of the blood ooze through the rubber skin of his wellington boots.

And if, at that moment, you had told Jason Morrow that a hundred years ago to the day his great-grandfather, William Morrow, had gassed himself in Room 406 on the top floor of the Station Hotel he would have been surprised. His surprise would have increased if you'd shown him great-grandad Morrow's signature on the bottom of the suicide note, because he would have seen the ghostly echo of it in his own signature, complete with the same vigorous zig-zag underlining. Although he would have been surprised he would have believed it all.

But if you had told Jason Morrow that by this time tomorrow he too would be dead—dead as the pig twitching and gushing blood at his feet—he wouldn't have believed you at all.

But both nuggets of information were true.

He nodded his head again. The axe came down. Jason Morrow moved across the killing floor.

And one by one the pigs, at last, stopped squealing.

3

Dr. David Leppington sipped his coffee and wondered whether to order another cake from the girl behind the cafe counter. It seemed shamelessly greedy—the Bakewell tart he'd just eaten had been huge—but now he was definitely gripped by the school's-out feeling and he was ready to make the most of his holiday.

I could walk up to the girl at the counter—pretty, blonde, red-varnished nails—ask her if she can recommend any good restaurants, then when she mentions a couple of names casually follow through and ask her for a date. Go on, David, urged a voice in his head. I dare you.

As the saying goes, he was as free as a bird since the break-up with Sarah; well, not so much a break-up, things just gently and gradually, very gradually, had dissolved over the last six months until they reached the point when they both had to agree that they were no longer an item. At least it was a painless separation for both parties. Even more painless because they weren't living together.

He watched the blonde waitress moving around the cafe, wiping down tables and straightening menus and sugar bowls. He'd begun to rehearse his opening lines when he noticed the glint of diamonds on the ring finger of her left hand.

Damn, he thought mildly. Oh well, there was still a fortnight ahead of him in Leppington; if the town held enough interest for him after all. Already he was thinking of perhaps moving on up the coast in a couple of days.

He sipped his coffee. Through the window he could see the great clot of dark cloud hanging over the quad towers of the Station Hotel. There was no sign of the crow now.

Another twenty minutes and he could check in. The lure of a hot bath seemed particularly strong now after the long train journey from Liverpool.

With time still to kill he pulled one of two letters from his pocket. It was from a Dr. Pat Ferman, one of the town's general practitioners; he was inviting David to consider taking over the practice on Dr. Ferman's retirement in six months. *I'm sure you'll enjoy working in Leppington*, ran the letter, *and would have much to gain professionally and socially, especially so as you have family ties that extend back many centuries* ... The letter was chatty and friendly and mentioned David's uncle, George Leppington, whom Dr. Ferman had known as a good friend and neighbour for the last thirty years, so the letter said. David hadn't seen his uncle since he left the town when he was six.

Would he accept the invitation to become a GP in this little town of his ancestors? He just didn't know. The idea of tootling round the lanes in a Land Rover like some medical version of Postman Pat was strangely appealing. There'd be no more nine-to-five in a mind-numbingly dull office at the Occupational Health Centre where all that was expected of him was to confirm or deny another doctor's diagnosis, or to advise businessmen to drink less booze and take more exercise. You might as well stand on a beach and recommend to the sea that the tide shouldn't come in today. The sea'd probably take more notice than the businessmen with expense accounts just itching to be used in expensive restaurants.

An elderly couple came into the cafe; they ordered toasted teacakes and hot chocolate, and sat down by the window. He noticed them glance in his direction. ('By heck, Ethel. There's a stranger in town"—no, it didn't need a mind-reader to know what they were thinking.)

David glanced at the clock above the counter. Ten minutes to check-in time. As he returned the letter to his pocket another envelope brushed against his fingers as if trying to attract his attention.

He'd not opened this letter yet, although he knew Katrina's handwriting well enough to realize who it was from.

OK, David, you're relaxed, you're in a good enough frame of mind to deal with it now; go ahead; read the damned thing; get it over and done with.

He pulled the white envelope from his pocket; quickly tore it open.

See, David, painless, isn't it? Read it, then tear it up and feed it to the bin in the corner.

But he knew he wouldn't do that. He'd read it a dozen more times before destroying it.

He pulled the letter from the envelope. The moment he opened it he knew he'd made a mistake. He should have postponed opening it that bit longer—postpone opening the damn thing until you've anesthetized yourself with a couple of beers, he thought, suddenly angry. You don't need this any more. You've not seen the woman in five years.

He opened the letter. The first thing that caught his eye was the housefly Sellotaped above the words "Dear David."

The fly's black body looked absurdly plump beneath the clear sticky tape. Its wings were missing. Not pulled off, he noted, but neatly snipped away with scissors. He jammed the letter unread back into the envelope and stuffed it again deep into his pocket.

A bitter taste welled up into his mouth.

4

From the deepest tunnels they surged upwards. They were hungry, eager for food. They moved quickly, purposefully, climbing upward to the passageways that ran just below the surface, and although they moved through absolute darkness instincts stamped deep into their very blood guided them.

When they reached their destination they waited, faces turned upward, knowing that in a second the deluge would come. Their sense of expectation filled the air; their bodies trembled with excitement.

Then it came, a torrent gushing down into a hundred or more open mouths.

The liquid sound filled the cave.

They fed. Their food was warm, wet, sweet. If there'd been enough light it would have revealed its colour. Red. Very red.

5

Wap!

The four tosspots lay at his feet in the grass. That had been a piece of friggin' cake. Easy or what?

The man ran his palm across his shaved head. The scar that ran like a streak of bright red lipstick from the corner of his eye to his ear tingled pleasantly. The way it did when he crushed vermin. He'd gashed the knuckles of his right hand planting his fist in one of the tosspots' baby-soft mouths but he didn't feel a thing. He wiped his bloody knuckles on a fistful of stinging nettles. Still he felt nothing.

"Listen to me," he told the four teenagers as they groaned and spat blood into the dirt. "From now on you'll do exactly as I tell you. All right?"

"Uh . . . ff-shit."

Wap!

He slapped the one struggling to his feet.

"You will do exactly as I say. Got that?"

"Fug off," one blubbered through a mouthful of spit, blood and drool.

Wap!

"I am . . ." *Wap!* ". . . the boss." *Wap!* "Now. Got it?" *Wap, wap.*

He yanked the kids to their feet and slapped their faces hard with the palm of his hand.

After five minutes' work, slapping their stupid heads, they started to come around to his way of thinking.

"Now, listen to me. Get up onto your knees. And kneel there until I tell you to move. Got it?"

Heads nodded.

"So what're you waiting for?"

The four, still wiping bloody noses and blinking tears from swollen eyes, dragged themselves to their knees, like they were kneeling in the presence of their king.

The scar on the side of the young man's head tingled even more strongly—like electricity was shooting from his eye to his ear. He felt good; he felt as strong as a monster from hell.

"I'll tell you this only once. I rule you now, okay?"

The four looked crushed. And all four nodded obediently.

Shit-hot, he thought, pleased. *Now I'm back in business.*

6

Electra Charnwood unlocked the basement door of the Station Hotel.

Electra? You can thank my poetry-loving mother for that pretty little posy of a name, she'd tell people, grinning. She was thirty-five years old, tall, sophisticated-looking, with black hair that reached her shoulders. She was also a cuckoo. Born bright in a dull town. It wasn't conceit on her part; it was just that she'd never felt as if she'd really belonged here, and that perhaps her parents had found her floating in a rush basket in the River Lepping. Maybe that wasn't so far off the mark; her dark hair, almost a bluey-black, and strong nose gave her a Semitic, perhaps even an Egyptian-princess look. In fact, she bore little resemblance at all to her parents who were mousy, freckled and anything but tall.

Electra was certainly no willow; she was big-boned and had drawn many an appreciative whistle from the brewery truck drivers as she'd hefted beer kegs into the basement lift. That was when her boozy, glass-backed cellarman hadn't shown up for work, as was his wont on a Monday morning. ('Must be the flu," cellarman Jim would snuffle into the phone; or "I think I'm going down with a migraine;" or "It's my bloody wisdom

41

teeth again; you don't know the pain I'm in.') Once she'd been so pissed off with the wisdom teeth one that she'd driven him to her dentist in Whitby, forced him into the chair and watched with a satisfaction that was near-monstrous when the dentist had told Jim that he needed more than a dozen fillings. The poor man's face had gone as white as snow. She could have sacked him for more reasons than she had fingers and toes, but when he did turn up to work he was conscientious enough—once she'd fed him enough booze. He didn't mind staying late to straighten up, empty ashtrays and wash the glasses. And, once she'd boosted his Dutch-courage levels, he was the only one brave enough to go down into the basement at night.

Electra switched on the basement lights. Light and dark in the basement had come to some kind of uneasy truce, she'd tell herself. When the lights came on the darkness would retreat, but only so far.

She walked briskly down the steps. She didn't want to be down there, she didn't like the hotel basement; she never had, ever since she'd been a child. But it had gone beyond fear now. A fatalism had soaked into her blood down through the years.

She checked the cases of wine, soft drinks and spirits. There'd be enough to see the hotel through to the end of the week. There would hardly be a rush of wine-quaffing tourists. Leppington wasn't on any tourist maps—unless slaughterhouses of titanic proportions were your thing.

Standing in the centre of the basement—as far from the walls, and their shadows, as she could possibly get—Electra let her sharp eyes roam over the cases of drink, beer kegs and plastic hoses that fed the beer to the handpumps in the bar upstairs. (One day she'd install electric pumps—but there never seemed a pressing need.)

She noted everything was in its place and as it should be. After the sounds she'd heard coming from down here last night she half expected to find the place completely wrecked. But then it was always like that. A lot of noise and fury, but she'd find not so much as a can of Pepsi out of place.

Now for the iron door at the end of the basement. Come on, Electra. You can do it. Best foot forward.

She steeled herself to walk the few metres into the shadows. You should have brought your torch, you silly mare, she scolded herself. But again that fatalism kicked in. If it's going to happen, it's going to happen, and there's nothing you can do about it.

She paused, licked her suddenly dry lips.

I shouldn't be here, she told herself. I don't belong here.

As if saying that would change the past. OK, so she'd been a bright young thing at school; she'd won the prizes for academic brilliance. She'd studied English at university. She'd landed the job as a researcher with a TV station in London. At twenty-five she was poised to be promoted front of camera as co-presenter on *Business Tonight*—but that was when it all went pear-shaped. Her mother died suddenly. (Dad had found Mum wide-eyed and cold on these very basement slabs, a broom clutched in her hand—by the brush head, not the handle.) Electra had come home for the funeral. Then, the day she was due to return to London to resume her glittering career (and take possession of the royal-blue Porsche she'd ordered from the dealer in Hampstead) her father had suffered a crippling stroke.

With no brothers and sisters to help out she'd taken over the running of the hotel, and effectively waved her TV career goodbye. Her father had been bed-ridden for the next six months, unable to walk, unable to go to the toilet himself, unable to even pronounce the letter "r."

"Electwa. Don't waste your time here. You've a caweer," he'd say—or at least try to say, fighting to get the words clear of his distorted lips.

"Don't worry, Dad. As soon as we can find a hotel manager I'll pick up the threads in London."

Her father had died that year, the same year as her mother. She'd watched his coffin being lowered into the ground, his voice still going around in her head: *Don't cwy for me, Electwa, twy not to cwy*.

She never had found that hotel manager. And ten years later she was still here in this shitty hotel. The career in TV was well and truly buried with dear old Dad. Damn. This hotel wasn't an asset; it was like a damn virus in her blood just waiting to go full blown. The noises in the basement at night—it was enough to drive a bloody saint to drink. Thank you, Mum, thank you, Dad. Why didn't you drive a stake through my heart when I was born and have done with it? The sudden upwelling of bitterness caught her by surprise. Her eyes pricked, she clenched her teeth and she found herself digging her nails into the palms of her hands.

Suddenly she walked forward into the shadows at the end of the basement where it narrowed until it was little more than a passageway to—

To nowhere, Electra. It goes nowhere. It's a dead end . . .

(Just like your life, kid.)

Now she could see nothing. She held out her hands into the darkness and walked forward.

Her fingers met it. It was cold and hard. The iron door that had frightened her so much as a child.

Frightened her mother, too. ('I can hear noises at the other side of the door,' her mother had said. "Sometimes I think I can hear people moving about through there." Dad had laughed it off, saying that there was nothing on the other side of the door but a section of disused basement.)

Mum claimed to have heard noises in the basement the day she died.

Found dead in the basement. She had died alone. Cold when they found her; eyes wide; brush head gripped in both hands the way the Angel Gabriel holds his sword when smiting demons. "There was a little pool of wee *spweading out fwom* her bottom," her father had mumbled towards the end, "a little pool of wee, Electwa. Can you imagine it? Your mother would have been so embawassed if she'd have known."

Well, she wouldn't know anything. She was as dead as a door-nail.

By touch, Electra checked the two padlocks that held the door shut. With a fatalistic shrug she gave the locks a good hard pull, almost daring them to come flying off in her hand.

When she was fifteen she'd seen a war documentary at school. It showed a soldier single-handedly firing a big field gun. Stripped to the waist, he lifted this big artillery shell up in his arms as if it was a baby, slipped it into the gun's breech, then fired it; the shock wave from the gun shook leaves from the trees. Most of her classmates wriggled or chatted—war documentaries interested teenage girls NOT! But Electra had seen something extraordinary. The single gunner's comrades all hid behind a mound of earth because the enemy were swarming over the hill and firing down at the lone gunner.

Fatalistically, that lone gunner, working in an exposed clearing in the wood, must have known that any second one of the hundreds of bullets buzzing through the air towards him would take his life. But he was beyond caring. He'd carry on firing the big gun until he was killed.

Even then Electra had a premonition that the clip of film was somehow significant. Now she empathized with that doomed gunner with an intensity that bordered on the monstrous.

She too felt as if she was fighting a losing battle (not the hotel; oh no, not the hotel, that was running at a profit).

Death's hurtling towards me, she thought, not in the shape of a bullet. No, it's something else. Just as lethal. She could feel it; just as she felt the blood running through her veins.

At that moment, the bell on the reception desk rang, breaking the spell.

With a sigh she stepped back out of the shadows and headed for the basement steps.

Maybe it's my Prince Charming; he's come to take me away from all this. But she knew it wasn't going to be as easy as that. Prince Charmings don't call on one-horse towns like Leppington. Just like the soldier in the documentary, she'd have to face the onslaught alone.

Chapter Five

Dr. David Leppington stepped through the doorway of the cafe into the fresh air. It was only a couple of minutes away from check-in time at the hotel across the market square. Now he really was looking forward to that hot shower.

He hoisted the holdall over one shoulder.

He'd taken barely a couple of steps in the direction of the hotel when he saw a middle-aged man in day-glo orange overalls hurrying towards him. One look at the man's tense expression told him something was wrong.

The man called to David, "Hey, mate, is there a telephone in the cafe?"

"I think so," David said, expecting there would be. Immediately there was a shout from his left.

"Tony! Best get the fire brigade out here, too. We can't shift him."

David shot a look left to where a knot of men in the same orange overalls—street cleaners, he guessed—were clustered over something where the road ended at the massive brick wall of the slaughterhouse.

David's instincts immediately joined forces with his professional training. A figure lay face down on the ground. Mentally he ticked off the possibilities: aneurysm, cardiac arrest, asthma attack, stroke, epileptic fit.

Heart beating faster as adrenalin squirted into his system, he hurried across the cobbled road to where the man lay.

The man wore street-cleaner overalls.

"What's wrong?" David asked crisply.

"Who are you?" The man who'd asked the question was more scared than aggressive.

"I'm a doctor. What happened to him?"

"It's our mate. He'd got his grab stuck down the drain." The man nodded at a metre-long pole with a mechanical clamp at one end on the ground beside a sloppy mound of silt; the device resembled an elongated set of forceps. "When he tried to free it, that's when he got his own hand stuck down there."

"Here, watch this, please." David handed his bag to one of the workmen and crouched beside the trapped man who lay face down on the ground, his arm thrust down into the drain. David could only see as far as the wrist. Oil-black slime covered the man's hand and fingers. The drain itself was nothing remarkable; a surface-water run-off drain you'd find set at the side of any road. The iron grating had been lifted clear and set on the ground just a metre or so away.

"Hello, I'm a doctor," he told the man. "Can you move your fingers?"

No response.

"Are you in pain?"

Daft question. David saw the man staring, eyes bulging, at his arm as it vanished into the water. His face was as white as

46

freshly fallen snow. The muscles stood out in his neck as if he was using every shred of will-power to stop screaming out loud.

"What's your name? Can you hear me? Tell me your name."

Again no response. The man stared down into the drain where his hand was trapped with all the astonishment of someone watching angels dancing on a pinhead.

David glanced up at the nearest workman—a man pushing fifty with grey stubble on his chin. "What's his name?"

"Ben Connor."

"How long has Ben been stuck like this?"

"Ten minutes. At first we thought he was just pulling our legs. You know, a practical—"

"You've tried pulling him free?"

"We tried. He's locked solid."

"Ben," David said gently. "Ben. Can you hear me?"

"He's only got his hand stuck," said one of the younger workmen; he wore a black jeep hat pulled down tight over his head; the man's expression was sullen.

"No, I don't like the look of him," David said quickly, his training in A&E coming rushing back. "He's going into shock."

"That serious?"

"Could be."

"Why?" the young man in the jeep hat asked in disbelief. "He's only got his flipping hand stuck."

"Shock is serious, believe me." David touched the man's skin: cold, clammy; it looked pale. Yep, classic symptoms of shock. He checked the pulse in the man's neck. It was rapid and far from strong. Shock. Definitely shock.

"We've got to get this man's arm out of there," he told the older workman.

"How? We've tried."

"Just give me a minute." He crouched down beside Ben who was still staring down into the drain as if something marvellous was going to emerge. "Ben . . . can you hear me?"

No response. The eyes glistened with a strange intensity.

"Ben . . . we're going to get your arm out of there."

Then the trapped man spoke with a morbid fascination. "My fingers . . . my fingers."

"Your fingers?" David said gently. "What about your fingers?"

47

The man swallowed. His eyes never flinched from his arm disappearing into the black drain water. "My fingers . . . something's *biting* them."

"There's something biting your fingers?"

"Rats," the young man said almost belligerently as he looked down at his trapped workmate. "Fucking rats have got him."

"There aren't any rats down there," the older man said. "I've never seen a single rat in them drains, or in the sewers here, in all my—"

"*Ah!*"

The man's self-control snapped. He looked down into the drain and let out a roar of sheer pain. He was panting but his face became even more pale.

"My fingers. They're eating my fingers . . . uh—uh . . ."

With another groan he slumped forward. David managed to get his hand under Ben's face before it hit the iron edge of the drain.

"What's wrong with Ben?" the old man demanded, frightened.

"He's fainted."

"Then he won't feel anything," the young workman announced in a self-satisfied way.

The next moment another workman ran up—the same one who had asked about the telephone in the cafe. "Fire engine and ambulance are on their way. Uh, what's the matter with Ben now? He's not—"

"No," David said quickly. "He's not. And I want it to stay that way."

"You mean—"

"I don't know what's happening to his hand down there," David said quickly, "but he's gone into shock."

"The fire engine will be here soon," said the young man in a way that was really starting to get up David's nose. "Why can't you wait until they get here?"

"Because he's showing signs of blood loss—this is a severe case of shock."

"But he'll be all right?" asked the older man, eyes wide.

"Only if we get his hand free. Believe me, shock can kill as efficiently as a bullet."

"What do you suggest?"

David nodded at the four strongest-looking men. "You, you, you and you." He felt in gear now; focused on saving the man's life. "Grab him by the overall. On the count of three, lift. Lift straight up as hard as you can. OK?"

"But—"

"Please do as I say. Your mate's life depends on it. OK, get a good grip. Make sure you lift straight upward, otherwise you'll snap his arm back against the elbow joint." He glanced at each face in turn; they'd follow his instructions to the letter. "OK, one, two, three—*lift*."

They lifted, with David holding the unconscious man's head. For the first few centimetres the body lifted easily from the floor. Then the arm pulled tight. David glanced down into the drain: the water surged round the man's fingers like black syrup. The hand remained locked tight. As if it had been set there in concrete.

"Next time pull harder."

The young man protested, "It'll pull his bloody arm out of its socket."

"Easier to re-socket the joint than restart his heart. His pulse is pretty weak." David took a deep breath while cradling the man's head. "Go on the count of three again. One, two, three . . . now."

This time the four men strained, clenched their teeth, veins standing out in their necks. They heaved like they were taking part in a tug-of-war.

The trapped man muttered; his eyes flickered open and rolled, showing the whites; even though he was unconscious the pain was punching its way through his brain.

"Come on. Pull harder."

David glanced back at the arm. It actually seemed to be stretching as if it was made from elastic; the strain on it was immense. He imagined the tendons cracking, the fibers stretched to breaking point.

Come on, come on . . .

Human beings are tough cookies . . . the arm shouldn't actually snap off . . . but, hell, look at the way it's stretching. The shoulder joint's going to pop any second.

"Yesss!"

Every man there sang out the second the hand snapped clear

of the drain; the man lifted as easily as a doll now; in fact, the sudden release almost threw the four men off balance.

"Right, listen carefully." David marvelled; his tones of quiet authority seemed to come from someone else. "Lay him down on the ground. Gently does it. Gently. Stand back, please." David expertly moved the unconscious man into the recovery position, lifting the man's leg that was furthest from him and rolling him onto his side. Quickly, he checked the unconscious man's airway: breathing still shallow and rapid, but otherwise tolerable.

"Jesus, look at his hand," one of the men said.

"Rats. I told you it was rats."

"And I told you there aren't no rats under here."

"All sewers've got rats."

"These haven't. I've been going down there for the last forty years."

"What had a go at his hand, then?"

David was too busy checking the man's vital signs to join in the great rat debate.

At last he could turn his attention to the man's hand. Gently he lifted the man's muscular arm in both his hands. Drain water blackened it to the elbow. He looked more closely.

Hell, what a mess.

The man's rubberized work gloves had been torn to nothing but loose strands that dangled from the cotton cuff of the glove.

"Told you, Doc." The irritating young man in the black jeep hat again. "Tell me that isn't the work of a rat?"

David didn't reply. The injured man needed his attention most.

The hand was smeared with that slick wet mud, black as oil, reeking thickly of drains. But overlaying the black were red smears of blood. He saw that the middle finger and forefinger were severed at the knuckle. The thumb had been cut through just above where it joined the hand. The stumps looked like chopped-up sausages. Splinters of startlingly white bone poked from the muck and blood.

David checked the tattered remains of the glove for any sign of the severed fingers. Nothing there.

Raising the man's arm to slow the bleeding, he looked up at one of the men. "The cafe will have a first-aid box. Please bring it . . . wait a second, I'll also need a roll of cling film, a plastic bag full of ice cubes and a couple of clean towels."

The man didn't question the list and sprinted away in the direction of the cafe.

The young man in the black jeep hat said, "Why haven't you used a tourniquet to stop the bleeding?"

"I *want* him to bleed."

"What?"

"I'm controlling the bleeding. The flow of blood is washing the dirt from the wound."

"But—"

"Shut up, Stevo." The older workman sounded tired. "Let the doctor work."

David looked up gratefully at the older workman. "What you could do for me is get as much material out of the drain as possible."

"His fingers?"

David nodded. "If we can find them the surgeon might be able to reattach them." As the man walked towards the drain David added, "Best use the mechanical grab. Not your own hands."

"Don't worry. No danger of that." The workman picked up the grab and lowered the business end into the drain where he began hoisting out silt and twigs dripping with that filthy, stinking water.

"Watch out for rats, Greg," the young man said.

"I told you, there aren't any rats."

"What got Ben's fingers, then?"

The old man shrugged and concentrated on pulling the mud out of the drain.

David kept quiet while he studied the man's wounded hand. True, rats *could* gnaw away fingers, but it would take hours for them to do this kind of damage—and usually the victim was long dead by the time they got to him or her, perhaps murdered and dumped in undergrowth where the rats could patiently work undetected. Also, this damage wasn't at all consistent with rat bites: the finger bones had been crushed to splinters, not gnawed. And now he'd carefully wiped away some of the mud from the hand he could see further bites on the man's hand and fingers. These hadn't punctured the skin, but they had left a

51

series of deep indentations in what approximated a letter C shape.

He recognized these bite marks clearly enough. Only it wasn't possible they'd been inflicted while the man's hand was down the drain. They must have been inflicted (possibly self-inflicted?) earlier in the day.

The workman returned with the first-aid kit, and the rest of the items David had listed.

As David worked, quite a crowd gathered to watch, their eyes wide. *It certainly beats TV medical dramas—why, you can almost taste the blood, can't you, Mrs. Jones?*

The voice in the back of his head tossed forward the odd flippant remark, but he didn't allow it to affect the way he worked—his own fingers moved swiftly, skillfully applying dressings to the still-raw wounds. The man's blood washed over his own hands to the extent he had to sometimes pause to wipe his fingers on the cafe's towel—which bore a picture of Whitby Abbey, some part of his mind dispassionately noted. He'd hand that over to the ambulancemen for incineration.

He called to the grey-haired workman clearing out the drain. "Any luck?"

"I've got everything out I can get with the grab."

"OK."

"Do you want me to try using my hand?"

"No. It's not worth the risk."

"What do you want me to do with this?" he asked, pointing at the pile of oozing silt.

"I'll go through it." David gently placed the injured man's hand down onto a folded towel.

"Would you like me to keep his hand held high?" asked a teenage girl eagerly. "That slows the blood loss, doesn't it?"

"No, thanks. He'll be fine like that." Ideally, the hand should be raised but he didn't want the man's blood being spread round any further than it had to be. "But if you could keep an eye on him and shout to me if his breathing becomes laboured or if he comes to. OK?"

She smiled and nodded, pleased to be put in charge.

"Thanks." David moved across to the pile of silt. If anything, it looked like a mound of sloppy diarrhoea. Trying to avoid breathing through his nose, to minimize catching the stink, he took a couple of pencils from his jacket pocket and held them like chopsticks. (See, David, he told himself, even all those boozy nights spent in Chinese restaurants weren't wasted.) With the improvised tweezers he quickly began to pick up anything that looked as if it might belong to poor Ben across there on the pavement. Twigs, leaves, cigarette butts, a spent cigarette lighter, a foreign coin—all dross washed into the drain from the street. Then he saw a stubby sausage-shaped object. Chopstick-style, he plucked it from the grue like it was a big, juicy prawn.

He held it up to get a better look.

Ben's thumb.

"Is it . . . you know?" asked the workman.

David nodded. "The thumb. There's no sign of the fingers, unfortunately."

He returned to his audience. As they watched, he began to wrap the severed thumb in cling film.

Stevo in his black hat said, "Aren't you going to wash it first?"

"No."

"Why not? It's covered in shit and stuff."

"You must never wash a severed limb. The hospital staff will take care of that." He looked at the teenage girl. "How's our patient doing?"

The girl flushed, pleased. "His breathing's slowing down . . . so's his pulse," she added quickly.

"You didn't touch his wrists?"

"No. I checked the pulse in his neck."

"Well done. Thanks." He shot her a smile; she blushed again, looking pleased with herself.

A good kid. Not like Stevo who sounded as if he was trying to pick a fight in a bar rather than show concern for his injured workmate.

"You've got to wash it," he insisted, "just look at the state of it."

"Trust me, it'll be fine."

"Are you sure you're a doctor?"

"Yep, I'm a qualified doctor." He gave the man a bright artificial smile. "Now, if you'd kindly hold this for me, sir."

He took Stevo's hand and placed the severed thumb—now securely wrapped in cling film—in his palm. The torn thumb-

53

nail, looking like a fragile seashell, showed through the transparent plastic; at the point of amputation, strings of meat were now sandwiched between cling film and skin.

As Stevo's eyes glazed David took the thumb back, wrapped it in his clean handkerchief, then carefully laid it amongst the ice cubes in the plastic bag.

Stevo watched the thumb nestling amongst the ice. His face paled; a second later he folded up onto the pavement in a dead faint.

"Hell's bells," said one of the man's workmates. "What shall we do with him, Doc?"

"Leave him." David suppressed the grin coming to his lips. "He'll come to in a moment."

He wrote the injured man's details—name, date of accident— on the back of his train ticket which he slipped into the bag with the thumb. They'd need the information in Casualty, when the ambulance—speak of the devil!—got him there. Blue lights flashing, the ambulance roared up the access road to the station. Seconds later the fire engine followed.

Now, at last, it was plain sailing. Within moments the injured man was stretchered into the ambulance; David handed over the bag of ice, complete with thumb, to the paramedic. He wished they'd managed to pull the fingers from the drain, but at least they had the thumb. Microsurgery was advanced enough probably to save the thumb, and with that all-important opposable digit, evolved by man and monkey alike, the injured man shouldn't be too handicapped in what he could do.

The ambulance roared away, siren whooping. The firemen turned their attentions to scooping more muck from the drain, but David doubted they would have any luck finding the fingers.

Stevo was sitting on the pavement, looking decidedly nauseous; he wiped his sweating face with the black jeep hat.

The other workmen thanked David and wanted to shake him by the hand, but he showed them his own bloody hands. Instead they slapped him on the back and promised to buy him a beer if they bumped into him in any of Leppington's thirteen watering holes.

With the live show over, the crowd had dispersed. Now David was left alone to retrieve his bag. He picked it up, realizing the handles were going to be pretty badly smeared with blood and drain silt. What the heck, it had felt good to be a useful cog in the great engine of humanity again.

As he crossed the market square in the direction of the hotel, he wondered just what *had* got hold of the man's hand in the drain and snapped off his fingers and thumb like they were breadsticks. No rat had done that.

As for the bite marks on the man's hand . . .

They couldn't possibly have been inflicted in the drain. David Leppington had no doubts at all. Those bite marks had been made by a human being.

Chapter Six

It was almost two in the afternoon by the time David Leppington actually made it into the hotel's lobby. The reception desk backed onto the curving wall that carried the dramatic sweep of the staircase. The receptionist, a tall woman with hair so black it carried tints of blue, was busy talking to a man.

The man, in shirtsleeves, wore a cellarman's apron; he was holding a couple of new, shining steel padlocks in his hands.

"Are you sure, Miss Charnwood?" he was saying.

"Positive, Jim."

"But the old padlocks are sound as a bell."

"Well, I'm asking you to fix another two to the door."

"The door in the basement?"

"That's the one, Jim."

"I've still to bring up the empties." The cellarman wasn't refusing, but it sounded like a job he wanted to put off—to the Twelfth of Never if possible.

"The empties can wait," the woman told him with an air of cool authority. "You put those new padlocks on for me."

"As well as the old ones?"

"Yes, as well as the old ones, Jim. And I'll make you a nice coffee . . . an Irish Coffee when you've done."

The cellarman nodded as the receptionist listed more jobs.

David took the time to let his eyes rove round the lobby. It was a hotel that had seen happier days. But it looked clean enough; it certainly wasn't seedy. The carpet was a plush yet muted purple; the tall windows were draped with velvet curtains, again in purple. If anything, it looked like a Victorian undertaker's.

"Dr. Leppington?"

The receptionist gave David a welcoming smile.

He returned the smile. "Good afternoon. I made a reservation by fax last week."

"Welcome to the Station Hotel. I'm Electra Charnwood, the proprietor." The woman, smiling broadly, came out from behind the desk and held out her hand in a gesture that seemed almost masculine.

"Sorry, I'd best not." Smiling, he put down his bag and held out both hands.

"Good heavens, it's not often a man comes into the hotel with blood on his hands."

She wasn't shocked; she smiled in a way that seemed peculiarly knowing. "Hurt much?" she enquired.

"It's not mine, fortunately, but this trip's turning out to be something of a busman's holiday."

"You're a surgeon?"

"No," he smiled good-naturedly. "A lowly doctor—strictly dicky backs and cholesterol levels."

"Yuk, that does look messy," she said breezily, looking at the hands. "You must wash. Follow me."

"Eh, thanks . . . but not the kitchen."

"You're the doctor. There's a sink in the utility room—no food's prepared here."

She held open the door, standing so he had to pass under her arm as if it were an archway. He was tall, but she was sufficiently statuesque to allow him to pass underneath without having to stoop too much.

"Do you have any disinfectant?" he asked, watching her turn on the taps for him.

"Will neat alcohol do?"

"That'll be perfect."

"Nasty stuff, blood. Especially these days."

"Better safe than sorry."

"I remember in my youth—"

She talks like she's all of ninety, he thought, but she can't be much past her mid-thirties, although her clothes make her look older. She was dressed all in black with an ankle-length skirt that lent her an Edwardian look as if she was on her way to a period costume party.

"I remember in my youth," she was saying, "if a friend cut themself you often obliged by sucking the dirt out of the wound."

"It wasn't a good idea even then. Are you sure you want to use that?"

The woman was unscrewing the top from a bottle of vodka. "Believe me, you wouldn't want to *drink* this. It's industrial alcohol. You see, I had to take over the running of the hotel in one heck of a hurry when my father fell ill," she explained. "In those days I was as green as I was cabbage-looking. I got fleeced more than once. On one occasion I bought twenty-four bottles of vodka from a dodgy wholesaler—of course, it wasn't really vodka at all. You'd probably go blind if you downed a couple of these with your tonic."

She poured the clear spirit onto his hands as he held them over the sink.

As he washed them clean she said admiringly, "Hell of a mess. Did you save a life?"

He smiled and briefly ran through what had happened across near the station.

"Something *bit* him?" she echoed.

"One of the workmen thought it was a rat."

"Some rat."

"The injury wasn't consistent with a rat bite. Also one of the other workmen swore blind he'd never seen a rat in the area."

"Oh, believe me, Dr. Leppington, there are rats aplenty round here. They pour into the hotel every night."

He looked at her, surprised by her frank admission. Then he saw the smile on her face.

"Oh, I take it these come scurrying in on two feet?"

"Correct, doctor. Their natural habitat is the public bar where they look for a mate," she continued. "But unlike rats that take a partner for life, this species of rat is only looking for one-night stands."

He looked at her face, wondering if he heard the bitter tones of first-hand experience. But she seemed quite nonchalant. She tipped more of the counterfeit vodka onto his hands. "That sufficient?"

"That'll be fine. I'll finish off with soap."

"Paper towels are in the dispenser."

"Thanks."

"Need anything else?"

"No." He smiled. "Clean as a whistle."

She appraised him with her blue eyes for a moment. At last, just as he was starting to feel uncomfortable, she said, "So: you're a Leppington?"

"My father lived here. In fact, I was born here."

"But you didn't stay?"

"My parents moved when I was six."

She smiled ruefully. "One of the lucky ones who managed to escape, eh?"

"My father was a biochemist. He went where the work was."

"Liverpool?"

David nodded as he balled the paper towel and pushed it down into a basket. "But I never acquired the Scouse accent."

"So what brings a Leppington back to his ancient stomping ground?"

"Curiosity. I haven't seen the place since I was six."

"And not everyone has a town named after them?"

"Well, I'm not sure if it isn't the other way round."

"Oh, believe me," she said, "your ancestors gave the town its name."

"Apparently they were a feisty bunch."

"They certainly made their mark on the place."

"I take it they're not remembered with tremendous affection?"

"It depends on who's telling the story." She toyed with a strand of that glossy blue-black hair. "Angels to some people, devils to others."

As David rolled down the sleeves of his shirt he said, "When I told an old guy that my name was Leppington he looked at me as though I should have a stake hammered through my heart."

She smiled. "He's probably sharpening one at home right now."

"You think I'll wake up in the middle of the night to find the locals walking up the street with burning torches, brandishing pitchforks and baying for my blood?" A joke, but he wondered if there was some antipathy that ran deep.

"A thousand years ago, perhaps. But today, Doctor, I'd steel yourself for nothing more lethal that a couple of cold stares."

"I'll bear it in mind."

Her smile broadened. "Seriously, I don't think you should worry. The real reason why the Leppingtons dropped in the local popularity poll was because the Leppington family sold off the slaughterhouse. A shady character took it on, but he wasn't interested in making money on the meat market. He raided the pension funds, then legged it to Monte Carlo."

"So it's not really our fault—the Leppingtons' fault?"

"The locals have got to blame somebody." She said it carelessly. "All clean? Good. I'll check you in, then I can show you to your room."

David followed Electra back to the reception desk. He knew little about his family's history—at least, the Leppington side, that was. It just wasn't mentioned. Now he had this gut feeling that he would find out more soon enough. From outside, there came a grumble of thunder as a chilling rain began to fall on Leppington town.

Chapter Seven

1

All right, David, he told himself sternly. Don't put it off any longer. It's time you staked this particular beast through the heart.

He dumped his bag by the hotel wardrobe, then sat on the bed.

Rain crackled against the window.

He pulled Katrina's letter from his pocket, opened it and

quickly read the few lines written in brown felt-tip. He read it with one hand over his mouth—an involuntary reaction to distress or unhappiness. Because to put your hand against your lips is to recreate the sensation of the mother's breast against the infant's mouth; for adults as well as children it's a way of comforting yourself. David would have recognized the action from his work on human behavioural psychology as a medical student. But this letter was a great leveller—now he was just another unhappy human being needing comfort.

When he'd read the letter twice, deliberately ignoring the fly Sello-taped in the top left-hand corner, he stuffed the letter into the drawer.

Why don't you tear the damn thing up and flush it?

Because I know I need to read it again before I destroy it.

Snap out of it, David. Why do you have to play the messiah? Why do you have to absorb the suffering of others?

It was an old argument he replayed inside his head each time one of Katrina's letters landed on his doormat.

He looked out of the hotel window, wondering whether to take a hard walk up into the hills, in the vain hope sheer speed would shake Katrina's ghost off his back—yeah, as if it would, David Leppington. Admit it, you're a haunted man.

The market traders were packing away as the rain fell harder. He saw the access road where just a couple of hours before he had fought to get the workman's hand from the drain. He thought about telephoning the local hospital to get an update on the man's condition.

So you can play the two-bit messiah again? And take some of the man's pain away from him and into you? Is that why you became a doctor? Not to heal. But to steal other people's pain? As if you're some kind of vampire? Instead of blood, you feed on their suffering?

Oh, give it a break, Leppington, he thought sourly. Katrina's letters always had this poisonous effect on him. Come on, for heaven's sake, you're a nice guy. Be nice to yourself for a change.

He moved across to a chest of drawers where there was a courtesy tray complete with kettle, sachets of coffee, jiggers of UHT and a little Cellophane pack of biscuits.

Now . . . my prescription is: forget the letter.

Easier said than done.

Katrina West had been his first real love. At school they'd been inseparable: did homework together, ate lunch together. And, eventually, slept together—his first real sexual experience. It had been a mind-blowing weekend in August when his parents had gone away on holiday, leaving him at home.

That was when being home alone could really be fun.

Katrina had come up with some plausible excuse for her parents and they'd spent an extremely hot and electrifying eighteen hours in his single bed. They'd both been seventeen.

Seventeen. That's an old man when it comes to losing your cherry, he'd thought. Better late than never. God, he'd walked tall the days following that duck-breaking weekend.

After school they'd gone their separate ways: he'd headed north to Edinburgh to study medicine. She went up to Oxford: she'd been the academic star of Loxteth High School—photo in the paper; met the mayor; opened a Summer fête—the works.

Within six months it had all turned to crap.

One day a letter arrived at his hall of residence from Katrina's mother saying that Katrina had suffered a nervous breakdown; he still remembered the letter verbatim. Obviously in a state of shock, Mrs. West had written in a series of staccato sentences resembling an old-fashioned telegram. *Katrina's in hospital. Very poorly. We're very worried.*

And that's where Katrina had stayed ever since. After months of tests and detailed observation the psychiatrist had eventually diagnosed paranoid schizophrenia.

Often schizophrenia is treatable with chlorpromazine, and more rarely with ECT. In Katrina's case it was a deep-rooted son of a bitch. All the symptoms were there: the delusions, the hallucinations, both audio and visual; she heard voices; she was convinced a shadowy figure that was part man, part animal followed her constantly. She created her own magical defence systems against attack from the beast-man: that was, she always wore blue, she had to brush her teeth in a very specific way (up and down six times, then from left to right three times while saying the word "blue-blue-blue" over and over). If she didn't follow these ritualistic measures she'd be terrified to the point of mania and would have to be sedated. After a while, she began to suffer from the delusion that the beast-man was her boyfriend,

61

David Leppington. That he'd undergone some kind of evil transformation. That he wanted to drink her blood and eat her heart.

At the request of her family he'd stopped visiting her at the mental hospital. That had been five years ago: the second she saw him walking across the ward, basket of fruit nervously clasped in palms that would sweat like fury—she'd shriek piercingly, then run away in blind terror. But that was when the letters started. At first, she'd write to him two or three times a day. They were always variations on the same theme:

Dear David,
I know what you want from me. I sense your passion and determination in wanting to steal my blood. Blood is precious; it is life in solution; it is red rubies; rubies are found in crowns, in the ground; the earth is thick beneath one's feet; that thick earth supported the blanket on which we lay when you forced your penis into me. I knew that penis would not give the seed of life; it would draw life from me; it was a tube that would drain me of my blood. My blood would be in your veins . . .

The letters rambled on, expressing a chaotic association of ideas (again, textbook symptoms of the schizophrenic which he had studied as a student. Only you never expect that the person you love will ever be held in the evil thrall of such a disgusting disease.)

I know you will kill me, ran the letters, *you will drink my blood, you will eat my heart; I will die in your strong arms . . .*

The classic persecution complex; a textbook symptom.

Your feet sound in the corridor outside my apartment (actually her room in the hospital); *bare feet with black pads on the bottom like a dog or Benji the cat . . .*

A schizophrenic often fails to distinguish fantasy from reality.

I pray for blue. Only blue can save me now. Blue is the colour of the sky and the veins under my skin; those veins you will bite and suck; your penis will invade my cave and draw my blood once more. You are a vampire-hearted man, David Thomas Leppington. Please eat him, not me (a blue line ran from the word "him" up the page to link up with the Sellotaped fly). *I will send you more. Believe me. Spare me. I will send more. I will send a kitten if I can. Eat him—not me. Although I am resigned, stoic, fatalistic. I know I will die in your strong arms . . .*

And so on. He tore open the pack of biscuits. The rain on the hotel room window had begun to irritate him more than was completely rational, and he knew it. Katrina's letter was corrosive. There was no other description. The bloody thing was eating into him. He'd have to—

There was a knock on the door.

He gaped at it for a moment, so wrapped up in his thoughts about Katrina that it felt as if he was waking from a dream—

—no, a damn nightmare.

The knock came again.

Snapping himself out of it, he opened the door.

Electra stood there with a a pile of clean towels in her arm. She smiled warmly. "Sorry to disturb you. I've just brought you more towels."

"Oh, thanks very much," he said and awkwardly took the towels while still holding the packet of biscuits in one hand and a half-eaten biscuit in the other.

"That trip up here must have given you an appetite." Her smile was vivacious as she pushed back a strand of her blue-black hair.

"I expect it has."

Would it be polite to invite her over the threshold, or would she get the wrong message? he wondered, feeling socially awkward now. It didn't seem polite to talk to her across the threshold of the doorway.

"I thought I'd mention we do have a laundry service if you need it. Also, because we don't have an in-house movie system, we can let you have a video machine on daily rental."

"I thought I'd try and give television a miss for a few days." He smiled back, wondering if he sounded pretentious. "Take advantage of the countryside, get some exercise. I've become a bit of a couch potato."

"Mmm, you look fit enough to me, Dr. Leppington."

"Eh, David . . . please. Just David."

"OK, David." She smiled as she turned to go. "Oh, nearly forgot. Would you like dinner tonight? No, not as a resident, but as my personal guest?"

"Ah, thanks. I hadn't made any plans." He heard a stammer

creep into his voice and wondered if he was blushing. This woman moves fast.

"There'll just be three people. You, myself and another one of my long-term inmates."

He hesitated. Reluctant to hurt her feelings but . . .

"We don't get much news from the outside world." She flashed that smile again. "The last guest we had for dinner astonished us all with news that man had just walked on the Moon."

He smiled, amused. "I'd be delighted, Electra."

"If you can make your way down to the lounge bar for around seven-thirty for a pre-prandial something or other—on the house, of course. You're a celebrity guest. Ciao." With another vivacious smile she swept away down the corridor.

David closed the door, unable to avoid asking himself if there'd be another knock on the door later that night. He imagined Electra standing there in the moonlight. If it came to the crunch, what would his reaction be then?

The time was four P.M.

2

At five-thirty Bernice stepped under the hot shower in her hotel bathroom. She loved the sensation of the needle-sharp jets of water as they struck her bare flesh. She'd spent the afternoon working with Jenny and Angie in the dispatch room, preparing the leeches for transit out to the hospitals. The mood had been light-hearted; the three of them had spent most of the time laughing over bits of juicy gossip served up by Jenny or Angie's reminiscences about her ex-husband's inept attempt to run a themed Dracula hotel in Whitby.

They'd asked Bernice if she knew any dark secrets about Electra Charnwood and if she indulged in any unspeakable acts in the hotel with travelling salesmen.

"Of course she does," Bernice had said, giggling, as she addressed leech containers, preparing them for the arrival of the courier that evening.

"Go on, then," they'd said, wide-eyed. "What unspeakable practices?"

"I can't tell."

"Why?"

"Because they're unspeakable."

Angie slapped a label on the plastic travelling box. "That Electra. She's a weird one, though, don't you think?"

"Leppington's answer to Morticia Addams," added Jenny. "Have you ever seen her with a man, Bernice?"

"Not a live one, anyway."

All three dissolved into giggles again.

When Bernice had walked into the hotel after work Electra had stopped her. "New guest, Bernice. Absolutely gorgeous. I've invited him to dinner tonight. I thought we both could do with a little stimulation." Electra had then smiled her wicked smile and added in a whisper, "I've put him in the room next to yours." Then she'd sailed away in the direction of the kitchen with a bright, "Drinks at seven-thirty. Put on your posh frock, and don't be late. The early bird and all that."

Bernice turned her back on the shower curtain, feeling the sting of the hot jets.

She closed her eyes and raised her face to the water.

Even though the sensation was pleasurable, Imagination, that first lord of mischief, was already trying to undermine her relaxed frame of mind.

Why do I always think of that scene in *Psycho*? she asked herself. Yes, *that* scene. The girl's standing in the water, steam billowing. Then the shadow appears on the shower curtain, a silhouette of a raised hand holding a knife. It's imagination again. Trying to spoil everything I enjoy. But—no—I won't allow myself to think of the videotapes in the suitcase. If I don't think about them now then I might not wake up thinking about them tonight. And I won't wonder what happened to the man who'd occupied my room. Mike Stroud with the blond hair and gentle voice . . . Stop thinking about it, Bernice. You see, it begins as insidiously as that. Think about the new guest in the room next to yours.

What he's like? Tall, dark, handsome? Or short and plump with hair growing out of his ears?

Bernice closed her eyes again and turned her back to the pricking shower jets. The water streamed down her skin, down her legs, taking the scent of her shower gel, and her body, as it gurgled away into the drainage pipes before it fell four storeys to the main drain.

Electra carefully applied mascara to her long lashes; in the mirror her hair glinted that gunmetal blue. Outside rain fell. When Cleopatra, Queen of Egypt and her lover Mark Antony lost the battle of Actium they knew the Roman army would soon reach their palace in Alexandria. They knew they would be hacked to death. But, instead of moping away their final days, they had held lavish parties, listened to music, made love. They were going to make the most of what was left of their lives.

Electra fastened a simple black-bead necklace around her long neck. She knew how Cleopatra and Mark Antony had felt. She would make the most of what time was left to her, too.

Below the hotel, in the brick-skinned tunnels of the sewer, water gushed in complete darkness. From an outlet pipe warm water joined cold water in the main channel. There, noses smelt the water, filtering the chemical odours from the human scents. A quiver of excitement ran through those that squeezed their thick bodies into the tunnel. Beneath the scents of shampoo, the shower gel—the cloaking devices of modern humanity—they smelt the real body beneath: it was sweet, rich, and spoke clearly of the hot blood that coursed through the body's veins.

Oh, how much they hungered. The need for that blood was a burning fire in their stomachs. Only human blood could completely quench that fire.

The time was coming. *He had promised* . . .

3

"What do you want to go out on a night like this for?"

He didn't want to. He had to.

"I promised some of the lads at work."

"I thought you didn't like to socialize with them?"

"I don't."

"Why are you going, then?"

Jason Morrow looked down at his wife as she sat in her armchair, impatiently flicking through TV channels, hunting for a programme that would occupy her for more than ten minutes.

"I'm obliged," he said. "It's John Fettner's leaving party."

"I thought you hated him?"

She was suspicious. She knew he was lying.

"I can't say I'm a member of his fan club." He slipped on his leather jacket. "I'll be glad to see the back of the lazy sod. But I'm management now. It's expected."

"How long will you be?"

Get the anglepoise lamp, why don't you, woman? he thought, feeling the heat rise through his gut. Use the rubber hose; beat a confession out of me. Christ, wouldn't you be surprised?

"Just a couple of hours," he told her, still managing to sound calm. "There's a bar of chocolate in the cupboard. Want me to get it for you?" Nonchalantly—at least, making a good act of nonchalance—he checked the cash in his wallet. There was enough if he had to pay for it.

She lit a cigarette and pinched it between her fingers. I bet she wishes that was my damned windpipe, he thought savagely. Bitch. You made me like this. You're to blame!

He forced a smile onto his face, but already he'd begun to rub the area of skin just above his left eyebrow; a nervous habit of old. "I'll see you later, love. Want a Chinese bringing back?"

"All right, then; if that's all I'm getting out of you tonight."

"You've got some beer left in the pantry?"

"Go on, Jason." She blew cigarette smoke up at the ceiling through the tight, spiteful ring of her lips. "Hurry up. Don't keep your friends waiting."

"See you later, then." She'd turned her attention back to the television by the time he'd lowered his face to kiss her. She didn't look up so he kissed the top of her head. The smell of the natural grease in her hair made him swallow. Cigarette smoke was preferable to that.

"I'll see you later, then?" he repeated.

"Expect you will."

At the door he paused, looking back at her. He rubbed his forehead. She was twenty-eight. She'd been beautiful once.

He was going to add, "Love you," the endearment that had lightly slipped from their lips in their honeymoon days. The words stuck in the back of his throat.

Quickly, he walked through into the hallway, then out the

back door to where his car was parked on the driveway.

God, he hated to have to do this. But he did have to. It was as if a poison dripped into his system. Every few weeks he'd feel the pressure building. Then he had to release it or he felt something would burst; that he'd spray all the poison, and this madness, this fucking dreadful madness all over the town.

He blamed his wife for his disgusting behaviour. He wished he didn't do this. He managed to forget about it for weeks on end. Then came the pressure: building and building, threatening to poison his life. For crying out loud, it's all that bitch's fault.

He unlocked the car door, sat behind the wheel, jammed the key into the ignition. Right, where should he try first? Which happy hunting ground? The strange grin that racked his face wasn't one of humour. It was a snarl full of fury and fright.

Christ, this was as much fun as playing Russian Roulette with five shells in the chamber. It'd only be a matter of time before some great bucket full of explosive shit would hit the fan then it would be all over. Finito. RIP.

Christ Almighty, Jason Morrow knew—knew exactly—why people killed themselves. They shit themselves into a corner. They can't get out. No escape. He rubbed the small ridge of bone over his left eyebrow.

If only he knew he'd inherited the habit from his great-grandfather, William R. Morrow. When his great-grandfather felt trapped he'd raise a stubby finger to his forehead; then rub the same bony bump above his left eyebrow.

No way out—no way out—no way out . . .

A hundred years ago Grandfather Morrow'd done the same in the room in the Station Hotel. He'd worked at the bump with his finger as he'd signed his name on the suicide note.

Then, still rubbing the bump . . . *no way out—no way out . . .* he'd turned on the gas. In those days the gas, produced by baking coal, was lethal.

William Morrow's great-grandson twisted the key. The engine started.

Jason rubbed the bony lump under the skin with his own stumpy fingers. No way out.

He knew that as clearly as if it'd been written on the side of his poxy house in letters of fire.

His great-grandfather had killed himself (although the great-grandson didn't know anything of the family history any further back than a great-uncle's exploits storming ashore at Normandy in 1944). Jason Morrow wouldn't have the opportunity for that act of self-deliverance, as they called suicide these days.

He was going to die soon. And badly.

Chapter Eight

1

David Leppington, casually dressed in a white cotton shirt and chinos, descended the main staircase into the hotel lobby. It was deserted; although, from one doorway, he heard a jukebox and the buzz of voices. That was probably the public bar. Electra Charnwood had invited him to the lounge bar. Sure enough, he found the glass-paneled door with the words "Lounge Bar" scrolled across the top in gold letters and went inside.

A girl with fair hair and striking brown eyes stood behind the bar shaking ice cubes into a large plastic head that sat on the counter. Above the plastic head's two staring eyes were the words "ICE TO SEE YOU," then came the brand name of an alcopop.

Katrina's letter still niggled away in the back of David's head. He thought of the fly Sellotaped to the letter.

Was Katrina even now rocking backwards and forwards on her bed in the mental hospital, humming tunelessly to herself, drool oozing from shapeless lips and imagining her ex-lover greedily tearing away the Sellotape so he could stuff the plump fly into his mouth? Maybe she was; or maybe she imagined he was pacing up and down outside the hospital room, just biding his time before he burst in to fasten his mouth on her neck and . . .

The girl was staring at him. She probably thought *he* was the one out to lunch, he realized.

Order a beer; smile, he instructed himself.

"Hello. A pint of Guinness, please." He reached into his pocket for loose change.

"You're Dr. Leppington?" asked the girl, replacing a plastic scalp on the head-shaped ice bucket.

News travels fast in Leppington. "Guilty," he said, smiling. "I'm in Room 407; do you need cash? Or can you put it on the room account?"

"Neither, I'm afraid." The girl smiled. "I'm a guest, too."

"Oh? Sorry. I thought you were one of the bar staff."

"I'm just helping Electra out. The cellarman's not arrived, so there's semi-organized chaos going on out back. Guinness, wasn't it?"

"Perhaps I should wait?"

"Electra said we should help ourselves. I'm getting a dab hand at this," the girl told him, picking up a glass and moving to the beer tap. "You know, the trick is tipping the glass to just the right angle. There . . ." She concentrated on the white foam pouring into the glass. "Also, when you pour Guinness you should only part-fill the glass, then leave it for a moment to settle."

He saw her glance at his hand that held the coins. "No, that's okay, Dr. Leppington," the girl told him cheerfully. "You're Electra's guest. This is on the house."

"Thank you very much."

The girl wiped her fingers on a bar towel and held out the hand. "Hello. My name's Bernice Mochardi. I suppose I'm an old-timer at the Station Hotel now; I've been here twelve weeks."

"David Leppington." He shook her hand and smiled. "Twelve weeks? You take your holidays very seriously, don't you?"

"I work here, in the town that is, for my sins. I'm still in the process of finding a house of my own, but the truth is staying in a hotel is making me lazy. I don't have to do my own laundry. I don't even have to make my own bed. Is that wicked or is that wicked?"

David found himself warming to her immediately. Her brown eyes were as vivacious as the smile; and she seemed such a friendly, down-to-earth kid.

"Take a seat," Bernice waved her hand to take in a dozen plum-coloured velvet chairs arranged around wrought-iron tables. "I'll just open a bottle of beer and I'll join you."

David chose a table closest to the bar. "Electra Charnwood's my idea of the perfect hotelier. But she won't make a profit out of us if she gives drinks away."

"It's not every day we have one of the famous Leppingtons come to call on us. From what Electra says it's almost on a par with a visit from royalty."

"Royalty? I'm afraid she might find me a bit disappointing. The only crown I possess is the one showing through where my hair's going thin."

She laughed. "Nonsense. You've a lovely head of hair." Then she blushed as if she'd been overly familiar. "You're here on holiday?"

"Just a short break. I was just curious to see what the town looked like."

"But you once lived here?"

By jimminy, news did travel fast.

"Until I was six years old. I can hardly remember the town. But I think I can remember eating a ham sandwich in this hotel once." He smiled. "It just shows the priorities of a six-year-old when it comes to memory. I recall the sandwich but not the building."

"Good evening, Dr. Leppington," Electra called brightly as she entered the bar. "Sorry, that should be David, shouldn't it? Good evening, Bernice."

"Hi," Bernice said.

David stood up, half-feeling he should bow. "Good evening, Electra."

"Bernice, you've taken care of our guest's creature comforts? Good."

Electra strode across the room, looking striking in black leather trousers and a flowing silk blouse in a dazzling crimson. Her perfume swamped the room.

"I'm ahead of schedule," she said briskly, making David think of an army officer outlining plans to capture Hill Seventeen. "So, if we dine in ten minutes. Oh, nobody's a vegetarian, by any chance?"

David shook his head. "Good," she announced. "Strictly speaking it should be fish because it's Friday, but seeing as Leppington was slow to shake off its pagan past I thought we'd murder a couple of bloody venison steaks apiece." Still talking, she swept energetically up to the optics behind the bar, fixed herself a whacking great gin-and-tonic, splashed in a chunk of ice from the ICE TO SEE YOU ice bucket then swept across to their table, her long leather-clad legs gleaming in the soft lights of the bar.

"It looks as if you two have become acquainted." She gave that collusive smile across the top of her glass before her red lips touched the rim. "You must have lots to talk about, seeing as you're both in a similar business."

"Hardly." Bernice laughed.

David sipped the Guinness, almost wincing at its iciness. "You work at the hospital?" he asked Bernice.

Grinning, girlishly, she shook her head. "The Farm."

"The farm?"

"Not just any old farm," added Electra swinging her athletic body down onto the chair next to David's. *"The Farm."*

"It's a leech farm," Bernice explained.

"Aren't leeches medieval, or what?" Electra took a hefty swig of gin-and-tonic. "I'll stick to the medicinal properties of Gordon's, thank you very much. What say you, Doctor?"

"Leeches are being used more and more in modern medicine. As well as their bloodsucking abilities, pharmaceutical companies extract an anticoagulant from their bodies for the drug Hirudin. I know, leeches don't sound so palatable, nor do maggots, but they have their uses."

"Ah, yes," Electra said brightly. "Maggots are sometimes used for treating burns, and for injuries where there's a danger of gangrene, isn't that so?"

David nodded. "Maggots only eat dead flesh, not living tissue. So if they are applied carefully to a wound—and I'm talking about sterile maggots here—they simply tidy up the wound of dead, possibly infective skin tissue. Once they've done their job they are removed and the wound generally heals faster, more cleanly and with less scarring than by using so-called modern methods."

"So we've a lot to learn from our forefathers," Bernice said carefully. "Leeches might be used when a severed limb has been sewn back onto the patient. Doctors have to ensure there's a good blood flow through into reconnected arteries."

"So Bernice's leeches might be used on the man you saved today," Electra said to David, fixing him with her cool blue eyes. "But Bernice doesn't know anything about it, do you, darling?"

David said, "Well, perhaps it's not an ideal before-dinner story."

"Nonsense. Our Bernice is made of strong stuff, aren't you, dear?"

David found himself retelling the story. He told it accurately, without embellishment. It felt good to have such an avid audience. Already the impact of Katrina's letter was softening.

"So *was* it a rat?" Bernice asked when he'd finished.

"Although a rat's incisors are harder than steel and can gnaw at a pressure of five hundred kilogrammes per square centimetre, the wound was inconsistent with a rat bite. There was evidence of crush damage, not gnawing."

"And there are no rats in Leppington," Electra added brightly. "Astonishing, isn't it?"

"Well, I'd find it hard to believe," David said, smiling. "This country is riddled with the brown rat. We don't see many of them because they tend to burrow down into the earth, or live in sewers, unlike the old black rat that prefers to live in the upper parts of houses or in hedgerows. By the way, I apologize if I'm sounding as if I'm giving a lecture. Part of my job is to give a regular talk on health and hygiene to water-company staff; once I start talking about rats I find myself starting to recite from my old papers."

"There are no black rats either." Electra went to the bar to fix herself another G&T. "Ask Rentokil. Leppington isn't even on their maps."

"Well, if you *do* see a black rat," David smiled, "give yourself a pat on the back because they're all but extinct. A couple of hundred years ago the brown rat flooded the country and wiped out the black rat population."

Bernice wrinkled her nose. "If it wasn't a rat that bit off the man's fingers and thumb, what did?"

David shrugged. He decided not to the mention the human bite marks. "All I can come up with is that there might be some kind of mechanical device buried under the pavement. Perhaps a pump that takes the drainage water to a higher level."

"But the workmen would have known about it, surely?"

73

He smiled and sipped his Guinness. "The mystery thickens. But there is no doubt about one thing."

"What's that?"

"I'm not sticking my hand down there to find out. Cheers." He lifted the glass.

2

Jason Morrow cruised through the narrow lanes that ran up into the hills outside Leppington. The car's headlights revealed bushes that shivered in the breeze. To Jason, they were pig-shaped and he would have sworn they were moving alongside the road as if running to keep up with the car.

He planned to visit the country park first of all. He might find what he was looking for there. Then he could get this burning, this burning, poisonous hunger out of his system for a while. Once purged, for a few weeks he would be content to sit and watch his wife eating chocolates and drinking beer as her piggy eyes devoured their endless diet of TV soaps.

The sign loomed out of the night: LEPPINGTON COUNTRY PARK. He made a right turn; tyres now crunched over shale.

Jason Morrow had maybe less than an hour to live.

3

The meal was a success. David had immediately warmed to Bernice, but his first impressions of Electra were that she tended to have a superior air; that she could be, at times, a prickly character. However, she soon began to relax (aided, no doubt, by hefty doses of gin-and-tonic, then by the red wine that came with the venison steaks). Talk was strictly small talk, although occasionally Electra would drop into the conversation an intellectual comment about a Shakespeare play she'd once seen or museum she'd once visited in Barcelona or Rome or somewhere equally exotic.

They ate the meal in a small private-function room separated from one of the hotel's public bars by a timber and frosted glass partition. David occasionally glimpsed the blurred shape of the head of one of the drinkers and heard the occasional burst of muffled laugher.

Bernice didn't have much of an appetite. As she ate, the picture of blond-haired and bespectacled Mike Stroud, the man in the video, seemed to dance before her eyes. She tried to keep up the small talk to take her mind off it. But already she found herself thinking about going down into the basement where she'd seen the man struggling with an invisible assailant. I'll go down tomorrow, she told herself, when Electra has taken the train into Whitby for a morning's shopping. Then I'll turn detective and investigate what happened to him.

As she sipped her wine she looked at David Leppington. He was smiling and chatting easily to Electra. A pair of dark eyebrows arched attractively above his bright boyish blue eyes.

When he turns those blue eyes to me, what does he see? she asked herself. This was an old game of hers. She could slip into it without trying. She would imagine she looked at herself through other people's eyes. Maybe he likes my brown eyes and fair hair? But he must think I'm awkward and unsophisticated compared to Electra, who could quote Shakespeare or recite a line or two of Keats or Oscar Wilde in that fluid and self-assured voice of hers.

And the blue nail varnish is a mistake, Bernice, she scolded herself, glaring at her blue nails as if they'd mischievously daubed themselves when she wasn't looking; it makes me look like a giddy fourteen-year-old. And now they're talking about a subject I know nothing about. Is Epstein a sculptor? Or a poet? Or even a painter? He could even be a minor character out of *Ren & Stimpy* for all I know. I wish dinner was over and I could go back to my room.

Bernice thought about the videotapes in the suitcase at the bottom of the wardrobe. She thought about the man in glasses. She thought about what paced outside her room at night.

I'll go down into the basement tomorrow. I will turn detective and find out who the man in glasses is—or was—and I will find out what happened to him.

"Electra? Could you come through to the kitchen, please?" Bernice snapped out of her daydream. One of the barmaids was talking to Electra.

"Can't it wait until after coffee?" Electra asked.

"There's someone at the back door asking to see you."

"Who?"

"He won't give his name."

"A man?" Electra gave wry smile. "Mmm, perhaps it's my lucky night." She dabbed her lips with the serviette. "If you'll excuse me just for a moment. Duty calls."

Electra swept out of the room followed by the barmaid.

"A formidable woman," David said to Bernice with a smile. "I wouldn't like to get on the wrong side of her."

4

Jason Morrow parked the car beside the Country Park's public toilets. The grounds were in complete darkness. He could only make out the tops of trees against the rising moon.

He paused only for a moment, rubbing the nubby lump of bone above his eyebrow.

Come on, get it over and done with. Then you can go back to that Miss Piggy and bury yourself in a bottle of vodka in front of the television.

He climbed out of the car, closed the door as silently as he could; here I come, he thought miserably, like a thief in the night.

Lightly, he walked towards the men's toilets.

He wasn't gay. In fact he'd punch anyone out who suggested it. Only he had this bizarre urge now and again. Once it was out of his system he'd be free of it for weeks, even for months. OK, so he'd have sex with a man. But still he told himself he wasn't gay. The idea repelled him. Only he had this vice . . . this addiction . . . this itch that needed scratching.

He walked into the public toilets. The urinals were dirty and stank of whatever pooled in the blocked drains. Illumination came from a single fluorescent tube that flickered and buzzed. This is where the local queers picked up their boyfriends . . . only he wasn't queer, he told himself grimly. This was just a bizarre urge he must exorcize every now and again. Why, one day he'd wake up and know he'd never have to do this again.

Maybe there'd be some rent boy locked up in one of the

cubicles; then he could get this over and done with in ten minutes flat.

Damn . . . the toilets were empty.

What now? Drive through to Whitby?

No, it'd take too long.

Maybe if he waited for a few minutes one of those filthy faggots would show.

He locked himself into one of the cubicles. The lavatory bowl was stained. Toilet tissue formed a damp mat on the floor. Graffiti had been scrawled over the fiberglass doors and walls.

The minutes rolled past. He waited in silence. Tense. Heart thumping. Sick with anticipation at the miserable, filthy, disgusting act he was about to perform.

Someone would scurry into the place. He knew it. There was a sense of inevitability about it, like the anticipation of a convicted murderer about to be taken to the chair.

The light buzzed, flickered. The stink bit into the back of his throat.

Then his heart missed a beat. He held his breath and listened.

He heard a light footstep outside the door.

At last someone was here.

Mouth dry, he eased back the bolt and opened the door.

That was the moment the light went out.

5

'Shall we keep him?'

"Pardon?" asked Bernice, puzzled. After Electra hadn't returned from the kitchen she'd gone to investigate. She found Electra looking out of the window and into the rear courtyard of the hotel, a strange smile playing on her face.

"Keep him," Electra repeated and nodded at the window. "You know, for a pet, a plaything?"

Still puzzled, Bernice looked out. Under the hard electric courtyard light she saw a young man. His face was covered with tattoos. He was moving crates of beer bottles from one of the outside stores to the back door. The halogen light cast his shadow so it appeared as a distorted yet gigantic beast shape that shambled across the courtyard walls.

"He looks as if he's just escaped from jail," Bernice said, shivering. "I don't like the look of him at all."

"Mmm . . ." Electra agreed dreamily. "He's got some compelling quality, though. You find yourself staring at him, don't you?"

"I think he looks like a monster. He's probably a mugger."

"At least he's making himself useful, seeing as Jim hasn't bothered to turn up again."

"Who is he?"

Electra shrugged. "He just turned up at the door asking for work in exchange for accommodation."

Bernice looked at Electra, shocked. "You're never going to let him stay here?"

"Why not?"

"He's a thug."

"Mmm, maybe. But he might make an entertaining diversion from the eternal ennui."

Bernice gave a nervous laugh. "Entertaining? You *are* joking, aren't you?"

"I'm perfectly serious, my dear. Have you seen those scars on his face? And those tattoos? Isn't that Man in his raw primordial state?"

"Electra, he looks like a wild animal. Why on earth would you want him staying in the hotel?"

"I'm sure I could come up with something." She smiled the collusive smile.

Bernice was appalled. She also wondered if there might be a streak of sheer insanity—suicidal insanity at that—in Electra's otherwise polished character.

"Please, Electra. Send him away. Just look at him. Don't you think he'll be dangerous?"

"Mmm, I *know* he'll be dangerous. Now, compose yourself, dear. Here he comes."

6

He pushed open the door with his foot. He carried the crates full of beer as easily as if they were feather-filled pillows. The two women in the kitchen couldn't take their eyes off him. The

78

tall one smiled. She wore leather kecks. Her hair looked as near to blue as black. The other one with blue nail varnish looked scared.

They had every right to be scared. Weird little bitches.

"Where do you want these?" he grunted.

"Just there, by the fridge," the tall one said, still smiling.

He knew she was going to ask his name. He also knew she'd let him stay there. He didn't know why he twatting well knew. Like he knew today was Friday, and tomorrow was Saturday. He just knew and that was that.

A name?

Which name would he give?

He set the crates down. The bottles rattled. Beer is piss. He didn't know why people drank it. All booze is piss. People hide inside booze like rats hide in a hole from dogs.

"That's great, thank you," said the long-boned bitch. "Oh, you've got blood on your hand. Have you hurt yourself?"

"No," he said. The blood wasn't his.

"Now that's a coincidence." The bitch smiled. "Two men come to my hotel on the same day and both have blood on their hands. Do you think that's an omen?"

He gave her a glassy stare. He didn't smile and he certainly didn't intend replying.

"Great." She still smiled but it looked forced.

Suddenly words popped into his head. *Well, thank you for helping out. You've really saved the day. Can I get you a drink, Mr—ah?*

He gave a quick smile. Sometimes the words came into his head like that before the bitches and the twats said them.

The tall bitch, still smiling, side, "Well, thank you for helping out. You've really saved the day. Can I get you a drink, Mr—ah?"

Now, giving names to people, to machines, to places is important. He knew that. At the Council home there was a woman who gave names to her cars. That impressed him. That was real power. Only powerful people gave names to things. He'd been right about the woman. She'd got herself elected head of the union. Then she got herself a new BMW. She'd named that, too. He'd learnt the lesson, all right. If you've got the power to give names to things you've got the power to do anything. He

79

wanted to give new names to rivers and to towns. Names that would live for thousands of years. The people who named this town would have been powerful. They would have had the power of life and death. He approved of that. That power was good.

So now he gave a different name to himself at each new town he wound up in. He didn't have to think for a name this time. It zipped straight into his head.

Just like that.

Just like it had been carried there by a bolt of lightning.

His skin tingled, as the name sizzled deep into his brain.

"Sorry, I didn't catch your name?" The tall bitch was getting nervous of his glassy stare now. And as for the smaller bitch with blue nails . . . hell, she was petrified of him.

Smile at the ladies, he told himself, make them feel more comfortable. He broadened the smile, but there was precious little warmth in it.

"My name's Jack," he told them. "Jack Black."

"Thank you, Mr. Black. I'm Electra Charnwood." The tall bitch held out her hand. Christ, she was a fearless one. "Yes, there's a self-contained apartment in the stable block. You can stay there; that is, if you'd like to be our new cellarman?"

He noticed the other bitch with the blue fingernails shoot a look of horror at her friend's offer.

Now he heard the voice inside her head clamouring away like frightened sparrows: *No, Electra. You're mad, you're absolutely mad. Don't let that thug stay here. He's an ugly monstrosity. He'll steal. He'll get into fights. Whatever you do, don't let him stay; he'll bring trouble.*

She's right, of course, he thought coldly. Wherever I go there's trouble. But it's too late now. Far too late. I'm here to stay.

7

Jason Morrow saw nothing in the pitch black. The light had gone out the second he'd opened the door.

But he sensed a presence there—a living, breathing presence. The man was here for the same thing.

80

He knew they both understood the game.

They were here to make a sexual transaction. There was no need to see the other's face, or hear a voice. There'd be a fumbled groping, then whoever was strongest stuck it in first.

The whole shitty fuck would be over and done with in minutes.

The unspoken rule was you'd leave the other time to make their getaway without being seen.

Outside the breeze moaned through the branches of the trees. Jason shivered.

The man standing there in the darkness, not just five paces away, might even be familiar. It might be one of the guys he worked with. He might be a policemen. Might even sell him his morning newspaper on the way to work. Not that it mattered, neither could see the other in this black hell-hole that stank of piss and disinfectant.

The other man's breathing was heavy. Perhaps asthma. Or maybe just the sheer excitement of a dirty, illicit and secret encounter in a men's pissoir in the middle of nowhere.

He steeled himself for the feel of hands grasping him. He'd accept that. But he kept his mouth closed. No kissing. He didn't like to be kissed by a man.

Quickly he unzipped his trousers. His penis was already erect. He freed it from his underpants, feeling cold air against the hot sensitive skin.

The breathing of the other man grew louder. He sensed movement in the absolute darkness. The man was bending down towards it.

Jason closed his eyes, waiting for the touch of the lips.

Now he could feel the blast of exhaled air against his skin.

Jesus. The man smelled bad. As if he'd slept rough in a basement or something.

Then came a sudden sensation of something being pressed against his penis.

Lips . . . was his first thought.

No.

Teeth.

"Hey! Stop th—*yuhhh!*"

He screamed. Bolts of agony—blue-white, incandescent— blasted through his head. Some detached part of him heard the click of two sets of teeth meeting after they cleaved through skin, meat, veins and urethra.

He screamed again; this time puke sprayed through his own lips; his arms flailed, his fists cannoned off the fiberglass cubicle doors. Then he was down flat on his back on the piss-slopped floor. He was screaming, writhing; but the grip was never released from the stump of his penis.

Only now did the sucking start.

8

A sudden breeze had sprung up. It whirled pieces of white paper around the courtyard. Bernice watched them flap beneath the halogen light like white birds locked into some mad dance.

She was angry, and frightened, by what Electra had done. Bernice watched Electra make a cup of hot milk for Jack Black—if that was the man's real name. She found it hard to stop staring at the tattoos on his face, or the big red scar that ran from the corner of one eye to the top of his ear. It looked as if someone had tried to draw a pair of spectacles on his skin with red felt-tip.

My God, was he going to be trouble.

The wind blew. It rushed around the hotel's Gothic roof shape, drawing forth a cold moaning sound.

Outside, the shreds of paper chased each other round in circles. Above the roof of the old stable block the crescent of the moon hung in the sky like a silver fingernail.

Bernice shivered. There was something peculiar about all this. The way the beast of a man stood in the centre of the room, his muscular arms hanging by his side. The way Electra stood holding the cup of hot milk out for him, like she was making an offering to a god.

Her scalp prickled. She thought: What's happening to me? Maybe it's lack of sleep; maybe that damn awful video has preyed on my mind too long. Why do I feel so . . . so weird . . . so incredibly weird?

She looked at the two people across the kitchen. Also she imagined she was looking at herself as if someone had videoed the scene. She imagined herself standing there, with her back to the wall, rubbing her forearm with her hand—a nervous, jumpy action, as if she half expected the tattooed man suddenly to snatch a meat cleaver from the rack and split Electra's face in two.

The wind blew harder. The moaning sound grew louder. It sounded like a mother grieving over a dying child. She shivered.

Time, it seemed to her, had slowed to a crawl. The man was taking forever simply to reach out and take the mug from Electra.

Through the window the moon shone brightly.

In the courtyard the pieces of white paper swirled around and around.

Then the door that led to the hotel lobby opened.

She saw David Leppington walk into the kitchen. He carried the stainless-steel bowl that contained the mashed potato. The lights behind him were over-bright, so that he appeared in silhouette—black and faceless. Distantly, as if his voice came from a hundred miles away, she heard him say, "I thought it was time I helped out."

Again she imagined herself into the uppermost corner of the kitchen, like she was some tiny spy camera planted there to capture this scene. There were Electra and the tattooed thug in the centre of the kitchen. Dr. Leppington with the steel bowl in one hand. And she imagined herself, wide-eyed, her back to the wall.

The scene was electrifying. She didn't know why. Her whole body tingled. And if she could have moved she would have run from the kitchen.

Then suddenly she understood.

This has happened to me before. I've stood in a room with these people, just like this. David had held the metal bowl in his hands—like he's doing now. Electra had held out the cup to the savage young man. The moonlight had shone through the window. The winds had struck the house; and that was the night that—

Bang!

It sounded like a gunshot. The wind battered the door open. Instantly the wind rushed into the kitchen, like it was a great raging spirit that had been held captive too long. It roared at them. Clattered the pans against the wall; ripped bunches of dried thyme from the walls. It tore at Electra's long hair; it hit Bernice in the face like an open-handed slap. Then it caught the red serviettes stacked on the work unit.

Instantly the air was filled with clumps of red that seemed to hang suspended there like drops of blood in water.

At that moment no one moved. It was as if fate had frozen the four people there, giving them time to imprint the memory of the scene onto their minds.

Yes. This has happened before, Bernice thought with a sudden tingling clarity. And the four of us have been together before. Now we are reunited.

David Leppington grabbed the outside door, then slammed it back into the door frame, shutting the storm outside once more.

Inside the kitchen, the air became suddenly still. The serviettes drifted down to the floor like blood-red snowflakes.

The silence was immense.

Chapter Nine

Eleven P.M. Bernice opened the wardrobe door in her room. She'd changed into her pyjamas and was determined to retreat to the warmth of her bed as quickly as she could. Already she had barricaded the room door with the chest of drawers.

Outside the wind moaned round the towers of the hotel; it rattled the window panes and she felt the draught rush in icy gusts from under her room door.

Quickly, she lugged out the tan suitcase with the silver clasps.

My God, she thought, I really am like an alcoholic now. Feverishly hunting the vodka bottle from its hiding place; ready for that first slug of the hard stuff.

But it was the videotape that was her vice. She craved to watch those opening shots of Mike Stroud, standing there in his white linen suit and glasses. There was a fire in her heart that only this video could quench. This miserable, stupid, vile video. She knew it had become an addiction. And for the life of her she didn't know why. She had to watch it. She had to peep over the top of her blankets from the fragile security of her bed and watch what happened to Mike; how he'd opened the door

—my door to my room, room 406—

and how something had reached in from the darkness of the corridor and wrenched him out of the room so violently his glasses had been flicked from his face.

Now, more than ever, she needed to know what had happened to the man in the video. Where was he? Was he alive? Was he dead?

Might that wonderful blond hair be green with moss and creeping things now? Was he lying cold, there in some corner of the basement beneath her very feet?

She switched on the television, turned the sound down low.

Oh, as considerate as ever, Bernice, she taunted, when are you ever going to stand up to people? You should have told Electra she was heading for one almighty disaster for giving that thug Jack Black the job of cellarman.

She pushed the video cassette into the machine, shivering as the loading mechanism eagerly snatched the tape from her hands to devour it.

The hotel and the machine and Electra and Jack Black are all in cahoots; they're planning to destroy you, Bernice. They want to see you suffer . . .

Stop it, she told herself, closing off the paranoid run of thoughts. It's your morbid fascination with this tape that's eating away at you.

Destroy the tape. Forget about it.

Easier said than done.

The thing was in her blood now.

She pressed the rewind button on the machine, then climbed into bed. She moved quickly, almost as if she'd prodded a sleeping—and possibly savage dog. It won't bite you, she tried to tell herself reassuringly.

Don't you believe it, Bernice. That video has got its teeth into your jugular—nice and deep, like a filthy vampire that's never going to let you go this side of doomsday.

As the tape rewound she heard a muffled clunk from next door. It was probably Dr. Leppington closing his bathroom door as he prepared for bed. Distantly she heard rushing water.

Probably brushing his teeth, she thought in a vain attempt to crowd out the frightening cluster of thoughts that always haunted her during the night. He's a nice man. Good-looking. Friendly, very pleasant. Single? Yes, Electra had pried that bit of information from him expertly enough. No romantic attachments? She didn't know.

If I ask him, perhaps he will take me away from here.

The thought struck her suddenly enough to surprise her. But she realized it must have been lurking there long enough. Suddenly she realized she wanted to leave this Gothic monstrosity of a hotel; she wanted out of Leppington.

But this's a damned roller-coaster ride—once you were locked into your seat you couldn't just get off. You had to stay on to the bitter end.

The tape clunked to a stop. She stepped out of bed to press the play button. Instantly the cold draughts rushing across the floor made her gasp at their icy intensity. It's like walking into a freezer, she thought, shivering from head to toe, her skin goosing beneath the thin material of her pyjamas.

She crouched in front of the machine: the television screen showed a fuzzy green "O."

Stop, Bernice.

Stop while you've got the chance.

You don't have to do this, you know.

You don't have to watch the vile tape.

You could go to bed and sleep.

But you know you won't sleep.

Insomnia's got its hooks into you.

So, think about what happened tonight.

You had the meal with Electra and the doctor.

That venison was tough as Old Mother Riley's boot.

No, it wasn't, you have a poor appetite, my dear.

Good heavens, I'm even thinking like Electra Charnwood now.

She's infected you.

I can lie in bed and think about how we were all in the kitchen together. Electra, Jack Black—all tattoos, scars and sinister deep-set eyes; Dr. Leppington had then walked in, carrying the empty stainless steel bowl.

At that moment I knew this had happened to me before. That

I'd been in a room with those people before. We'd stood in those same positions. Dr. Leppington had carried the bowl. And there had been such a charge in the atmosphere; an electricity. My muscles had snapped so tight with tension I thought I would explode. Something was going to happen; something incredible.

That's when the door had burst open. The wind had caught the red serviettes and whirled them round the room so it looked as if the air itself was full of blood—flying clots of blood, red, living blood.

Later, when everything had been straightened and the thug Black—oh, I bet he's served time in prison, she thought—had gone off across the courtyard to his new apartment in the stable block, she and Electra and Dr. Leppington had returned to the function room where they'd drunk their after-dinner coffees.

Electra and Dr. Leppington had chatted light-heartedly about the incident.

Electra had mentioned the thug's name, Jack Black.

Dr. Leppington had looked up with a surprised smile. "Jack Black? You're joking!"

"No," Electra had said. "What's so funny about the name?"

"Oh, just coincidence, I suppose."

Electra smiled. "I don't follow."

"Just going back to what we were talking about earlier: the rats, and the mystery of whether or not rats had bitten off the workman's finger."

"So?" Electra shrugged her shoulders. "What's Jack Black got to do with all this?"

"Nothing, really." Dr. Leppington had given a gentle laugh. "It's just that a certain Jack Black was once, by royal appointment, rat-catcher to Queen Victoria."

Electra had laughed. "But that won't be our Jack Black, unless he's far older than he looks."

"True. But it looks as though both Jack Blacks are colourful characters. The royal rat-catcher Jack Black was covered in scars from rat bites."

"Ugh, charming."

Dr. Leppington had slipped an After Eight mint from its envelope. "Mr. Black's official title had been 'Rat and Mole Destroyer to Her Majesty Queen Victoria'." And he was paid three pence from the royal purse for every rat he caught."

Bernice had pulled a face. "Nice work if you can get it."

"Personally, I prefer rats to your leeches, my dear. At least rats wear nice little fur coats and are warm-blooded."

"But seething with bacteria and all kinds of nasty viruses," Dr. Leppington had said.

"Aren't we all, dear?" Electra had gazed thoughtfully at her coffee cup.

Now, back in the hotel bedroom, Bernice looked back at the play button of the video machine.

Press me, press me . . .

It might as well have been crying that. Bernice knew she'd have to watch the videotape again.

I'm caught in its dark spell, she thought morbidly. Oh, well, here we go again . . .

She pressed the button. The screen flickered.

Quickly, almost fearfully, she scooted back to her bed where she pulled the blankets up to her chin, as if shielding her body from anything that might lunge out of the screen at her.

This has got to stop, she told herself unhappily, this has really got to stop . . .

Not tonight, it wouldn't.

She watched the video. There was blond-haired bespectacled Mike Stroud smiling into the lens . . .

And there outside in the corridor someone—or something (something dark and nasty and wet and dead)—paced up and down outside her door. She was convinced of it.

One night I'll open that door, she thought. Then I'll see for myself.

The wind boomed around the hotel's four towers, before dropping to a broken-hearted moan just outside her window.

I might open the door tomorrow night, she told herself. But not tonight. Tonight the evil video had claimed her. Claimed her blood, body and soul.

Chapter Ten

1

Saturday morning. The Station Hotel restaurant.

Bernice looked across the table at Dr. David Leppington as he ate breakfast. They'd bumped into each other on the hotel landing so it had seemed perfectly natural that they should share the same breakfast table. There were no other guests so they had the run of the restaurant. A teenage girl served the food. Electra had already left for a morning in Whitby.

Bernice picked at her grapefruit, then went straight on to the toast. She watched, almost admiringly, as David launched himself wholeheartedly into a cooked breakfast of bacon, eggs, black pudding, mushrooms and fried tomato.

"You know," he said, smiling at her in a way that made her tingle. "Wasn't it bizarre last night? When the wind blew open the door?"

She nodded. "It was as if the whole storm had come rushing into the kitchen." She had felt far more than that. The scene last night of the four of them in the kitchen had electrified her. She was tempted to tell David of her experience. Already she had begun to trust him. But he'll probably think I'm mad if I begin claiming it had all happened before and somehow we'd all been in the same room together in the past.

But what David said next surprised her. "The funny thing is," he said, heartily forking egg into his mouth, "I had the strangest sense of . . . of déjà vu. You know, the I've-been-here-before kind of feeling?"

She stared at him. He smiled. "Perhaps it sounds a bit eccentric. It's just that . . ." He shrugged, the smile still on his lips. "It's just that when I saw the three of you standing there it was just . . ." He shrugged again, as if the words wouldn't come

89

easily. "I could have sworn we'd all been in that room together sometime in the past."

Bernice said in a low voice, "Perhaps we have."

"I think I would have remembered a colourful character like Jack Black, wouldn't you?"

Bernice shuddered. "I think you would. I don't like the look of him at all."

"Strange choice for cellarman. How long has he worked here?"

"When you saw him? All of ten minutes."

She saw David raise his eyes in surprise as he cut a fried tomato in two. "Electra hired him just like that?"

"Just like that," Bernice said with feeling. "I don't know what made her do that. God knows what he'll get up to once her back's turned."

She wanted to return to the subject of the sense of déjà vu David had experienced, but she realized the subject had moved on and he was chatting about his plans for the day that involved visiting an old uncle who lived up in the hills outside town. She had thought of suggesting she show him round the town. Then, in a rush of enthusiasm that seemed almost brazen, she'd decided to ask him to lunch at the Chinese restaurant. But the more he talked the more it seemed the day would be absorbed by the duty call on a family he'd not seen since childhood. Maybe tomorrow, she thought.

He said, "My old uncle lives at a place called The Mill House. Do you know it?"

Pretend you do, Bernice, offer to stroll there with him. Tell him about the videotape and the night visitor that paces outside your room. Instead she found herself saying, "No, I'm only just starting to get my bearings in the town."

"Well, I should be able to find it. My father sent me instructions before I left. He says it's about a fifteen-minute walk from the centre of town."

"You might be best taking a taxi. It's looking like rain."

"No," he smiled warmly. "I'm going to grit my teeth and walk. The exercise will do me good, and—" He looked down at his empty plate. "I need to burn off these calories."

Go on, Bernice, ask him to dinner tonight. He won't bite . . .

He pulled a timetable from his pocket. "If I get my family

visit out of the way, I might go into Whitby. I hear the views from the clifftop graveyard are legendary."

Damn, you've missed the boat. Bernice, you idiot.

He poured himself a coffee from the jug. "Want a top-up?"

"Please, yes. Thanks." Suddenly she felt as awkward as a child in the company of a strange adult.

He hesitated for a moment as if something was on his mind. "You know," he said, thoughtfully. "Just going back to when we were all in the kitchen last night. When I held that bowl of mashed potato in my hand, and I saw you all standing there, I had this bizarre urge to turn the bowl upside down and put it on my head. Isn't that just a mad impulse? Could you imagine me standing there with an inverted stainless-steel serving bowl on my head with mashed potato in my hair?"

He smiled and she laughed politely, but she realized the experience had, inexplicably, had a deep effect on him. Suddenly, she again wanted to tell him about the videotape. But in a serious way, not this polite edging round a subject that was troubling them both. And she wanted to talk about the man in the video; she desperately needed to get this off her chest. Perhaps David could help her find out what had happened to the man.

David continued, "Perhaps that wine of Electra's went straight to my head."

OK, Bernice: go for it. "David. This might sound strange. But I found a videotape in the hotel. I can't . . ."

She noticed David was not listening now, but looking over her shoulder at something behind her.

She glanced back. Jack Black—all tattoos and scars and oozing menace—had just walked in. He carried a plateful of fried potatoes and bacon. Without even acknowledging the two other people's existence he sat at the opposite side of the restaurant and began eating in a way that was nothing less than ferocious.

David smiled and switched his attention back to her. "Sorry, you were saying?"

The moment was well and truly gone. The air of intimacy where secrets could be revealed had vanished. Blown away as violently as those red serviettes the night before.

"Oh, nothing," she said, hearing the return of the polite, almost formal note in her voice. "They certainly don't stint on breakfasts here, do they?" she said as David helped himself from a plate piled with toast.

"They don't. Normally, I have a bowl of cornflakes and that's it. Or if I'm feeling particularly energetic on a weekend I'll make myself a sausage sandwich." He smiled. "Now, if I can walk all this off I'll have an appetite for dinner." He paused as if suddenly struck by a thought. "I heard food at the Magpie restaurant in Whitby is pretty extraordinary. If you're not doing anything tomorrow night, Bernice, would you like to come with me?"

2

Shit. The bacon tasted like shit. He shovelled more into his mouth. The hotel looked like shit. The town was shit.

But he'd pull on this old tit of a town until it was dry.

Car radios, TVs, videos, computers—they were milk in the tit and he'd pull on it until there was nothing left, then he'd move on.

The only thing that pleased him was the name he'd given himself. Jack Black. Jack Black. He liked its rhythm. Yeah, a dark rhythm it had. Jack Black. Jack Black.

Go up to some old freak in the street and say, "I'm Jack Black." Then *wap! Wap!*

Punch their friggin" teeth out.

Yippee—aye—ey.

He doused the bacon with ketchup.

Blood-red it was, and thick. Just like blood from an old man's head.

He grinned and shovelled the ketchup-reddened bacon into his mouth.

Sometimes he would imagine he stood on a rock to talk to a load of people who watched him with love and respect. He'd tell these imaginary disciples incidents about his past.

"Once I swallowed a mouse. Yeah. A live one. With eyes like two little black beads, a pink tail, legs no thicker than match-sticks. I held its body between my finger and thumb. I pushed it into my mouth nose first.

"Its little legs were kicking and it were screaming—

92

" 'Leppington! Leppington! Leppington!' "

No, was it shit.

It was just squealing.

"Anyway, I pushed it down my throat and swallowed it.

"I could feel those legs scurrying like mad.

"Its body was twitching and fluttering and struggling inside my stomach.

"I could feel it inside of me. I could even feel its heart-beat in my guts. It was still moving ten minutes later."

His congregation, gathered before him, would look up in awe, mouths hanging open.

Cool.

. . . That's settled then. I'll tell David all about it. I must trust someone. Watching that stupid video will eat me up; it's poison; it's . . .

The shit was coming out of the head of the twat with blue fingernails. She was sitting with the other guy from last night, drinking coffee.

. . . I wonder if Mike is alive. Did he die in the basement? Lovely eyes . . .

Jack Black started on the fried discs of potato. They were so hot they'd have had anyone else rushing for a glass of cold water. He didn't feel it.

The mouse must have bitten the inside of his intestine. He didn't feel that, either.

Vaguely, he was aware the two on the other side of the restaurant were talking about some old shit. Words didn't matter. He knew they were both frightened of him.

Good thing, too.

He was Mr. Bad.

The scar on the side of his head tingled. An idea was surfacing inside his head; it was shooting up from the depths of his mind like some kind of torpedo or something.

It was one of those sudden insights that sometimes blasted through into his consciousness as if they'd been fired in there by the Almighty. It must have been memories of eating the mouse.

(How it wriggled and tickled inside of me.)

The tingling along the scar intensified. Suddenly he thought: This town's swallowed those two people like I swallowed the mouse. Only they don't know it yet. The mouse had gone down twitching and struggling and heart going da-da-da-da-da, eighteen to the dozen, maybe it was thinking it would still have a chance to survive. Only as soon as it went down into my throat it had gone beyond the point of no return. Those two are just like the mouse. The town's swallowed them; they've gone beyond the point of no return. Only they don't know a shit thing about it. They don't know they've just entered a long black tunnel that they might never come out of. They don't know nothing.

They couldn't see what he saw when he looked out of the window. He saw lightning flickering over the horizon; only this was lightning like you'd never seen before. This was black lightning; it sent great pulses of darkness across the town, like the flickering shadow of death itself. No, they didn't know—they didn't know fuck.

But they'd find out soon enough.

He was sure of that.

He swallowed a cup of hot milk in one go, lit a cigarette, then started on the toast, folding a whole slice before pushing it into his mouth.

Soon he'd go find the four guys he'd slapped into submission yesterday. He needed to educate them some more before he began work on the town.

There'd be videos, TVs, hi-fis, power tools from garages and . . . and something else.

He paused in his munching.

Something else he had to do whilst he was here. Something that needed to be done. His skin tingled, reinforcing the idea.

Yeah, shit. He had to do something else while he was here. Something more than robbing a few TVs and videos.

But for the life of him he couldn't think what it was.

It was like he'd forgotten something really important.

Maybe it was to do with the black lightning throbbing across the hills? He'd seen nothing like that before.

He shrugged and returned to his breakfast.

It would come to him soon enough.

David Leppington left the hotel. He was surprised to find the big smile he'd suddenly sprouted after breakfast hadn't gone yet. And he was singing to himself under his breath.

My God, he thought, as he fastened his coat, you know why you feel so good, Doc?

No, tell me, Doc.

You've only just gone and pulled, my old son. She's agreed to go out for a meal with you, tonight. You handsome old devil, you.

The smile broadened as he walked along the street with its trickle of Saturday-morning shoppers. Come on, David, he told himself, you're not a sixteen-year-old who's just copped a quick grope with a girl behind the greenhouse. You're a civilized man of almost thirty; you're going out for a meal with another human being. That's all there is to it.

He paused and checked the piece of paper on which his father had jotted directions to his uncle's house. He'd just passed Cardigan Street on his right. The bridge that took Main Street across the River Lepping was dead ahead. After that he took a left onto Hangingbirch Lane that would wind uphill, taking him out of town to The Mill House. He supposed he'd visited his uncle's house as a child but, for the life of him, he couldn't bring it to mind.

Even though he'd spent the first six years of his life here in Leppington nothing looked particularly familiar. Oh, there was a shop doorway here or an iron railing there topped with something like iron acorns that stuck some chords, but on the whole it was as if he'd never been here before.

Outside a Georgian town house he suddenly stopped. A flight of just three stone steps led up to the front door straight from the street. There, just outside the door, he saw an iron boot-scrape. The thing looked like a cast-iron boomerang lying on its back and welded to two vertical iron bars that were set in a stone block.

The voice rang with a luminous clarity inside his head: "David, will you come down from there? You'll fall. Now . . . hold my hand; we're late for your Uncle George's as it is."

The voice was his mother's. Suddenly he had a vivid snatch

of memory of him climbing up onto the bootscrape and balancing there, arms outstretched. He'd been making fighter-plane sounds at the top of his six-year-old voice. In his hand had been a little die-cast jet fighter. The grey paint had been scraped off, he'd played with it so often (mainly chucking it off the garage roof, he recalled, smiling to himself). The plane, denuded of paint, had shone silver in the morning sunshine.

His smile broadened. Perhaps with enough stimuli like this his memory would loosen up.

As he started to walk uphill, the memory surged back vividly. Yes, he'd jumped off from the bootscrape, lost his balance, fallen to his knees. The plane had shot out of his hand to land in the gutter.

In a second, he'd jumped up and run to retrieve his precious toy.

It had landed on . . . on? Yes, the grating of a drain at the edge of the road.

He looked down. There it was. A big old-fashioned cast-iron grate where the surface water ran through when it rained. In fact, it was pretty much like the grating he'd seen yesterday when the man had lost his fingers to some old drainage pump. (Well, he reasoned, it had to be something like a drainage pump; surely the man couldn't have put his hand knowingly down into the drain to have his fingers bitten off, could he?)

The memories came back with a kind of pungent strength that sent a tingling across his skin.

He clearly remembered all those years ago when he'd retrieved the toy plane from the top of the grate. (Phew! That was a close one, Davy, nearly lost your Lockheed Starfighter and Captain Buck there.) But as he'd looked down into the grate he'd seen a strange sight.

He remembered laughing and turning to his mother; she'd stood holding out her hand to take his. Now he clearly remembered asking his mother this question: *"Mum, why is the drain full of white balls?"*

"Full of what, David?"

"The drain's full of white soccer balls."

With a sudden vividness he recalled it all as he looked down into the black iron grate that, now anyway, held nothing but darkness.

White soccer balls. He'd seen dozens of them moving through that same darkness below the iron grille.

A sudden shuddering took him by surprise. It felt as if he'd suddenly dipped a bare toe in an Arctic sea. He shivered again. A violent shivering that made him catch his breath.

My God, it had been full of white balls flowing steadily from right to left.

But all those white balls? How did they get down into the drain?

Uneasily, he looked down into the drain, half-anticipating that same flood of white balls flowing beneath his feet again.

He thought of the workman yesterday crying that something was eating his fingers.

He recalled twenty-odd years ago pointing excitedly down through the grating into the drain and shouting, "Mum, mum. Where's all them balls come from? Where did they all come from? Mum!"

His mother had advanced across the pavement. A frown creasing her forehead.

"Mum? Why is there all them white balls down there?"

She'd stooped. Then grabbed his hand.

"I told you, David. We're late for Uncle George's party. Now come on."

"Mum . . . the balls. Where've they come from? Mum . . ."

She'd never looked; instead, she'd dragged him away up the lane.

He found himself, a twenty-nine-year-old man, staring down into the darkness, his teeth clamped together, his fists bunched.

Where did all those white balls come from?

If they were balls.

What could they be? he asked himself. What else could they be?

He shivered. Beneath his clothes a bead of sweat trickled down his chest. He shivered again. Then, with almost a physical effort, he wrenched his gaze away from the pit of darkness descending into the earth beneath his feet.

He suddenly realized that looking down into the drain was scaring him. Why? For Godsakes why should a common or garden street-drain scare him?

All those white balls. Filing by below. That's why.

With a strange shudder that ran to the pit of his stomach he turned and walked quickly up the street.

The memories were returning.

And they were all black.

Like crows darkly flapping towards a battlefield to feed on the dead.

Chapter Eleven

10 A.M. Saturday.

Bernice Mochardi killed time. She'd decided after all that the blue nail varnish made her look fifteen and she'd taken it off with remover.

Then she'd mooched downstairs to the Dead Box, half hoping there might be another piece of luggage belonging to Mike Stroud, the film maker with the blond hair and glasses. She'd found nothing but the usual stacks of cheap suitcases and the ancient vacuum cleaners lined up against the wall.

I promised myself I'd watch the video in daylight, she thought; I could do that now. Would it be different? After all, it never seems exactly the same twice. As if someone secretly sneaked the tape from her room to add more footage or edit out earlier scenes.

Instead, she drifted through into the public bar. At this time of day the hotel served coffee and sandwiches to elderly shoppers.

Unable to settle there as she sometimes did with a coffee and a magazine, she moved back into the lobby where she eyed the door to the basement like a child eyeing brightly coloured berries on a bush. Like that child wanting to eat one of the shiny red berries, she wanted to go down into the cellar. But as berries on ornamental bushes are probably poisonous so that cellar door emitted danger signals too. She could feel them coming to her in cold waves.

She looked at the clock above the reception desk. Ten-thirty.

Already she'd decided to confide in Dr. Leppington. Now she wanted desperately to tell him what she'd experienced in the hotel. At the first opportunity she'd suggest that they watch the videotape together.

Bernice mooched across to stand on the steps of the hotel where she gazed out at the hills, imagining what the doctor's reaction would be when he saw the young man in glasses being dragged from the room.

The wind gusted, sending sheets of newspaper gliding across the market square. She shivered and walked back into the hotel.

2

Rain had begun to fall by the time David reached his uncle's house. Well, it didn't so much fall, he thought, as fly horizontally in the stiff breeze gusting up the valley. Rain drops cracked against his coat like bullets.

The moment he saw the three-storey house he felt that tingle of recognition. Like most of the older properties in the area it was built of stone beneath a roof of orange and red pantiles. But this one resembled a fortress. A high wall, probably higher than he could reach with his fingertips, surrounded the house and gardens.

He pushed open the heavy iron gate (that's the kind of gate to keep folk out, he thought—or your lunatic cousin in), and walked into a garden that was neat without being fussy. Rose bushes were pruned almost to the black earth; a dozen apple trees shifted restlessly in the wind like they had secrets that they needed to get off their chests.

Behind the house a hill rose almost as steep as a cliff. The top of the hill was smothered in black cloud. As he walked up the path he saw that to one side of the house ran a fast-flowing stream; he guessed this was the stream that had once powered the mill itself, although there was no sign of the mill building now.

The rain struck him harder, stinging where it hit bare skin.

Hell of a fine day for a walk, he told himself, as he hurried along the path to the front door. You should have taken the taxi after all. And missed the fun of finding that old drain again? And remembering how you'd once seen all those white footballs floating through the darkness?

He smiled and shook his head. Memory can play strange tricks.

He was probably muddling reality with a dream he'd had when he was a child.

Didn't he used to dream he was being chased down a long dark tunnel by a man—or at least a great shadowy figure? The dream used to come as regular as clockwork—probably after a supper of cheese on toast, he shouldn't wonder.

He paused at the front door. Hell, it must be a long time since I had that dream. Probably the last time was at university.

Fixed high on the door was a heavy black iron ring. He raised it and let it fall. The huge sound it produced went echoing into the deepest recesses of the house.

Enough to wake the dead, he thought with a smile. Come on, Uncle George. Don't leave your nephew out in the cold.

After the knocking for the third time he realized there was no one home. He had sent a brief letter a few days ago to let his uncle know he'd be there for ten-thirty. He'd even followed it up with a couple of telephone calls. Only there'd been no one there. Still, he'd left messages on the answer machine.

Half an hour ago he'd been relaxed about the idea of strolling up here on the off chance his uncle would be in, but the walk had turned into more of a hike up the steep lane out of town. Now, with the rain coming down, he realized this wasn't going to be fun. Not one little bit.

Maybe the old man's at the back of the house? He must be eighty if he's a day. He imagined a wizened old man, shuffling round the kitchen in baggy checked slippers, perhaps taking the weight of his ancient bones on a Zimmer frame.

Then again, he might even have had a fall. Maybe he was lying flat out at the bottom of the stairs, too weak to haul himself to his feet or to cry out when anyone knocked.

He clattered the iron ring against the iron stud in the door.

Damnation. Now his imagination had supplied the picture of the old man lying half dead, perhaps with a fractured hip, David knew he would have to satisfy himself that there really was no one home.

So much for duty visits.

Forget it, Doc, said a voice in the back of his head; just turn round and head down into town; remember those lovely gooey buns in the cafe. Treat yourself to one. You can always come again. Better still, just tell your father that whenever you came up here there was never anyone in. He'll understand.

David sighed. No. He couldn't just walk away. He'd have to nose round the back first to make sure nothing was amiss.

Hunching his shoulders against the rain, he followed a stone-slabbed path to the rear of the house.

Through the windows he could see tidy but gloomy rooms—a sitting room with cream leather suite, a stuffed owl on the windowsill; then a kitchen—quaint farmhouse-style worktops with an iron range that combined open fire and oven. The back door was locked.

Bugger.

Cold rain trickled down his neck.

Then he noticed a row of substantial outbuildings built of the same stone. From one pantile roof poked a chimney. Blue smoke puffed out in distinct round clouds.

David headed for it.

He was met at the doorway of the building by a man. He was carrying a long sword whose tip glowed orange. When the drops of rain hit it they sizzled and turned to steam.

David was suddenly unsure what to say. "George Leppington?"

The old man nodded, then turned and walked back into the building.

For a moment, David stood there; perhaps the old man didn't want to see him after all? It was a good twenty years since they'd last met.

More than once recently he had wondered if there was any ill-feeling between his father and George Leppington. His parents sent the old man Christmas and birthday cards but there were never any cards in return.

Uh-oh, big mistake, David, he thought. Perhaps you should just sidle out of the garden and head back towards town. Console yourself with a whacking great bun in the cafe.

Then he heard a surprisingly low voice from the outbuilding. "You know, David, it's drier in here than it is out there."

That seemed something approximating an invitation so he went inside.

3

His uncle stood in the centre of a blacksmith's workshop. There was an anvil, leather bellows, a forge glowing yellow with coals—the fire cast out a wall of heat that pressed against the front of David's body like it was a solid thing. A great iron hood drew away the smoke. On the walls hung all kinds of tools that David wouldn't in a month of Sundays be able to put a name to, with the exception of a dozen or more hammers of differing sizes—from a tiny pee-wee-sized one that looked good for nothing more than breaking toffee, to a huge device that looked as if it could hammer down the gates of Hades itself.

The old man lifted the sword he was making and examined the point with a look of fierce concentration. "Well, the beastie's taking shape, but it'll take a lot of work yet."

He rested the sword down on a workbench and took off his leather apron.

"You look cold, great-nephew. Come and sit near the fire."

Any closer and I'll burst into flame, thought David, his face tingling from the heat. Nevertheless, he sat down on the stool his uncle had pulled across the dirt floor. He watched his uncle as he hung the leather apron on a nail in the wall. He was a giant of a man and showed none of the shrivelling entropy of a man of eighty-four. At that age the hands should be frail, possibly arthritic, certainly liver-spotted; those were the hands of a man half his uncle's age. And the man was bursting with vitality and energy. He looked strong as an ox. His face was lined and weather-beaten, but the blue eyes shone with a fierce brilliance beneath a pair of shaggy white eyebrows. And falling down over the forehead was a thick fringe of that same pure white hair. If there was an elixir of life then this man took a damned good swig of it every day.

"Well, you look like a Leppington. So, there's life in the old gene yet. How're your parents?"

"They're fine. They're taking the boat down to Greece this week."

"Sailing it down?"

David nodded. "It's been in dry dock over the winter. My Dad was itching to get back to sea."

"Ah, that's the Nordic blood in his veins. It's in mine and yours too. Good red Viking blood. Tea?"

"Please." David watched the old man take a heavy black kettle and sit it amongst the glowing coals. As they waited for it to boil the old man would ask questions—the polite sort you'd ask a distant family member. He didn't smile, and spoke in a bluff no-nonsense way.

David found himself answering guardedly.

The old man asked, "Sugar? Milk?"

"Just milk."

"You don't want a slice of lemon in it?"

"No, thanks."

"Good. If you'd said yes I'd have picked up that sword over there and taken your head clean off with a single swipe."

David stiffened, and shot a look at the door.

For the first time the old man smiled. "Pardon my sense of humour, great nephew. But I expected you to come here dressed in a pink tie and flimsy little loafers and reeking of pissing aftershave." He shot David a keen-eyed glance. "They didn't ruin you by taking you off to the city, then?"

"Liverpool? Well, we lived on the outskirts of it. And after all Liverpool isn't Paris or San Francisco."

"Glad to hear it, great-nephew." He spooned loose tea into a pot. "By the way, I can't keep calling you great-nephew, can I now? Should it be Dr. Leppington?"

David smiled. "No, just David."

"And don't call me bloody Uncle or I'll be swinging that sword again," the older man said gravely. "You're a man now. Call me George."

He strode across the floor and thrust out his hand. David shook it. The man's skin was hard and the grip like iron.

"George." He nodded, smiling.

His uncle—George, David corrected himself, call him George—nodded at the sword. "I started making those when I sold up the business a couple of years ago. I wanted something to keep me busy. I didn't want to start to rot before my time. What would the medical advice be for that?"

Good God, he only retired two years ago—when he was eighty-two? David warmed to the man. He smiled. "You're obviously healthy enough, and if you enjoy it, do it."

"My feeling exactly." George spoke heartily. "I couldn't let myself seize up until you got here."

"Until I got here?" David looked at the old man, puzzled.

"You *are* coming to live here?"

"Well, I'm here on holiday."

"Yes. But you got the letter from Pat Ferman, the GP?"

"Yes. He was inviting me to consider taking his practice."

"He's a she, by the way."

"Sorry?"

"Dr. Ferman is a woman. But then, most professional titles don't reveal gender, do they?"

"No . . . but . . ." Suddenly David felt as if he'd lost some significant strand of the conversation. His uncle was talking as if he should have received some long letter of explanation. Only it had never arrived.

"You're taking the practice? You're coming to live here?"

The old man locked his blue eyes onto David's. The force of the stare was almost shocking.

"It's early days yet," David said, taken aback. "I haven't decided anything."

The old man stared hard at David. The wind blew, drawing the fire with a roar. The heat hitting David in the face made his skin smart.

Then the old man broke the stare with a sigh. He turned his back on David as he poured boiling water from the soot-black kettle into the teapot.

"I should have known," George said in a low voice. "Your father was never one for meeting a challenge head on."

"I'm sorry?" David felt as if he should defend his father. But from what?

"Your father should never have taken you away from Leppington."

"But he—"

"Yes, yes. Went where the work was. I know the reasons. Or at least I heard the excuses."

"Look, George. You've lost me completely."

"No. *We* lost *you*. Your mother's made of something harder

104

than this." He picked up the sword and tapped it against the steel vice. "She came from outside and cut your father's roots."

"Look, I think it might have been a mistake coming here. My father passes on his best wishes. But I'll have to be getting back to—"

"Sit down."

"No. The rain's stopped. If I go now I can—"

"Sit down." George's hard voice suddenly softened. "Sit down, son. Drink your tea."

David was ready to walk away but something in the old man's voice made him pause. There was a note of sadness mixed in with the gruff no-nonsense tones. "Please, David. Have a cup of tea with me first."

David nodded, but he knew his body language was telling the old man that he'd politely drink tea with him, then he'd leave.

"There you go, David." He handed him a mug of tea that looked brutally strong. "You know, son, the last time I gave you something to drink was at the Station Hotel down in the town. You and your mother and father were early for the train."

"I think I remember," David said in a low voice. "You bought me a ham sandwich."

The man nodded, the tough expression softening. "Your mother was in such a hurry to rush the pair of you out of town that she hadn't had a chance to get you any breakfast. By heaven, you wolfed that sandwich down like there was no tomorrow. Although I had to do some verbal arm-twisting to get them to spend a few minutes with me in the hotel. Your mother was adamant she'd get the pair of you onto that train and away from here for good. Remember?"

David shook his head and gave a small smile. "Sorry, I only remember the ham sandwich."

"You were a good lad. Remember when you rode on my shoulders all the way up to the top of Berrick Crag? Pissed it down all the way back, ha!"

Again David shook his head, his smile broadening. "I don't remember that, either."

"Ah, all those memories are in there somewhere. They'll come back."

"I remember you carrying me out of the house one night to look at the chimney."

"By God, yes! I remember. The thing caught fire."

"It looked like a firework. Sparks were shooting out of the chimney pot."

"Aye, and they even set fire to the grass in your neighbour's back garden. Anyone else and they'd have complained to high heaven."

David shrugged, puzzled. "Why didn't they complain?"

"Because we're Leppingtons. They're frightened of us."

"Frightened?" He shook his head with a puzzled smile. "Why?"

George sighed sadly. "They've told you nothing at all, have they? None of the family history?" He took a swallow of his powerful brew of tea. "I used to talk to you a lot when you were young. Right from before you could talk. Remember anything of that?"

David shook his head, even more puzzled than he had been a moment ago. He sipped the hot tea as his uncle gazed thoughtfully up at the ceiling, blue eyes impenetrable beneath the thick white eyebrows.

Then he nodded slowly, reaching a decision. "OK. I'll tell you. Only there's one thing." He shot David a stern look.

"And what's that?"

"You smile too much. Leppingtons never smile. At least, not in public." Then the old man laughed, a deep rich sound that trickled down to vibrate the soles of David's feet.

Was that some old Leppington family joke? he wondered, unsure of whether he was supposed to laugh along with it or keep stone-faced.

George stopped laughing and rewarded his nephew with a suddenly broad grin. "OK, David. Pin back your ears and listen to this."

Chapter Twelve

George Leppington sat on an upturned crate, facing David. He rested one booted foot on the anvil, the mug of tea gripped in both his hands. Whenever the wind surged up the valley the fire roared in its grate, and the coals turned from red to an incandescent yellow.

David sipped his own tea, trying not to grimace at its strength. He found himself wanting to avoid giving his uncle the impression that he was some kind of soft, dandified city fop. He also found himself liking his uncle. He reminded him of a robust, outspoken version of his father.

George spoke with blunt strength. "David. Did you know that in the slaughterhouse there are sixty-four drains that take the blood from the killing floors straight down into tunnels under the town?"

David shook his head, feeling bewilderment begin to creep back in.

George continued, "Your great-great-grandfather designed the slaughterhouse himself. Every day something like five hundred gallons of blood goes gushing down the drains, right under the town."

"But surely modern health regulations prohibit dumping blood and offal into the sewers? The rats would—"

"Ah! The blood doesn't feed *directly* into the sewer system. And, besides, there are no rats in Leppington. Not a single one."

"So I've heard. But I still find it hard to believe there isn't at least one rat somewhere round here."

"Take my word for it, David. Here, let me top up your mug."

George swung out a long arm and plucked the big teapot from the workbench, then poured more of the amber liquid into David's cup. David steeled himself against the taste of the strong tea and took a sip.

George refilled his own mug. "So, David. They told you nothing about the family? And nothing about the town?"

David shook his head, wondering why it should be so important to know anything about the family history. Most people bump along perfectly well, thank you, with only the sketchiest idea of what grandma and grandad got up to in the dim and distant past.

"What do you think of Leppington—the town?" asked his uncle.

"Seems pleasant enough. Quiet. But I imagine it's seen better days?"

"True. The town's dying. The only employer of any size is the slaughterhouse. But that employs no more than a couple of hundred. Fifty years ago it employed more than a thousand."

"But we—the Leppingtons—have no interest in it now?"

"No financial interest. The family sold out in 1972. Sold it to the biggest shyster they could."

"Oh, I heard about that," David nodded. "He raided the pension funds, then legged it to the South of France, didn't he?"

"The bastard. If I ever clapped eyes on him again, I'd take this to him." George picked up the sword he was making and David didn't doubt for a moment he would. All his old uncle needed was a cloak and a helmet set with a pair of bull's horns and he would be a Viking warrior incarnate.

His uncle continued, occasionally stroking his fingertips along the blade of the sword as he spoke. "The demography of Leppington town shows clearly enough what's happening. The population is shrinking. Young people, if they can, move out—usually to the cities. Soon there'll only be a town full of retirees hobbling up and down the streets on their Zimmer frames, grumbling about the weather and the price of Horlicks."

"It's not that bad, surely?"

"Believe me, David, the place's dying on its feet."

"Local government aren't running any initiatives to encourage new businesses?"

"Nothing to speak of. We fall under the protective wing of Scarborough Borough Council which is way down the coast. Their initiatives and financial support don't filter this far north. No. Leppington's always had its back to the wall, fighting for its survival ever since the ancient Romans packed their bags and left 1500 years ago."

"As a community it's pretty much off the beaten track anyway. Small towns dependent on a single industry like coal mining or a single factory can easily go belly-up if the coal runs out or the factory goes bust."

"Nevertheless, the outside world has always done its best to shaft us. We've always had to fight to keep this town together by the skin of its teeth. Without us the town would have vanished a thousand years or more ago."

The realization clicked. *Us*, David thought. The old man was referring to the Leppington family—or should that be dynasty? His uncle clearly believed the Leppingtons were responsible for the town's survival.

"One thing I did mean to ask," David said. "Did the Leppingtons get their name from the town or was it the other way round?"

The old man gave a dry smile. "So you *are* curious about family history? Ah, there's a tale to tell. See the stream in the garden when you came through the gate?"

David nodded.

"That's the source of the River Lepping. A dozen or more streams feed into it down the hillside. But that stream out there is where the Lepping starts. Our ancestors came across in longships from Germany in the fifth century. They gave the river their name, the town too. Only then it was known as Leppingsvalt."

"So we can claim royal blood?" David spoke lightly.

The old man looked at him levelly. "No. Not royal blood. The Leppingsvalt family claimed *divine* blood."

David, despite himself, felt a buzz of surprise. "Divine blood? That's quite a claim!"

George nodded and ran his fingers along the stone. "This is the story. Our family lived on a mountain in Germany. They were blacksmiths. One night, a long time ago, maybe two thousand, maybe five thousand years ago, Thor, the Norse god of thunder, awoke to find his hammer had gone missing. So he borrows the Goddess Freya's cloak of feathers so he can fly across the world and look for it. He never does find it. Instead he arrives at the house of Leppingsvalt high on the mountain. The blacksmith is an unhappy man. His wife can't give him a son. That means the family name will die out. Which is a terrible, terrible calamity for a proud Norse man. Thor, god of thunder, tells Leppingsvalt that he has lost his fabulous hammer of the gods, and that it will take a mountain of flint to produce a new one. Leppingsvalt says he will make a better hammer. One of iron. So he sets to work and beats raw iron for a dozen days and nights until he creates a new hammer for Thor. To this hammer he gives a name: Mjolnir—which is the name it is known by today."

"An interesting story."

"Aye." George was no longer smiling. His eyes were far away.

"And in return—as a reward—Thor lay with Leppingsvalt's wife. Later she produced a son."

"And that's how we come to have divine blood? We're descended from the Viking god, Thor?"

"We are indeed, great-nephew."

David looked at his uncle more closely, trying to decide whether the old man was taking these folk tales seriously or if it was his dry sense of humour coming to the fore again.

"It was a story we Leppingtons believed in implicitly for centuries."

"That we were the descendants of a god?"

"Why not? It was the religion of the time. Many people today still believe in the Christian angels or the miracles of Christ— water into wine, making the blind see by spitting on their eyes, raising a child from the dead. Six hundred million Hindus believe that when the soul is born, its first incarnation will be in something as lowly as a plant or even a mineral. Only in later incarnations does it migrate upward into animals and eventually man."

"But those religions are still alive. The Norse religion is dead."

"Well, son, perhaps it just went underground." He gave that dry smile. "Also, legend has it the old Norse gods retreated into the rivers when Christianity gained the upper hand."

"But you don't believe we're really descended from a mythical deity?"

George shrugged. "Ask me that question in public, I'd laugh and make a joke. Ask me in private . . ." He shrugged again. "Your grandfather—my brother—believed."

"Wasn't he headmaster at the Church of England school in the town?"

"Indeed he was. But I saw him on feast days—on the old feast days, that is—throwing a handful of new pins or coins from the bridge into the Lepping."

His uncle must have read David's puzzled expression.

"To throw coins or even pins into a river is a way of making a sacrifice to the old Norse gods."

"Even so," David said, smiling. "Most of us avoid walking under ladders and we'll throw salt over out left shoulders if we spill some."

"Oh?" George lightly ran his strong fingers the length of the sword blade. "A harmless eccentricity, then?"

"Probably. You wouldn't believe the number of sick people I see who wear lucky charms—four-leaf clovers, St. Christophers, holy talismans."

"So the old religious beliefs aren't completely dead?"

David shrugged. "When a doctor prescribes a medicine—one manufactured in a computerized factory in Canada, Switzerland, wherever—he knows full well that thirty per cent of that drug's effectiveness is the patient's belief it will cure them. If a man superstitiously believes a rabbit's foot will cure him of a migraine, well, perhaps he's thirty per cent on the way to recovery."

George smiled. "So you medics will allow us our little portion of magic?"

"OK," David smiled back warmly. "In a scientist's hands magic doesn't exist. But in our *minds* perhaps traces of it do still linger on."

"And perhaps a little in the modern outside world, too." With a chuckle George slapped his huge palm down onto the anvil. "You arrived here yesterday?"

"Friday, yes. Why?"

"Friday is named after the Norse goddess Frig who was the wife of Odin."

"I remember the origins of the names of days from school. Wednesday was named after Odin, the father of the Norse gods, and Thursday is really Thor's day. Am I right?"

"You're right, son. More tea?"

"Eh, no, thanks. I've still some left."

"Bit on the strong side for you, hah?"

"Not at all."

"Come on, you can't pull the wool over your old uncle's eyes. Fancy something stronger?"

I don't think you'd find anything much stronger than this tea, Unc, he thought, the tannin still tingling on his tongue. It's probably industrial strength already.

"Give me your mug, son." He took the mug from David and flicked the contents through the open door where it fell in a heavy brown splash. He then reached up onto a shelf and brought down a bottle of Irish whiskey. "This will fire up your insides," he said with a hearty chuckle. "You know, I never thought I'd share a real drink with you. But I remember you coming into that kitchen—" he nodded his grey head in the direction of the house "—you'd climb up onto the stool, and I'd pour you out a glass of Coke. I even cut you a slice of lemon. You know, you used to rush down the drink just so you could eat the lemon. Gobble it down like it was chocolate, you did; skin an' all. Never knew a kid like you for that. Most only want sweets. You'd eat anything sour—sourer the better. It was all your Auntie Kathleen—God bless her—could do to keep you from eating the apples before they were ripe."

Auntie Kathleen—God bless her? Which god? wondered David. One with a horned helmet and that filthy great hammer that was named Mjolnir?

He vaguely remembered his Auntie Kathleen—a big woman, as hearty as her husband George. David thought she'd died about fifteen years ago.

George talked enthusiastically now, eyes twinkling, fingers gliding up and down the massive blade of the sword. "We never had children of our own, of course, so it was a real treat for her to cook you a big roast when you used to come up here for dinner. You ate like a wolf. Then we used to go and sit by the stream in summer. You'd sit on the big rock in the middle. Sometimes I'd come out of the house and find you singing to the water."

"Singing to the water?"

"You'd have been about four then. I suppose a Christian minister would claim you were singing in tongues. Anyway, we used to sit there, me on the bank with my pipe, you on the rock.

You always asked me to tell you the story of how the Leppingsvalt family came to this country." The man was away now, David thought. He's probably seeing me as that four-year-old singing on the rock again. Now this, at last, was typical of old age. Where the distant past is more vivid than the present.

"Fifteen hundred years ago one of our ancestors was working at the anvil when Thor once more appeared to him. He was told to take his family across the sea to a new land. There he'd find a cave in a hillside. Deep in the cave would be a lake in which lived a monstrous fish. Inside the fish would be a sword which he must take for himself. Then he should build a temple and a great city."

"Ah," David nodded. The pieces were falling into place. "The Leppingtons—sorry, Leppingsvalts came to this country and founded the town?"

"Indeed they did," said the old man.

"But I take it all this sword-in-the-fish business was pure folk myth?"

"Well, family legend does have it that Leppingsvalt and his sons went down into the cave, battled with the fish, then cut a sword from its stomach, which also contained gold and precious stones."

David suspected a lot of old myths and fairy tales were muddled up with the family history. Guardedly he said, "The story has parallels with the story of King Arthur and the legend of Excalibur, the Sword in the Stone."

"The sword of the Leppingsvalts, drawn from the belly of the fish, did have magic powers." The old man ran his finger along the blade.

"What happened to the sword?"

"It was handed down from father to son for centuries. But—" He shrugged. "It was stolen by the Normans in the eleventh century."

Bummer, David thought. There goes the divine inheritance out the window.

"And that's when the town began its long slow decline."

"The city of Leppington that never was," David said, then regretted it, wondering if he'd sounded brutally flippant. Obviously the family stories were a source of comfort to the old man now.

"Last year I dreamt about the sword," the old man said. "I dreamt I found the sword driven through the front door of the house. When I awoke I remembered the sword in every detail and decided to make a replica."

"A replica of the dream sword?"

"A replica of Helvetes, which is Norse slang for 'bloody' or 'blood-soaked.' Helvetes. A sword that could slay an army with a single cut or bring down a hail of burning stones on our enemies." The man looked along the blade of the sword with a deep satisfaction. "Or so the old stories ran." He smiled up at David. "Quite a sword, mm?"

"Quite a sword," David agreed, feeling more than a little drowsy—a mixture of the fire and the whiskey. Then he remembered something long ago. He remembered sitting on a rock, dangling his feet in the numbingly cold water of the stream. "But there was another part of the story you haven't mentioned," he told George. "What was it now?" He sipped the whiskey from his mug. "That's it. Weren't the Leppingtons given some divine mission or quest?"

The old man smiled warmly. "I told you you'd begin to remember."

"Something about a new kingdom?"

The old man, still smiling, shook his head. "Not a kingdom: an empire." He stood and tipped the remains of the Irish whiskey in his cup into the fire. Purple flames blossomed and rose into the chimney.

And don't you bet that gesture, pouring whiskey onto a fire, is a sacrifice to the old gods, thought David, easily; the whiskey buzzing in his veins.

George said: "The head of the Leppingsvalts was ordered by Thor to conquer the world, build a great new empire. And the little town there in the valley would become a city to rival Rome or Athens. It would become capital of the world."

"Quite some undertaking."

"Yes, quite an undertaking. And for that, the Leppingsvalt clan needed a vast army."

"Or an army of supermen."

The old man looked at David. "You are remembering."

David smiled, expansive after the whiskey. "Remembering what?"

"Remembering what you were told. About what happened in the past." He took a key that hung from a nail above the work bench. "And you'll remember what will happen in the future."

"You mean the Leppingtons still have a God-given appointment with destiny?"

"If you like. Come on. You can stretch your legs. I'll show you something now that might jog your memory."

Chapter Thirteen

David Leppington followed his uncle out of the workshop. The rain had almost stopped by now, although the wind still surged up the valley in powerful gusts, shaking the trees and making a droning sound as it swirled round the roofs of the outbuildings.

George—all of eighty-four with a bushy head of snow-white hair—strode energetically across a yard to what David at first took to be an old stone-built garage that backed onto the hillside. At the front were twin timber doors painted in a dull green colour.

David watched as George unlocked one door then held it firmly back so the wind wouldn't catch it and smash it against the hinges.

"Inside," his uncle said in that bluff no-nonsense way. "I'll close the door behind us, otherwise this wind'll have it over York by this time tomorrow."

The garage was empty. Then David saw to his surprise that it was impossibly empty. The place seemed to defy physics. The garage stretched onward perhaps for thirty metres before becoming lost in darkness. Then he realized what he was seeing.

"It's the mouth of a cave?" he asked George who was lighting a Calor gas lamp.

"The very same cave that led to the subterranean lake where the fish lived. Follow me. Keep to the concrete path in the middle. The floor of the cave gets soaked this time of year."

David followed, seeing the back of his uncle in silhouette.

The lamp filled the cave ahead with a brilliant white light while hissing loudly.

The walls of the cave were of a black rock, possibly granite. Delicate veins of white ran from ceiling to floor. Unlike most caverns where you had to keep ducking your head when the roof dropped low, this was big enough to drive a van through. David guessed it had been enlarged by hand at some time in the past.

After they'd been walking for no more than three minutes, George stopped. "This is as far as we go, son."

David immediately saw why. An iron railing formed a barrier. It ran from wall to wall and ceiling to floor. It looked like the bars of a cage. A substantial cage at that. You could have safely kept a pride of lions on the other side of the bars.

The light from the lamp illuminated another twenty metres or so of cave before the shadows finally got the upper hand.

David found himself straining his eyes into the darkness beyond those bars, half expecting to see a hideous figure shambling towards him.

"There is a lake down there?" David asked.

"There is. It's the size of a tennis court. But it's deep. Very deep. The bottom's never been plumbed."

"And the underground lake's the real source of the Lepping?"

"You are starting to remember?"

David shook his head. Even so, he sensed a faint tingle of recognition. Something about the iron bars; and the darkness beyond.

It should look different somehow.

And the iron bars made a noise.

He frowned.

Come on, David, how could iron bars make a noise?

Again he realized how strange the world must appear to a six-year-old. As a twenty-nine-year-old he found himself glimpsing these surroundings through his six-year-old self. He began to remember.

There had been a strong smell.

Like the zoo.

Or a stable.

No, a pigsty.

And the railings in front of him weren't silent.

He looked at the railings in the lamplight. They cast a heavy black shadow back into the cave. Then he noticed a steel peg as long as his forearm. It was tied by a length of white plastic-coated washing line to one of the horizontal bars. The bars there carried slight dents.

Suddenly he knew why.

The memory flashed back. Hard and clear. His uncle standing, holding young David's hand while he rattled the steel peg backwards and forwards to produce what seemed to six-year-old ears a deafening, clanging sound.

But why on earth did his uncle do that?

Again David looked through the iron bars into the dark bore of the tunnel running away into the hillside.

There's something there, he suddenly told himself; something there in the darkness watching me. I can sense them.

Them?

Why had he thought "them"?

The air in the cavern seemed suddenly colder. He shivered. A breeze—no, not quite a breeze, barely more than a draught, but cold, so icy that cold had begun to ooze up into his face.

When he breathed into his hands to warm them vapour blossomed into the air, a dazzling white in the light of the gas lamp. He shivered again. His heart began to beat harder as if deep down he knew something was going to happen at any moment. There was a deep-rooted sense of anticipation. It was so strong he felt as if he could reach out and clasp his fingers around it.

What is this place?

Why does it have such an effect on me?

Why couldn't he take his eyes off that dark core of the tunnel running away to God knew where?

Which God, David? The God of angels and light?

Or a God of darkness and screaming and bestiality and blood?

He found himself thinking back an hour or so to when he'd seen the drain that had unleashed that bizarre twenty-three-year-old memory of seeing white footballs bobbing through the darkness beneath the grating in the street. Was that weird or was that weird? He wondered what other memories might come surging to the surface.

"Those who make contracts with the gods must keep them," his uncle spoke in a low voice as he hung the lamp on an iron hook screwed into the ceiling where it hissed and pulsed with such a brilliant light that David could barely keep his eyes open.

"Remember what I told you," George said in a low voice that was almost swamped by the hissing of the gas lamp. "The thunder god, Thor, gave the chieftain of the Leppingsvalt clan the task of creating a new empire that would cover the whole world. The chieftain complained that he had no army, so Thor offered him one, providing he would begin the invasion of the world immediately the winter snows had melted." George poured more whiskey into David's cup. "You see, already the Nordic gods felt their powers diminishing as Christianity spread like plague throughout Europe. The Norse temples were being destroyed, the old rituals were no longer performed. The chieftain of the Leppingsvalts agreed. And so the contract was forged. Immediately, Thor summoned the Valkyries—these were the warrior maidens of the gods—and he ordered them to fly to the battle-fields of the world where they would collect the dead warriors and bring them back to these valleys."

"But what use would a collection of old corpses be?"

"Ah, but here we have the working of a god—an old and very powerful god. With the edge of his knife he split his tongue, then with his mouth full of his own blood he kissed each fallen warrior in turn and restored them to life."

"And these resurrected soldiers would obey the Leppingsvalt chieftain?"

"Absolutely."

"So what happened when the invasion took place?"

"The army wasn't ready. They lay in the caves throughout that winter of a thousand years ago, feeding on the blood of bulls to regain their strength. Remember, Thor had told the Leppingsvalt chieftain to attack when the winter snows had cleared."

David felt warmed by the whiskey once more. His uncle had become a silhouette against the brilliance of the lamp that hissed and pulsed until David could almost believe that a fragment of the sun had been brought down into the cave.

The old man continued. "Then, on the night before the invasion, disaster struck. The chieftain sat in his feasting hall with his sister and his bride-to-be. Also there was his lieutenant, Vurtzen. Now Vurtzen was a Goth warrior. By all accounts he was a gigantic savage of a man whose speech was closer to that of wolves than human. Then—and it is never made clear why—the chieftain and Vurtzen began to argue. The argument grew more and more ferocious until they drew swords and fought each other. The battle raged all night. At some point a huge wind blew open the door and extinguished the candles. But still they fought on—only now it was in utter darkness. Both men were expert swordsmen; neither could better the other. You can imagine them fighting there in the dark: the clang of steel blades echoing from the walls; the flash of sparks as sword crashed against sword. However, with neither of them realizing it, the chieftain's sister and the bride-to-be were accidentally killed during the duel. Neither the chieftain nor Vurtzen knew who struck the fatal blows. In remorse Vurtzen fled the country. Chieftain Leppingsvalt reacted differently. Mad with fury, he burned down the temple to Thor, blaming him for the deaths of the women."

"But the god wouldn't take that lying down?"

"No. Thor appeared, ordering Leppingsvalt to begin the attack on the Christian kingdoms."

"Using what amounted to a vampire army?"

"I suppose an army of vampires might be as good a description as any," the old man agreed softly. "An army of dead men fed on living blood. Perhaps you can allow your imagination to run freely, David? You can picture a hundred thousand men; they're clad in armour that had begun to rust as they lay dead on the battlefields. Their leather boots may have been rotted from their feet, their eyes may have been pecked out by crows; but there they are, made magically alive again and as strong as the bulls on whose blood they've feasted. They are ready for Leppingsvalt—your ancestor, David: your flesh and blood—to lead them into a war against the living."

"Quite a story," David said, sipping from his cup.

"Quite a story," the old man agreed. He took hold of the steel spike where it hung by the length of washing line from the bars. For a moment he gazed at it thoughtfully. "Yes. Quite a story."

"But Leppingsvalt never gave the order to attack?"

The old man didn't reply.

"There never was a vast empire with Leppington at its centre becoming a new Rome?"

The old man tested the weight of the steel spike in his hand. "Leppingsvalt refused to honour his deal with Thor. So he ordered his army—his vampire army—to return to their lair deep inside the mountains. So consumed with grief was he at the loss of his bride-to-be that he told Thor there never would be an invasion."

"The deal was off?"

George nodded his grey head. "The deal was off." Carefully he let go of the steel spike. It swayed gently, in the cool breeze. "But whatever you do, you must always honour your contract with the gods. In his fury Thor struck Leppingsvalt with the hammer. Legend has it that the blow smashed every bone in Leppingsvalt's face, leaving him resembling a pig. The injuries were so painful that even the touch of spider's web on one cheek would leave him howling in agony."

David shrugged thoughtfully. "So there ends the Leppingsvalts' quest for a world empire."

The old man turned to David and his face wrinkled into a dry smile. "Not quite, great-nephew. Remember, the blood of Thor, the thunder god, ran in Leppingsvalt's blood. No matter how disobedient a son is, a father won't hate him forever. And, to all intents and purposes, Chieftain Leppingsvalt was a son of Thor: he was half mortal, half god." The old man was speaking quickly, and somehow, to David, the voice sounded incredibly fluent, almost musical, the tongue loosened, no doubt, by the whiskey. "Years later, Leppingsvalt lay dying in his crumbling palace, the furniture rotting from neglect, the birds nesting in the ruined roof, the fireplace now eternally cold. As his final breath of life came Thor appeared to his son. He must have looked down on his son's broken face with its piggish snout. At that moment Thor's heart softened. He told the dying man that for a thousand years the fortunes of the Leppingsvalts would continue to slowly fall into ruin, the family would dwindle. Then, when all hope seemed to have gone and the once great family lay broken and scattered and dying, one of its sons would return from exile. He would take back the sword of Helvetes from the Christian kings. Then he would unleash his terrible army of dead warriors, sweeping away all of Leppingsvalt's enemies."

"And creating the vast empire presided over by the old Norse gods?" David recognized an inherent paranoia in the story. It was a legend told to Leppingsvalt children by the fireside down through the centuries to explain why the family was steadily losing its grip on the ability to generate wealth. And it continued to be told when the Leppingsvalts' name changed to Leppington. The story was an excuse for the Leppingtons' failure. Maybe the old man found a perverse comfort in it. By repeating it you were saying the reason for the family's decline came from outside, it was everyone's else's fault—the local Christian rulers of the time; betrayal by their own gods; market forces outside the area; why, even the government's income-tax policy would do. David wondered if the old man allowed the story to prey on his mind now that he lived alone in the house on the hillside. You never knew, the fixation on the story might be an early symptom of senility.

David looked back at the old man who gazed through the bars into the darkness beyond, lost deep in his own thoughts. Perhaps the old man spends hours in the cave, David thought, nursing his bottle of whiskey while brooding over the past glories of the Leppington family—possibly imagined past glories at that.

Still, he mused, you don't get to know you have divine blood in your veins every day. I wonder what the guys and gals at the tennis club would make of that?

He found himself smiling, then quickly killed it: he didn't want to hurt the old man's feelings. He did like him. And after all, everyone grows old one day. With the wrinkles and aching joints comes the fixation on ideas that younger people might find peculiar. Weren't winters colder and summers warmer in the old days? That's what many a grandmother would maintain. And grandfathers always claim beer tasted better, that rum was thick as syrup, that neighbours were friendlier, that money went further and so on and so on . . .

In the light of the lamp David watched his great-uncle's brooding eyes as they continued to watch the darkness.

Come off your high horse, David, he suddenly told himself. Quit the arrogance. He's an old man living alone. His wife's long dead. He has no close family. What else has he got left?

David felt a sudden fierce loyalty to the old man. His uncle had loved him like a son. He'd taken him for walks out into the countryside as soon as David could walk, bought him birthday and Christmas presents. George had probably babysat for him and his stepsisters. His Uncle George must have been broken-hearted when David's parents had moved what was left of the Leppington family to Liverpool.

And now you stand here coolly assessing him as if he's some stranger who's walked into the clinic with a bunion. Remember, David. This old man is family. A blood relative.

He lightly touched the old man's arm. "Uncle George. Is it possible to see the lake?" The old man might brighten up if he showed an interest in the family mythology.

The old man shook his head. "Not anymore." He touched the metal bars with a strong finger. "Nothing will get through these."

"Isn't there any other way into the caves?"

"There's a couple more entrances like this on the hillside. Colonel Leppington had them blocked off with these steel bars more than a hundred years ago."

"Why?"

"Too dangerous."

"Too dangerous? How?"

"Children were forever wandering in." He shrugged, sounding suddenly tired and old—incredibly old now. "They became lost. Place is a maze down there. Tunnels go on for miles." He shook his head; his voice now dropped to a whisper. "Too many children. They got lost in the dark. Never came back. So . . ." He gave the iron bars a slap; they hummed as if he'd tapped a huge bell. Quickly—almost anxiously—he quelled the vibrating bars with the palm of his hand. "So, Colonel Leppington had all the entrances fitted with these steel bars. Made a damn good job, too." With a deliberate effort the old man was making himself sound more cheerful. "Well, we'll catch our deaths malingering away down here. Come on, I made some bread yesterday. We'll toast it over the fire in the forge. You used to love that when you were about so high. How's your mother keeping? I kept meaning to drive across to Liverpool to visit one day, but . . . well, you know how it is. You lose touch. But it's been grand to see you, lad. You've not got yourself spliced yet, eh?"

He reached up a muscular arm and took down the lamp from the hook. Then, making nothing but small talk, he led David back to the surface, the hissing lamp surrounding them in a globe of light. David walked quickly to keep at the old man's side. The darkness behind deepened. The shadows seemed to follow them, as if eager to escape the cold loneliness of the cave.

Chapter Fourteen

1

This was the part Jack Black liked best. The moment of entry. The instant of penetration. This was the NOW! when what belonged to someone else became his.

Bang.

His foot had gone clean through the plywood panel at the bottom of the back door. Another two kicks and there was a hole big enough for one of his maggots to climb through.

The maggot complained. "Did you have to make so much noise?"

"Inside. Open the door," Jack Black ordered.

"What if someone heard?"

"No one heard."

"Look, I'm on bail. If I get caught again the bastard judge'll send me down."

"You won't get caught. Inside. Open the door."

Jack Black stared down the maggot. He knew the maggot wouldn't protest that much. The maggot still had the scabbed nose and black eye from when Jack'd put his maggot band together.

The other two maggots stood sullenly along the path. Jack Black knew they didn't like him. But they feared him. And he'd promised them a good cut of the proceeds so that was enough to be sure of their loyalty.

These maggots thought small-time. They smashed a car window and stole a radio. If they broke into a house they took what they could carry in their hands—which wasn't much: maybe a video, portable TV, a bit of jewellery. Jack Black would show them how to do it big-time. He'd rented a transit van from Whitby. Then he'd picked a house stuck in the middle of fields. Shit, this was easy meat. *Wap! Wap!* Kick in the flimsy plywood panel at the bottom of the door; send in one of his maggots to unlock the Yale. Then he was in.

That was what he liked: walking into some shit's house and thinking: this is mine. For the next couple of hours I own you. I'm taking what I want.

And the secret of making house-breaking pay is taking every piece of shit that's worth money—cash, jewellery, TV, radios, computers, clothes if they're half decent, furniture, vases, antiques, even the bloody pictures off the walls. Strip the fucker bare if need be.

"Are you waiting for a handwritten invitation or what?" he asked the maggots. "Follow me. Everything I touch, take it out to the van. OK?"

They nodded, stone-faced. "OK, boss."

Christ, I hate the fucker . . . I'm going to grass him up to the cops first chance I get. My fucking nose. He hurt my fucking nose so much. I'll kill him. Or I'll tip off a cop. No. Wait and get the money first.

Jack looked at the kid with the ginger beard and checked lumberjack shirt.

Jack Black. What kind of fucking name is that? I'm going to tear out his liver. I'll hurt him worse than he hurt me . . .

Jack knew what the kid was thinking. And that's no figure of speech, he thought to himself. The kid's thoughts rabbited away through Jack's head.

I'll cut him open; rip out his fucking liver. Kick his fucking liver all over the fucking street . . .

"Oi." Jack pointed at the kid with the ginger beard. "Try anything . . . any fucking thing. And I'll have your liver. I'll roast your liver over a fire and make you fucking eat it."

The bearded kid looked at Jack in nothing less than shock. His mouth dropped open—all stupid and wet-lipped. Now that had surprised the maggot; when you let them know what they're thinking.

Jack grinned, feeling the scar on the side of his head tingle.

"Now, you lot, move it," he ordered. "We're going to get all this over to York by this afternoon."

"When do we get the cash?" whined one of the maggots. "I need some blow. My head's like full of shit. I need a line of coke or speed."

Wap!

Jack slapped the maggot—an open-handed slap. Christ, aren't I the merciful one today?

"Shut up, and follow me."

He moved through the house, feeling calm, serene, like he was gliding through the rooms on golden wings. Lightly he laid a finger on a painting of a horse on one wall, ignored another, touched a green jug on the mantelpiece while he didn't even give a pair of brass candlesticks a second glance. He'd got an instinct for this. He selected the valuable; ignored the rubbish.

This haul would convert into cash—heaps of cash. After the share-out he'd do what he always did. Keep back a couple of notes for expenses, then pay the rest into his account through the cashpoint. His maggots, he knew, would blow it all on birds, booze and drugs within twenty-four hours.

But not me, he thought, gliding through the room, tattooed fingers lightly touching a chair here, a china figurine there. Money is power. His accounts—under half a dozen different aliases—now totalled over seventy thousand pounds.

Now that is power—real power. And that's what he needed. More than anything else.

2

Bernice Mochardi was hot on the trail of the man in the video.

In her hotel room she carefully unpacked the suitcase belonging to Mike Stroud that she'd found in the Dead Box, laying out the contents on her bed. There were shoes (good-quality Italian black loafers, size tens); two pairs of Levis, underwear, a black T-shirt, a couple of white cotton shirts, then a toilet bag containing razors, shaving foam, aftershave (she smelled it: once, twice, three times; then dabbed a little on the back of her wrist so the scent would stay with her).

The wind gusted outside, sometimes bringing a rattle of rain drops against her window.

I'll find what happened to him, she thought. There has to be a clue here.

There were no address tags on the suitcase, and no documentation of any kind inside. She picked up the three reporter's spiral-bound notebooks. They were all new; the pages blank. As she flicked through them a small snapshot-type photograph fell from the back of a pad.

She smiled, pleased with the discovery. It showed Mike—blond-haired, bespectacled and smiling—standing outside a Whitby hotel. Written in pencil on the back were the words: "Me outside the Royal, Whitby. The hotel where Bram Stoker conceived Dracula."

This is a find, she told herself, glowing with pleasure. A real find. She thought she might show it to some people she knew in the town; it was possible they might remember him. The person to ask would be Electra. Only if she did ask her she knew the woman would tease her about having a crush on a stranger.

No, it's more than that, she thought, gazing at the man's smiling face in the photograph. I will meet him one day. I know it.

A shiver ran up her spine.

Then, before she could even stop herself, she'd taken the video cassette from its case. She had to watch the tape again. And this time she would make notes in the reporter's notepad. There must be clues that would tell her more.

3

David Leppington left his uncle's home that afternoon. The old man had insisted he stayed for lunch—and that was after a huge pile of toast made over the forge fire. In the kitchen the two of them had sat down to a huge fry-up of mashed potato mixed with cabbage and bacon. Conversation had been of the kind anyone might have had after not seeing a close relative for a number of years. There was no return to the family saga involving Norse gods and new empires—to David's relief: he had begun to wonder if his uncle was harbouring some deep brooding obsession about the Leppingsvalt—now Leppington—divine mission to overthrow Christendom. But the old man now seemed quite light-hearted and delighted in showing off bottles of home-made elderberry wine, or asking David about his work and life.

David found his liking for his uncle deepening. Glimmers of old memories were surfacing. He remembered his uncle taking him fishing, or driving into Whitby to the museum at Pannett Park, or simply pumping pennies into the amusement arcade slot machines before going for ice creams down by Whitby harbour and watching the fishing boats chugging out to sea.

After promising to visit again, David had shaken the man by his powerful right hand, then walked down the lane to town. He felt good, as if he was walking inside a warm envelope. He decided to call on the man again in a couple of days; he'd take along a bottle of whiskey and they could chew the fat.

The wind was still blowing hard, but David didn't feel it. He carried a bag containing a privately-printed family history that one of the female Leppingtons had produced thirty years ago. There was also a bottle of the elderberry wine. His uncle had promised the wine was good and David believed him.

Humming to himself, he crossed the River Lepping and walked back into town.

Chapter Fifteen

1

She walked down beside the river. Her sandals slipped on the sandy path; she fell backwards and her rump hit the ground hard.

"Ow . . . bastard."

The jolt wasn't bruising, but it brought Friday night winging back firmly into her memory. Dianne Moberry got to her feet and dusted her bum. Don't look like a slag, Di. You don't want to scare him away, do you, honey?

127

Her cunt was sore. That was from spending six hours being fucked by Joel Preston. Most boys spurt off after ten minutes but Joel Preston fucked like a machine.

It had been fun when she'd started the affair with him six months ago but now the sex was monotonous. He'd pump solidly away between her legs for an hour and a quarter. Even after half an hour she'd be dry as a prune. Now the fucking just fucking well hurt, OK?

Even so, she was reluctant to dump Joel just yet. Yeah, he was dull, he was mechanical, he fucked missionary style with as much finesse and passion as a sexton digging a fat man's grave but he was affable enough; he tolerated her turning up late, or borrowing money from him for her hair restyling—like the blonde flashes she now wore, and, my God, they were expensive. She'd gone to Whitby's finest for that one. He'd even bought her these sandals. They were cute enough to die for. Little slender criss-cross straps—they made her bottle-tanned feet look tiny and golden.

But they were a bugger to walk in—especially when you were on a mission down by the riverside.

Last month Di Moberry had worked in a hotel bar in Whitby. This week—after being caught by the manager's wife giving him a blow job in the back of the car—she was kicking her heels in good old Leppington.

Christ, my cunt's sore, she thought again, as she threaded her way along the path. It was the kind of path that didn't want to be a path at all. It wanted to be a roller-coaster track. There were no level parts to it. Either you went down steeply to the edge of the River Lepping that gurgled and sang over the boulders. Or the path climbed up the banking. And everywhere there were willows.

Fucking willows. She hated them. The branches tried to catch her hair. The roots snagged her sandals. "If you bust a strap I'll fucking shampoo you with weed killer," she snarled at a tree.

And sometimes the clumps of willow grew so close together the path meandered away into darkness. And it's only the middle of the afternoon, she grumbled to herself. Once you got down in a hollow with all those willows it might as well be midnight. If I tread in some dog shit . . . bloody stupid dogs.

Reason for this mission, Di?

Come on, spill your gourd.

You're on a mission to get laid.

But this would be no boring missionary fuck, with old fish-faced Joel Preston.

Christ, my cunt is sore. If I don't end up with thrush it will be a miracle. She decided to give herself a damned good squirt of Canesten B when she got home—that's if dear old Dad hasn't got it muddled up with toothpaste again. She grinned, remembering how the old bugger had gagged the last time he'd mistakenly brushed his teeth with thrush cream.

Di Moberry had turned twenty-one last month. She'd got the key of the door and a damn sight else besides. Her thick and luscious swathe of hair, widely spaced blue eyes, raunchy hips and full breasts gave her what a poor education couldn't (but her twagging off school two or three days a week hadn't helped). If she smiled and flirted at interviews—providing the interviewer was a man—then her lack of qualifications was often overlooked. So, on the whole she took a better job than her plain but well-qualified cousins. Only Di Moberry hadn't got the knack of holding on to a job. They slipped through her fingers like water.

When she got tired of having two or three men on the go at once—in five or six years, she'd tell herself vaguely—then she'd snare a husband with a good career. Then it's a lady-of-leisure life for me. She pictured herself driving a Range Rover down to York for a day leathering that Visa Gold card.

But today she was hunting down some fresh blood.

She smiled. Someone filled with spunk. Who'd be exciting; who wouldn't dry her out so much she developed friction burns on the lips of her vagina.

Ow . . . my cunt *is* sore. Itchy, too.

The river bank path now took her into Leppington town behind the Bath House, the library and—wait for it, wait for it—the Station Hotel. This morning she'd spotted the sexiest piece of meat she'd seen in months—he was all brawn and tattoo and scars. And his eyes were so fierce and penetrating she'd felt herself go immediately moist. Her intelligence network—the girl who cooked the hotel breakfasts—had revealed that this stud was the new cellarman. That he was probably screwing Electra Charnwood, haughty proprietress of the hotel.

But who cares, thought Di, providing I get my share of that meat.

She imagined him looking down at her with those eyes full of ice and menace. She shivered with delight. Now she could almost feel his tough fingers cupping her breasts, then sliding up and down her bare stomach before tweaking her nipples.

God, he can tweak them hard, she thought, heart thumping. Hard as he damn well likes.

I like my nipples to be touched, then pinched. Then nipped between a good set of teeth, while fingers slide down between my legs.

Oh . . . shit. Oh, shit. I can't wait. I can't wait.

There'd be no messing around. Get in there, girl.

The plan?

That's easy, Di.

"Just like you, honey," she told herself in a louche, have-me-any-which-way-boys kind of voice.

She giggled.

No, Di. The plan. Just turn up at the back door of the hotel. Tattooed lustboy will probably be humping crates of beer from the cellar ready for Saturday night which was the big piss night in Leppington. Well, soon you'll be humping me, lustboy. She imagined the rounded mounds of his buttocks; she could almost feel herself gripping them as he pumped into her.

The soreness between her legs gave way to a mad tingling.

Oh, God yes, like a thousand pinpricks ding-dinging away down there in her crotch.

Her feet moved faster. Up one stretch of banking, brick wall of the back yards to her left, river gurgling to her right. Then . . . down to the water again. Down under the dark, dark willows . . .

Where boys and girls play doctors and nurses.

Mmm . . . she remembered that. Being fucked under the willow trees by what's-his-name . . . the boy who worked the potato wagon.

Excited now, she moved faster, little sandals slipping on the sandy banking. The banks of the river were deserted. Only commercial buildings backed onto the river. The residential waterside developments of the upwardly mobile hadn't touched Leppington yet.

Here there was only silence—apart from the giggling whisper of the river; that silence mated with a sense of isolation even though the main street with the market square would only be a stone's throw away at the other side of the line of buildings that included the Station Hotel.

Ahead, she could see the gap in the three-metre-high brick wall that led into the rear yard of the Station Hotel.

She was breathing heavily now.

My God, Di, are you gagging for a shag or what, girl?

The soreness of her cunt had now most definitely been replaced by an itch. That old, old itch she knew so well.

Like a cow with an itchy hide she wanted to rub against something hard. Something damn hard . . . *oh, yes.*

Another twenty paces and she'd reach that gateway. She didn't doubt she could charm the pants off Mr. Jack Black in ten minutes flat. There was just one dip down into a clump of willows. Then another ten steps in her dainty sandals would take her up to the entrance of the hotel's back yard.

Christ, that itch. It needed scratching—scratching hard; fucking HARD.

She slithered down the sandy path into the gloom of the willow trees. Again she slipped.

"Bollocks."

She stood up in the half-darkness and rubbed the muck from the skirt stretched drumskin-tight across her backside.

"Have you hurt yourself?"

Oh-Shit-God-Almighty!

She looked round, gasping with shock.

A man stood there in the gloom. He wasn't even on the path but standing on the edge of the water. Willow branches formed a frame around him. For all the world he could have been a portrait hanging on a wall.

"I'm sorry, I didn't mean to startle you."

Her surprise was double-barrelled. The man's voice was so polite, considerate. It was also American.

"Are you OK?" The voice was silk to her ears.

"Fine . . . phew . . ." She fanned her face—a deliberately pretty action. "I'm fine, thank you. You took me by surprise, that's all." She peered hard at the man. Why was it so dark down here at the water's edge?

"Are you fishing?" she asked prettily.

"You might say so."

"Well . . . either you are or you aren't."

The words could easily have come out harshly, but Di liked the man's voice—that American purr set her skin a-tingling. Instead, her voice acquired a sassy huskiness.

"Oh," the man said lightly. "I was just waiting for a pretty little girl to come by."

"Perhaps if you're patient she'll come."

"Perhaps she already has."

"And she might come sooner than you think." Hell, Di, that's racy even for you.

But there was something about the voice that melted even the hard core of her cynical heart.

My God, I feel like I'm fifteen again. When the lad from the potato truck humped me on the dirt over there. I'm all breathless and hot, and my heart is positively purring.

She screwed up her pretty eyes in an attempt to see him better.

There stood a slender figure (willowy, she thought, pleased with an adjective that was so poetic and apt, considering they stood in a copse of willow).

Jack Black up there in the hotel was already shunted onto the back burner. A bird in the hand, she thought. Yeah, a bird in the hand, right?

Anyway, Jack Black won't blow away in a breeze, will he? He'll be around tomorrow night.

Now she felt good in the presence of this stranger with his polished American accent. She sensed his smile rather than saw it; imagined his soul music.

Now that is poetic. Soul music. She'd never heard that before. But this man had it; he was playing it for her.

And she felt good in his presence.

She walked down towards the water's edge beneath the dense ceiling of willow branches.

Now she saw his softly curling blond hair. His face was strong as if the muscle beneath the skin was superbly toned. A pair of ever-so-faint marks at either side of the bridge of his nose suggested he might, on occasion, wear glasses.

When he reads music at the piano, she thought. And he's so

tall. The image of a Victorian artist. Romance streamed from him like water from a spring.

I'm in love. For the first time ever, I'm really in love. I love this man. I want to dissolve in his heart blood.

"You've wonderful hair," he said. "It looks as if it has golden lights burning inside the strands."

"Thank you," she said prettily, allowing herself to be flattered. "Aren't you cold without a coat?" She noticed now that he wore just a shirt and light-coloured chinos. For a moment she thought they looked stained but no, perhaps it was merely the shadows.

She would have looked again, but he was gazing at her with the most intense pair of eyes she'd ever seen. The eyebrows were surprisingly dark for someone with blond hair. And it was the eyes . . . she'd never seen eyes like them. They're fixed on me so . . . so . . . say it, Di, say it! she thought with a thrill . . . they're fixed on me so *passionately.*

"You live here?" he asked smoothly, beaming a beautiful smile at her. "In the town, that is, not the river?"

She giggled the ever-so-pretty-little-girl-am-I giggle. "Yes. For my sins. Do you?"

"For your sins? You're never a girl who knows anything about sin, are you?"

"Well . . . I didn't fall off the back of the cabbage truck yesterday."

"You do have wonderful eyes, don't you?"

"Thank you." And yours are, too, she thought, feeling a kind of dreamy warmth rise over her. His eyes were so wide; so vast. She couldn't take her own eyes off them.

He did not blink. Not once. The eyes were bright, wide-awake looking.

Wonderful, wonderful eyes, she thought. Her heart purred; her blood ran warm and thick in her veins; she felt such . . . such tranquillity; such a sense of well-being.

"What's your name?"

"Dianne."

Her voice was a whisper now. Nothing else existed but his eyes. She marvelled at them. They were brighter than any diamonds she'd ever seen. And he does not blink, she thought. My love does not blink. Not ever.

"Dianne. It suits you."

The muscles around his eyes altered their shape from second to second. Now the eyes seemed to pulsate. One second they were huge white discs, centred with blue. The next the white of the eye vanished and all she could see were the pupils. They became black holes; deep, ineffably mysterious.

She found herself leaving the path.

Never once did she take her eyes from his.

Those eyes . . .

Warmth, love, serenity, sweet music: the music of angels filled her.

Then a beautiful thing happened.

The murmur of the river, the song of the birds, the breath of the wind that sang gently through the willow branches. All of that vanished into his eyes. A sliver of her went with it.

He sees me as beautiful, she thought, overjoyed. I want to surrender myself to him. I want to give him everything. But what can I give? I have nothing special that he could possibly want, have I?

His eyes were huge shining globes.

His smile was warm, loving, wanting.

Hungry.

His arms moved slowly, gently, lovingly through the gloom to enfold her. They might have been a pair of vast wings wrapping her in a glorious warmth.

She opened her mouth and awaited that first kiss.

It was Saturday afternoon; the time, three o'clock.

2

Saturday. 3:15 P.M.

"David. Join me for coffee."

Electra Charnwood's voice sailed across the hotel lobby to greet him.

He let the door swing shut behind him, sealing off the sounds of the market and the traffic. "Don't mind if I do." He smiled.

Electra walked from behind the reception desk with a heavy silver tray on which were loaded cups and a cafetière containing a richly dark coffee.

"My," she said, with a warm smile. "It looks as if you've had

134

the cobwebs well and truly blown away; have you walked far?"

"Only just to the edge of town. Family visit."

"Oh, that would be Mr. George Leppington. An uncle?"

David nodded. "I don't know what you feed yourselves on round here but you're looking pretty good on it. He must be mid-eighties but he looks a heck of a lot fitter than me. Here, let me move the vase."

He moved the vase from the centre of the table as Electra set down the tray.

"Do you know George?" he asked.

"Know *of* him, really. See him in town occasionally. Now, David, you sit there and amuse me, I've just slogged round Whitby looking for a new dress and I can't find a thing to fit me. Oh, damn the girl. White flowers."

"Pardon?"

Electra picked up the vase that contained a pair of white carnations. "I've told her again and again: no white flowers." She shot David one of her direct gazes. "Did you know in China a white flower is a symbol of mourning?"

He shook his head and smiled. "They don't make the place look funereal, anyway."

Electra sighed. "Perhaps the girl has had a premonition or something. Now, allow me to be mum. Milk?"

"Black."

"A man after my own heart. Don't be shy. Grab a biscuit."

"Is it always this quiet on a Saturday afternoon?"

"Always. Dead as a doornail, isn't it?" She waved her hand to take in the deserted hotel lobby with its sprinkling of red upholstered chairs and tables. "So, we've got the run of the place. What shall we do? Swing from the drapes, or bite the heads off these ghastly white carnations?"

Her eyes twinkled mischievously, making her look years younger. David couldn't help but laugh.

"You know what I've always wanted to do?"

"Go on, Doctor, shock me."

"Use a tray as a sledge and ride it downstairs."

Smiling, she nodded towards the silver tray. "Go on, be my guest."

"I think I'd need something stronger than coffee before I did that."

She laughed, then asked in that no-nonsense style of hers, "What do you make of Leppington?"

"Quiet."

"As a grave?"

"I like it."

"More than Liverpool?"

"Liverpool can get a bit mad, you know."

"Oh, give me the big city anytime," she said, stirring sugar into her cup. "I like the anonymity of crowds. Here you feel as if you're constantly in the spotlight."

"You're not a fan of the town, then?"

"I hate it!" she said with feeling. "I hate this hotel, too. Big, bloody awful place it is."

David reached for a biscuit—not hungry after the huge meal George had fed him—but unsure how to respond to Electra's sudden outburst. "It doesn't seem such a bad place to live—the hotel or the town."

She toyed with a strand of her blue-black hair, her eyes thoughtful. Steam rose from the coffee cup. "The hotel's a place where people come to die."

He raised his eyebrows.

She smiled. There was more than a hint of the grim in that smile, he thought.

"Sounds morbid, doesn't it?"

"And a tad melodramatic." He smiled, trying to lighten the mood.

"But true. Too many people have died here over the years." She sipped her coffee. "I grew up here. As a child I kept a list of people who had come here only to leave feet first. Some were suicides. When I was eight years old, a girl was suffocated in the room next to mine. Her boyfriend was convicted of the murder but he claimed he was innocent."

"They always do."

"My aunt climbed out of an upstairs window and threw herself down into the courtyard outside. Died of a broken neck."

He decided to let her speak. Clearly she had to get this off her chest.

Uh-oh, David, playing Christ again, aren't we? Absorbing other people's pain? No, he reasoned. Perhaps Electra didn't have close friends or family to speak to; this was a form of catharsis; so why not allow her blow off a little steam?

Electra continued, speaking faster now. "My mother died in the hotel's basement."

"An accident?"

"Heart failure, so the coroner said."

"You believe that?"

"No. I think she died of fright. Do you know why?"

Stop her now, a voice said in the back of his head. Her voice was thickening with emotion. What are you afraid of, David? he asked himself. That she'll burst into tears and you'll have to comfort her?

"People do die suddenly," he said gently. "Sometimes even doctors don't know why it happens."

"I know," she said, controlling the emotion in her voice. "I remember seeing a death certificate for my great-grandfather who dropped dead in that very doorway. In the box headed cause of death the doctor had written: Died as a result of a visitation from God. That's how they used to describe a death from unknown causes, wasn't it?"

David nodded, wishing someone would walk into the lobby or the phone would ring. Anything that would help snap her out of this mood.

"Died as a result of a visitation from God," she repeated colourlessly. "Now that is a picturesque way of putting it." She took a deep breath; on the surface she seemed calm. "You see, Doctor, my mother heard sounds coming from the basement."

"Sounds?"

"Yes, banging. Like someone clamouring to be let out. She'd been hearing these for weeks."

"Did anyone else hear them?"

"No. At least they pretended not to. Well . . . these noises terrified her. She dreaded having to go into the basement. But she had to. She ran this monstrosity with my father. She didn't want to be seen as a silly, neurotic woman. So she kept going down into the basement. And she kept hearing the noises—thumping, banging, like someone hammering on a door."

David nodded, realizing that despite himself he was slipping into the doctor-and-patient role.

"Then, a week before she died," Electra continued, "she became convinced that she was going to die. No, she had no aches or pains or shortness of breath—no physical symptoms of ill health—she suddenly knew as surely as night follows day that soon she would die."

"And she connected this with the sounds in the basement?"

"Yes. For her the noises were death—Death personified; the Reaper himself was coming for her. All neurotic fantasy after all, what do you say, Doctor?"

"She didn't confide in anyone?"

"Only her diary. I have it now, in my chest of treasures upstairs. She was a poetic soul, my mother." Electra sucked her coffee spoon before laying it back on the silver tray. "But a few days later she was found lying dead in the basement. Not a mark on her. But she held a sweeping brush in her hand as if she'd been swinging it like a club. Dead in a little pool of cold urine. Now isn't that a sad, miserable way to go?"

"You know," David said gently. "It sounds as if this is unexpressed grief. I'm sorry to sound like the doctor now, but I think you've been bottling this up for some time."

Electra shrugged. "I never cried over her, true. But I'm not the crying sort." She gave a sudden smile. "Now, drink up your coffee. It's getting cold." David thought the time was ripe to change the line of conversation, but before he could speak she looked quickly up at him and said in quite a matter-of-fact way, "Those noises in the basement." Fear suddenly bloomed huge in her eyes. "The ones that troubled my mother. I've started hearing them, too."

3

Saturday. 3:30 P.M.

The road over the mountains stretched out before them. Above them clouds raced like dark phantoms on a mission from hell. Jack Black drove the van steadily. Nice and easy does it. Nothing to attract attention.

In the back of the van his maggots sat amongst the furniture and electrical goods they'd taken from the house. In another hour they'd hit the city of York, then they could unload this on a crooked dealer in exchange for a nice wad of cash. After that the maggots would head for an almighty piss-up. Jack Black

138

would pay his share into the hole-in-the-wall machine and maybe spend the weekend cruising the city streets.

Then it came right out of the great shining blue to hit him.

He was going the wrong way.

He stopped the van at the side of the road.

"What's wrong? Why've you stopped?" asked one of his maggots.

"I'm going back the other way," he announced in a low voice.

"Going back? We've got to get this shit to York."

He shook his head. "I'm going back to Leppington."

"Leppington? For Godsakes, why?"

Why? He didn't know why. Only he had this need—this burning need to go back there. There was unfinished business. Again he didn't know what but it gaped at him like a great, raw unhealed wound.

4

Saturday. 3:40 P.M.

Dianne Moberry thought: *I am dead.*

She wasn't. But perhaps it would have been better for her if she were.

She wouldn't like what was going to happen to her next.

A moment ago she'd opened her eyes. She thought she was waking in bed, that she'd been dreaming about meeting a beautiful blond-haired man on the river bank.

Reality came clunking back—as cold, as forceful, as brutal as a runaway truck.

Jesus-oh-Jesus. Help me.

Her clothes had been stripped from her body. Now, naked, she stood facing an iron gate. Water swirled round her feet. She looked round, her mind juddering back to full consciousness.

The river flowed past behind her. Overhead willows arched. She realized she was standing in what must be a culverted stream that ran beneath the town before finally flowing out into the Lepping through a huge drain. The drain lay in darkness beyond the bars of the gate.

But why am I standing here? Why am I naked?

She shivered and tried to move back, away from the gate.

She couldn't, she realized with muted surprise. She couldn't move so much as a centimetre. It took a moment to push understanding through her fogged brain. But at last she understood: she couldn't move because someone was forcing her, face forward, against the bars of the gate; her bare stomach, breasts, hips pressed against cold metal.

She felt sick. She only wanted to get away from here. There was an unpleasant animal smell oozing through the gate. Oh, why is he holding me like this? He's using his body to hug me against the iron bars. I'm going to vomit; I'm cold.

And frightened. Incredibly frightened.

"Let go of me," she begged. "Please . . . I—I'll do anything."

Without a shadow of a doubt she knew it was the blond man holding her tightly there against the gate.

But why?

Then, ahead in the darkness, she sensed movement.

Dazed, she found herself asking, "Who's there?"

No reply.

Now there was a flurry of movement in the darkness of the tunnel. There were gleams of white—bluey white, like blood-starved skin. The movements grew quicker.

All of a sudden she sensed, rather than saw, figures moving out of the darkness towards the gate. She heard feet splashing the shallow water of the stream.

Dianne Moberry closed her eyes.

She knew things were going to happen to her. Nasty, awful things. Knew it absolutely. But, no . . . oh no, she couldn't watch.

Water splashed up against her bare body. She flinched.

Eyes closed—keep them closed!

She screamed the words through her head. Keep them closed! You don't want to see what's—

Ah!

She gagged in pain.

Pain speared through the tips of her breasts.

Her teeth clicked as she clenched her jaw.

A hand folded over her mouth. She couldn't even scream now. But, oh, she wanted so much to scream. She wanted to roar out her agony and fear.

She tried to push herself back from the iron gate. The agony grew even more intense.

Her eyes snapped open at last. The image she saw was impossible.

Blood. There was plenty of blood, lashings of blood, spurting, covering her bare arms.

But it was what else she saw that refused to make any sense to her splintering mind.

Two tubes—all white and softly fleshy—had grown out of her chest. They ran straight out through the bars of the gate to where something white as bone bobbed and shivered.

White tubes. For Godsakes, what were they?

She gasped, shuddered, as she stared down over the hand clamping her mouth.

Then she knew what the white tubes were. Something had gripped her breasts as they'd been forced through the bars of the gate. Now it pulled hard. And no way would it let go. Not ever. She knew that absolutely. Her nipples felt as if they were gripped by red-hot pincers. Now her breasts were drawn out as thin as a pair of baby's arms. Blue veins showed through the skin.

And here and there that white skin was smeared with blood.

The blond man still held her tightly, face forward against the gate.

The only way she could escape would be to tear away her own breasts.

But she couldn't fight it any more.

She stopped trying to push herself back; immediately the pressure exerted by the man slammed her body forward against the metal bars.

Pain—aching—exhaustion—submission; and with that there came something else, too. A sweetness; a deep, penetrating sweetness that oozed back from her breasts, to her heart, to every single cell of her body.

Once more she closed her eyes.

As Dianne Moberry, she had seen the last of this world.

Chapter Sixteen

1

David Leppington took the lift to the fourth floor of the Station Hotel.

The ancient lift seemed little larger than a coffin. The fact that it was lined with a dark varnished pine only added to the effect.

Normally he'd have taken the stairs but the huge meal he'd eaten at his uncle's (and the whiskey he'd drunk that fired up a warm glow in his veins) made him feel drowsy. In one hand he held the carrier bag containing the bottle of home-made wine, and the self-published book, *The Leppington Family: Fact and Legend*, by Gertrude H. Leppington.

As the lift bumped and squeaked slowly, slowly up the shaft he thought of Electra's sudden outpouring in the lobby below. Both her parents had died when she had been young. Despite her air of sophistication and cynicism there was probably a vulnerable little girl inside her that was still bewildered and hurt at being orphaned in her twenties.

It was only the arrival of a couple that had interrupted Electra. They wanted a room for the weekend. Both had been flushed and glittery-eyed from drink. The girl had kept repeating, over and over: "A double room, it must be a double room. Do you have a sunken bath? A four-poster bed? Oh, Matt, we must have champagne . . . make them send champagne up to the room." Giggles.

He found himself liking Electra. Once she dropped that tough shield she was a nice, warm human being. He pictured her: the blue-black hair, the strong nose, a dark, almost Egyptian colouring. I wonder if I should—*shit*.

The single light in the coffin of a lift went out. There was instant darkness.

The lift gave a groan.

Stopped.

Oh, shit.

Great.

Now I have to bang on the door and shout and end up feeling a right prat when the fire brigade at last winch me out.

He looked up. Though there was little point. The darkness was absolute. There, above the roof of the lift, he pictured cables running up to the lift motor. The winch motor was smouldering, rats were nibbling at the brakes, a psychopath was hacksawing his way through the cable that held this little pine coffin three storeys above the ground.

OK, OK, he told his runaway imagination, don't forget the werewolves and the zombies, too.

He reached out to where he judged the control panel would be—no, David, a little more to the left. First came the edge of the door; then his fingers found the raised edge of the metal plate where the buttons were set. Then he found the buttons, feeling oddly like cool nipples in the dark.

Cool nipples. Now, David, he thought, suddenly grinning, does that or does that not show you've not been getting any lately? Comparing lift buttons to nipples?

You need the love of a good woman (well, a *bad* woman would do). He smiled again. Hell, this is one way to spend a Saturday afternoon. Groping lift buttons in the dark.

By touch he found the lowest button on the panel. That, he guessed, would be the alarm button.

OK, here goes. He pressed the button. He listened, anticipating the sound of a distant bell to come ringing down the shaft—the "Hey, everyone, listen to this, there's a stupid prat stuck in the lift" alarm.

Nothing.

He listened.

Total silence.

He hit the button again. Once, twice, three times.

Bingo!

Suddenly the light came on. Immediately the lift juddered; somewhere above him the electric motor of the winding gear hummed into life.

Only the lift was descending. Not going up.

143

He shrugged. Oh well, might as well enjoy the ride.

The lift whirred down floor after floor. Yawning, he leaned back against the pine wall of the lift, waiting for it to stop. Then he could press button number four and try to get back to his floor. He was ready to crash out on his bed where he could stare at the ceiling and lazily plan what to do with the rest of the day.

The lift bumped to a halt. The doors slid open.

David stared.

He'd expected the hotel lobby and a view of reception with Electra sitting behind the desk.

Instead there was only darkness.

He blinked. Then checked the button he'd pressed. It was marked with a "B."

Oh, you've got the basement, you idiot.

He pressed button four.

Then he stood waiting for the doors to slide shut, the carrier bag dangling in his hand.

The ancient lift mechanism was in no hurry.

He found himself looking into the darkened basement, seeing a stack of black plastic crates alongside one whitewashed wall. Beyond that there were only indefinable shapes in the gloom. These were humped, suggestive of figures standing there watching him.

"Come on, lift."

He spoke lightly enough.

Even so, there was something not too pleasant about that solid wedge of darkness beyond the little radiance spilled by the light in the lift. The darkness looked near-solid. The air seeping in had an icy bite to it. It didn't smell pleasant: a wet organic smell that hinted at rot.

That uneasiness came back. The same sense of unease he'd experienced when he'd looked down the grate in the street that morning and recalled seeing the white footballs bobbing by as a six-year-old. That sense of unease that had been reinforced by the walk into the cave behind his uncle's house.

"Come on, I've had enough of dark underground places." He spoke flippantly to himself, but the truth of the matter was that he didn't like the basement. All too easily something could run out of the darkness and into the lift.

Just what, for crying out loud? he asked himself, irritated by

144

his stupid flight of fancy. This is a hotel basement, not Castle Frankenstein. Out there are empty crates, beer barrels, junky pieces of furniture, not razor-toothed monsters or gore-hungry ghouls.

He tried to shrug the creep of cold fear off his shoulders; but even so he found himself pumping the lift button with his finger.

"Come on. Time to take daddy home, baby."

At last the doors slid shut.

But not before the conviction gripped him that something small and verminous would scuttle out of the dark and into the lift.

The doors shut.

The relief he felt seemed absurdly large. A second later the lift was rattling its way back to the fourth floor.

Suckers, you didn't get me that time.

He smiled to himself. And tried to ignore the shiver running up his spine.

2

In the back of the van the maggots were complaining—they wanted to go to York, they wanted their share of the money, they wanted to get pissed, they wanted to get laid, they—blah, blah, blah: same old story.

Jack Black switched off. Now he didn't hear their voices coming from their mouths, but he did still catch the buzz of dissatisfaction humming inside their heads. He'd been able to hear what people said with their minds as well as their mouths all his life.

And it was all shit.

Humanity. He hated it all.

As much as it hated him. He expected tomorrow to be like yesterday. And next year to be the same as last year. He didn't expect his life to get better or worse. Once, when he had realized he was the only one he'd ever met who could hear the voices in other people's heads—mind-reading, they called it—he had wondered if it was something he could exploit, but the psychiatrists who visited the care homes didn't believe him. And when he freaked kids out at the foster homes he was booted out to another foster home, or shunted back to the Council care home. Now he kept his trap shut.

The road rolled out in front of him across heather-backed hills. Storm clouds stained the sky with blacks, purples and greens, like someone had given God Himself a damn good kicking.

Jack Black shifted down a gear as the van started to chug up the incline.

A sign said: LEPPINGTON—6 MILES.

He drove faster. It was as if the town was calling his name.

3

"Did you hear anything?"

"It'll be the couple in Room 101, they were so hot for each other they were practically disrobing in reception."

"No, it sounded like a scream."

"Then it probably *was* the couple in 101."

"You don't take anything seriously, do you, Electra?"

"Just what is there to take seriously, honey?"

"Life?"

"Life is cheap."

"You're the most cynical person I've ever met."

"Cynical?"

"Yes."

"Nope, dear. Realistic."

"Realistic, my foot."

"When you get to my age, dear."

"What, all of thirty-five, Electra?"

"When you reach the grand old age of thirty-five, Bernice, you will realize that you are an unimportant cog in this universe. No, you're not even a cog. A cog is a serrated wheel that drives another serrated wheel; that suggests you are a vital component in this windy great star-spangled cosmos. Therefore, no, we are not even cogs. We are dust motes blowing in the wind. We are sludge particles oozing along a river bed. Did you know that this entire universe was created by a simple fluctuation from the norm? Ask an astrophysicist. We are a blip on the screen, a bubble in water, a random event. We—"

"How's that? Too tight?"

"Yes."

"I'll slacken them, wait."

"No, they feel better laced tight like this. There, Bernice, what do you think?"

Electra stood in the middle of the hotel kitchen and raised her skirt to above the knee to show off her new boots that laced from the toes to just below the knee.

"Don't you just love black leather?" Electra gave a sudden wicked grin. "Kinky, or what?" She sighed impatiently. "Bernice, I said kinky, or what? What do you think?"

"Mmm . . . sorry. I thought I heard it again."

"What, dear?"

"It sounded like someone crying out in the back."

Electra looked through the window into the courtyard. "All deserted."

"I'm sure I heard crying. You know, sort of high, like they were being hurt?"

"Kids," Electra said carelessly and topped up the wine glasses.

"Oh, Electra. I said I'd only have one."

"Live a little, honey, for tomorrow we die."

"I'll be fit for nothing but bed."

Electra gave a licentious wink.

"Now don't start that again."

"Don't you find him attractive?"

"Who?"

"Why, the old man who collects the empties. OK, so he's got a boil on his forehead and cotton wool in his ears but I hear he goes like a train."

"Electra!"

"No, silly. I'm talking about Dr. David Leppington, of course."

"The purple's better than the white," Bernice said, holding up the two silk scarves.

"I kept the receipt, I'll change it next week. Now, stop changing the subject. The good doctor. Are you interested?"

As Saturday afternoon slid into Saturday evening the two made girl-talk in the kitchen. Over the last month or so it had become a tradition. Saturday afternoons Bernice would share a bottle of wine with Electra and they'd show each other clothes they'd bought that morning or simply chew the fat. At first Bernice had been easily embarrassed by Electra's teasing. Now she realized it was all in fun. They got on well together, enjoying each other's company.

Electra tried on earrings she'd bought from that craft fair in Whitby's Church Lane, pushing back her long blue-black hair with her fingers.

Bernice tilted her head slightly to one side, listening. She was sure she'd heard a thin cry coming from the direction of the river that flowed behind the high brick wall of the courtyard. It could have been children, she supposed. Even a bird. And yet the sound of it had been strangely shocking. Like someone experiencing incredible pain.

As Electra tried to prise out what she, Bernice, thought of Dr. Leppington she gazed out of the window. Dark clouds were bubbling up over the mountain tops. There was a storm coming.

"Maybe he will invite you out to dinner one night," Electra was saying. "Would you accept?"

Bernice had intended to say nothing about this to Electra, but she couldn't resist seeing the look on her face. "Oh, he already has," she said, quite casually.

"No!" Electra's look of astonishment was immensely satisfying. "You said yes—you did, didn't you?"

Smiling, Bernice nodded.

"Oh, child." Electra beamed. "When?"

"Tomorrow evening. We're going to the Magpie in Whitby."

"Oh, good choice. My, I'll get my tool kit out tomorrow afternoon and we'll put so much work into you that he'll swoon with desire."

Chatting happily, they planned what Bernice would wear for the dinner. Outside, the dark clouds slid over the town. For all the world they looked like the wings of a vast bat, stretching out as if they could obliterate the whole of humanity.

Chapter Seventeen

1

SEX. SEX. SEX!

Oh, God, I love it. I love him doing this to me. I love the words he uses. Dirty words. But it's so exciting. I wonder if I dare go down on him?

There has to be a first time for everything, doesn't there? she asked herself. *Yes, go on: do it.*

Fiona Hill stretched luxuriously in the bed, allowing herself to be kissed from her forehead to the soles of her feet. Room 101 of the Station Hotel was warm—they'd warmed it, steaming the windows.

"Now I'm going to kiss your breasts," her lover was murmuring. "Then I'm going to kiss your stomach, then I'm going to kiss your hips, then I'm going to . . . yum, yummm-mer . . ."

Fiona Hill squirmed her legs against the sheets, loving every sex-soaked moment of it. She was twenty-nine years old.

Believe me, she thought, this is way, WAY overdue. She weighed just over seven stone. She was slim, small-boned, brown-eyed. Hair? A mousy brown. Not unpleasant, she thought. Normally she wore thick, blue-framed glasses—not today though, you won't. You've earned this. You've earned being the centre of attention for once. You've earned being the object of desire: a hot, sexual—yes, yes, say it—animal desire.

You've earned being . . . being . . . go on, she told herself. Don't hold back. Say that naughty word.

Fucked.

You've earned being fucked.

Now she breathed the naughty word out loud. "*Fuck* me, Matt . . . *fuck* me, please."

Fuck.

The word seemed peculiar in her mouth—exciting and strange and dirty all at the same time.

Fuck.

In all her twenty-nine years she hadn't even been able to think of the word without blushing hotly. Then she would rush into confession as if Lucifer himself was chasing her. She'd tell Father O'Connell everything. About these wicked feelings in the pit of her stomach, the magazines the girls at work would leave open on her desk, and how—and where—she'd soap herself in the bath, when she'd known that her skin was already clean; but she loved the slippery feel of soapy fingers on her skin.

Sex.

But now the floodgates had opened. She'd bumped into Matt at a friend's engagement party. He'd driven her home—well, part-way home. Suddenly he'd stopped the car and kissed her— Heavens, she'd been nervous; she'd felt as if a balloon had expanded inside of her: growing bigger, bigger, bigger until it almost burst.

Then something *had* burst.

It had all been mad—just completely mad.

Within two minutes he was on top of her, filling her with himself until she thought she'd split wide open—was I in ecstasy? Was I in agony? Did I go mad?

I loved it, she'd thought later. Twenty-nine years old, still a virgin.

But not any longer.

Sex.

She opened her eyes, a smile playing on her lips. The setting sun had broken through the cloud; now a shaft of red light came through the window to flood the hotel room wall. It glinted off the glass on the framed picture of naked boys swimming in a lake. The scent of the single red rose in the champagne glass reached her. Ineffably sweet, it seemed to flow through her skin to warm her blood. Her heart sang with pure happiness.

Love.

Here I am in Room 101, she thought, relaxing, feeling incredibly delicious, and wanted. I want to stay in Room 101 forever. I want him to fuck me until I melt and flow into the carpet and furniture and walls. I want time to freeze the next time I orgasm and for that orgasm to last for eternity.

Perhaps this is what heaven feels like?

An eternal sensation of coming? A billion-year orgasm?

Mmm . . . I hope so.

Thoughts like that would have sent her running to Father O'Connell with his ears bristling with white hairs and dour Scots voice. Not any longer, Fiona, not any longer. I have my true love now. I'm warm. I'm safe.

Yes. There were problems. The twenty-year age gap didn't worry her. But Matt was married. He was a director of the civil engineering group that employed her.

But the future didn't matter.

This weekend would last forever, wouldn't it?

Fiona gazed fondly down at the head of steel-gray hair as it moved from side to side, licking her flat stomach. She moaned with pleasure when he kissed the curl of downy hair between her legs. One of his big hands moved up to gently knead her breasts. His big gold wedding ring glinted in the red sunlight.

Matt moved up her body until his eyes—as bright as chips of ice shining in sunlight—looked into hers. His body lay on hers. It felt warm and firm and oh-so-comforting.

"Fiona," he whispered. "Do you trust me?"

"Yes."

"Do you believe me when I tell you I love you?"

"Yes, I do."

He kissed her on the lips. She smelt champagne and cigar on his breath. "Now," he breathed. "I'm going to make love to you. Ready?"

"Ready." She slid her hands round his wide back, her knees raised.

Oh, she wanted this to last forever.

As she felt him slide magnificently into her, the sun crept below the horizon and night began its stealthy entry into the room.

2

Three storeys above the lovers in Room 101 David Leppington sat in his room. He'd pulled the armchair across so he could sit with his feet casually on the bed. A coffee steamed near his elbow. In his hands was the book his uncle had given him, *The Leppington Family: Fact and Legend*. As a family history went it was incredibly thorough with family trees, photographs of his Leppington forefathers—stern patriarchal Victorians with moustaches bushy enough to sweep a carpenter's floor—and Leppington matriarchs in bustles and dresses that touched the ground. They all glowered sternly from the photographs as if lives depended on them not breaking into a smile.

The exceptions came later, with photographs of his father and his uncle George—his father would have been in his teens, his uncle perhaps thirty-something—both sitting in a rowing boat wearing easygoing grins and straw boaters.

The legend of the Leppingtons being the proud possessors of divine blood was recounted as matter-of-factly as the marriages and deaths. Then came Uncle George's potted biography, telling how he built up a successful business in Whitby, importing cheap shoes from the then Soviet Bloc countries. Running parallel to the business of importing shoes was a chain of shoe shops stretching from Bridlington to Saltburn.

On page fourteen there was even an engraving of some ancient Leppington of a thousand years before kneeling before the Thunder God Thor, complete with Mjolnir, the hammer. Thor was handing the man what appeared to be a rolled-up newspaper (although obviously it couldn't have been). In copperplate print beneath ran the words: *Great Thor Bestows The Word Upon Tristan Leppingsvalt AD 967*. David examined the reproduction in the book. It looked Victorian and had the appearance of a Christian church's stained-glass window rather than blood-and-guts Nordic art.

He turned over a page and, at random, chose a paragraph.

My gift to you is an army undying, feasted on the blood of bulls, obedient to the word of Leppingsvalt, and eager for the new Kingdom that kneels before Thor, not Christ.

David scanned the page, reading a sentence here and there. It was obviously an account of the vampire army Thor had given to his ancestors with the intention of conquering the Christian kingdoms of AD 1000. No doubt Thor, enraged by Chieftain Leppingsvalt's refusal to begin the invasion, had obviously decided to take his proverbial bat and ball back to Valhalla with him.

Bummer, David thought smiling. He remembered when one of the students at university had sauntered into the lecture room and announced he'd just inherited a cool million from some distant auntie. Smug bugger. Just think if, after this holiday, I can saunter back into the clinic in Liverpool and just as smugly say, "Guess what I inherited, guys?" Then, with a theatrical gesture towards the window, show them his vampire army standing obediently out in the car park, their rusty swords and axes at the ready.

He smiled and shook his head. A vampire army? The idea appealed to his at times flippant sense of humour.

That flippant sense of humour was something he'd developed at medical school. After all, when you're nineteen years old and you suddenly find a corpse there on the dissecting room table and the anatomy lecturer is saying to you, quite straight-faced but no doubt inwardly blabbering with laughter, "Now, Mr. Leppington, perhaps you would be so good as to remove the spleen for your fellow students' examination. Come, come now, Mr. Leppington. Dead men don't bite."

My God, yes, there are times when a sense of humour is as essential as the air you breathe.

The hotel room had grown gloomy. He switched on the table lamp, took a sip of coffee, then returned to the book.

3

As David Leppington read, in the room next door Bernice Mochardi tried on clothes she'd found in a storeroom on the same landing.

They were Electra's clothes, she had no doubt of that. They were stored neatly on shelves. Bowls of salt had stood on each shelf to prevent damp creeping into the delicate fabrics.

My God, she thought, Electra must have more clothes than a princess. Surely she never gets to wear everything?

It was early Saturday evening. She had nothing to do. Boredom eventually outweighed any notion that it might be improper to try on someone else's clothes without asking. Besides, Electra would be busy opening the hotel bars downstairs and supervising kitchen staff.

Surely it wouldn't do any harm to take a few items to her own room, Bernice reasoned, try them on, then return them neatly folded to the storeroom. Why, I imagine Electra no longer knows she has these clothes. There's probably storeroom after storeroom in this hotel containing clothes that Electra had bought and never even worn.

And I need to take my mind off that stupid video, she thought firmly. I can't keep brooding over it. Or wondering what happened to the man in the video. It might have been nothing more than an elaborate joke. Don't some people take photographs of themselves in coffins, pretending to be dead? Every day hospitals remove cucumbers, Coca-Cola bottles, and God knows what else from people's anuses. It's a strange, strange world; people are driven to do strange things . . .

. . . like watching that vile video; like barricading your door at night; like imagining that a man—green with graveyard mould and eyeless—paces outside your door, Bernice.

Shut up, she told the voice in her head. I don't need this. Why should these mad, these bloody mad thoughts preoccupy me?

Leave this town, said a sudden cool voice in her head. Leave this town if it's the last thing you do.

The clothes.

Busy yourself with these. Occupy your mind.

Bernice gathered up armfuls of blouses, dresses, scarves, gloves from the shelves, then walked quickly across the hotel corridor back to her room. She closed the door behind her.

4

In Room 101 Fiona panted on the bed. Matt was a great gloomy shape above her. He thrust himself into her body. The bed creaked to the muscular rhythm. She surrendered herself to pleasure.

He looked down at her, eyes glinting in the near dark. Nothing else existed but that friction between her legs—that delicious friction that made her heart pump harder, brought out her breath in hard spurts. She gripped his buttocks in both her hands, pulled him into her. He panted a string of words at her; they were loving, sexy and dirty all at the same time.

God, she was coming.

She looked up at the ceiling, her mouth and her eyes wide. The ceiling rose blurred, contracted to a grey spot, then seemed to explode into a million colours as the orgasm roared through her body.

5

Saturday night. Within the brick walls that formed its unyielding crust, the Station Hotel continued its existence on this Earth.

An animal is composed of internal organs that are, in turn, composed of living cells. The animal's heart beats, circulating blood through arteries that might be as thick as a hosepipe or thinner than a hair. The digestive functions continue; lungs aspirate, valves open and close, electrical impulses flicker across the brain carrying sensations—warmth, pressure against skin. If that creature is human those electrical impulses transmit ideas—whether to write a poem about the waves on the ocean or the intention to watch a concert on TV.

The hotel mimicked the life process of the body. Food entered through the door, waste was flushed down the drains.

As microbes in a body follow their own agenda, the hotel's four guests went about their business. In Room 101 the two lovers entwined upon the bed; in Room 407 David Leppington drank coffee and read his book; in 406 Bernice Mochardi slipped on black lace gloves that reached up over her elbow. The kitchen staff peeled, diced, chopped; they stirred pans that billowed steam; Chef was already on this third whisky-and-lemonade. Electra moved svelte as a cat amongst the tables in the dining room, greeting the clientele.

And as an animal is unaware—at first—when a virus invades its body, so no one noticed the thing that crept through the back door into the hotel, bare feet padding softly on the carpet. Someone seeing it on the landing might have believed they could describe it—the long arms, the way its toes curled back beneath its feet so it walked on them, the two burning eyes, the scalp curling with thick blond hair, red pressure points at either side

155

of the nose that suggested glasses had been worn once. But its biology was as alien to man as anything that pulsates on the ocean floor; or even holds fast to rocks upon worlds beyond the stars.

6

Fiona lay warm and safe in her lover's arms. He was asleep. She relaxed as drowsiness pulsed up within her in warm, pleasant waves. Her body throbbed. This was so right; so absolutely and so perfectly right. She'd found love at long last. Everyone deserved to be loved and to fall asleep warm and safe in the arms of a lover as tender and considerate as this.

She closed her eyes. She was happy, content, warm. Sleep stole across her brain as stealthy as a fox.

7

Bernice stood in front of the mirror. She was dressed in blacks and in purples so dark they bordered on black. She wore black lace gloves that reached above her elbows. The fabric felt oddly seductive; she could feel the pressure of it enclosing her hands, wrists and forearms. There was something sexy about it; just the feel of the pressure. The blouse was silk. Almost black, it was shot through with fibers of that dark electric purple that imbued it with the same kind of glint you find in a beetle's carapace. And the blouse was definitely on the big side for her, tailored for Electra's statuesque frame. The skirt would have come to Electra's calves. On Bernice it came down to her feet.

Now, I could pass for a Victorian lady she thought, pleased with the effect and swishing the skirt from side-to-side with an elegant sweep of her hand. I am the mistress of the house, the lady of the castle. I can do what I want—go where I want. This is my home.

She experienced a giddy thrill, dressed like that; suddenly she lifted the skirt to admire her black lace-topped stockings. Now she wished someone could see her dressed like this. She wanted to share the effect: primly Victorian yet smoulderingly sexy; the fusion of opposites.

Bernice smiled in the mirror, her brown eyes sparkling, her teeth catching the light. A euphoria buzzed through her veins.

I can do anything, she thought, I can knock on David Leppington's door and sweep into his room to lie back on the bed kicking my black-stockinged legs in the air and laughing at his surprised expression.

Just then she wanted to shock.

She thought of sweeping elegantly into the bar downstairs just to turn the heads of the slaughtermen on their night out on the town; then she'd sit at the bar, order red wine, as lusciously red as her lips, and wait to see who approached her first.

Too tame, she thought, skin tingling, eyes glittery.

I want more.

So much more.

Her skin burned hotly.

Her heart beat faster.

She wanted to live dangerously.

If the blond-haired man from the video appeared at my door, I'd kiss him on the mouth and pull him onto the bed, she thought outrageously.

If only I could find the man from the video.

Electra probably has him chained away somewhere.

She keeps him as a sex slave.

Where?

In the basement, of course!

Those words seemed to come from outside her head. In fact, they came so strongly she thought someone had spoken them in the room.

With a surprised gasp she looked round. No one there. The room was still the same: the star-shaped crack in the window above the bathroom door, the framed painting of a girl knee-deep in the river on the wall, the suitcase containing the video tape lay snug in the wardrobe . . .

And William Morrow, eyeless and dead as can be, stands outside your bedroom door.

No. Stop those foolish thoughts. There's no one outside the door, Bernice. Just you wait, I'll prove it.

Before she could stop herself she fearlessly opened the door.

Standing outside in the corridor, black, hard-edged, was her shadow, thrown from the light behind her.

Otherwise the corridor was empty. Stretching along the corridor was the old scarlet carpet (where bare, dead feet tread); no, they don't, she told herself firmly. Keep your imagination under control, Bernice.

Nevertheless, blood buzzed through her veins. She felt in a strange, almost alien frame of mind, as if an external force guided her actions.

A cool, sane splinter of herself told her to return to her room, shut the door, get changed, wash her face and telephone one of her friends from the Farm. The voice told her she needed company. She needed a normal, bog-standard conversation to bring herself down to earth.

But something had got a hold of her. She wanted to do something that was dangerous and exciting.

But what?

The basement.

Go down into the basement.

You might find out a secret. Just what has Electra done to Mike Stroud, the blond boy from the video?

Again, the sensation came that the words had originated from outside her head.

You don't want to go down into the basement, Bernice, said the voice of reason, it's dirty, dark, rat-infested . . .

But she found herself walking quickly along the corridor, her sandalled feet whispering across the carpet. Then she was at the stairs; she walked quickly down them, feeling that strange buzz of excitement; she could have been a spy on a mission of national importance. Her heart beat faster.

Go back, Bernice, go back.

She ignored the voice of reason and hurried down to the lobby, breathless, excited.

The lobby was deserted. The doors to the public bars were locked to prevent the rowdier elements invading the peace of the hotel. Customers would use those doors of the bar that opened directly onto the street. Electra would be in the restaurant. Through the closed doors she could hear the occasional burst of boozy laughter along with the mushy bass beat of the karaoke machine in the bar.

She tried the door of the basement.

Locked.

Fine. Damn fine.

She glared at the door impatiently as if it barred her from meeting a lover.

Quickly, she looked in the cupboard behind the reception desk. A huge bunch of keys lay on the shelf.

Oh, come to momma, she thought, feeling a near-delirious burst of pleasure.

It took no more than three attempts to find the right key, then the basement door swung open.

Stone steps led down into a darkness that seemed to pulsate with a velvety blackness.

She looked round the lobby. The light from the chandelier seemed far too bright, the normally muted red of the drapes seemed hideously garish. It was like when you have a drink of wine in a gloomy bar, then go outside where the daylight seems brutally over-bright because your dilated pupils refuse to contract to restrict the gush of light onto the optic nerve.

What's happening to me? she thought wonderingly. This really felt just so weird, as if she'd been injected with some potent stimulant.

Go back, Bernice. Knock on Dr. Leppington's door. Tell him something peculiar is happening to you. Don't go down into the basement . . . don't go down into . . .

She went down the basement steps in a rush. Darkness enfolded her. She stared around the place, wide-eyed, seeing only gloomy shapes.

The darkness . . . I've never seen darkness like this before, she thought, awed; it seemed to be veined with a deep, deep red.

She reached out, feeling at that darkness, as if it would be solid as a wall.

Then a warning voice shunted into her head: You're going to reach out and touch a face. The voice of reason was fighting back through that giddy excitement. It was beginning to make progress, too, but not nearly enough.

Impetuously, she walked into the darkness, one hand in front of her, the other gripping the keys.

Any second, you will touch a face. It will be Mr. Morrow, the man who killed himself in your room, Bernice. He'll be standing there, face bloated with pus, his eye sockets empty as fresh graves . . . he's waiting for the kiss of living lips; he's been all alone in that grave for a hundred years—oh, he's so cold and lonely he'd sacrifice his niche in heaven just to press his maggot-thickened fingers onto your bare breasts, then slip his tongue—slippery as a dead fish—into your mouth . . .

She gasped.

Her fingertip pressed something cool in the darkness.

Mr. Morrow's dead face . . .

No.

No, the wall.

Inside her head the voice of reason spoke louder. Bernice, what are you doing in the basement? In the dark? Unable to see so much as your hand in front of your face?

This is madness.

And she realized that's exactly what it was.

The heat from her earlier excitement quickly dissolved into the darkness. Now fear crept into her veins. A cold fear of unreasoning dread.

She found she was moving deeper into the basement, still in absolute darkness. She couldn't stop herself. A greater power had control now.

She smelt the damp; the fustiness of air imprisoned by the five floors of the Victorian monstrosity above her, and by the subterranean rock that lay behind the walls of the basement.

This place is bad, she thought. I shouldn't be here. This is a bad place where bad things happen. This is where a hundred years ago the owner of the hotel raped his servant girls. Then threatened them with the sack if they told. This is where children were pushed crying and terrified against a wall; this is where they heard a zipper being opened in the darkness; this is where they were told to open their mouths and warned not to bite when . . .

Oh, dear God, this is a terrible place.

The cold rolled at her in dark waves.

She looked round, unable to see a thing.

The darkness was liquid. Veins of deeper darkness wormed from the damp brick beneath her feet to take root in her feet. She felt those roots of darkness work up through her legs, her stomach, her chest where they snaked cancerously into her heart.

160

She blinked, seeing purple bloom in front of her eyes.

I'm going to scream.

She took a deep breath. I'm going to scream. I'm going to keep screaming until someone comes.

You're going to project that scream through two metres of solid brick? No one's going to hear you down here, Bernice.

Like no one heard those children. Or the shrieks of those fifteen-year-old maids when their hymens were brutally torn.

The blond man screamed in the video.

No one heard him.

So why on Earth should they hear you, Bernice?

When the terrible thing happens to you in the next five minutes, no one will hear. You're going to suffer this alone.

In the dark.

Now her senses turned in on themselves. Deprived of sight, she became exquisitely sensitive to her body. She felt the firm grip of the lace gloves around her hands, fingers and wrist. The silver droplet earrings felt like splashes of icy rainwater against her neck whenever she moved her head.

She heard the soft squelching beat of the pulse in her neck. Acutely, she was aware of the sensation of her blood running through her body; from the arteries that were as thick as her thumb and fed her heart to the capillaries in her finger-tips that were thinner than a hair. Even there, she felt her lifeblood whisper through those tiny blood vessels. And she heard the blood that pulsed through her body, driven by the solid beat of her heart. If ungodly creatures lurked in this basement then now, surely, they could hear that beat; that hypnotic rhythm thudding up through her chest, through her neck to fill her head. It sounded as loud as a drum in a marching band.

Boom-boom-boom . . .

The keys chinked in her right hand. Her left hand moved in a motion similar to someone polishing a window, a circular motion; her sensitive fingers passing over shelves—bearing soft bundles in the utter darkness. (Victorian underwear of crisp white cotton spotted with blood; a severed hand tied up in a rag; dead babies in sacks: the terrifying images flowed incontinently now.)

She found it hard to breathe. The cold was intense.

Her fingers touched brickwork; she felt the icy feathers of saltpetre that grow from basement walls.

A hard protrusion.

A staring eye.

No.

No. A light switch.

Jerkily, she swiped down at it.

Damn . . . it didn't work. The switch was a dud.

No, you were clumsy. You didn't push the switch fully down.

She tried again, this time grasping the cold piece of plastic between finger and thumb before pulling.

A bulb flashed on above her head; after the darkness it was screamingly bright. Dazzled, she looked round. There were stacks of crates containing empty beer bottles. The basement walls curved inwards above her head to form a series of vaults shaped like barrels lying on their sides. Here and there were shelves piled with pieces of old sacking, workmen's tools, buckets, old bundles of brewery invoices, redundant kitchen equipment, half a dozen white plastic toilet seats.

The darkness was gone; along with the imagined bundles of dead babies and severed limbs.

The spell was broken.

Why was she down here?

She felt such an idiot now.

Maybe she'd drunk too much wine with Electra this afternoon after all. On an empty stomach, too.

She looked at the sleeve of the silk blouse. The purple fibers gleamed under the light of the single 100-watt bulb.

There was a white mark from the saltpetre on the walls. The same white powdered the fingertips of the lace gloves she wore.

Now she felt angry at herself—and guilty: she'd no right to mess up clothes belonging to someone else.

She looked up, realizing she'd heard something.

A soft sound it was; like a note quietly played on a glockenspiel, not with a hammer, but with a bare knuckle.

The sound came again.

She looked towards the direction from which it came.

Her eyes widened in surprise.

There, right at the end of the basement, almost concealed by the stagnant shadow, was what appeared to be a door.

She moved towards it, her head tilted to one side.

The door was of steel; a single great chunk of it like a piece of armour-plating from a battleship.

It was hinged at one side.

At the other side four padlocks held it shut. Two of the padlocks had begun to rust; the other two were shiny and new, as bright as mirrors in the glare of the light bulb.

Now, where on earth does that lead? she thought. Lightly she touched the cold steel, sensing its great thickness; metal like that would stop cannon shells.

As she touched the metal door a vibration tingled her fingers; simultaneously, she heard the glockenspiel note again.

Someone's knocking on the other side, she thought. The realization came to her quite coolly, even matter-of-factly. Somehow, someone's got themselves locked in on the other side. I've got to let them out. I'm the only one who can do it.

But who's there?

It's me.

Instantly she imagined the blond-haired man on the other side of the door. Somehow he was trapped. He needed to escape the cold void that lay beyond that steel door. He'd been lost in there for months.

Again that drowsy giddiness came. The idea of someone—a beautiful young man with beautiful blond hair and a beautiful smile—of someone being lost underground for months didn't seem strange. The simple fact was that he *had* got lost, he was hungry—oh-so-hungry after all this time. Suddenly she felt protective towards him. So incredibly protective. As if he was a lost child, his eyes all big and dewy and trusting. She would bring him out into warmth and safety. She would feed him, look after him.

The keys, Bernice.

The voice seemed to ring through the metal door at her and straight through the bone of her skull, bypassing her ears entirely.

Use the keys, Bernice. Open the door.

She held up the bunch of keys.

So many keys. Which ones opened the padlocks?

A sense of urgency infected her blood. She had to get the man out of there. She imagined him pale and shivering. Hunger

163

had made him weak. Only she could save him now.

. . . don't do it, don't do it, the voice of reason was faint again as if something—that power from outside—had subdued it . . . don't do it, don't open the door. Open that door and you will see something that will split your mind in two; then something will be done to you that should remain nameless. Pain and despair will become your universe . . .

There were two new-looking keys on the ring, glinting as brightly as the padlocks. Try these first, she thought, drowsily.

She carefully, with slow, oh-so-slow, deliberate movements, slipped the first shiny key into the bright new padlock. The key turned a fraction, then stopped.

Try again, Bernice. You can do it. Oh believe me, you are beautiful; I can't wait to touch your face. The voice trickled like electricity through the steel door.

She used the same key on the second new padlock. It opened smoothly.

With that same mechanical slowness she singled out the other shining key and tried the first padlock again. With a satisfying click the mechanism released the hasp. Unlocked.

Now for the old padlocks.

She frowned slightly. These might be more difficult: the mechanism might have rusted.

Oh, you can do it, Bernice, the voice encouraged. A prickling sensation ran across her skin under her blouse, tingling to the tips of her breasts. A wonderful, silky voice. She recognized it. It was the man from the video. She recognized the cultured American accent. Such a kind voice. She imagined that voice whispering to her beneath the bedclothes.

If the padlock mechanism has seized you'll find a WD40 aerosol somewhere in the basement. Spray a little on the padlock. It'll open.

She worked her way steadily through the bunch of keys, her eyes huge in her face and staring glassily in front of her as if she was sleepwalking.

There was no fear now. Only a kind of dull anticipation. This was what her whole life had been working towards. This was what she had been born to do. To release the blond man from whatever dark place lay beyond the basement door.

The padlock mechanisms hadn't rusted after all.

One by one she unlocked the remaining two.

They dangled by their C-shaped hasps through the steel loops in the door and steel door frame. Once she'd slid them from the loops she could open the door. Simple.

She removed the first one. Easy.

Second one. It squeaked a little, the loops there were a tight fit.

Third.

Slowly does it. There.

One left.

Then she could swing open that heavy steel door and see him standing there.

Come on, Bernice, the voice seemed to sigh at her. *That's a girl that's a beautiful, beautiful girl. I always believed in you. Not like the others who thought you were awkward and clumsy; who thought you weren't good enough for them. We are soul mates. I've always loved you . . . always will love you—*

Quickly now she worked the hasp loose. Rust slowed its release; it squeaked—a thin, mouse-like sound. In a second it would be free.

That's it, Bernice. Open the door. I can't wait any longer; I'm so cold and tired and I want to—

"STOP IT!"

The voice boomed down at her.

She screamed with shock and spun round.

A great shambling figure loomed out of the darkness at her.

Chapter Eighteen

1

Bernice screwed her eyes up against the light. But all she could see was the monstrous silhouette bearing down on her along the barrel of the basement.

Frightened, she demanded, "Who is it?"

"Me."

The figure slid out of the shadows with a near-reptilian smoothness. "Give me the padlocks," came the voice; it was low and simmered with menace.

"Jack?" She shielded her eyes against the glare of the light.

"That's me," the voice agreed, as unfriendly as ever. "Padlocks."

He emerged from the dazzling wash of light to stand in front of her. The mean eyes glared into hers; the tattoos on the face stood out as if they were some mutant tracery of thick, blue veins.

"Padlocks," he prompted and held out a massive paw.

Despite her fear of the brutish-looking man, she felt intense annoyance. She'd decided what to do—to open the steel door—and now this ugly ape of a man had decided she had no right to do so; in fact, he'd assumed the authority to tell her what she could or could not do.

"I heard a noise behind the door," she said. "I think someone's trapped in there."

"So?"

"So?" She laughed in disbelief. "So we've got to check. Someone might be hurt!"

"The only person who'll get hurt is you."

This was more a threat than a suggestion she might have an accident, or might be in some kind of danger. Again, a sense of resentment flared.

"I'm *going* to open the door," she said defiantly. "I think there's someone trapped in there."

She turned round and tugged at the remaining padlock.

A pair of huge arms appeared at either side of her; one hand brushed her own hands away with a careless ease as if they were nothing more than a pair of fragile butterflies; then his tattooed fingers gripped the padlock hasp and snapped it back into the mechanism with a sharp *snick*.

"Padlocks," he repeated, his voice low; he wasn't going to be deflected from what he saw as his God-given duty.

"Oh." She nodded sharply at a shelf beside the door. *"There."*

Fuming, she watched him replace the padlocks one by one. Now, what infuriated her most was the realization that he was the one with power—she was the one who was powerless.

He's taken away the right for me to decide what to do. In two seconds flat he'd gained control of her. She clenched her fists.

"Keys," he said in that flat unemotional voice. "Give them to me."

"Who gave you the right to tell me what to do?"

He didn't reply, merely held out a muscular paw for the keys; his beast-like eyes fixed coldly on her.

"I'm going to tell Electra. What are you going to do about that?"

"Keys. Give them to me."

With a savage sigh, she slammed the bunch of heavy keys down into his hand.

In a low voice he said: "Piss off. Don't come down here again."

"What did you say to me?" Her face burned with fury. "What did you say?" Angrily she locked her eyes on to his, trying to stare him down.

He stared coldly back: bullets wouldn't have dented the icy expression.

"*Shit*," she spat, broke eye contact and stormed out of the basement back to her room.

2

Jack Black returned the bunch of keys to the cupboard in reception. The lobby was deserted. He stood there for a moment, sensing the pulse of the building—it was slow, old . . . dying. Like the town.

Jack Black didn't translate the feeling into words. Words only got in the way of what was real. From the bars and restaurant off the lobby came the buzz of conversation and the muffled thump of music. In the Silver Suite there was a meeting of something called the Royal Order of Buffaloes (antediluvian branch): they were a bunch of old blokes, squashed uncomfortably into suits and half strangled by ties that they only wore for their shit-stupid meetings and funerals.

In the women's toilets, scribbled on the tampon machine,

167

were the words: *"Question: Why is Electra like a pendulum? Answer: Because she swings both ways."* In a cruder hand someone had scrawled: *LESBO!*

And all through the hotel electrons flowed along old wiring, and water pumped through furred pipes to bathrooms like blood through elderly arteries.

Black lifted his hands. Feeling the vibrations come trickling through his skin, he raised his deep-set eyes to the ceiling.

On the counter an advertising flyer for the hotel stated: *The Station Hotel's architectural style is strictly Victorian Gothic, designed by G. T. Andrews and built in 1863 in the typical railway hotel manner to cater for the rail traveller of the day who demanded something grander than the coaching inn of yesteryear.*

You could have told him all that, but when he pictured the hotel in his mind's eye all he saw was the skull of a huge animal resting on a windswept plain. Inside crawled insects feeding on the remaining shreds of skin and brain. And in the earth beneath the skull were yet more creatures waiting to feed on the insects.

He licked his cracked lips. The scar on the side of his head that ran from ear to eye like a streak of bright red lipstick began to tingle.

He sensed the people in the hotel scurrying to and fro with no more insight into their existence than the insects in that great rotting skull.

Thoughts trickled down through five floors of brick and wood:

—dem bones, dem bones, dem dry bones—

". . . can't treat me like that. I'll tell Electra as soon as I see her. After all, what's she running here? A hotel or a doss house for moronic thugs like Jack Black—and if that's his real name, I'll eat my hat—now, eyeshadow, eyeshadow. Where did I put it?"

He closed his eyes. The Bernice bitch was in her room, trying on the other bitch's clothes. He sensed her anger at him for preventing her from opening the steel door in the basement. That anger was now slipping into an unfocused feeling of rebelliousness. He saw her sitting in front of the dressing-table mirror, wearing a long black dress, the near-black blouse shot through with purple thread. She was applying make-up, slipping on silver rings over the black lace gloves that reached above her elbows. The silver rings bore designs of bird skulls, human skulls, magic eyes.

Bernice Mochardi's thoughts ran through his own shaven head. "He's no right to tell me what to do. He's probably on the run from the police, probably got his hand in the till. Electra's a fool. Now, there: my dear, don't you look a Gothic princess? Welcome to Castle Dracula. Come freely. Go safely. And leave something of the happiness you bring . . ."

The lift door opened with a rumbling sound.

He watched the man step out—Leppington, they called him. He had the same name as the town. Jack Black watched the man cross the lobby to the reception desk. There was something fascinating about him. Jack Black had to watch him even though it made the man uncomfortable.

—so bloody what, Black thought coldly; *I could slap him flat on his back with just one punch.*

Go on, do that now; give the runt a slap, you know you'd love to see the blood come oozing thick as treacle from his busted nose.

Leppington, dressed in jeans—clean jeans, all neatly pressed—and expensive sweatshirt was going to leave his key at reception.

But because he's seen me here he won't do it, Black thought, because he's thinking the moment he's gone I'll take his key, go up to his fecking room and rob his fecking shoes and razor and stuff, then piss on his fecking bed. As if!

Now he's slipping the key into his pocket, even though it's got a big chunky red plastic fob wired to it and it'll dig into his leg every time he sits down; now he's pretending he's come all the way down here to pick up a tourist leaflet from the desk, and now he's going to walk by me as if I don't exist.

Give him a slap. Go on. There's something about that Leppington twat that's got under my skin; he's making my arms itch; my scars are tingling like a line of ants is running along them. Hit him: deck the fucker!

"Jack . . . Jack. We need more mineral waters in the bar." It was the bitch, Electra. "I think the people of Leppington are turning all virtuous on me and are drinking sparkling water instead of beer."

Jack grunted and shambled off in the direction of the basement door.

Electra shot a grateful smile at him.

She's frightened of me, he thought, but she's fascinated, too. Just look at her, she can't take her eyes off me.

He shot a look back at the guy, Leppington. And he can't stand the fucking sight of me. No doubt about that. He's imagining me being cuffed by the cops and hauled away. He'd like that.

David Leppington saw the vicious look Jack Black shot him before he opened the basement door.

Jack Black was going to be trouble before long, David told himself; Bernice thought so; for the life of him he couldn't understand why Electra had so eagerly employed him.

Come on, David, he thought, I think you can hazard a guess at the real reason. Electra lives alone. Many women would find a tattooed, muscular mesomorph like Jack Black sexually exciting.

Even so, weird the way David had come out of the lift to find Jack Black standing there, big ugly tattooed face raised to the ceiling, hands raised, too, like he was communing with the divine or something.

Electra swept across the lobby after giving Black his instructions.

"Good evening, David," she said, elegant as ever in a black blouse and leather trousers. "Can we tempt you into the restaurant tonight?"

"Not tonight, thanks. I thought I'd try the local cinema."

"Don't let me be the one to put you off, but the latest Arnie extravaganza's getting a pretty lousy press."

"No, I thought I'd try . . . what do they call it?" He searched his memory. "The cinema club?"

"Ah, Cinema Society. They show the classics in the little library theatre."

"That's the one."

She smiled. "That's not too bad. There's even plenty of leg room. What's on the bill?"

"Duel."

Her forehead creased. "I don't know it. Western?"

"No, the early Spielberg film with Dennis Weaver. Basically

it's about a man being chased across country by a big truck."

"Ah yes, it's a Spielberg month."

"They're running it back to back with *The Colour Purple*."

"Ah, now I *do* know that one. An episodic film, unabashedly literary too. I love it. Anyway, have a pleasant evening."

"Thanks."

Electra smiled as David left the hotel through the revolving door. She thought: now why couldn't more of her guests be like him? Weekdays she got sales reps who looked glum, were often homesick and would get quietly drunk in the bar. Weekends it tended to be couples away for some illicit tryst. Like the pair in Room 101. Now *there* would be a mattress that would take some airing on Monday.

"Bring the bottles straight through into the bar," she told Jack Black as he hefted the heavy crate as though it was made from nothing more than duck's eider. "You locked the basement door after you?"

"Yes." He looked at her with those eyes with their unfathomable depths.

Mmm . . . perhaps he's undressing me mentally, she thought, with a wicked little tingle. I wonder what he's like under the duvet? A real beast, I shouldn't wonder. "Jack?"

"What?"

"When you've taken those into the bar would you move the sacks of potatoes from the kitchen to the store?"

"OK."

"Chef will show you which ones. And Jack?"

He looked at her, eyes burning into her face.

Go on, Electra, invite him up to your rooms for supper later. The thought had been dawdling around the back of her head for the last twenty-four hours. There was a big question mark hanging over the man. She wanted to find out more about him. He fascinated her.

"What do you want?" he asked—as unsubtle as ever, she thought, trying to steel herself to take the plunge and ask him to, what . . . a bite to eat? Then plunge into bed together? My God, Electra, that man would be a white-knuckle ride.

"Ah, give Mary a hand collecting glasses in the bar. Jo hasn't turned up tonight."

With a small nod of acknowledgement he moved off to the bar.

Chicken, she scolded herself, the time was ripe; you should have asked the big monster up your rooms; think of the fun you could have had.

Yeah . . . he looks like the kind who'd slap a girl round and not think twice about it. Electra, are you developing a death wish or what?

The phone on the desk rang. Slipping off her left earring she answered it.

"Hello."

Heavy breathing rasped from the earpiece.

A naughty phone call. Thank God for that.

A red light on the desk unit indicated it was an internal call.

"Hello," Electra repeated politely. "Reception. Can I help?"

Heavy breathing. A giggle. Followed by a scraping sound in the earpiece. "Oh . . . ah," a female voice gasped as if suppressing a giggle. "Champagne . . . bottle of champagne, please. Room 101."

Electra raised her eyes to the ceiling, partly an expression of stoicism born from dealing with tipsy or sex-addled guests, and partly imagining she could see through the ceiling as if it was glass, where she pictured the two guests in Room 101, naked limbs entwining on the bed with the telephone lying on the pillow beside their heads. Always good for a thrill, she thought philosophically, telephone reception during sexual intercourse.

"Certainly," she said politely. "Room 101. Which champagne would you like?"

"Oh?"

"We have Bollinger at twenty-five pounds, Moët et Chandon at—"

"Oh, any. Any will do. And two glasses, please."

"I'll bring it straight up. Thank you."

Within forty-five seconds Electra was climbing the stairs to the first floor. She carried a tray on which were the glasses, ice bucket and bottle of champagne swathed in white cloth.

As a Saturday night it was pretty much of a muchness. Nothing out of the ordinary.

Even so, she couldn't help but think of the story of King Damocles who sat upon his throne with a sword hanging over

172

his head by a hair. Something lethal seemed suspended in the air above the hotel. The hair was breaking . . .

She tapped on the door of Room 101. It was immediately opened by a flushed-looking woman with a bath towel wrapped around her.

"Oh, thank you," the woman said. "Let me take it from you."

Electra smiled as she handed over the heavy tray. "I hope you enjoy your champagne. If you need anything else just give me a call."

"Yes. Thank you." The woman was eager to close the door.

"Would you like me to add the champagne to your room bill?"

"Yes. Thank you. Goodnight."

"Goodnight."

Fiona closed the door with her foot.

"Champagne," she said to Matt who lay face down on the bed, naked as the day he was born. "And it's ice-cold."

He smiled, chuckled. "And just what are you going to do with it, pray?"

"Drink it. And you, dear, shall be my cup." She set the tray down on a table then, lifting the bottle from the ice bucket, poured a little into the hollow of his back where it pooled, fizzing.

"Yikes." The man's legs muscles spasmed.

"Cold?"

"Very cold."

"Here, let naughty girl lick it off you."

"Is naughty girl in a licking mood?"

"Naughty girl is. Mmm . . ." She licked the champagne off his skin, the bubbles pricking her tongue. "Anything else you require licking, sir?"

"Now you come to mention it . . ." With a broad smile on his handsome face he turned over onto his back.

Fiona felt a pang of excitement. This is it. There really was a first time for everything. She dribbled a little champagne from the bottle onto his penis; licked her lips; then lowered her head down onto him.

Outside the wind blew hard; rain spattered the window. Thunder growled like an ancient demon across the hills. The storm was just about to break.

Chapter Nineteen

1

From out of the darkness the gale tore down from the mountainside, bending trees, shearing branches, rattling car ports, buffeting drinkers walking along the street, carrying away newspapers high over the town. A front page hit a window of pebbled glass on the first storey of the Station Hotel, momentarily pasting itself there.

"What's that?" Fiona asked, throwing a startled glance at the bathroom window. A white object flapped against it, looking like a huge bird against the night sky.

"Just a piece of paper . . . now, are you going to get in this bath or not?"

She smiled. "It's not big enough."

"You can sit on my legs."

He grinned as he ran his fingers through his iron-gray hair. "Come on, plenty of room for two."

Steam hung in the bathroom, misting the mirror and the tiled walls. Matt sat in the bath, champagne glass held in his strong fingers.

Giggly from the champagne and six hours of sheer unadulterated sex, Fiona leaned over the bath to kiss his forehead.

"I don't want this weekend to end," she said.

"Me neither."

"Will you still notice me on Monday?"

"I will."

"I won't be just another girl in the office?"

"You won't."

"Promise me, Matt."

"Promise."

"How will you show it?"

"Tell you what, wear a short skirt, no knickers."

She giggled as he spoke.

"When I walk into the office, I'll drop my pen. As I bend down you cross your legs and give me a flash of that sweet little thing of yours."

He reached out of the bath and touched her between her legs.

"Oh." She trembled at the feel of his fingers. Slippery with soap and hot water they glided over the lips between her legs and slid inside her. She kissed him passionately. She wanted him out of the bath and on the bathroom floor where she could straddle him and feel his beautiful—oh, say it!—his beautiful cock sliding into her with all the firmness of a column of rock.

She kissed him hard and ran her hand across his chest.

"Fuck me," she said breathlessly. "Now. Fuck me on the floor. Christ, I want you so much. I want to—"

"Damn."

There was knock on the door. Quite low; almost a secretive knock.

He scowled, and there was a hardness in his eyes she'd never noticed before. "Who the hell can that be?"

"Ignore it, Matt."

He sighed. "It might be about the car."

"It won't be. Don't worry, we've bolted the door, they can't get into the hotel room."

The knock came again.

"Oh, damnation," he grunted. "I best see what they want."

"Matt . . . ignore it. They'll go away."

"It might be about the car," he said again woodenly. "I didn't like the look of the car park. It's too far from the hotel."

"Matt . . ."

He ignored her. "All I need is another insurance claim. Clarice'll nag."

He climbed out of the bath, dripping water onto the floor. Muttering about the car being broken into, the CD player being stolen, the leather upholstery being slashed, he wrapped one of the big white bath towels around himself. Now the expression he wore on his face looked the way it did in the office when he was preoccupied with profit and loss and winning new contracts or sourly shaking his head over Jackson's sloppy accounting.

Suddenly she didn't want him to go. Even in that dozen seconds she felt she was losing him.

"The car'll be fine," she said, hearing the note of pleading in her voice. "Stay in the bath. I'll soap your neck."

He shot her a smile—the suddenness of it made her wonder if it was artificial. "Don't worry, love. I'll find out what they want . . . and if it's that woman with the champagne bill I'll send her away with a flea in her ear. Spooky cow." He swathed his fine stomach and hips with the towel. She watched him walk out of the bathroom and into the room with its wildly disordered bed and clothes strewn across the table and chairs.

She loved the look of his broad wet back, shining from the lamp on the table. She wished there was a way to keep him loving and warm; she didn't like the sudden glimpse of his hard side, with the glint of managerial cruelty in his eyes.

Matt pulled back the bolt on the door. Suddenly she realized she was standing there naked in the bathroom doorway. Quickly she stepped back into the bathroom, closed the door.

Sliding the bathroom bolt across was simply habit.

Oh well, she thought, in a couple of minutes he'd be back. It was probably only the proprietor of the hotel asking if they wanted breakfast in their room or something. She hoped Matt wouldn't get angry with her; she didn't want to hear his voice turn hard and cold-sounding. She wanted it to be soft, loving, warm. She picked up the champagne glass and stood there in the middle of the bathroom floor, sipping the cold liquid and wanting Matt to come back and hold her.

Beyond the bathroom door she heard the clunks and clicks of Matt twisting the key in the lock of the room door, then turning the door handle.

She imagined beads of water trickling down his back.

She glanced up at the pebbled glass window above the bathroom door. A soft yellow light from the table lamp glowed through.

There was a flicker of shadows, no doubt from Matt opening the door.

She heard his voice. "Yes?"

Then . . .

A sudden silence.

Only a little one. But striking in its . . . its completeness.

176

She stared up at the pebbled glass, feeling an inexplicable shock.

At the same time a cold draught blew under the gap between the bottom of the bathroom door and the carpet.

Matt's voice, annoyed. Surprised? "What on earth do you want? Is this some kind of joke? How the hell—"

Fiona's blood turned icy, even in the steamy heat of the bathroom. She shuddered. Something was wrong. Terribly wrong.

She put the glass down on the side of the bath and hurried to the door.

Now there was a thumping sound. Matt started to say something, then he made this odd little cry that sounded like a cross between a laugh of disbelief and an expression of fear.

Crash.

Something hit the door of the bathroom—it sounded like a piece of concrete. Or—or

—a body.

Then she knew Matt was being attacked.

"Stop it! Stop it!" she yelled. "Leave him alone! I'll call the police. The police are coming!" It was a stupid thing to yell, but in her sudden panic it was the first thing that came into her head.

There were more crashes; it sounded as if Matt was being thrown around the room like a cloth doll.

Another crash as a body hit the bathroom door, shaking it against the bolt.

"Please . . ." Matt's voice sounded high and frightened. "Please, Fiona. Let me in. Please, for Godsakes let me in . . . let me in!"

She heard hammering as he pounded on the door. She ran to it, reached out to grab the bolt.

Then paused. She was naked. Unarmed. What could she do?

If they're muggers, they'll take his wallet and go. The voice of reason came as clear as a bell. If you go out there naked it won't help. Why, they might take one look at you and decide to . . .

"Oh, God, Fiona . . . Fiona!"

Matt was crying her name through the thick timber of the door.

"Fiona . . . Fiona. Don't let them . . ." Then came garbled

words. The door shook as Matt either pounded on it—or (the thought sickened her) or his head was beaten against it.

She dropped to her knees. She had to see. This not knowing what was happening out there was indescribable; she felt she would burst.

What were they doing to him?

How could anyone make a strong man like Matt cry like a child in sixty seconds flat?

There was no keyhole in the bathroom door.

Still on her knees she looked up. The pebbled glass set above the door was no way transparent enough to see through, even if she could reach it. All she could see against it were flickering shadows.

There was a lot of movement going on in the bedroom.

"Fiona . . . Oh, oh . . ."

"Leave him, you bastards," she screamed. *"Leave him!"*

A cold draught blew against her bare knees as they rested against the carpet.

She looked down. The gap between door and carpet was quite wide.

Quickly she bent down like a Moslem at prayer, pressed the side of her head against the carpet and looked through.

Bare feet. That was what she saw first. With toes nearest the door.

They were holding Matt face forward against the door.

"Leave him, you bastards. I've called the police." Again the impossible claim, but what else could she say? "I've called them. They're coming! They'll get you, you bastards!"

She looked under the gap in the door, eyes watering from the force of the icy draught.

Now she saw other feet. They were a woman's feet. They were dirty, but she saw the woman wore a pair of expensive sandals, her toenails varnished red.

Then came another pair of feet.

These were bare.

Another pair of bare feet?

This didn't make sense.

Fiona slapped the door and screamed. "I've called the police, get out, you bastards!" No reply. "Matt, you'll be all right. Oh God, you'll be all right. I promise."

Matt made no reply.

She pressed her face harder to the carpet, trying to see the muggers. She thought: the police will need a description. But, oh, the police? Now Matt's wife will find out about the affair.

Even as the thoughts of being confronted by a hysterical wife ran through her head, there was a sudden flurry of knocks against the bathroom door.

Then a face thumped down against the carpet. It was only centimetres from her own. She could have even slipped her fingers under the door and touched it. Through the gap between carpet and door she could see the iron-gray hair, the forehead still wet with bath water, the eyes . . .

They stared back sightlessly.

She backed away from the door, still on hands and knees. She backed until her bare rump came up against the toilet. She couldn't retreat any further.

A volcanic pressure was building inside of her—coming from her stomach, up through her chest, to her throat, fighting to burst from her mouth.

. . . tap tap . . .

Eyes wide, she looked up at the pane of glass set above the door.

. . . tap tap . . .

Blurred by the pebbled glass, two heads appeared.

. . . tap tap . . .

A finger rapped against the glass.

They wanted her to open the bathroom door. They wanted her, too.

. . . tap tap . . .

That's when the volcano inside of her erupted—she opened her mouth and began to scream.

2

High above the naked dead man, and the screaming woman in the bathroom of Room 101, Bernice applied a blood-red lipstick.

She had thought of slipping out to the wine bar and turning some heads. But the rain blasted from out of the darkness like machine-gun bullets to rattle the window panes. Thunder rumbled. The wind screamed round the towers of the hotel.

Filthy night. Filthy, terrible night. She dabbed her lips with a tissue and admired the result in the mirror.

No, she'd stay in her room. Safe and sound.

3

Down in the hotel bar Electra nursed along another vodka and tonic. Was this number three . . . or six?

Oh hell, who's counting?

Got to live a little before you die, haven't you? She helped herself to ice from the *Ice To See You* bucket and watched Jack Black collecting glasses from the tables. The other drinkers watched the tattooed beast of a man with a mixture of fear and fascination.

Nice bum, she thought, eyeing his tight jeans.

She smiled to herself, sipped her drink.

Despite the Godawful weather the bar was buzzing. Maybe business on Saturday nights was picking up. A couple of teenage girls in leather miniskirts were murdering an old Rolling Stones number on the karaoke:

"SATISFACTION . . . YEAH!"

They were loud enough to raise the dead.

Electra returned to her currently favourite pastime: watching Jack Black walk around the bar collecting those empty glasses smeared with foam and lipstick. He moved fast, aggressively, like a crocodile.

The thugs who normally came into the bar to get drunk and start fights were behaving themselves tonight. They were sitting like a bunch of nervous schoolkids in the corner of the bar as if frightened to draw the attention of the great and terrible Mr. Black to themselves.

I'm glad he's here, she thought, surprised by the idea; it's as if he always should have been here. There was a piece missing from this hotel; he fills it. He's an integral part of its structure. A keystone.

Oh, getting poetic, are we? she thought. Time for another drink. Steadily, showing no sign of being at all drunk, she raised the glass to the optic and injected another splash of crystal-pure vodka into her glass.

A red-haired girl sitting alone at the end of the bar lit a cigarette and smiled a certain kind of smile at Electra. A smile that had all the secret coded meaning of a Freemason's handshake. Electra cold-shouldered her with a colourless glance. She wasn't interested. Tonight she only had eyes for Mr. Black.

4

When the end titles for *The Colour Purple* began to roll, David joined the dozen or so other cinemagoers as they headed for the exit. As evenings out go it hadn't been heart-stoppingly exciting; however, he'd enjoyed it. He felt relaxed, and ready to turn in.

And yes. OK. Leppington town was pleasant enough in a faded, attenuated kind of way. But he didn't see enough to keep him here. Not for the rest of the holiday. Nor professionally. The invitation from Dr. Ferman was still in his pocket.

If anything, he'd like to spend more time with his Uncle George. He guessed that for the first six years of his life the old man had been like a second father to him. It would be an act of meanness to simply move on just like that. But he supposed he could promise to keep in touch with his uncle, more than just cards at Christmas and the occasional phone call. He could even invite the old man to Liverpool for a couple of days.

At the main exit, David hung back in the warmth of the foyer. In the darkness outside rain blasted the pavement. Thunder rumbled, a jagged spike of lightning split the night sky. The storm had well and truly broken.

Chapter Twenty

1

This was Leppington at midnight. Rain lashed the black slate roofs. Lightning flashed, turning, for a split second, those black-as-coal roofs silver—a dazzling silver. Saturday night revellers had made it home for late-night television, Chinese takeways, tipsy love-making or simply to sleep. In the chip shop in the wonderfully named Tiger Lane, Chloë and Samantha Moberry were punching Gillian Wurtz in the face. Gillian had joked that Dianne Moberry had run off with a gypsy lover. Now Gillian lay flat on the tiled floor, covered in steaming chunks of cod, chips and vinegar; blood streamed from cuts on her face opened up by the Moberry sisters' rings. She'd hide the scars with make-up on her wedding day; but she'd still remember the beating in the chip shop fifty years from now on the day she died. There's no way of completely hiding scars on the mind.

Lightning blossomed again in great shimmering airbursts of silver. Thunder barrelled down the hillsides, rattling windows and waking babies and dogs, raising a howl that mated human and canine.

The River Lepping, engorged with rain, wormed through the town like a thick artery, bloated to the point of rupture.

The wind blew hard. It sighed around the eaves of the Station Hotel. When it gusted harder it rose into a moan, before ebbing into a broken-hearted sob.

A sparrow caught out in the fierce gale tried desperately to make the safety of a hollow beneath the church guttering. Beating its wings it tried to escape the bruising wind and rain. Lightning flashed, disorienting it. The bird flew down instead of up.

Its wings brushed the headstones in the cemetery. Flowers

torn from urns flew with it in a mad flock of red and yellow petals. Thunder thumped the earth like a hammer blow. It sent vibrations down through the headstones, down through the moist soil to the coffins two metres below the turf. The bones of the dead shivered in mystic sympathy with those great hammer blows of thunder that rained down upon the wet town.

The wind gusted. The sparrow beat its wings, striving to escape the storm before the cold and damp ate into its body and froze its heart.

In a flurry of feathers and spinning petals it flew high into the sky towards the silvery bursts of lightning in the cloud.

Perhaps its brain processed the information received via eyes and ears incorrectly. Perhaps it thought it was locked inside some cave and the flashes of lightning were the opening of the cave and daylight.

Blinded by rain it beat the night air with its wings.

The Station Hotel reared up before it, monstrously scab-like in the darkness. Lightning flickered silver. That same silvery flicker was reflected on its wet brick walls.

The sparrow flew harder.

A square of pure silver suddenly shone in front of it.

Freedom.

The sparrow flew at it.

A second later, neck broken, it spiraled down to the pavement below.

2

David Leppington looked up as he rolled his socks into a ball.

It had sounded as if someone had thrown a ball at his window. He'd distinctly heard a muffled bump.

He pulled the curtain to one side. Beads of water rolled down the glass. When the lightning flashed, some of the beads looked pink.

Blood, supplied the ever-vigilant professional side of his brain. How the hell does my window get sprayed with blood at midnight? Especially when I'm five storeys up?

Lightning flashed. Thunder WHUMPED! down against the roof.

A bird, he supposed. Probably lost in the dark, it had flown into the glass.

He opened the drawer and dropped his socks into it.

Yawning, he looked at his watch. Ten past midnight.

He was drowsy but doubted if he'd be able to sleep with the gods playing some celestial version of footie across the night sky. The racket was awesome. Every WHUMP! of the thunder sounded like a hammer blow against the hotel.

It made the floorboards vibrate beneath his bare feet.

He sat on the bed, yawned again, wondered whether to switch on the TV.

Best not, he thought, thunderstorms and television don't mix. He remembered, when he'd been twelve years old, how lightning had struck the TV aerial as he and his parents watched *Star Trek*.

The screen had flashed, then cracked in two with a tremendous bang. Following that the room had dramatically filled with smoke. The dog had hidden under the sideboard and they were still trying to coax him out with biscuits and rawhide twists two hours later.

So he pulled the aerial plug from the back of the set and went to brush his teeth.

As he did so he happened to glance at the bottom of his door. A shadow moved along the gap between the carpet and the brass carpet grip.

Now, as far as he knew the only other guest on this landing was Bernice Mochardi. She was probably returning to her room after a night on the town. If he was quick he could just put his head round the door, wish her goodnight and remind her about tomorrow. Floating diffusely in the back of his mind was the hope he could get a conversation up and running. Then perhaps invite her in for a coffee; then—

Oh no, you don't, David, he told himself with a grin. You never played the predatory sex fiend particularly well. Nor are one-night stands as much fun as people pretend.

But with the thunderstorm playing merry hell on the hotel roof, he'd never get to sleep yet, so a chat and maybe a homely cocoa or something would pass the time until the storm blew itself out.

Quickly he made it to the hotel room door, turned the key and swung it open.

"Bernice—*oh*?"

The eyes that locked onto his from across the corridor oozed menace.

Thunder crashed. The lights went out.

3

David froze in the doorway, one hand resting on the frame. The sudden darkness was total. The thunder drowned out any other sound.

A second later the lights flickered back on.

And there stood Jack Black.

I'd bet any money you're not up here to turn down the beds, thought David sourly. The thug was probably on his way to slip into someone's room to steal their wallet.

Jack Black's face was even more ugly in the flashes of lightning. The tattoos and scars stood out vividly from his head. His grey eyes burned with a kind of ice fire that seemed even more menacing than before.

David knew he'd have to say something to the thug—just what, he didn't know exactly; but he'd have to be careful it didn't sound provocative or as if he was threatening him. Last thing he wanted was to have a fist fight with the monster.

Jack Black stood in the middle of the corridor staring expressionlessly at him.

He's waiting for me to speak first, thought David. OK, say something diplomatic, something completely inoffensive, then get rid of the man.

Before he could say anything another door rattled down the corridor; a block of light fell on the carpet.

"David?" Bernice stepped out into the corridor; she shot David a smile, but it faded the second she saw Jack Black's hulking form in the corridor.

David glanced at her then looked again in a surprised double take. She wore dark eyeshadow around her eyes, her lips were bright red—a startling blood-red—and she wore clothes that looked distinctly Victorian: a long black skirt, a blouse, also black and glinting a deep electric purple; and she wore a pair of startling black lace gloves that reached above her elbows. The effect was solidly Gothic.

Deliberately ignoring Jack Black, she looked at David. "My lights went out. Did yours?"

"It must be the storm," David replied. "Perhaps we ought to ask Electra for some candles just in case." He turned to Black. "Do you know if there are any candles in the hotel?" He spoke politely.

Jack Black stared at him with eyes that burned yet were strangely cold.

"We'd best have some candles," David repeated in an even voice. "It looks as if we might be heading for a power cut."

"Don't bother, David. You won't get any sense out of that moron."

Oh, great move, Bernice, thought David, appalled by her open insult. There'll be trouble now.

The man turned his eyes at her, locked them onto her face. A shiver ran up David's spine.

The thug would never hit a woman, would he?

David wasn't so sure.

Slowly, the man raised a finger and traced the line of the livid red scar that ran from his eye to his ear like a spectacle arm. It was as if the scar tingled. Jack Black appeared to be considering some problem.

David stepped slowly sideways to put himself between Bernice and the man.

If he attacks, David thought, I'll simply grab him, then yell to Bernice to phone the police.

Meanwhile you'll end up a bloody punchbag.

Christ, some holiday this's turning out to be.

Jack Black looked up, his eyes narrowed; he'd reached a decision.

David took a step back.

Here it comes, he thought grimly.

Jack Black spoke in a low voice; but there was clearly force in it. "Go back into your rooms," he said. "Go inside and lock the doors."

Bernice's eyes flashed angrily. "Why don't you just piss off?"

"No . . . go into your rooms. Lock the doors."

"OK," David said diplomatically. "We'll do that. But it's time you were in your own room . . ." So far, so good. No sudden flurry of blows from the thug. "You're staying in the converted stable block, aren't you?"

He didn't reply. The man's eyes suddenly lost their focus as if he was listening to a voice speaking to him from far away. After what seemed a long while he very slowly nodded as if agreeing with the voice . . . or as if he was beginning to understand something that had been troubling him.

"It's the lightning."

"Sure it's lightning," Bernice said, irritated. "Anyone can see that."

"No." Jack Black shook his head as if preoccupied with some great problem. "This lightning is different. It's not the lightning you can see," he said as, on cue, lightning flashed, filling the corridor with a silver brilliance. "This is black. Black lightning. It's bringing those things to life. They're going to break out." He took a deep breath; his eyes sharpened as they focused. "Go into your rooms. Lock the doors," he repeated in a whisper. "That is what you've got to do."

"Yeah," Bernice snorted. "Nice one. What then? You pick the locks and nick all the televisions on this floor?"

"No." Again he wore that dreamy faraway look. "You're both in danger. Go back to your rooms."

"We'll go back to our rooms once you've gone downstairs," David said calmly. "There's no reason for you to be up here, is there?"

"There's you," Black said obliquely, then rubbed his fingers across one of his massive tattooed fists. "So I've got to stay up here."

David looked back at Bernice. She pointed a lace-clad finger at the man. "You know what he's going to do? He's going to rob us. Why did Electra do such a crazy thing as hire him? She's insane, isn't she? Just bloody insane."

In a quiet voice David said to Bernice, "We can't stay here all night."

"I will if I have to."

"I'll phone reception."

"Fat lot of good that will do."

"Why?"

"No one there. I'll ring Electra in her own apartment."

David looked back at Jack Black. He seemed really out of it. Hardly the professional observation of a medical expert. But that was the perfect description. He seemed out of himself. Away somewhere else. Preoccupied with a voice that David couldn't hear.

Thunder rumbled.

Suddenly Jack Black's expression cleared and he looked David in the eye; then he looked at Bernice.

He turned his head to one side and touched the red scar. "My mother did this when I was six hours old. She kicked over the hospital incubator when she saw me. Imagine that. Little baby in one of them plastic fish-tank things they have in maternity wards? Kicks it. Tips me out. Splat I go on the floor. Head split from there to there." He pointed at the side of his head, speaking low and fast. "When I was six days old she poured a kettle of boiling water over me. A week after that she tried to swap me for a packet of cigarettes." He shot David a look. "Why do mothers do that? I didn't do a full day in school after I turned eight. I can draw, though. I can draw really good . . . really, really good. And . . ." He stabbed another look at David. ". . . and I know what you're thinking. And then there's the black lightning. It's all over the town. I saw it the day I came here. It's nuthin' to do with the weather. The black lightning's coming out of the ground. And no one else can see it. Only me," he breathed. "Only me."

Drugs. That was the word that popped crystal-bright into David's brain. Lots of drugs. The man was obviously traced up on something.

David glanced in the direction of the lift door. Perhaps he should get Bernice into the lift. Otherwise they'd have to pass Jack Black to reach the stairs.

He backed casually away from Black who'd suddenly stopped talking and wore that preoccupied look again, as if striving to remember something important.

"Bernice," David said gently. "Would you press the lift call button, please?"

"I'm not leaving my room unlocked."

"OK, just pull the door shut. It's got a Yale; it'll lock itself. Then I think we should go downstairs and talk to Electra."

"I haven't got the key."

"Electra can unlock it later for you. Just pull the door shut."

"What about your room?"

"It'll be OK."

"But—"

"Don't worry. It'll be fine."

Bernice stood behind David, close by the lift door. David didn't want to turn his back on the thug. Now the man ran his fingers over his lips, still working through the problem, his lips moving as he talked to himself. "Black lightning. Things moving under ground. Not good, not good . . ."

Behind him he heard clicks, then a hum, as the lift machinery spun reluctantly into life.

Jack Black stood there in the centre of the corridor, his huge figure framed by the walls and ceiling. Lightning slashed silver along the walls; thunder boomed.

At that moment the lift door opened.

For a second David thought the sudden screams he heard were somehow generated by the storm.

Then he saw a pale shape burst through the lift doors. For a second he stared at the naked woman who threw herself down at Bernice's legs, wrapped her arms around them, then clung there with a savage desperation. And all the time she screamed, her mouth wide open, her eyes as round as discs.

Blood smeared the woman's arms.

David snapped himself out of the shock. He crouched down beside her. "What's happened? No, it's OK, you're safe. Can you tell me what happened?"

The woman looked up through mascara streaked eyes. "Don't let them hurt me . . . don't . . . don't let them hurt me like Matt . . ."

4

Five minutes later the woman—Fiona was the name David had managed to coax out of her—sat on Bernice's bed. She shook violently, great tears rolling down her cheeks. And she wasn't making a lot of sense as she tried to tie the pink towelling dressing gown Bernice had given her.

189

"Here," Bernice said gently, crouching down beside her. "Let me." She tied the towelling cord for her. Bernice looked up at David, eyes full of concern. "Can you tell if she's hurt?"

David came from the bathroom with a damp flannel and towel.

"As far as I can tell, no. The blood on her arms doesn't look to be hers. Has she said anything else?"

"No, she seems completely scrambled. Has she been—*attacked*?"

He realized what she meant. Raped. "I can't be sure. Not until she can tell us what happened." During a brief examination, he had noticed the redness of her vagina—and the smell of semen was unmistakable; but that might be attributable to consensual sexual intercourse. The situation was fragile enough without yelling rape.

Bernice stroked the woman's hair. Gently, she asked, "Fiona. What happened? Has someone hurt you?"

"I—I . . . oh, Matt . . .'s impossible, impossible, impossible . . ." She spoke in a stuttering, gasping kind of way. "I can't believe this happened to us . . . it isn't fair . . . it isn't." She began to rock backwards and forwards.

Bernice looked up at him. "Black did this, didn't he?"

"We can't be sure."

"And he's still out there?"

"Yes," David said. "At least, he was a minute ago."

"What's he doing now?"

"Just standing in the corridor like he's on sentry duty or something."

"He's mad . . . Christ, the cruel bastard. How could he do this to a woman?"

"Look," David said in a low voice. "I'll phone for an ambulance."

"And the police."

"The police as well," David agreed. He picked up the bedside phone.

"That's no good."

"Why?"

"You need to get reception to give you an outside line."

Bernice stood up.

"Wait," he said, "Where are you going?"

"Down to reception. I'll use the phone there."

"You can't," David said, horrified.

"We can't sit here until Doomsday, can we?"

"Look, Bernice. Someone attacked this woman. You can't roam about the hotel alone."

Bernice looked really in gear, driven by anger from seeing the bruised and naked woman; he thought she'd sail out of the room alone.

She sighed. "OK, point taken. What do you suggest?"

"I'll go down. You lock the door after me."

"What about Black?"

"Look, I don't know if he's done this. He's not behaving like someone with a guilty conscience, is he?"

"David, he certainly isn't behaving as if he's sane."

"Point taken."

Their eyes met and an understanding flickered between them. He gave an appreciative smile. They were working together on this now.

"Bernice," he said in a low voice. "On second thoughts, I think all three of us should go down to reception. We can phone from there. We'll get Electra up, too."

"Right." She glanced in the direction of Black beyond the doorway. "It's time she grabbed the bull by the horns."

"OK," David said. "Give me a hand with Fiona; that's it, take her other arm. Careful with her elbow; that graze will be sore."

Gently Bernice said, "Fiona . . . Fiona . . . we're going downstairs. Can you stand by yourself?"

She looked round for a moment, confused as if she wasn't sure where she was. "Where's Matt?"

"Is Matt your husband?" David asked.

She shook her head. "He was with me . . . they came in . . . they just . . . just hurt him . . . they'd have got me, too. I ran when they pulled him out of the room; I got in the lift. I just hid inside there . . . I thought it would be all right when I came out. I used to have magic words when I was little—Pomerania, Beetlejuice, Antimacassar—I said those when Grandad took off his belt."

"It's OK," Bernice said soothingly. "Come on, stand up."

"Pomerania, Beetlejuice, Antimacassar. I said . . . I said those words when Grandad took his belt to me. If I hid in the lift and

191

said it long enough and—and with enough . . . conviction, it would be all right. Matt would come back. He'd be alive. Pomerania, Beetlejuice, Antimacassar, Pomerania . . ."

"She's in shock," David said to Bernice. "Pulse is shallow, she's breathing way too fast."

"Beetlejuice, Antimacassar. Grandad took his belt off, took it off, went down, fell . . . doornail-dead—uh!—dead as a doornail."

"Come on, sweetheart," David said gently. "We'll get you downstairs." Then to Bernice he added. "Don't be shocked if she faints on us; she's looking a bit groggy."

"Groggy? Me, too."

David looked at Bernice. She was doing a good job, helping the distraught woman, but she'd started to shake.

He gave her as big a reassuring smile as he could. "You're doing fine, Bernice. Almost at the door."

"What about Black?"

"Ignore him."

"And the boyfriend? Matt, was it?"

"Once we're in reception and I've made those phone calls I'll check the room."

"What do you think happened?"

He shrugged, but he was deeply troubled. "I don't know . . . I really don't know."

5

They guided Fiona to the doorway of the hotel room. David used his heel to pull the door open as fully as it would go.

Now Jack Black stood about ten paces down the corridor. His back to them, his arms dangling loosely by his side.

Damn, it really did look like the man was standing guard. What the hell had happened? Had Black attacked the woman? Perhaps even raped her? Where was the boyfriend, Matt? Maybe he'd roughed up the girl after an argument?

The woman's thought process was really screwed.

She still mumbled, "Pomerania, Beetlejuice, Antimacassar . . ."

"Is the lift there?" David asked.

"Gone. It automatically returns to the ground floor."

"Never mind. Can you manage to reach the call button?"

"Yep, got it."

Christ, he thought, don't we make a strange sight? Bernice made up like the Queen of Goth complete with blood-red lipstick and over-the-elbow black lace gloves; I'm wearing no shoes or socks; and we're both supporting a grazed and bruised woman between us who's mumbling magic words from her childhood.

And to top it all there's Jack Black standing in the corridor, shaved head in grim silhouette; he's staring in the direction of the stairs as if the bogeyman's going to jump out and shout YA-HOO!

He looked at Bernice; she was biting her lip and watching the illuminated lift counter—a green numeral enclosed by a little brass frame just above the wood-effect doors. The numeral told them the lift had reached the third floor.

David shot a glance down at Jack Black. He still stood there—a weird statue of skin, bone and tattooer's ink.

Thunder rumbled. A deeply ominous sound.

David joined Bernice watching the numerals climb as the antique lift clunked its way up the lift shaft. Now at the fourth floor.

He looked back at Jack Black who stood with his head tilted to one side looking for all the world like a Rottweiler guard dog who's just heard a stranger's step.

Black suddenly turned to look at David, eyes fierce.

"They're coming up the stairs," he said quickly. "Go into your room and lock the door."

"No," David said, losing his patience at last. "We're taking this lady down into reception."

"In the lift?"

"Yes."

Jack Black nipped his bottom lip with a thick finger and thumb, considering. "OK," he said bluntly. "Get in the moment the door opens."

He really is traced up, thought David in exasperation. What was it? Solvent abuse? E? Nitrates? This guy's on another planet.

But as Black walked towards them—a rapid pace, savage as

193

a crocodile's—David couldn't see any of the usual signs of substance abuse. No staggering. No goofy grin. No vacant expression.

The lift door opened.

At that moment, the woman sagged, almost pulling Bernice off balance.

"Oh hell," Bernice said, shocked. "David, she's gone, she's gone."

"Don't worry, she's only fainted."

Black kept shooting glances back at the staircase. "Hurry up. They're almost here."

"*Who*'s almost here?"

"Stand here another two minutes, you'll find out."

Jesus H. Christ, thought David. This I don't need. "Bernice, hold the lift door for me. I'll—uph . . . no, Jack, it's OK; I'll hold her."

But he might as well have tried reasoning with a crocodile.

Jack Black took the woman under one of his massive arms and carried her into the lift. She hung there limp as a cloth doll.

"Stay inside," Black told Bernice as she tried to get out of the lift, a look of fear on her face.

"Let go," she said, frightened. "Let—"

"Stay," Black grunted. Then he looked out through the doors of the lift at David. "Inside, Leppington."

David hesitated.

"Get in the lift now," Black ordered.

David felt as if events were whirling out of control. It was a sickening experience. He was used to being in control; for Godsakes, he was *trained* to be in control. All this had become a bizarre, no, a downright lunatic ride, with the madman Black at the steering wheel.

Just then he heard a noise from the far end of the corridor. Shadows played on the wall opposite the stairwell. Someone was climbing the stairs to the fourth floor.

"David. Get in, please," Bernice pleaded from the corner of the lift.

"Someone's coming up the stairs," he said.

"Get in," Black ordered. "Now."

"It might be Electra," David told him.

"It isn't," Black grunted through his thick lips. "Now get in the lift."

For an instant David was ready to run to the end of the corridor to see exactly who was climbing the stairs, but at that moment some residual sixth sense kicked in. His skin prickled: instinctively, he found himself backing away, his eyes locked onto the shadows cast on the wall as someone, with a ponderous slowness, climbed the stairs.

This isn't rational, he thought, shivering. Why are you afraid of those shadows?

His gut feeling overrode that rational segment of his mind.

He backed towards the lift, shooting a glance over his shoulder as he did so. Black carried the still unconscious Fiona under one arm. The dressing gown had pulled open, revealing her bare legs and pubic hair. Bernice was wedged into the corner of the lift behind Black's broad body. She peered over his thick arm with frightened eyes. She was shooting silent pleas to David to get into the lift, and not wait any longer in the—

Then her face was gone.

David stared at the lift door sliding shut.

"Open the lift door," he called. "Press the hold button."

"I am pressing it," Bernice cried. "I am! It's not working. It's . . ."

The door closed. Then they were gone.

Lift motor humming, barely audible above the thunder. He looked as the green numeral morphed from four to three.

He heard a muffled clunk—as if a heavy object had been dropped on a carpeted floor.

It came from the direction of the stairs.

David Leppington's mouth turned dry. Again he couldn't explain this current of fear surging up inside of him. The clunking sound came again.

He had no alternative now. He turned to see what was coming up the stairs.

Chapter Twenty-one

1

Bernice could hardly move. The lift was tiny enough as it was. The pine-lined box rumbling down the brick shaft was as narrow as a coffin.

With the huge form of Jack Black standing there, solid as an iron statue, the unconscious woman clasped in one of his big tattooed arms, there was hardly room to breathe.

Bernice reached out, squeezing herself between Black's body and the pine lift wall, and pressed the lift button marked with the number four.

"What are you doing?" Black asked in that flat, sinister voice of his.

"I'm going back for David."

"That won't work. The lift'll go down to the ground floor first."

"I can try," she said defiantly.

He shrugged; in his arm the bruised woman rolled her head. Her eyes—matted and blackened with lumps of mascara—were closed. Even so, she muttered: "Pomerania, Beetlejuice . . . Anti—" Then muttered something Bernice couldn't pick up.

"Can you move to one side?" Bernice asked, glaring up at the back of the shaven head. "I can't breathe."

"Soon be there."

She let out an angry breath of air. He thinks I'm just a stupid little girl, she thought. She tried to feel anger, but all she could feel was a kind of despairing acceptance, as if her imagined observation was the right one. I must look like an idiot, dressed like this—long black dress, lace gloves stretching up over my elbows, make-up caked on like I'm Dracula's daughter or something. God, I must look stupid.

Why *did* I dress up like this?

Because I wanted to hide my body.

I don't like the shape of my body.

It embarrasses me, so I wanted to hide behind as much lace and satin and make-up and bright red lipstick as possible.

Suddenly the clothes and make-up seemed transparent to Jack Black's eyes. She felt as naked as this poor girl here in his arms had been.

Naked and stupid . . . and deeply unattractive.

The lift bumped.

"Almost there," she said, feeling she had to break the silence. "Another two floors."

He said nothing. She looked at his bullet-shaped head.

Again she wondered if Jack Black had attacked the woman.

And here I am alone with him . . . well, as good as alone.

She felt intensely uncomfortable. Black's masculinity was a force of nature—like gravity: she sensed it pressing down on her with a Godawful weight.

Oh, come on, lift . . . hurry up . . .

The moment the doors opened she'd run across the lobby to the reception desk, then she'd have that red phone in her hands.

. . . dial the police first. Then ambulance. She wanted the hotel flooded with solid-looking policemen.

They'd take Jack Black away in handcuffs . . . lock him in a cell . . .

He said: "They won't, you know."

"Won't what?"

"The cops. They won't take me away. I didn't do this to the woman."

She felt a swirl of confusion. It's almost as if this thug had read my . . .

The lift juddered. The lights dimmed, flickered, brightened.

She shot a look at the floor counter. The numeral morphed to one.

Nearly there.

Thank God.

Once they were out she'd send the lift back up to David.

"It's not stopping," Black said in a low voice.

"What?" Shivers shot through her scalp. "Press the button. The ground-floor button."

"I did. It's not stopping."

197

This is absurd, she thought. She couldn't move in the lift. She could hardly breathe, pressed there into the corner of the pine walls. The bruised woman muttered.

Bernice swore. "Just when you need it, the lift goes haywire. Damn thing."

She pushed by Black again and punched at the button marked with a letter "G" as the "G" flicked up on the floor counter then blanked as the lift trundled on downward.

"It's not working," he said.

"I *know* the damn thing isn't working. We're going down to the basement."

Basement.

The word seemed suddenly shocking.

Memories of her going down to the basement earlier in the evening and unlocking the steel door came rushing back . . . someone was behind that door, she thought. He's waiting in the basement now. He must have pressed the call button down in the basement. He knew we were getting into the lift.

Aghast, she looked back at the door as the lift shuddered to a stop.

Oh my God, someone *is* down there. That same someone who attacked the woman. The realization came thundering through into her head. Wide-eyed, she stared through the gap between Black's arm and the lift wall at the doors.

Any second they'd slide open. She'd see . . .

She pressed the lift buttons; it was a frantic, panicky action, her lace-covered fingers seeming to slide off the buttons without making proper contact.

A letter "B" flickered up onto the panel. The lift light flickered, too. Went off.

Darkness.

The light came back on—only more dimly.

"Turn round," Black ordered.

"Do what?"

"Turn round."

"No—why? Why are—"

"Do it."

He turned around in the confines of the lift. Still holding on to the unconscious woman, he used his free hand to grab Bernice by the shoulder.

198

She resisted but found herself being effortlessly pushed face forward against the back of the lift.

He doesn't want me to see, she thought frightened. Why?

The lift door opened.

Instantly she heard a loud hissing. Like air escaping from an air hose at the garage.

She felt rather than saw Jack moving behind her. Desperately she tried to turn her head. But she couldn't twist her neck enough to see out. She only saw the grain of the pine wall in front of her.

"Pomerania, Beetlejuice—*ah!*"

The woman's incoherent muttering jerked up into a sudden shrill cry.

Then the lift door closed.

Oh my God, Bernice thought, bewildered. He's thrown her out of the lift.

He's just gone and thrown her out into the basement.

Why? For Godsakes, why?

At last Black released her. She turned round.

The doors of the lift had slid shut once more.

Shocked, she looked round the tiny lift.

She was all alone with Jack Black.

2

David had watched the numerals on the wall, indicating the lift's descent—

—4, 3, 2—

The speed of events had dazed him.

Now, there seemed to be people coming up the stairs. Only they came up slowly, furtively.

Perhaps muggers had slipped into the hotel and robbed the couple in Room 101. That seemed the most likely explanation.

But why were they venturing so high into the hotel? Surely they'd have turned tail and scarpered when the naked woman ran screaming blue murder from the room?

David thought about simply going back to his room and locking the door, then perhaps trying to raise Electra or reception on the internal telephone system.

But, strangely, he felt a sense of guilt at the thought of hiding away. What would his Uncle George have said to that? A Leppington with Viking blood in his veins, hiding in a hotel room?

Where is your pride?

David realized what he was going to do was stupid. There might be a gang of psychopaths roaming the hotel.

But he gritted his teeth, then walked quickly along the corridor.

He'd almost reached the top of the stairs when he heard a flurry of sounds.

It was the sound of feet going down the stairs at a run; an eager run like hungry kids hearing the dinner gong, and now they couldn't wait for their hamburger and chips.

David found himself running, half hoping to catch sight of whoever it was . . .

(to give a description to the police, supplied the rational side of his brain)

. . . and half of him hoped not to see what was running down the stairs. Again that vestigial sixth sense told him the last thing he wanted to do was confront whatever was running down the stairs. It was unpleasant; it was dangerous . . .

Whatever—whoever, he corrected himself—was running down the softly-lit stairs was just a few steps ahead. Every dozen or so steps the stairs turned sharply round a corner then descended again. The person was always just out of sight.

David reached the ground floor panting. The main door to the street was shut—and no doubt firmly bolted; as was the revolving door. The other doors leading from the lobby were shut, too.

So where had they gone? They can't have just evaporated into—"

He froze.

The door to the basement stood open.

If they'd gone into the basement there was—he guessed—no way out. The muggers had effectively trapped themselves.

Mouth dry, he walked cautiously towards the open doorway. Beyond the door lay an inky darkness; thick, almost solid-looking.

Across the lobby came a clunking sound followed by a whispery hiss.

He turned to see the lift doors slide open.

Only two people stepped out: Jack Black and Bernice Mochardi.

He shook his head, puzzled. "Where's Fiona?"

Black strode past him without a reply. Bernice walked out of the lift as if she was sleepwalking. She moved to one of the velvet upholstered chairs and sat down heavily in it. She stared straight in front of her, locked up in pure shock.

"Bernice," he demanded more loudly. "What happened?"

Not blinking, she slowly shook her head.

He heard Jack Black's voice behind him. "Leppington. Did you open this door?"

David turned to see Jack Black standing by the basement door as if he expected armed terrorists to come bursting from it.

David shook his head. "It was open when I got down here. Now, what happened to—"

Jack quickly reached out, grabbed the door handle like he was grasping a poisonous snake, slammed the door shut.

He held it there. As if expecting someone to try and tug it open from the inside. Someone obscenely nasty.

"Get the keys from the cupboard," Black ordered.

David hurried to the reception desk. "There's someone down there?"

"Hurry."

"The keys. Whereabouts are they?"

"In the cupboard. There, under the desk."

"OK . . . got them. Which one?"

"Just keep trying them until you can lock the door."

Jack Black wasn't letting go of the handle—he gripped it with both hands and leaned back with a foot jammed against the door frame.

"Hurry it up," he grunted.

David quickly worked his way through the keys, ignoring the Yale keys and going straight for the mortise key.

It seemed to take forever.

Any moment he expected to hear a clatter of blows coming from the other side of the door—someone furiously clamouring to be let out.

David fumbled through the keys, trying one, discarding it.

"Where's Fiona?"

"Just get the door locked."

David shook his head. Sooner the police got here the better.

"Got it." David turned the key; it gave a satisfying *clunk* as the mechanism drove the lock into the door jamb.

"Locked?" Black asked.

"Yeah."

"Sure?"

"I'm sure."

"You better be."

As David turned round he noticed a figure at the top of the stairs. It was pale-faced; the eyes looked dark and doom-laden.

"Electra," he said with a mixture of relief and surprise at her expression.

She looked down for a moment before asking, "Has it happened again?"

3

David watched Electra come down the stairs. She was dressed in a black kimono that touched the ground; her feet were bare; her blue-black hair was mussed around her shoulders; without make-up her face was a startling white.

"Electra, I'd like you to phone for an ambulance," David said quickly, yet calmly. "The police, too."

"Why?"

"A girl came up to the fourth floor; she'd been attacked."

Electra looked round. "Bernice?"

"No, some other girl . . . Fiona. One of your guests."

Electra nodded, stone-faced. "Fiona Hill, Room 101. Where is she?"

"That's what I've been trying to find out. She went down in the lift with Bernice and Jack over there. When I reached the ground floor via the stairs the lift doors opened but only Jack and Bernice got out."

Electra looked at Bernice, saw she still stared in front of her in shock. She turned to Black. "Where did she go?" she asked him bluntly.

"The lift went down to the basement," he said in a flat, emotionless voice. "She got out."

"She got out?" David echoed. "She got out in the basement? Why?"

Jack Black shrugged, his face expressionless.

"Liar." Bernice snapped out of the trance. "Liar. You threw her out of the lift!"

David shook his head, bewilderment flooding through him. "Threw her out? What on earth for?"

Bernice stood up, a fierce look returning to her eyes. "Ask him. Go on, ask him."

"She got out," Jack Black said evenly.

"Did she hell," Bernice snapped. "You *threw* her out." She stood up and advanced across the carpet towards Black, her eyes glittering. "Your friends were down there. You threw her out to them like she was a piece of meat being thrown to a pack of dogs. That's what happened, isn't it?"

"Whoa." Electra held up her hands. "Stop just there. Look, there's got to be a rational explanation for all this."

David said, "And I think Bernice has just supplied it. Black knew there was someone in the basement; he just locked them down there."

Electra looked at the door to the basement, then looked back at the lift with the table pushed halfway in to hold the door open. "Did Jack do that?"

David nodded.

"Electra," Bernice said urgently. "For crying out loud, call the police."

"No."

"No?" David echoed, shaking his head. "Electra, for heaven's sake, there might have been a murder here. We might even know the culprit." He glanced at Black who stood motionless by the basement door, face still expressionless but eyes fixed on David.

"Jack's not responsible," Electra spoke firmly. "In fact, you might be thanking him before too long."

"Electra. You've lost me. What's happening here?"

"We can talk about that later. First, I think we should take a look in Room 101. A man should have been staying there with Miss Hill." She glanced at each of them in turn. "I think we all should go up there together. Don't you agree?"

After a little pause David and Bernice nodded. Black simply

walked across to the foot of the stairs and waited for them.

David added, "Perhaps we should check on the other guests, too?"

"No need. With the exception of Miss Hill and friend, you and Bernice are the only guests." She climbed a couple of steps, then turned to look down on them. "I'll go first. Jack, you follow behind David and Bernice, OK?"

He nodded, his tattooed face an unsmiling mask.

David felt Bernice touch him on the arm. It was a gesture made to reassure both of them. He gave her a grim little smile.

"OK, follow me." Electra walked slowly up the steps. They could have been a family going to pay their last respects to a dead grandparent in a chapel of rest. There was something darkly funereal about all this.

The rain pattered against the glass. In the distance thunder was a dismal grumbling sound, so deep it was felt rather than heard.

Inside, David felt cold, subdued. The prospect of going to Room 101 was forbidding. He realized it was a fear of the unknown. He didn't know what he would find there.

Chapter Twenty-two

The four of them sat around the table in the kitchen. Coffee steamed from mugs on the table. Milk spilt from a clumsily torn-open carton formed little puddles of white on the wood. Jack Black rocked back on two legs of his chair while he looked up at the ceiling, a cigarette clamped between his thick lips.

Electra must have noticed that Bernice was wearing her clothes—the long black skirt, the silk blouse, and black lace gloves that snugly enveloped her hands and forearms—but she made no comment or even gave an indication she had noticed.

"Electra." David spoke in a low, even voice. "Let me get this straight. You won't phone the police?"

"No. I will not."

Bernice leaned forward, elbows on the table, earnestly looking Electra in the face. "Electra, for heaven's sake, why not?"

"OK, Bernice, David. I call the police. What do I tell Sergeant Morrow when he steps through that door?"

"Tell him what happened. That's easy enough, isn't it?"

"But what *did* happen, Bernice? You tell me."

Bernice sighed, going over the story for the third time. "The woman stumbled from the lift. I grabbed her as she fell—"

"No, no, Bernice. Later. What happened to this woman—this Fiona Hill—when she got out of the lift?"

"In the basement?"

"Yes. Where did she go?"

"She didn't get out. Not of her own accord. He—" She stabbed a finger at Black. "—he pushed her out."

"She ran out of the lift," Jack said sullenly.

"What?"

"She ran out."

"But there was a struggle!"

"Yeah . . . she struggled away from me. I tried to stop her running away. Like Doc here says, she needed to go to hospital."

"Electra. Look." Keep this calm, David, he told himself. Talk this through nice and easy. "Look. The woman appeared to have been attacked. She was bruised, she was bleeding. Here, at the elbow; she was in shock. We've just been up to the room she occupied."

Electra said, "And who did we find there?"

"No one, granted. But the place was a mess. There was blood on the bed sheet and blood on the bathroom door."

"But no Mr. Smith?"

"No, but what did you expect? A disembowelled body?"

"Maybe I did," Electra agreed with a little shrug. "But we found nothing."

"You call the room in chaos and the blood *nothing?* And where are your guests?"

Electra sighed. It was a weary sound; worldly, too, as if she had at last to explain the facts of life to a curious nephew. "David. I run a hotel. And sometimes bizarre things happen. Sometimes two men check in wanting separate single rooms. In the morning, chambermaids find only one room has been slept in, and the sheets are . . . well, in a bit of a mess. Bernice, David,

205

this is the real world. Hotels aren't just for families requiring accommodation on the way to Disneyland. Don't look at me like that, Bernice: yes, I am sounding patronizing. But the fact of the matter is some people *do* check into hotels for adulterous liaisons; sometimes they can be pretty kinky. Sometimes people enjoy getting rough when they have sex; then blood gets onto sheets and furniture, and yes, Dr. Leppington, Vaseline might be found smeared on a chair leg or we may even find safety pins covered in blood. You know as well as I do there are sadists and masochists as well as God-fearing folk who religiously uphold the missionary position and kiss with their mouths closed. We find tab ends of reefers in waste bins or scraps of burnt foil, so we know drugs get used in hotels—ask any motel or hotel manager anywhere in the world. Sometimes a lover gets carried away—the other lover freaks and runs from the hotel room. They might be high on drugs, or get cold feet at having their nipples stapled or—"

"You're saying," David interrupted, "that this couple might just have been indulging in some kind of S&M sex play that got out of hand?"

Electra nodded. "Possibly."

"But that girl was *terrified*," Bernice said, gripping her coffee mug as though, if she held it tightly enough, it would squeeze some common sense into Electra. "She fainted in my arms, she was rambling . . ."

"Doctor. Might not a drug have that effect?"

David conceded with a slow nod. "LSD. It might have that effect, depending on the person's state of mind."

"But that still doesn't explain where this Fiona Hill and Mr. Smith vanished to."

Electra gave a little shrug. "Bernice, you know guests sometimes do a runner from hotels."

"In the middle of the night? And the girl was only wearing my dressing gown!"

"They were embarrassed: she might be a schoolteacher; he could be an archbishop for all I know. After all, I doubt very much if Mr. Smith was his real name. In those circumstances wouldn't you want to get out of the hotel fast before the newspapers had a field day with you?"

"They left their clothes," Bernice insisted.

"So. You've seen the Dead Box?"

"The Dead what?" David asked, mystified.

"The Dead Box. Tell him, Bernice."

Bernice's expression looked more glum now than shocked: Electra had an answer for everything.

"The Dead Box," Bernice said, "is the name of the room off the lobby. That's where suitcases and other belongings are stored when people leave without paying."

David raised his eyebrows. "This happens often?"

Electra replied, "You should see how full the room is. It's packed from ceiling to floor. Believe me, Doctor, it's been happening ever since this hotel was built. People decide they don't want to pay their bill . . . or they suddenly realize Mr. Right is Mr. Wrong and *ffftt* . . . away they go: leave everything behind."

"But this Mr. Smith and Fiona Hill arrived by car. So the car will be parked out back?"

"They said they arrived by train, but seeing as there was no train due around the time they reached the hotel I suspect they came by car and hid it in a side street somewhere. They were very discreet."

David realized that Electra was neatly explaining everything away. She didn't want any trouble with the police. If that was the case. And she wasn't hiding something. He glanced at Black. He didn't take any part in the discussion. His expression, as wooden as ever, was partly hidden by a thick cloud of cigarette smoke.

"Anyone like more coffee before we turn in?" Electra was all sweetness and reason. Probably inwardly gloating that we'll never find where the bodies are hidden, thought David. But he knew he wasn't allowing his flippant humor to run away with him. He suspected Electra did indeed know something. There was a secret hidden here in this hotel. David wanted it outed. "Half a cup," he said and pushed the mug across the table. Electra smiled and topped it up from the jug.

"I can make you a sandwich if you like?"

David shook his head, smiling too. But determined not to let Electra sweep the whole thing under the carpet. He didn't believe for a moment that embarrassed lovers had simply quit the hotel.

"I suppose they left a fake address on the registration card?"

Electra gave that characteristic little shrug. "I guess."

"And they paid cash?"

"Mmm, a deposit anyway . . . in advance."

"So no credit-card receipt. Handy."

"Run of the mill, I'm afraid," Electra said soberly. "Adulterers are a devious breed."

Bernice shook her head with a long sigh. "They might never have been here at all?"

"No wallet. No papers. Nothing," was Black's contribution.

David looked at the man for a moment as he sat wreathed there in cigarette smoke. "That's all the questions answered but one," he said.

"Oh?" Electra sipped her coffee. "Which one's that?"

"When I saw Mr. Black here just after I'd reached the ground floor, he wedged the door of the lift so it couldn't be used. Or couldn't be called from another floor. Also, he went straight to the basement door, shut it, then held it shut until I locked it. Who did he think was in the basement?"

"His friends," Bernice said with a dark bitterness. "Accomplices might be a better word."

"The door needed shutting," Black stated woodenly as if that was an eloquent enough answer.

"Is there another way into the basement?" David asked.

"Through the service lift in the yard. That's padlocked from the inside. No one can get in."

"Or out?"

"Or out," Electra agreed.

"And there's no other entrance to the basement?"

"No, none at all."

David thought Bernice had shot Electra a surprised look, as if the woman had not told the whole truth.

But that didn't really matter. He'd made up his mind what he was going to ask next.

"Electra."

"Yes?"

"Do you mind if I check in the basement?"

"No, but you'd best leave it until morning."

"Why?"

"It's really not safe down there. Some of the lights aren't working."

"But you will be able to lend me a torch?"

She said nothing but he sensed her resistance to him searching the basement himself.

"Look," he told her, "the girl ran out of the lift into the basement. She might have hurt herself, passed out, whatever—she was really in a bad state when we first found her."

"She's not there." This time it was Electra's turn to sound wooden.

David persisted. "Nevertheless, I think I should check."

There was a pregnant pause while Electra considered. He knew she would try and talk him out of it. The cigarette smoke hung heavily in the air. The clock on the kitchen wall tocked steadily on, showing the minute hand edging up to the two. Thunder still rumbled through the night air.

There was a timelessness to it all; as if some immense occult machinery was meshing great dark gears in a world beyond this one in order to slow down time. Someone—or something—apart from Electra didn't want him in that basement.

And at the end of that long drawn-out moment, which was as silent as the proverbial grave, the telephone rang.

Chapter Twenty-three

1

David sat around the kitchen table with Bernice and Jack Black as Electra went to answer the telephone in reception. Jack Black nipped out the cigarette between his finger and thumb. Then lit another, his ugly face suddenly a bright luminous yellow in the light of the flaring match.

Drops of rain crackled against the window. The time was ten past two.

David knew he couldn't even begin to drop the question of where the girl had gone until he'd satisfied himself she wasn't in the basement.

He glanced at Bernice, noticing fully for the first time the Victorian-style clothes she wore and the black eyeshadow and blood-red lipstick. He realized he was looking at her in a kind of wide-eyed stupid surprise; he'd simply not taken in her Goth clothes, make-up and vampire-bat jewelry until now. Obviously because of that crazy performance upstairs with the blood-stained woman; then Electra's calm denial that anything criminal had happened in the hotel tonight. (Bizarre, perhaps, Electra would concede; but criminal? Definitely not.) Now the full effect of Bernice's clothes and blood-red lipstick struck him: it was darkly erotic; in other circumstances, he would admit (at least to himself), that it was turning him on.

Suddenly he realized Bernice had seen he was staring at her; her cheeks flushed pink as if she was embarrassed to be seen dressed like that. He quickly looked away from her to the clock on the wall as if checking the time had become the most important thing at that moment.

Seconds later he glanced back at her. She deliberately looked across the table at him, making eye contact. The message he read there was clear enough:

Black and Electra are hiding something: they know what happened to the girl.

2

Bernice sipped the coffee. It was lukewarm now; it didn't taste that pleasant but her mouth was so dry. It must be something to do with the shock of what had happened tonight.

David Leppington was looking at her across the table. She wondered if he was thinking the same as her: Something terrible had happened to the girl. That Electra knew more than she was telling. That Jack Black had thrown the girl from the lift into that black heart of the basement, like he was throwing a scrap of meat to wolves.

She'd enjoyed staying at the hotel. She liked Electra. But this was all too much.

She told herself: As soon as I can, I'm going to check out of this hotel. It's a madhouse . . .

As soon as I can I'm going to check out of this hotel. It's a madhouse . . .

The words trickled clearly enough into Jack Black's brain. It was the weird bitch thinking that shit. Doc Leppington was thinking words like: *Contusion. Fiona was showing signs of shock. Best check the basement as quickly as possible.* Then Doc Leppington's mind wandered; there was a tingle of lust trickling through the man's brain; he was thinking: *Why on earth does Bernice dress like that? Christ, I can't take my eyes off her lips—they're so red; and just look at the shape of her hips showing through that long black skirt; you can see her breasts through that . . . oh, give it a rest, David. You're not a schoolboy getting a hard-on over a girl you've seen in some sticky old magazine. Concentrate on the matter in hand. What happened to Fiona Hill? Where is she now?*

Black listened to the man's thoughts rattling away now with all the speed and purpose of an express train. Shit, the man had a brain like a machine.

Black searched their heads for one word that had lodged inside his for the last twenty-four hours.

He didn't know where that word had come from. But it wouldn't go.

It was like when he heard the name Leppington.

Then he knew he had to come here 'cos the name went around and around in his head: *Leppington, Leppington, Leppington.* His brain bleated it over and over.

Jack Black wouldn't get his tongue around words like prescience or destiny, or even fate. But he knew he had to come to Leppington—there was something here for him; something important; something connected with the black lightning that he'd seen (and only he could see it) flowering in great dark airbursts over the town. Yeah, it was to do with that, all right . . . only he didn't quite know what.

And just as the word Leppington had gone around and around his brain like a wasp trapped inside a glass jar, now a new word went around and around and around and round . . . buzzing so furiously it wouldn't let him sleep. The new word didn't mean that much to him. Overuse and misuse had robbed it of its meaning. Except, when the word buzzed insidiously through his head, it brought other ideas associated with it. Something verminous, bloated . . . purple veins . . . hunger . . . pain . . . disease. The word buzzed inside his head now.

And that word was:

VAMPIRE.

4

Electra walked into the kitchen. Her movements were quick. David saw that once again her composure had deserted her. She swept across the kitchen floor, the gold roses on the black silk kimono catching the light.

"David," she said sounding almost breathless. "I'm terribly sorry, I've bad news."

He stiffened. The phone call . . .

Images shuttled chaotically through his head: His parents' boat had capsized, his half-sister's baby was dying of meningitis, burglars had ransacked his Liverpool flat. Katrina had hanged herself in the mental hospital grounds . . .

"On a night like this, too." David forced himself to concentrate on what Electra was saying; her eyes were full of compassion.

"That was the hospital. Your uncle, George Leppington, was admitted to casualty a couple of hours ago. They're asking if it's possible for you to go up there. They need to speak to a member of the family."

David was on his feet, heartbeating faster. "Is he ill?"

"They wouldn't say."

"Are they still on the phone?"

"No, they're assuming you'll go there straightaway. I can telephone them back if—"

"No. Thanks, anyway. I'll go straight to the hospital." Suddenly he realized he was barefoot. "I just need to go back to my room for a moment first."

"Of course."

"Can I use the key on the hotel room keyring to get in through the front door?"

"Yes. Use the one marked 'Residents' Door' to the right of the revolving door."

David felt once more that he'd become a straw thrown on a fast-flowing stream; events were carrying him along. He could only go with the flow. Running concurrently with these thoughts was a concern for his old Uncle George. He liked the man. He found himself hoping that for whatever reason he had been admitted to hospital it wouldn't be serious.

"Don't worry about things here," Electra said quickly—and confidently. "We'll take care of it."

He glanced at Jack Black. The man sat there with his characteristic wooden expression. Bernice sat with her hand over her mouth, looking up at David with concerned eyes. She genuinely felt for him; and again he experienced a sense of empathy when their gazes locked briefly.

"One detail, though," David said as he pushed the chair back under the table. "Where is the hospital? Can anyone give me directions?"

Bernice jumped in. "Electra. Can I take your car? I'll drive David there, if that's OK?"

Electra nodded readily enough. "Yes. Good idea. Keys are on the hook by the door. You're used to the clutch? It can be fierce."

"Yes, I've got the hang of it now."

"Thank you." David nodded gravely at Electra, then said to Bernice, "You don't have to. It's pretty late."

"No worries," Bernice said quickly. "I'll meet you in reception in five minutes."

For a moment David felt as if he was demanding too much in having Bernice chauffeur him to the hospital at this time of night. Then he realized she badly wanted to get out of the hotel. She didn't feel safe here anymore.

And certainly he didn't want to leave her here alone. He wondered if he should ask Electra to call the police after all. But there was an air of collusiveness between Electra and Black now.

And what about Fiona Hill? he asked himself. Why didn't Electra want him to venture down into the basement? Maybe the reasons were mundane—perhaps she bought illegally imported beer that she stored down there; maybe there were a couple of dirty mattresses where she romped with the thug Black and his equally dodgy mates? Who knew?

Saying goodbye to Electra and Black (who merely grunted, eyes expressionless as ever) he headed into the lobby. The lift was still jammed open by the table, so he ran lightly up the stairs. Now his thoughts were for his uncle. He wanted to make sure George wasn't seriously ill. Perhaps they could take him home tonight. He was sure there would be a spare room up at Mill House where he, David, could stay so he could look after the old man. But what about Bernice? He didn't want to leave her to go back to the hotel alone in the middle of the night.

With the questions flitting unanswered around his mind he returned to his room, pulled on socks and shoes, then ran back down to reception where Bernice stood in the long skirt and lace gloves, the car keys clinking in her nervous fingers. The look of relief on her face when she saw him was obvious.

Poor kid had been frightened, waiting there alone in the lobby. Where were Electra and Black? Returned to the scene of the crime?

No, he told himself. Leave the speculations. His uncle was what mattered now."

"Ready?" asked Bernice.

"Ready," he replied walking rapidly across the lobby toward her.

"The car's out back," she said and led the way through the kitchen to the back door.

5

They went out to the black Volvo parked in the rear courtyard. Beads of freshly fallen rain stood like pearls on its roof. Discreetly stencilled in gold on the passenger door were the words: *STATION HOTEL, LEPPINGTON. WEDDINGS, CHRISTENINGS, PRIVATE FUNCTIONS*.

Bernice unlocked the doors. The central locking device clicked and the lights flashed as the alarm system disarmed itself.

She climbed into the driving seat; David climbed in wordlessly beside her and fastened his seat belt.

God, I must look like a fright dressed like this, she thought, catching a glimpse of herself as she adjusted the rear-view mirror. The lipstick seemed to glow a luminous red while her eyes were darkly shaded almond shapes centered by whites that glistened in the gloom. Do I look like Dracula's daughter or what? she thought. Perhaps I could wait in the car at the hospital. I shouldn't be traipsing about like this in public.

"Is it far?" asked David in a flat voice.

"About five minutes."

That was as far as the conversation went. She felt she should say something reassuring, but she knew it would end up sounding absurd or somehow grossly unsympathetic.

She started the engine and drove across the courtyard, the car's headlights shining off the brick walls of the hotel.

Seconds later she took a right, following Main Street past the station and the vast brooding pile of the slaughterhouse.

Rain splotched the windows, and she set the wipers to intermittent.

Main Street was empty of traffic. The wet road reflected the orange street lamps. A cat slinked along the pavement with a broken-necked sparrow in its jaws. The only people she could see were a couple of middle-aged men walking unsteadily along the street, while a third paused to urinate in the doorway of the delicatessen.

The man pissed a great steaming pool onto the mat on which was printed the word WELCOME.

And you're welcome to it, thought John Doyle, boozily magnanimous, as he shook himself before zipping up his flies. Piss. It's the only thing I've got plenty of. Piss, piss and piss, not forgetting the drop that always runs down your leg. He belched. I shouldn't have bet every penny in my damned pocket on that last hand of poker.

Bloody stupid thing to do.

Blame the beer.

Beer always makes you do stupid stuff. You're forty-six years old, for bugger sake. Don't you ever learn?

Too much damn' beer. Pub for three hours, then across to Sad Sam's for poker and more beer. Sad Sam's mongoloid son served it up in any old glass he could find. Of course he sucked the froth from it in the kitchen. You pretended not to notice.

215

But you could taste his spit on the rim of the glass because Sad Sam's son ate nothing but Polo mints all night—crunch, crunch, crunch . . .

And Sad Sam's mongoloid son always wore a cardboard crown on his stupid ugly head. It was gold with day-glo orange writing on it that said *Burger King*. Now is that a stupid thing to do? Wear a cardboard crown? Even if you are missing a chromosome or something?

Oh, got to ease up on the beer, old son. Bladder can't take it anymore.

He wrinkled his nose at the steaming piss in the doorway; it flickered gold and sunlight-yellow under the street lights. Looks quite pretty really. Quite pretty.

He hawked and spat into the puddle of liquid his liver and kidneys had doggedly spent all evening processing.

And so Jesus turned water into wine.

Well, li'l ol' me turned Heineken Export into water . . . salty old water . . .

He realized he was leaning forward, resting one hand on the shop door for support.

Where were them other buggers?

With an effort he stood on his own two feet, then walked with considerably less aplomb than a thirteen-month-old taking its first baby steps.

"Hey!" he shouted thickly as Smith and Benj strode away down Main Street. "Hey! Way up, lads . . . way up for us, can't yer?"

Groggily, he followed them. "Hey, way up, me laddi-owes."

They didn't hear. Kept on walking.

"Cloth ears," he grunted, and walked faster, one foot squelching where he'd walked through a puddle somewhere on the way back into town.

He put his head down and zig-zagged solidly forward. He was perhaps twenty paces from the bridge, his two mates had just reached the other side, when he felt a hand lightly catch his sleeve.

"Excuse me, have you the time?"

He stopped and turned his whole body to see who it was standing in the darkness of the alleyway.

He screwed up his eyes. It was a girl with light fluffy hair, shining gold in the street lights. A pair of beautiful eyes looked up into his.

John Doyle felt a sensual prickle go tingling up his spine.

"Have you got the time?" she repeated. God, the girl's voice was pretty.

"Time," he echoed, his tongue feeling stiff in his mouth. "Time?"

"Yes."

"Aren't you Moberry's lass? Samantha?"

"No, I'm Dianne, Sammi's older sister."

He looked down at the cleavage exposed by the open buttons of her blouse. Dear heaven, he could even see a black lacy bra— just a flash of it.

He'd not seen underwear as pretty as that on a living person ever . . . dimly he pictured his wife's heavy-duty no-nonsense industrial-strength bras.

God, he even sensed the woman's body heat: it came at him in waves—a sexual energy radiated from those eyes that burned up at him.

He swallowed. "Dianne Moberry . . . yes . . . yes . . . I remember you. You're—you're beautiful . . ."

"Thank you. Thank you very much."

She fluttered long eyelashes. All wrapped into one, she was girlishly innocent yet a mature woman—worldly, experienced, sensual.

The eyes held him. They shone, huge and round in the street lights.

She was beautiful and—

And, oh God, he wanted her. He wanted her more than anything else in the world. Every cell of his body screamed out to him to touch her; he imagined putting his face next to hers and feeling the heat radiating through her skin.

"I've always liked you, Mr. Doyle," she whispered huskily. "You always looked so strong."

"Did I?"

He gazed into her eyes, hypnotized, feeling his soul leaking out of his body and into hers.

"I bet you could lift me up as if I was as light as a feather."

"I could, yes . . . I could," he breathed, loving her sense of presence.

She stepped back into the shadows of the alleyway.

"Mr. Doyle. Why don't you try?"

"Lift you up?" His heartbeat fast, blood roared through the arteries in his neck, rivalling the roar of the swollen Lepping foaming around the rocks just paces away.

"Yes," she whispered from the shadows, her eyes burning like twin lights. "Lift me up, Mr. Doyle. Please."

He stepped from the pavement into the gloom of the alleyway, guided by her burning eyes.

He reached out, finding her narrow waist by sense of touch.

Then he lifted her up.

Oh . . . He breathed in deeply when he felt her lips touch his bare throat.

6

"The hospital's just up there on the hillside," Bernice said as she turned off the main road and followed a lane that snaked uphill. "Warm enough?" she asked, her fingers resting on the fan switch.

"Uh? Yes, fine. Sorry, I was miles away," David said with a smile.

She smiled back, feeling a sudden intimacy with him there alone in the car. My God, she thought, why aren't we riding out into the countryside under different circumstances?

Not this grim drive up to the hospital, not knowing if his uncle is alive or dead.

The night seemed intensely dark, she thought, somehow darker than normal. The street lights appeared to have difficulty in casting their orange glow more than a few miserable paces.

They were now driving uphill, the lane flanked by houses, all in darkness, their occupants deeply asleep and oblivious to the fun and games at the Station Hotel tonight, she thought.

All except one. There stood a semi with a bedroom light lit. A second later the door opened, casting a block of yellow light onto a front garden lawn.

Jill Morrow recognized the sound of her husband's knock on the front door—a furtive apology of a knock made by a weak-as-water man; she opened it straight away.

Join the Leisure Horror Book Club and

GET 2 FREE BOOKS NOW—
An $11.98 value!

┌─────────────────────────────────┐
│ **— Yes! I want to subscribe to —** │
│ **the Leisure Horror Book Club.** │

Please send me my **2 FREE BOOKS**. I
have enclosed $2.00 for shipping/han-
dling. Each month I'll receive the two
newest Leisure Horror selections to
preview for 10 days. If I decide to keep
them, I will pay the Special Members
Only discounted price of just $4.25
each, a total of $8.50, plus $2.00
shipping/handling. This is a **SAVINGS
OF AT LEAST $3.48** off the bookstore
price. There is no minimum number of
books I must buy and I may cancel the
program at any time. In any case, the
2 FREE BOOKS are mine to keep.

— Not available in Canada. —

NAME: _____

ADDRESS: _____

CITY: _____ STATE: _____

COUNTRY: _____ ZIP: _____

TELEPHONE: _____

E-MAIL: _____

SIGNATURE: _____

If under 18, Parent or Guardian must sign. Terms, prices, and conditions subject to change. Subscription subject
to acceptance. Dorchester Publishing reserves the right to reject any order or cancel any subscription.

Would he pay for this!

She'd wring the money and domestic chores out of him until he bleated.

"Jason," she hissed, seeing him straightaway as he hung back in the shadows. "Do you think I can't see you hiding there?"

He didn't reply.

The breeze blew, opening the split of her cotton dressing gown and sending an icy draft up her bare legs as far as her waist.

"Jason. You better have a damn' good reason why you didn't come home last night, or you'll never come through this door ever again."

"Jill," her husband's voice was low, whispery. "Let me in. I'm cold."

The voice sent a shiver down inside her stomach.

"What's your excuse this time? And what have you done with the car?"

"Jill . . . *love* . . . let me in, please. I'm cold."

His voice sounded so familiar, yet so different. That whispery quality sent a shiver—a sensual, erotic shiver—deep down inside her. It made her conscious of the cool breeze around her bare legs, and the slight, almost tickling, friction of her T-shirt across the tips of her breasts. She folded her arms in front of her, aware her nipples were hardening and rising.

The pressure of her dressing-gown collar at the base of her neck became a caress. She shivered again. Her anger ebbed away. In place of that vanishing anger she now felt a sultry warmth. She wanted to see her husband again.

He's been gone too long, she thought. I want to run my fingers through his hair; just like I did when we were courting; I want to see his cute habit of rubbing the nub of bone above his eyebrow; that sexy smile.

"Jill. Aren't you going to ask me inside?"

His voice was warm, pleasant and deeply, deeply loving. The sound of it made her skin feel so exquisitely sensitive. The breeze moved each hair on her legs. The material of her T-shirt touched and clung to the curves of her stomach, bottom and breasts; her thighs tingled.

Again he spoke, lovingly and patiently; an effortless patience. He would wait there until apple blossom filled the trees in the orchard if he had to. The idea pleased her; he'd wait there devotedly, like a medieval knight; he'd be chivalrous, courteous, completely devoted. Images from the romance books she'd read—and loved for their escapism—blossomed like summer roses deep within her heart.

"Jill," whispered her husband from the shadows. "Can I come inside the house?"

"Yes," she said eagerly. "Come in, Jason." She stepped back from the threshold and beckoned him.

He stepped into the hallway. Then, as if a weight had been lifted from his shoulders, he smiled.

Now his eyes never left hers. They were huge: they filled his face. They shone.

Her heart melted. She was in love again.

In a moment he had swept her into the living room. Her heart clamored.

He was peeling off her dressing gown; then he gripped the neck of her T-shirt. In one fluid movement he tore it wide open. Feeling her legs go weak, almost watery, she allowed him to sit her naked in the armchair. Never once did he take his eyes off her—those wonderful eyes, shining like they contained living flames.

Then he was holding her tightly. She felt a pressure between her legs—a sweet pressure, strong, firm, purposeful.

Then . . .

He was inside her.

And he felt so marvelous.

He entered her more deeply than he'd ever done before.

She felt him sliding, sliding, sliding, sliding—

—in, in, and in.

Oh.

Her heart swelled, the blood thickened her arteries and filled her lips.

The curtains were open: she saw the hospital on the hillside blazing with light.

Still he pushed inward; he seemed to flow into her—a one-way motion, going into her deeper and deeper. Now she felt him so deep inside she felt a pressure just below her ribs, warming her.

Then she felt a sting from inside—a sting that, although intense, felt strangely sweet; as if he was drawing out a thorn that had been deeply embedded inside her womb.

Now his lips closed over her nipple. The sting came there too.

But she was too drowsy, too warm, too much in love to protest.

She turned her face to the uncurtained window. The lights of the hospital in the distance were growing dim.

I know what's happening to me, she thought sleepily, and I don't care. This is love.

Her eyes closed, leaving on her retina the dying image of car headlights moving like a star into the grounds of the hospital.

7

Bernice slotted the car into a white-painted space in the visitors' car park. She didn't switch off the engine.

David looked at her. She noticed how large his irises were in the dark like round dark pools.

"Are you going back to the hotel?" he asked. She detected a hint of reluctance in his voice as if he thought it would be a bad idea.

"No," she said with a small smile. "I'll wait here in the car."

"I don't know how long I'll be. You know what hospitals are like."

"I could get a coffee or something in the waiting room," she agreed. Then she thought of her Gothic-looking clothes, complete with the long lacy gloves. "Electra's sheepskin coat is in the back. I'll wear that, then at least I'll look half decent."

He gave a little smile. "You look nice."

"Oh, I think I still need that coat."

They climbed out of the car. Bernice slipped Electra's coat on; it was big and warm; the cuffs came down to the ends of her fingernails. Then, side by side, they walked to the twin doors marked CASUALTY.

Chapter Twenty-four

1

David walked across the car park to the door marked CASU-ALTY. Already his stomach muscles were tense with apprehension. His uncle was an old man in his eighties: strokes, embolism, heart attacks were all too common at that age.

The wind gusted across the hillside, driving drops of rain with stinging force.

He glanced at Bernice. She wrapped herself deeply into the warm sheepskin coat; he glimpsed her lace-clad fingers poking just below the cuffs.

He was grateful she'd come. Visiting a sick relative in casualty at three in the morning is a hell of a lonely thing to have to do.

They went straight to the hospital reception desk where the clerk—a middle-aged man with tufts of gray hair brushed across a balding crown—took David's details (while shooting a couple of glances at Bernice, David noticed: the man was no doubt wondering what the low-down was about her, with her blood-red lipstick and heavily shadowed eyes from the make-up).

"A nurse will be along in a minute, Dr. Leppington, if you and your, ah, companion would like to take a seat." The clerk indicated the usual drab rows of gray plastic chairs that inhabit many a hospital waiting room: they were dotted here and there with people—mostly men, mostly drunk, with tissues clamped to bleeding noses, eyes, ears. The exception was a child in a dressing gown, flanked by two anxious-looking parents. The little boy had a papier mâché bowl on his knee; there was a whiff of vomit in the air, vying for dominance with an aroma of now stale beer.

"We might be in for a long wait," David told Bernice as they sat down. "You like a coffee or something?"

Before she could answer, a tall nurse, as thin as a pole, swung aside a pair of rubber doors. "Mr. Leppington?" she called, "Leppington family?"

Instantly all the drowsy heads in the waiting room perked up and looked round, the glazed eyes now sharp with interest.

A Leppington? Here? David could almost read their minds.

He stood up, acutely aware that a dozen pairs of eyes had fixed on him. "Here," he said.

"This way please, Mr. Leppington. Cubicle five." The nurse held open the rubber door for David and Bernice to pass through. In front lay the standard casualty cubicles fronted with green plastic curtains. That hospital smell immediately flooded his nose. The walls were covered in notices that were instantly recognizable to him from his days on A&E in Liverpool: a hand-written notice on a cupboard ran FLAMAZINE CREAM— ONCE OPEN DO NOT PUT BACK IN CUPBOARD BUT IN BIN. Then there was the faithful notice, many times pored over when a suspected overdoser was brought in: this was headed MANAGEMENT OF ACUTE PARACETAMOL OVERDOS- AGE. Even though the building was strange to him the para- phernalia of the casualty ward was keenly familiar.

The nurse hurried on ahead. "Dr. Singh," she called to a young Asian dressed in surgical greens complete with hat and with a surgical mask hanging loosely down against his throat. He was standing at the end of the corridor scrutinizing a sheet of paper. "Dr. Singh, Leppington family for patient in number five."

"Ah, thank you, nurse." Smiling, he strode forward. "Mr. Leppington? Quite a famous name in these parts."

David nodded and decided to correct the title—not for ego's sake but because it would make things easier for them both if they could avoid the usual doctor-to-patient pidgin. "It's Dr. Leppington." David smiled and held out his hand. Dr. Singh shook it.

"Ah, a medical doctor? Good, good. Lazy man that I am, I can rely on jargon now."

David added, "This is my friend Bernice Mochardi."

"Absolutely," said the doctor with an understanding nod. "This way, please." He held open the curtain. "Don't be alarmed. Your uncle is still in something of a mess. We don't

223

get the chance to clean our patients too thoroughly at weekends. Casualty tends to get rather lively after the public houses close, you'll understand, doctor?"

David nodded. Friday and Saturday nights, hospitals—whether in inner cities or peaceful-looking market towns—might as well be in war zones for the number of blood-soaked casualties that are stretchered in.

When Dr. Singh moved to one side David got his first good look at his uncle lying on the bed.

The old man was unconscious and lay with a sheet pulled halfway up his bare chest. He breathed rhythmically, although there was a wet bronchial crackle coming from his mouth. David noticed an airway tube had been inserted.

Then he saw the blood.

Damn . . .

It had turned George's snowy gray hair into a mat of reddish brown. David moved around the bed, automatically checking the color of the skin—pallid, almost the color of lard with that same shiny white characteristic of shock; the lips were bluish.

Then he saw what appeared to be a pair of sanitary towels bound to the side of his uncle's head with a crêpe bandage. Initial treatment in casualty favors the effective rather than the pretty. Blood had soaked through the white dressings in dandelion-shaped blots of red and brown.

"What happened?" asked David, looking up.

Dr. Singh tilted his head slightly. "No one knows precisely. There's a gash in the side of the head. Unconsciousness resulted from the blow; while—"

"He was attacked?" David asked, shocked.

"That's not for us to say."

"Skull fracture?"

"Not possible to say, either, until we can get him up to X-ray."

"When will that be?"

Dr. Singh shrugged. "I'm sorry, it's Saturday night."

"Look, I think you need to give his case priority. He's more than eighty years old."

"I appreciate your concern, doctor, but we have our priorities, too."

"Where are the police?"

"They have been informed."

"Are they in the building? Can I talk to them?"

Again, Dr. Singh could only make the reply that was sounding increasingly painful to him. "It is Saturday night. I'm sorry."

David put his fingers to his mouth and looked down on his uncle; the old man's brow was furrowed as if some mighty problem still weighed on him even in the depths of concussion. The white—the worryingly white—bloodless eyelids twitched and fluttered, occasionally exposing the glassy sheen of an eye. He felt a hand on his forearm. He looked down to see Bernice's oval face looking up at him. Her eyes were full of concern.

David breathed out slowly. So this is how it feels to be on the other side of the fence in casualty: the relative of the patient. It felt shitty; he didn't feel in control; he was becoming emotional. He took a deep breath and said evenly, "How seriously hurt is my uncle?"

Dr. Singh's large brown eyes were sympathetic. "It's not at all possible to say."

Oh, for Godsakes don't say "Because it's Saturday night" again, David thought with a sudden fury.

"The injury doesn't appear to be overly serious. But, then again, you must appreciate his considerable age is a factor. Eighty plus, you say?"

David nodded. "Eighty-five, I think. Who brought him in here?"

"Ambulance. Apparently, after he was injured he managed to telephone."

"Then he was able to speak when he telephoned?"

"No. Emergency services heard him . . . make a noise. That was all, the telephone remained off the hook so they were able to call up your uncle's telephone number and address on the Telecom computer, then dispatch police and an ambulance. They showed great initiative, don't you think?"

"They did," David agreed. "After X-ray he'll be taken to a ward for observation?"

"Yes, unfortunately I can't say precisely when. It is, after all—"

"Saturday night. David gave a small smile; he felt calmer now. "I know," he said in a way which he hoped was under-

225

standing, not sarcastic. "I did my casualty spell in Liverpool's Royal. You have my sympathies."

The curtain swished crisply to one side. It was the tall nurse again. "Dr. Singh. The duodenal in cubicle one. Looks as if she's hemorrhaging. There's a sixty-year-old arrest in eight. And there's a cooking-oil burns in three."

Dr. Singh gave an apologetic sigh. "I'll be back as soon as I can. Please . . . sit with your uncle if you wish. We have a vending machine in reception should you require refreshment." He stepped through the curtain, then paused. "One word of warning, I would avoid the oxtail soup if I were you." He smiled. "Back as soon as I can."

Then there were three, David thought. He fought down an inappropriate smile that was straining at his mouth. Saturday night in casualty is when patients are no longer referred to by name but by the ailment or injury they are suffering from. And the only diagnosis a doctor feels confident to make with any degree of certainty is which hot drink to avoid from the vending machine. And despite it all, the world still manages to keep on revolving smoothly around the sun.

Bernice lifted a pair of plastic chairs alongside the bed. He felt grateful—enormously grateful and touched—by her willingness to join the night vigil.

They sat there side by side watching the sleeping man; hearing the wet sound in the back of his throat; breathing in the antiseptic fumes of the hospital; seeing the blood dry to a flaky skin on the old man's face. David felt an impulse to reach out and hold Bernice's hand. It would feel so good to feel the pressure of another human's skin against his.

But that typical English reserve kept both his hands resting palm down on his knees.

The hands of the clock on the wall reached ten past three. And at that moment George Leppington opened his eyes—they were wide, staring glassily at the ceiling; his lips cracked open, too; his jaw strained as his mouth opened wide.

And that was when he began to speak.

The old man spoke quickly, clearly, in a breathy kind of voice: "Thrutheim, come I; Vlaskjalf, Sokkvabekk, Valholl, Thrymheim. Briethablik are my many houses. Here I wait for Ragnarök; here I will fight with Fenrir beneath the tree of the world. This is Grimnismal . . . this is where I wait for Ragnarök with the eight hundred." He breathed deeply; his eyes swiveled down and fixed on David. The eyes were bright and shining, as if the old man had seen something as fascinating as it was horrible. "David . . . I am Ishtar; I have broken down the gates of the underworld and set the dead upon the living; forgive me, I had no choice . . . no choice . . . I'm sorry, David. But time was running out."

"What's he saying?" Bernice asked. She sounded frightened by the old man's words. "What does he mean?"

"He's confused. He's taken quite a knock on the head—haven't you, uncle?" He lightly touched the old man's hand that lay motionless on the blanket. "Uncle George. Can you tell me what happened? Were you attacked?"

"Attacked?" He shook his head. "No. Dynamite."

"Dynamite?"

"I set charges on the iron fence in the cave. Thought I'd given myself enough distance. The explosion threw me against the wall."

"But what on earth were you using dynamite for?"

"I had to open up the caves." He looked at David, the eyes glassy. "I had to break down the gates of the underworld. I had to set the dead upon the living."

David glanced at Bernice. Her eyes were fixed on his uncle's face; she concentrated on every word he said with an intensity that was puzzling. The old man was confused. He'd been dreaming, surely.

"David." The old man gripped David's hand. "I should have brought you to Leppington earlier and explained everything. It's my fault I've left it too late."

"I'm here now, uncle, relax."

"No. There were things I should have told you. I started when you were a baby. I talked to you from the day you were born, because I knew you understood speech even then. I told you our history and our destiny. I was still telling you when your mother took you away from Leppington. She shouldn't have done that, but she was an outsider . . . she was frightened of the truth; she didn't want to be involved."

"Uncle, I'll find a doctor. We need to get you X-rayed as soon as possible."

"No." The grip tightened on David's hand. "Will an X-ray show you the words inside my head? David, listen to me: the time has come. Don't you remember?"

David shook his head. The old man was verbally coherent but his mind must have been scrambled by the blow.

"David. Remember when you were young? Four—five years old? I took you into the cave. I beat the bars with the iron rod. What did you see coming toward you out of the darkness? What did you see walk up to the bars?"

David shook his head. The old man's eyes had a strange glittery quality; yet the face was expressionless, as if the man spoke in a trance.

"David, tell me what you saw then?"

"I saw nothing, uncle."

"You did. There in the cave. What did you see?"

"Nothing. I saw nothing."

"Listen to me, David. Read the family history I gave you. The Leppingsvalt legend is all there."

"I'll read it when I get back to the hotel. Now relax, please, uncle."

"Ah . . . don't humor me. You can't avoid the truth now."

"Uncle."

"Your mother has built a brick wall in your mind. It divides you from your memories of what you saw here when you were a little boy. It's time to break down that wall. You've got to remember."

David turned to Bernice and said, "Will you find a nurse or Dr. Singh?"

"No. Listen to me. Listen. Open your mind." The grip tightened painfully on David's hand. "It's up to you now, David. You must take control of them. You must lead them. If you don't they will kill everyone. They will be a disease that destroys humanity."

"David," Bernice spoke in a small voice. "What's he saying?"

"I don't know. He's concussed."

"David. You are their king. Take control. If you don't everyone will die. Do you hear me. Everyone will die. This will be Ragnarök—the end of all . . ."

The old man's grip suddenly relaxed on his arm; the eyes that had glittered and stared so brilliantly closed.

"Oh, my God," Bernice said hushed. "Is he . . ."

"No." David felt the old man's pulse. "He's sleeping again. His pulse is strong."

"What did he mean about you being king—about taking control?"

David didn't have a chance to reply. The curtain rings rattled and swished behind them.

"Ah, Dr. Leppington." Dr. Singh beamed as he entered the cubicle. "How's our patient?"

"He's been conscious."

"Conscious?"

"He was speaking to us before you came in."

Dr. Singh gave a smile of disbelief. "Speaking? Really? I believed he was deeply unconscious. The concussion really appears quite severe. Are you certain he was speaking?" Again the quizzical smile as if he suspected a joke was being played on him.

"Yes," Bernice spoke earnestly. "He sounded completely lucid. He was telling David . . . Dr. Leppington . . ."

She trailed off.

"Telling him what?"

"My uncle was confused. I think he was mixing reality with a dream."

"Oh," Dr. Singh nodded as if he understood, but David noticed the way he rocked forward. That's an old trick you learn in casualty, rock forward onto the balls of your feet, to surreptitiously try and smell alcohol on someone's breath.

With a prickle of sudden anger David realized that Dr. Singh suspected that he and Bernice were either drunk or high, or both.

"Well, that's that, then," Dr. Singh said (patronizingly, David thought: he was obviously dismissing the notion of the injured old man talking just now as a delusion on their part). "I've just had the call to take your uncle up to X-ray. Then we can find him a more comfortable bed."

David looked down at the sleeping old man, with the red-stained dressing fastened to the side of his head. The prickling sensation still continued across his skin. This time it wasn't anger. He felt as if a sudden tug-of-war had started up inside him—the two opponents were memory and forgetfulness.

At that moment he realized there *was* a memory deeply hidden inside his head. Something he'd rather stayed forgotten. But it was tugging relentlessly toward the surface.

He stood back as the hotel porters came into the cubicle to wheel the bed to X-ray. His skin prickled as though insects were marching across his stomach and his back.

And at that moment fear—cold and blue and terrible—began its stealthy creep through his body.

3

Daylight had just begun to gray the sky when they left the hospital—Bernice still red-lipped and wrapped warm in the big sheepskin coat.

His uncle hadn't regained consciousness again and now lay in an observation ward. David had satisfied himself that the man's color was good, that his respiration and pulse were strong and even. Now there was nothing else they could do but wait for nature to run its course. With luck the man would simply wake up of his own accord in a few hours. He'd have a headache like the mother of all hangovers, but at least he'd be back on the road to recovery.

As they climbed into the black Volvo in the car park David said, "Before we go back to the hotel, do you mind if we check on my uncle's house? I want to make sure it's all safely locked up."

Bernice nodded, but there was clearly something troubling her. "Your uncle seemed to be warning you. What was all this about you taking control and if you didn't we'd all die?"

"Oh, it's a long story." David gave a tired smile. "A fanciful fairy story, at that."

Bernice smiled back, but her voice was serious. "Maybe I believe in fairy stories." She looked at him steadily. "Why don't you run this one past me?"

"OK," David nodded, wondering why she was so interested in what the old man had said. "I'll tell you what he told me."

As Bernice slipped the car into reverse and backed out of the parking space, David began to talk.

Chapter Twenty-five

1

The sky was a solid gray by the time they pulled up at Mill House. David had related the family legend to Bernice during the ten-minute drive. She'd listened intently. Almost as if what she was hearing had importance and relevance to her own life.

David didn't know why the story should interest her so much. Divine blood? Vampire armies? God-given quests to build new empires? David had written off the story as nothing more than an unusual curiosity.

After switching off the car's motor Bernice sat there for a moment, pale oval face serious as she digested the story. Not for the first time David felt as if he'd turned over two pages in the book and missed some vital element of the plot. Was he too dense to see it? Why did he have the feeling that all these events—Electra's confession that she heard noises in the cellar of the hotel; the disappearance of the couple from Room 101; his uncle's injury—all added up to form a coherent picture? Only for some reason he didn't see what that picture was. Or he was seeing it from the wrong angle.

The wind blew, rocking the car slightly. The trees surrounding his uncle's house shook like great shaggy beast-shapes. The monsters are waking up, he told himself. *The monsters are waking up.*

What monsters?

The trees. Because that's what they looked like. Great woody monsters, waking from a night's sleep, shaking the dew from their skeletal limbs.

231

No, he thought, I sense something else waking.

Monsters are waking.

They are coming to life.

He shook himself out of the cold sensation that had been settling on him ever since he had heard his uncle speak in the hospital.

"It's nearly morning," he said, deliberately breaking a silence that was becoming almost palpable. "Tired?"

Bernice gave a little smile and shook her head. "Too much excitement."

He opened the car door; cool air gusted in. "This shouldn't take long. Coming?"

"Just try and stop me," she said obliquely.

They entered the garden through the gate set in the fortress-like walls. The wind sighed through the branches of the trees, shaking off big drops of water. Bernice pulled up the collar of the sheepskin coat.

David had been given the house keys (they'd been collected by the police, then handed into hospital reception). He checked the doors of the house. They were all soundly locked.

"Picturesque." Bernice spoke in a small voice, as if the surroundings made her feel tiny. "Look, there's even a stream flowing through the garden."

"The source of the Lepping, so I'm told," David said. "Wait here, I'll just lock the workshop door."

The door had been left open and swung in the wind.

"Nothing been tampered with?" Bernice said, arms tightly folded as if she was feeling the cold.

"I don't think so, but I'd best check. The last thing my uncle needs is to come back and find the place ransacked by burglars."

"Does he live up here all alone?"

David nodded. "His wife died about fifteen years ago."

"Nothing seems to have been touched." David looked quickly around the workshop. The bottle of whiskey was still on the shelf; the fire in the forge was now out but he could feel the heat still radiating from the stones. The sword his uncle had been making lay across the anvil.

"Very Arthurian, eh?" he said, nodding at the sword. "My uncle was making a replica of the magical family sword."

"Oh, the one found in the fish?"

"The very one." David tried to sound light-hearted about it, but the atmosphere of the whole place seemed pregnant. As if something colossal was waiting to happen. *The monsters are waking . . .*

"I'll lock up," he said and they both stepped back outside through the heavy door. He locked it.

"So why was your uncle using dynamite?"

"He was using it to destroy steel bars that had closed off a cave entrance in the hillside across there."

"But what on earth for?"

He stopped and looked at Bernice. She looked back at him, her hair blown across her face in the wind; her eyes large, serious.

"Like the man said," David told her. "To set the dead upon the living. He's unleashed the vampire army on us all."

"You believe that?"

David laughed, yet he felt a touch of sadness too. "Of course not. The poor old boy's probably been out here on this windy hillside far too long. The old Leppington fairy stories have been preying on his mind." Suddenly he shot a surprised look at her. "Why, do you?"

As she opened her mouth to answer a loud bang echoed across the back yard. It came from the building that capped the opening to the cave. David saw that the heavy doors were blowing backward and forward in the breeze; every so often one would slam back into the timber frame.

He sighed. "I should think my dear old unc has made a mess of the cave. Dynamite? Good grief, I imagine the police will be asking him a few questions about that one." He walked toward the stone building with the twin timber doors flapping to and fro in the breeze.

"Careful," Bernice said. "If there's been an explosion the cave might not be safe."

"Don't worry." He smiled. "Wild horses wouldn't drag me inside. I'd best lock the doors, though, in case any kids take it into their heads to go exploring."

He held one door shut, then slid the bolt down into its drilled hole in the floor to hold it. Then he grabbed the other door, ready to lock it.

He paused for a moment, looking into the dark throat of the

cave that lay beyond the entrance. On the floor were drops of blood. He imagined his uncle dynamiting the steel fence that sealed the cave: the force throwing him back against the wall, then him staggering groggily from the cave to the house where he managed to telephone the emergency services, blood streaming down his face.

The maw of the tunnel drew his eyes back. He found himself staring into utter darkness. A darkness that seemed more than just absence of light. That darkness seemed a palpable thing veined with purple. That darkness had presence; it had form.

Bernice stared too, he noticed. As if there was something hypnotic about that dark roadway into the heart of the hill. And who knew what lay beyond? The caverns. The lake of the legend; complete with a great silver-sided fish that swam around and around the underground lake in sluggish circles.

There was a quality so compelling about it. You just wanted to walk forward; to go into the cave; to allow that velvet dark to swallow you.

Bernice said in a low voice, barely more than a whisper. "David. Your uncle asked you to remember what you saw in the cave."

David nodded, mute.

"He said it was important. That when you were little he'd take you into the cave and strike the bars of the fence with an iron rod."

"Yes."

"Why did he do that?"

"I don't know."

"You might rattle the bars of a cage to attract the attention of an animal locked inside, mightn't you?"

"Yes." David's voice was a whisper. His muscles had locked up tight. Suddenly the world seemed distant; Bernice's voice could have come from the bottom of a deep, deep pit.

All his attention was fixed on the cave running away into the hillside like an artery worming deep inside a man's chest to connect with his beating heart.

"Do you remember what you saw as a child, David?"

He shook his head slowly, feeling that the world had turned dreamlike.

"You saw something in the cave, didn't you?"

"No."

"You stood in there with your uncle. He rattled the bars of the cage—clang, clang, clang—then what did you see?"

Suddenly he gripped the door hard, his teeth clicking as his jaw muscles clenched. There was a sense of something rushing inside his head. A wall had come down; now whatever lay behind it came gushing through.

"David. What did you see?"

"I saw *them*. . . ." He turned to Bernice. Inside he felt cold, very cold. "I saw *them* . . . they were coming out of the dark."

"*Them*, David? What are they?"

"People." His throat muscles had clenched as his body had made a last-ditch attempt to prevent the memories coming out. He shivered convulsively. "In the cave. There were people. Dozens of people. I remember the faces . . . they were white. White as a piece of bone." He locked his eyes onto Bernice—wide, frightened eyes. "And they were monsters."

2

Leppington, the town, made the transition from night to day. Already the newsagent's was open. Paper boys pedalled through town, their bags heavy with Sunday newspapers that were fat with supplements their readers would never get through.

The vast slaughterhouse glowered over the town, its red-brick flanks still shining after the storm. Inside, the huge killing rooms were silent. Floors were clean, the air still and heavy with disinfectant.

The River Lepping, swollen with rain, gushed noisily over boulders, the waters turning white with froth.

Most houses still wore their curtains closed as people slept late.

Briefly, in the Moberry household on the council estate at the edge of town, Dianne Moberry's father woke. He stared at the shadowed ceiling for a moment, listening to the breeze gusting up the valley. Dianne hadn't come home last night. Another boyfriend, he supposed. She was probably away on another of her frolics to Whitby or Robin Hood's Bay or wherever. The proper parental attitude would be one of disapproval, he thought.

Primly, most mothers and fathers would tell a gallivanting daughter of twenty-something to settle down; get married; have babies. But life in Leppington was shackled to monotony. Most newly-weds lived on this estate on social security. He watched teenage mothers pushing their babies in buggies. Those mothers looked as if they had had the vitality sucked right out of them; already they wore the tired expression of put-upon housewives who faced another day of mechanically going though their chores—washing, Hoovering, ironing, nappy changing, you name it. These people were bloodless; if he let his imagination freewheel away from him he could picture them as the modern living dead. They had bugger-all to look forward to.

At least Dianne's life was different. Wherever she was, who-ever she was with, he prayed she was having fun.

Then he turned over and went back to sleep.

3

The drive back to the hotel was a mixture of silences and quick-fire bursts of conversation. The world, to David Leppington, still seemed dreamlike, even in this hard, iron-gray light of dawn.

Bernice Mochardi spoke quickly, like a detective on the very brink of solving some particularly baffling murder mystery. "Do you remember anything else?"

"No . . . nothing."

"You said you remember seeing people in the cave when you were a little boy?"

"Yes."

"As if they were caged in there? Prisoners?"

"I suppose so." The dreamlike sensation wouldn't quit. David bit his lip. He felt so . . . so bizarre . . . there was no other de-scription for it.

Bernice indicated a right turn and swung the car onto Main Street. "You said you thought they were monsters."

"Monsters? Yes, well, that was the six-year-old me's inter-pretation of what I saw."

"But what are these monsters? Where did they come from?"

"Bernice, look. I don't know if what I saw all those years ago was real."

"What do you mean?"

"I might have imagined it all—or I might be remembering a childhood nightmare."

"David. You had a repressed memory. Now you've released it. I've read books where people—"

"Where people under hypnosis recall being abducted by UFOs or remember being sexually abused by their Scoutmaster." He smiled—at least he tried to: this smile felt a watery effort. "Yes, we covered repressed memory at university."

"So you had a repressed memory about the people you saw caged up down there. Now it's been released. You remember your uncle calling them by banging on the bars?"

"Not necessarily."

"But you remember it in so much detail, the way your uncle struck the bars, what they looked like, even the clothes you were wearing. You're not going to tell me that was just some old nightmare you had when you were six years old, are you?"

He sighed, and looked at her as she drove. Her face had a brittle quality. As if she was composing her expression through will-power alone. And why was she so keen to believe in the underground-people story so strongly? It was almost as if she were clutching at it like the proverbial drowning man clutching at straws scattered on the water. He realized all of a sudden this repressed memory of his was important somehow—to her at least. It was something she was clutching at to stop her drowning.

As she turned the car into the Station Hotel car park he said gently, "Bernice, there's something called false-memory syndrome. There's evidence to suggest that a lot of these so-called repressed memories that have been recovered under hypnosis or through therapy are false."

"But you recalled everything in such detail, didn't you?"

"That's all part and parcel of it. But the truth of the matter is, Bernice, some of these memories are just phantoms; they're products of imagination. In the light of false-memory syndrome some notorious child abuse cases are going to have to be overturned."

Bernice parked the car. One look at her set expression told him she refused to doubt what he had remembered—*apparently* remembered, he corrected himself, up there at the mouth of the cave.

"Well," he said, deliberately striving to sound down-to-earth. "I think we've earned a good day's sleep after all that excitement."

She nodded, her face still tight.

He smiled. "I'll see if I can find Electra and tell her what happened; she's probably wondering what's happened to us."

"David?"

"Yes."

"That book you mentioned—the family history. May I borrow it?"

"Yes. Of course."

"Now?"

"Sure." He smiled. "I'll push it under your room door. It is rather a slim volume."

She gave no answering smile. Her face was earnest. As if she'd been given a tough problem to crack. And as though lives depended on her coming up with the right answer.

Hell, he thought as he climbed out of the car. What is it with this town? It's as if eccentricity has suddenly become infectious; people were deadly serious about some old piece of family folk-lore.

In the gray light of day the night's events, and that torrent of memory—false memory, he corrected himself—seemed nothing more than a bizarre dream.

That's it, he reasoned to himself. False-memory syndrome; that was the neat, all-encompassing explanation. Tie it all up in the sensible ribbons of modern-day science with a neat double bow on top: False-memory syndrome. Pure imagination. Some remembered childhood nightmare. Nothing more.

Nevertheless, as he followed Bernice across the courtyard to enter the hotel by the back door, the words continued to circle around in his brain: *the monsters are waking up.*

4

Within ten minutes David had handed the book, *The Leppington Family: Fact and Legend*, to Bernice at her door, then he'd retired to bed. The curtains were thick and admitted little daylight. Hell, it was a long time since he'd stopped up all night. He still felt . . . weird: that was the only word for it.

The monsters are waking up . . .

Electra had left a note on the kitchen table, saying not to worry about the couple in Room 101. But David doubted somehow they'd turned up sheepishly in reception: this was more a sweeping-everything-under-the-carpet kind of operation. The PS at the foot of the note added that Electra had gone to bed.

And why is Bernice so interested in my family history? he asked himself. At one point he was reluctant to hand the book over—the intensity of her manner suggested she was in the early throes of developing one humdinger of a fixation about the thing.

He pulled the bedclothes higher. Perhaps after a few hours' sleep the peculiar, no, he corrected, the downright bizarre night he'd just experienced wouldn't seem so strange. He yawned. The time on his bedside travel clock read 7:17 A.M.

By 7:18 he'd entered a deep, dreamless sleep.

5

7:19 A.M. In her suite of rooms on the first floor Electra Charnwood slept in her bed alone. Naked, she lay face down. In the throes and turns of the dream the duvet had slid partly off, revealing a breathtakingly long back. Her blue-black hair formed a dark wash across her pillow.

The mantelpiece clock that had been a wedding present for her mother and father ticked resolutely on in the sitting room. If she had known that subsidence in the town cemetery had split open her mother's coffin and that baby rabbits now scampered across the skull and through the still-moist ribcage she would have given a little laugh; that was all. Electra Charnwood knew that real life was shot through with threads of the macabre. In the midst of life we are in death, she'd tell herself a half-dozen times a day. She found death and all its trappings fascinating. The Egyptian mummy room of the British Museum was one of her favorite places in all the world. There she could stand and stare in a dreamy fascination at the three-thousand-year-old dead: the women bound in linen with their jewelry, and the bones of their still-born children between their knees.

Now she dreamed of a dark figure with great leathery wings that erupted from a grave in the town cemetery. She couldn't tell whether it was male or female. Only that its face was beautiful and its skin was as smooth as PVC.

Now, in her dream, it slipped smoothly as a snake through her bedroom window and crept onto the bed beside her, wrapping those great bat-like wings around her body, binding her so tightly she couldn't move. The eyes were as bright as light bulbs.

From the beautiful face that straddled the borderline between the feminine and the masculine it breathed silkily into her ear: "I love you, I love you, I love you . . ."

6

7:20 A.M. Bernice Mochardi was in bed. But she did not sleep.

She held the book that David had lent her so tightly that every so often she had to make a conscious effort to lay it down and flex her aching fingers. She felt as if she was close to making an important discovery.

For weeks now she'd obsessively watched the videotape she'd found in the Dead Box downstairs. She thought and she'd dreamed about Mike Stroud, the blond-haired man in the video. It had preyed so intensively on her mind that she'd been frightened that she was going mad. Now all these events—the video, imagining that someone stalked outside on the landing at night, what had happened to the couple in Room 101; everything— were like fragments of a jigsaw that were swirling like fury in front of her. She knew they'd all fit together into a single coherent picture if only she could find more clues. She had to solve this puzzle. For the sake of her sanity. Now she was determined to work on it until she had an answer.

And perhaps that answer lay in these pages.

As the gray light brightened she settled down to read the book.

Chapter Twenty-six

1

By four o'clock on the Sunday afternoon David was sitting in the kitchen of the Station Hotel. He'd slept for a good seven hours after going to bed that morning. Already he was experiencing a mild disorientation from a disturbed sleep pattern. Nevertheless, he'd visited his uncle at the hospital (this time taking a taxi and going alone). There was no change. His uncle lay in the side ward, deeply asleep, the dried blood now washed from his face; all the doctor could tell him was that the X-ray had revealed nothing; that the old man's vital signs were within tolerable limits (that is, they didn't believe he would die on them just yet) and that they'd continue to observe him (that was, a nurse would, every now and again, put her head around the side-ward door and look in on him to make sure he wasn't awake and asking for his breakfast).

For the last thirty minutes David had sat in the kitchen (which he now realized was the nerve center of the hotel). Electra stood at the cooker, ladling stew into bowls. Bernice Mochardi sat across the other side of the big well-scrubbed table. David noticed how young and vulnerable she looked now that she'd removed the Goth make-up and changed into a plain gray sweatshirt and black jeans.

Jack Black was working out back, moving in that mechanical way of his as he manhandled empty beer kegs across the yard to the store.

Already they'd had time to swap their stories about the events of Saturday night. Electra was sympathetic about his uncle's accident—and she was nothing less than goggle-eyed when she heard how it had happened from a dynamite blast. Electra's recollections of Saturday night were fairly scanty. In a nutshell she'd seen nothing, heard nothing. Now she was playing the mother role with the aplomb of an experienced actress.

"Here, you must eat. Both of you," Electra said firmly as she set two steaming bowls in front of them. "It's a beef-in-ale stew. A good hearty recipe of my own; it'll put new life in you. I made it all myself, chopped up the ingredients. And don't look at me like that, Bernice. I haven't put the occupants of Room 101 in the pot." She smiled as she laid a soup spoon by each bowl. "I'm roasting them on a spit out back tonight."

"With an apple in their mouths?" David added; then instantly regretted the flip remark.

"Naturally. And with a sprig of rosemary up the bum."

"I don't think that's funny," Bernice said, her face looking tight. "If you'd seen the mess that girl was in you wouldn't joke, Electra."

"Bernice, I'm—"

"She was bleeding, bruised. Raped. I really thought she'd been raped."

Electra sighed. "Point taken. Sorry. I was just trying to lighten the mood a little. Any bread to go with that, Dr. Leppington?"

"Please."

She's striving to be light-hearted, David thought, looking up at her as he spooned some of the rich stew into his mouth. Something, however, was still preying on her mind.

"So, David," Electra said as she sat down at the table with a cup of coffee, "what's it like to have divine blood coursing in your veins?"

He smiled. "Oh, Bernice has been telling you about the Leppingtons' colorful family history?"

"She has, but we heard the stories from our grannies here in Leppington."

"Stories to be told on a dark and stormy night, eh?"

"Something like that. Stories about vampire armies to frighten little children before bedtime. Charming. But the Leppingtons' claim to divine ancestry? You have to admit it's something to boast about it, isn't it?"

David's smile broadened. "I did plan to add it to my CV."

"I approve." Electra flashed a vivid smile back. "Anything to improve one's career prospects must be good, I say." She sipped her coffee. "Unfortunately we Charnwoods can't boast anything so grand as having a Norse god for an ancestor. The only thing handed down genetically in our family are our petite ears." She flicked back her blue-black hair to reveal a small ear, from which dangled a jet drop earring. "Cute, eh?"

"Well, to be honest." David smiled. "My mother said the only thing that ran in our family were noses." He touched his own prominent nose.

"And the only thing to run in our family were feet," Bernice said, a smile at last warming the serious expression on her face. "Which has to be the most feeble joke ever."

David laughed, Electra too. The laughter was loud and David suspected those feeble jokes were providing an outlet for the emotional tension that had been building over the last few hours. Laughter—friendly laughter, not mocking laughter—is also a way of bonding a group of people together. But as they sat around that table David was once more struck by the sensation that he'd met these people before.

When he stopped laughing he looked at the two women, going from one face to another. They were looking back at him, too, and he sensed a growing empathy: as if some subliminal communication flashed from one to another, some spark of understanding as if they shared the same secret.

And what could that secret be? Perhaps, deep down, all three of them were thinking the same thing: *The monsters are waking up.*

2

And it was at that moment that, by some kind of instinctual and unspoken agreement, the three of them decided the time was ripe to bring out into the open the secret that weighed on their hearts like a rock.

For a few moments they made small talk. The sun broke through the heavy cloud that lay like a gray rug above the town; shafts of sunlight fell onto the hillsides, then moved toward Leppington, playing on the rooftops like searchlights being shone down from the sky.

As they talked Jack Black—all tattoos and bad attitude— walked into the kitchen, took milk from the refrigerator and sat

243

on a stool by the worktop, drinking straight from the carton.

And now we are four, thought David. The team is complete. The notion surprised him. However, it seemed oddly *right*. And again the impression came strongly that the four of them had interacted in the dim and distant past.

Electra took Black's arrival as a cue to change the topic of conversation.

"Bernice was telling me that when you were up at your uncle's you experienced some kind of flashback."

"Oh, *that*," he said, trying to make it sound as if it wasn't of the slightest importance. He looked at Bernice who leaned forward clasping her hands together on the table as if in prayer. Her eyes were troubled.

Electra continued in low, even tones. "That you remembered what you saw in the cave when you were a child?"

"*Thought* I remembered," David corrected. "Yes, I imagined I saw people in the darkness beyond the railings of the fence."

"The fence that your uncle dynamited last night?"

"Which I'm sure will get him into trouble with the police."

"The fence has been breached?"

"I don't know. I didn't check."

"But if it has, then the people you once saw in the cave are free to come out."

"Come out?" He shook his head, bemused. "Electra. I was no more than six years old at the time. I probably imagined seeing those . . . people, whatever they were."

"You described them as monsters," Bernice said quietly. "Didn't you?"

"Yes, monsters. So, I was remembering some old nightmare."

"And now your uncle has dynamited the gate and let them out." Bernice pinched her bottom lip between finger and thumb as if allowing the full weight of the truth to sink in. After a moment she added, "George Leppington said . . . let me get this right . . . he said, 'I am like Ishtar. I have broken down the doors of the underworld and set the dead upon the living.' "

Electra nodded, eyes narrowing as she considered what Bernice was saying.

David felt increasingly bemused; and underlying the bemusement a sense that the world—the reality he knew—had assumed that dreamlike quality again. "Now wait a minute," he said, still smiling, but he felt a tension creeping into his stomach. "Who the heck is Ishtar?"

Without hesitating, Electra said, "The Ishtar-Tammuz myth dates from the Akkadian civilization that flourished in the Middle East around four thousand years ago. Ishtar was a goddess who fell out with her fellow gods and goddesses and threatened to break down the gates of the underworld and, therefore, set the dead upon the living with the intention of wiping out humankind. Your uncle employed the story as an apt metaphor for his actions."

"Wait . . . wait . . ." David rested his fingers against his suddenly aching temples. "Have I missed something here? Or have I gone mad and I'm imagining all this?"

"I can pinch you if you like," Electra said crisply. "And I've got a jolly hard pinch, believe me."

He looked at Electra. She was no longer joking. She gazed back at him levelly, her expression serious.

"Wait a minute." He looked from Electra to Bernice. "Are you telling me you believe all this? You believe the fairy stories about the Leppingtons having divine blood, and . . . and—for crying out loud—that there's a vampire army lurking somewhere in a cave?"

Electra's gaze did not flinch. "Don't you, Dr. Leppington?"

He gave a laugh; to his ears a strange barking sound in the tiled kitchen. He shook his head. "You can't be serious. Tell me this is some kind of wind-up!"

Gravely, Electra said, "But you've *seen* these creatures, haven't you, David?"

David glanced at Black, hoping at least to hear mocking laughter from the tattooed man. Black's face was like stone. All he did was wipe the milk mustache from his thick lips and light a cigarette.

David took a deep breath. "Like I told Bernice, this is obviously a case of false-memory syndrome. Yes, I agree, I can close my eyes now and picture my uncle beating a steel peg against the bars—like you'd rattle the bars of a cage to attract an animal—then I remember looking into the gloom beyond the bars."

"And?"

"Yes, I remember—*appear* to remember, I should say—seeing dozens of people—men and women—sort of shambling forward. Their faces were white—as white as that plastic bowl across there. Eyebrows seemed heavy and as black as the bristles on a paint brush; as for their eyes, they had a bruised quality to them: the skin was dark, very dark, around their eyes. This made the whites stand out—so much so that they actually seemed to shine, as if they were lit from inside."

Electra sipped her coffee. "That's a very detailed description of what you're now claiming is a dream or imagination."

"Just a facet of false-memory syndrome. Many people claim they've been abducted by space aliens. Psychologists now realize these so-called abductees genuinely believe they have been whisked off to a spaceship. And these so-called abductees are just as detailed in their descriptions—yes, the aliens had big, dark almond-shaped eyes, they wore silver rings in their ears, they had five fingers but no fingernails, they smelled of onions. Yes, the details are there, but it's sheer imagination; they never were abducted by aliens—which shows the mind is a wonderful thing, doesn't it?"

Electra spoke calmly. "What else do you remember?"

"That the clothes they wore were ragged. Where the fabric was ripped their bare skin seemed to gleam through a bluish white that was almost luminous in the lamplight. Their teeth seemed too big for their mouths, which resulted in them being unable to properly close their jaws. Oh . . . and there was one other thing." David held up a finger. "I think this might be significant."

Both Bernice and Electra leaned forward, listening intently.

"They were led by a tall guy." David paused thinking hard. "Jet-black hair, slicked back. He was wearing a long black cape and went by the name of Count Dracula."

David heard a grunt and the crash of the stool being kicked back. "He's taking the piss," Black grunted furiously. "If he can take the piss I can take the fucking smile off his face."

David stood up, his skin turning cold as the blood drained from it. Shit, he's going to attack me, he thought, looking around for a weapon. Although he knew as sure as jiggery you'd need a sawn-off shotgun to stand any chance of stopping that monster.

"Jack." Electra spoke calmly, yet with complete authority. "Sit down."

246

"He can't bollocks us around like that. He knows fucking nothing."

"No. He knows everything," she said calmly. "Only, at the moment, Dr. Leppington is in denial. His rational side won't allow him to believe."

"I'll knock some bollocksing belief into him."

"No, you won't, Jack. We can convince him, can't we, Bernice?"

Black sat down, his face sour.

"Jack. There's some cigarettes in the drawer. No, the one to your left. Now . . ." She turned to look at David. "Please, will you sit down?"

David felt his face set in a grim expression. "I think it's time I checked out."

"Please sit down, David."

"I'm checking out. Or are you and your friend," he stabbed a look at Black, "going to stop me?"

"No."

"Will you prepare my bill, then? I'm going upstairs to pack."

"David, please."

He turned to look at Bernice as she spoke, still sitting at the table, her fingers knitted together in anguish.

"David," Bernice said in a voice that was desperately close to pleading. "Please sit down and listen to what we have to tell you. I . . . I really need you to hear this." She looked up at him, her eyes huge and pleading. "I'm frightened. And I think you're the only person who can help."

3

David sighed deeply, then sat down. "OK. Say what you have to say. Then I'm going upstairs to pack."

Electra, still sitting at the table, moved the bowls to one side. A spoon fell from the bowl and clattered onto the floor with a high ringing sound. "Even in the midst of high drama we're confronted with the mundane," she said obliquely and, without moving the chair, bent to pick up the spoon. "God uses the mundane to remind us of our lowly position on Earth."

David said dryly, "OK. Get on with what you want to tell

me. There's a train to Whitby in an hour. I'll be on it."

Electra assented with a nod. Bernice's eyes were large and scared; the expression childlike. David instantly felt protective toward her, regretting that Electra had somehow trapped her in this collective madness. Divine blood. Vampire armies. The destruction of the human race. OK, Mulder and Scully. Over to you. Fangs for the memory and all that. David adopted the expression of the doctor patiently listening to a hypochondriac's list of imagined ailments.

The time was a little after four-thirty. Jack Black pulled deeply on a cigarette, shrouding one end of the kitchen in tobacco smoke. The late-afternoon sun pierced it with a ray of light that reflected dazzlingly from the stainless-steel work surfaces.

"David," Electra said in a quietly matter-of-fact voice. "In a few minutes I'm going to show you some . . ." She tilted her head a little. "Something in the basement."

He gave a small, neutral nod.

Electra continued, "Yesterday, David, I told you how my mother, God bless her, complained of hearing noises in the basement. That she was terrified of the place. And that one day she was found dead in the basement."

Again David gave the neutral "Go on, Doctor's listening" kind of nod.

"Officially the cause of death was a heart attack."

"But you disputed that?"

"The only person I told was myself. But I knew my mother died of fright."

David nodded. "And you mentioned that you hear noises from the basement?"

"Yes, I do," Electra agreed. "You can sometimes hear them up as far as the second floor. A frantic hammering like somebody pounding on a door to be let in."

David said, "You've checked that it's not kids playing a prank?"

"Believe me, these aren't children, David. The noises I hear are the same ones my mother heard, the same ones that frightened her to death."

"But does that prove the story about vampire armies waiting

underground for the call to march out and . . . and do God knows what?"

"No. But you realize what I'm doing." She pushed back a strand of the blue-black hair that had fallen across her eyes. "This afternoon I'm laying my cards one by one on the table. That is to say I'm giving you sufficient evidence to reach your own conclusions."

David spoke gently. "You've heard noises in the basement. I believe you, Electra, but what does it prove?"

"Bear with me, David. Bernice. What happens to you?"

Bernice hugged herself, looking cold. "I don't sleep very well at night. More than anything I feel with a complete, utter conviction that the building—that the whole town is infected with something. There's a sense that an evil force is just waiting to break out."

"Bernice. Can you tell David about the videotape you found?"

"I found it in a suitcase in the Dead Box. That's basically the room where Electra stores lost property or, more often, just simply abandoned property."

David felt himself nod again. "You mentioned it before."

"Well . . . in there I found a videotape, you know, one of those small camcorder tapes? On the tape is the rough edit of a travelogue an American was making. I only know that his name is, or was, Mike Stroud. Well, to cut a long story short, he was staying in a room in this hotel. My room, I think?" She looked to Electra for confirmation. She gave a small, sober nod. "He was convinced, as I am, that at night something paced outside his door—up and down the corridor all night. He could feel that conviction working through his blood like it was a virus or something. I feel it, too." Bernice clenched her fists earnestly as she spoke. "I took to barricading my door with the chest of drawers. I sensed that thing outside my door—whatever it was— was reaching into my brain, calling me out into the corridor.

"Anyway," she said after a deep breath. "This American, Mike, decided to catch this . . . this nightstalker on video. One night he set the camcorder to record what happened when he opened the door."

"What happened?"

"He did exactly that. He opened the door, then . . ." She put her hand to her mouth. "Something grabbed him, dragged him out into the corridor." She swallowed. "David, I've got the tape upstairs. I can get it if you want."

"Maybe later, Bernice." He rubbed his face and sighed. "Electra, do *you* know anything about this Mike . . . Mike?" He looked to Bernice to supply the surname that had slipped his throbbing head.

"Stroud."

"Mike Stroud."

Electra gave an emphatic Gallic shrug. "He checked in for three nights. Left after two without paying the bill. All I know, he was American, that he left a few anonymous belongings which I stored in the Dead Box. That was two years ago."

"You're saying he disappeared off the face of the planet and no one ever asked about him or inquired after him?"

"No."

"No friends or family or lovers?"

"Not a soul."

Again David sighed. The throbbing in his head grew worse. "Has anyone seen anything . . . untoward . . . well, to call a spade a spade, has anyone seen a monster?"

All three looked steadily back at him.

"Well, *has* anyone?" David pressed.

"Only one," said Electra slowly. She pointed at David. "You're the only one."

He shook his head, a smile of disbelief breaking out on his face. "Imagined? Dreamed? You name it."

"And there's what happened last night," Electra said. "The couple from Room 101. What happened to them?"

David sipped his coffee. "Electra. You yourself said they might have just got carried away with some sex game. Why change your tune?"

"Because I realized last night I'd been denying the truth for far too long. Belatedly, I know it's time I came clean and told people what's happening."

"And what *is* happening?"

"Guests have been disappearing from the hotel for years. For a hundred years we—the Charnwoods, that is—have been brushing it all under the carpet. We've tut-tutted, we've pretended it was just guests who skipped paying their bills. We stored away their belongings into the room under the stairs.

Then we oh-so-conveniently forgot all about them."

"Didn't the police become involved?"

"Occasionally, although not as much as you'd think. If an adult goes missing and there's not much to suggest foul play they don't worry about it overmuch. If you don't believe me, go into a police station and report someone missing."

"Well, what happened to the couple last night?"

"Something—and I use the word accurately: not some*one*—*something* came into the hotel and attacked them." Electra looked him in the eye. "Something wanted their blood: literally."

"Oh, come on now," David protested. "You can't be serious?"

"Believe me, I *am* serious."

"But who—or what—wanted their blood?"

"Those things you saw in the cave all those years ago."

"Vampires?"

"Yes," Electra gave that sober nod. "Yes. For want of a better word: vampires."

"But really," David held out his hands, pleading for common sense. "Vampires?"

"Vampires. Or if you prefer—vampire-*like*. That is, creatures that have certain qualities usually attributed to the vampires of folklore. Granted, these creatures here in Leppington do not originate from Transylvania. I doubt if they are troubled by garlic or by crucifixes. But, as I said, they are vampire-like. They move by night. They don't grow old like we do, nor do they die. And they *do* feed on blood."

David rubbed his temples while shaking his head. He said, "And these vampiric creatures took the couple from Room 101 last night to drink their blood?"

"Not exactly, I think whatever beings came into the hotel were merely procurers. They took the couple to the other ones that live—for want of a better word—underground."

"Like they were rounding up cattle for a farmer?"

"If you like."

"Electra." David shook his head. Christ, this was weird . . . so weird . . .

"And now your uncle has used dynamite to destroy the gate that has kept them caged for so long . . ." She gave a slow shrug and left the sentence unfinished.

251

"So you see, David," Bernice said in a frightened voice. "You've got to help us."

"Why me?"

"It's obvious. You're the only one who can help," Bernice said. "You are the last Leppington."

"Wrong."

"Your uncle is in hospital, and it was he who set them free."

"There's my father."

"And where is he?"

"On a sailing holiday in Greece."

"I think he's pretty much washed his hands of the whole town, don't you?"

David found himself shivering from head to toe. The rational side of his brain—that Johnny-come-lately frontal lobe, evolved over the last thirty thousand years—that was the seat of rationality and learning and logic and modern-day conscious thought was busily saying: David, don't listen to this superstitious tosh. They're barking mad, all three of them. They actually believe a ridiculous folk tale. Pack your bags. Leave town.

But the old part of his brain, tucked deep inside his head, was braying out a different message. It spoke from his heart and his guts: *Every word is true, David. You can sense the town is pregnant with evil. You saw those shambling white-faced things in the cave all those years ago. They're real and you know it.*

Electra looked at him, those dark eyes reading his eyes. She knew she was winning.

"Jack," she said calmly. "Tell Dr. David Leppington here what really happened last night."

"Everything?"

"Everything," she agreed, "then we'll take him down into the basement."

David listened to what he was told next. There was no melodrama: it was all matter-of-fact. Black might as well have been a TV weatherman describing a cold front moving down from the north or announcing squally showers over the hills. Jack Black was telling it how it was.

Black pulled on the cigarette, veiling his scarred and tattooed face with smoke.

"Last night," he told David, "I knew something was wrong. I had this feeling, here, right in the pit of my gut. Something told me I had to stay up on the top floor."

"He was standing guard," Electra explained. "Outside your doors. He probably saved your lives."

"You said something told you," David asked. "What, exactly?"

"Just something right inside here." Black twisted his finger against his temple like his finger was a screwdriver.

"Oh, there's more to Mr. Black than meets the eye," Electra told David. "He has some very recondite talents."

David raised a questioning eyebrow.

"We'll go into those later. OK, Jack, continue."

"You lot came out and started banging on about me going downstairs, remember?"

David gave a nod.

"You thought I was going to rob your rooms or some bollocks like that, didn't you? Anyway. That bird from downstairs charged out of the lift. You took her into the room to clean her up and put her in a dressing gown and stuff. Then we got ready to go downstairs, right?"

"Right," David agreed.

"Only when me and her," he nodded at Bernice, "got in the lift someone pressed the lift call button from the basement." He spoke a little faster now. "I had the woman under my arm 'cos she'd flaked out on us. Bernice was stood behind me in the lift. Anyway, it went right down into the basement. The lift doors opened."

"And?"

"And it was dark. No lights on down there. Black as coal it was. Then out of the darkness I saw some figures coming at us. And it was us that they wanted. I knew that as sure as shit sticks to your fingers."

"What did they look like?"

"Weird. Fucking weird."

"What happened then?"

"This Hill woman . . ." he pantomimed looking at an unconscious woman in his arms, "I chucked her out at them. I thought better her than us."

David looked at Bernice. Her eyes glittered, her lips were pressed tight together.

He looked back at Black. "You mean to say you threw her to them? So while they were busy with her it would give you time to get away?"

Black nodded as if it was the most natural thing in the world. "Aye. That's right. The bollocking lift door took ages to close. I figured that if I lobbed her out and they got busy on her it would give the lift door time to close, then we'd be on our way back upstairs." He spoke with more than a hint of pride, as if it had been a job well done.

"Dear God," David breathed. "Did you see any of this, Bernice?"

She shook her head. "He held me to the wall—with my face to the wall . . ." She held a trembling hand up in front of her face. "I couldn't see anything. But . . . but I know he's telling the truth now."

"You've been talking to Electra this afternoon?"

"Yes."

David rubbed his face. It felt oddly stiff, as if the muscles had become rigid with shock beneath the skin. He began to speak; in fact he tried three times, but the words wouldn't come out. He sighed, shaking his head. "Crazy . . . crazy . . ." was all he could manage.

Electra stood up. "Now, before it gets dark, I think it's time we showed David what we have downstairs in the basement. This way, please." She paused. "Jack. Bernice. I think we all should see this."

David, in a kind of queasy daze, followed Electra from the kitchen, across the deserted lobby to the basement door.

Chapter Twenty-seven

1

David followed Electra down the stairs into the basement. He was followed by Bernice, then by Black, who looked even uglier in the naked light of the electric bulbs hanging from the barrel ceilings. The light shone through the stubble on his scalp and gleamed on his great bony skull, highlighting scars on his head that looked like the contour lines on an OS map.

Electra led them along the barrel vault of the basement, talking in a low voice as if, bizarrely, this was some conducted tour of cruddy North of England hotel basements. "This is where we keep the beer for the bars upstairs. See the pumps and the pipes running up there. Apart from that, what you see is largely junk. Careful you don't trip over the step." She took a torch from a shelf and shone it ahead of her to where the walls narrowed as they walked into a vault that was basically wedge-shaped.

Saltpetre clung like white feathers onto raw brick. The air was cold, so cold that David saw his breath turn vaporous. He shivered, then turned to look back at Bernice. He liked her. He didn't like to see her as frightened as this. Why had Electra filled her head with this horror story?

"There." Electra shone the torch on the end of the vault. "See that?"

The vault didn't end in a wall. Instead, David saw with some surprise, there was what appeared to be a door made from a solid sheet of iron. Hinged down one side, it was locked in place by four stout padlocks—two old-looking ones, brown with rust, and two new shiny ones that glittered silver in the light of Electra's torch.

"It's solid," she said, rapping the metal door lightly with her knuckles. It made the sound of a glockenspiel being struck by a hand; a near-musical chime that became slowly attenuated until David could no longer hear the vibration. Electra struck it lightly again, then stopped. He saw her shiver that someone-just-walked-over-my-grave shiver. After a moment's pause she spoke again, as if to reassure herself as much as anything; once more she sounded like a professional tour guide. "This door was made a hundred years ago in a foundry in Whitby where they made ships' anchors. That door could stop an armor-piercing shell."

David nodded, "So, it's quite a door." His voice echoed back at him eerily; even the metal door vibrated in sympathy, humming like a tuning fork. "Where does it lead?"

"Do I have to tell you, David?"

"I guess you're going to tell me it leads into a tunnel that runs up to the cave at the back of my uncle's house. Am I right?"

"You're absolutely right. In fact, there's more to it than that. There's a whole complex of tunnels running under the town. The rock under here's nothing more than a big Swiss cheese full of holes running for miles."

"And that's where our vamps hang out?"

"Your denial is sounding a tad hollow now, David."

"Are you going to open that door for me?"

"I don't think that would be a very clever idea. We don't know what's squatting on the other side of the door, waiting for us to do just that." She looked at the door and gave a little shiver. "It's probably listening to what we're saying at this very minute."

"Well. You've shown me no evidence that there are legions of undead, biding their time under the town. If undead is the right name—what else can we call them? Nosferatu? Children of the night?"

"Believe me, they're down here. At least, they were until your uncle blew one of the fences to smithereens with dynamite. Where they might be now is anyone's guess."

"I know where they are. Do you know where they are, Electra?"

"Tell me, doctor."

"Where they always have been. Inside your head, Electra."

"Doubting Thomas." She said the words lightly, but there was a coldness to them. Certainly no humor.

"Can I go now? Or do you want to hold me down here in leg irons until the day my toes curl up and I die?"

"Your flippant remarks are sounding more like whistling in the dark, David."

"Whatever."

Electra continued speaking, almost breezily now as if she wanted to close the discussion once and for all. "After you left for the hospital last night with Bernice I moved the chair from the lift. You recall? Jack had very wisely prevented the lift from operating simply by wedging the chair across the door. Unwisely, as I've told you, I moved the chair. Instantly the door closed. The lift descended to the basement. Clearly, someone had summoned the lift. I heard the doors open down in the basement. Someone, I conjectured, got in and pressed the ground-floor button. The lift ascended. With me standing there like silly Nelly's aunt waiting for whatever was inside to step out right in front of me. Fortunately, what I could do was switch off the lift mechanism with my key."

"Handy you'd got it with you."

"Still flippant, aren't we, doctor?"

"So what happened next?"

"I switched off the lift motor and isolated the lift between floors, trapping whoever—whatever—was in the lift until daylight hours."

David stopped and looked at her, his skin prickling. For all the world a great cold slug of a thing could have just slid across his body. "Electra. Tell me you're joking."

"No joke, David." Electra paused by the door of a lock-up store. The door was stout and there were a couple of equally stout padlocks holding the thing firmly shut against a hefty balk of timber that served as the frame.

"Electra . . ." he began, feeling a trickle of fear become a flow.

"Bear with me," she said and swept her hand down across a row of light switches. There was instant darkness. He heard Bernice gasp.

What the hell was Electra doing? He sensed Black's ominous presence behind him in the darkness and he didn't like it one little bit. "Electra," he said.

The torch flashed, lighting a slab of brickwork. Electra found another light switch by the door, clicked it. "Just taking sensible precautions," she said quietly. "I'm keen to avoid putting too much strain on the ring main down here. The fuses might blow if we overload them. We need just enough to see by. Out here, in any case."

There was no light in the basement now except for Electra's torch. "Jack," she said, "unlock the padlocks for me, please."

"Electra," David said tensely. "What is this? What are you doing?"

Black unlocked the padlocks that held the storeroom door shut, his thick, tattooed fingers moving deftly.

"Come closer, David. I want you to see what we have here." Arm straight out, she pushed open the door. Then she switched off the torch.

From the store room shone a hard, brilliant light. He followed Electra inside. A halogen light, of the sort you might use to illuminate a pub car park, blazed. The glare was so fierce it cruelly dazzled David's eyes. He couldn't look directly at the halogen lamp but he guessed it had been screwed to the ceiling of the store.

Then he stopped. Fixed to one wall at little above waist height was a broad stone slab that served as some kind of work table. Perhaps in more unsanitary times meat might have been butchered here for the kitchens upstairs.

On the stone table was a sheet.

Below the sheet, David saw, was a body.

David's eyes were now becoming at least partly accustomed to the brilliant glare. He glanced round. Electra, Bernice and Black stood against one wall of the storeroom, hands raised to their eyes in an attempt to protect them from the fierce blue-white glare of what must be a 500-watt bulb.

Electra said coolly, "Take a look under the sheet, David. We found it in the lift this morning. When the sun was shining."

2

Cautiously. Slowly. As if he was lifting the covering stone from a nest of venomous snakes, David Leppington pulled back the sheet.

The body of a woman lay flat on her back. Just as if she lay on a mortuary slab. Her eyes were closed, her hands crossed across her chest.

In the mercilessly brilliant light of the halogen lamp her skin looked completely white, while the veins under the skin appeared brown rather than blue. Her lips were gray. She was, he guessed, somewhere in her twenties.

The brilliance of the light and the bloodlessness of the corpse made it a ghastly figure—a nightmare simulacrum of a human being rather than an actual one of flesh and blood. Only the hair, which was fluffy, soft and gleaming with blond highlights, looked human.

"She's shrunk since we brought her in here."

David turned to Electra, startled. "Shrunk?"

"Yes; earlier this morning she was bloated. Her stomach was so swollen she looked eight months pregnant."

Black grunted. "Full of blood. She must've gorged on it. It was all around her mouth. She's licked her lips since then."

"Jesus Christ," David said in a hushed voice; he was horrified. Turning to Bernice, who stood with her arms folded, shivering against the doorway, he said, "Did you know about this?"

Bernice shook her head, swallowing; she looked nauseous.

"Electra," he snapped, "what the hell are you playing at?"

"I decided this was the best place for her."

"You decided? Jesus Christ, Electra, this belongs in a morgue. You've got to inform the police. Didn't that occur to you?"

Electra shook her head. "This is one case where the police won't be able to do a thing."

David looked back at the grisly white body on the slab. "Who is she?"

"Dianne Moberry. A local girl. A sassy thing, if the rumors are true."

"What happened to her?"

"We found her in the lift, completely unconscious. Only she was, as I said, quite bloated with fluid, her stomach absolutely distended. We found the hatchway from the yard to the basement open; that must be how they've been coming and going."

"Electra, do you know what happened to her? How she was killed?"

"No, I don't think she's dead. Not dead in the way you learned at university, doctor."

David looked back at what lay on the slab. It still looked like a corpse to him—and he had seen plenty; he'd even dissected one from the crown of its head to the end of its toe as part of his anatomy training. Yes, he told himself, this is a corpse, a corpse, a corpse. Lying there cold and stiff.

He reached out and lightly touched the corpse's face.

Damn.

He withdrew his hand quickly.

"What's wrong?" Bernice cried, frightened.

Electra gave a tight smile. "Hot, isn't it, Doctor Leppington?"

"Yes . . ." He spoke in wonder. "Yes . . . burning. Like a fever."

He pulled the sheet back down to the waist and lifted the arm. It was pliant, relaxed like that of someone asleep. No sign of rigor mortis.

Baffled, he looked more closely at the upper torso of the woman.

The body was bare to the waist, the skin very white, translucent even, with a marbling effect; almost the same effect you get when you pour milk into water. He looked even more closely—there were no signs of injury, nor the characteristic bruised effects from when the blood of a corpse settles in the lower parts of the body.

He lifted both the arms—they were peppered with tiny black hairs. The bare breasts were large in proportion to the slender body. The nipples very dark.

Hell . . . he hadn't noticed that the . . . *uh, damn.*

Wrinkling his nose in disgust, he looked at Electra. "Have you seen that?"

She took a step toward the body but still kept her distance, as if afraid to get too close.

"What is it?" she asked.

"The nipples are missing. These are scabs."

"Dear God."

"From the rough edges of the wound I'd say they weren't removed with a knife." David shook his head, grimly. "My guess is her nipples were bitten off."

Bernice groaned. "Uh . . . Christ. I can't take any more of

this." She shook her head, with her hands over her mouth.

Electra asked gently, "Would you like to go upstairs?"

"Not alone."

"We'll only be a couple more minutes, dear," Electra said. "It's starting to get late."

"I'll wait outside in the main part of the basement. I can't . . . I can't look at that thing anymore." She shot a sickly glance in the direction of the corpse.

"Don't switch on the lights," Electra said, still managing to sound composed. "The fuses might blow with this halogen lamp burning . . . the Station Hotel's electrics are a bit on the antique side."

"She can't stand out there in the dark," David protested.

"Take this," Electra handed Bernice the torch. "Don't worry. We'll be no more than a couple of minutes."

When Bernice had stepped through the doorway David looked back at the corpse—if corpse was the right word.

But if corpse wasn't the right word, what word did describe the thing on the slab? With its hot skin and scabs where the nipples were chewed completely away?

The word slid into his brain as slickly as a worm:

VAMPIRE

That's the word to describe it, isn't it, David?

VAMPIRE

Quelling the sense of unease rising inside him, he forced himself to feel the thing's long, swanlike neck for a pulse.

He found it immediately; beneath his fingertips he felt the slow but strong squelching pulse of blood feeding through the artery. "There's the pulse," he said in a flat voice. "But it's slow; impossibly slow. And yet I can't find any trace of respiration."

"Would you describe her as alive?"

He shrugged, bewildered. "I don't know. There are some vital signs that . . . that, well, mimic life. Pulse. But impossibly slow. A very slow heartbeat. But strong—incredibly strong." He continued the examination with a deliberate effort to suppress a feeling of revulsion welling up inside of him and—let's not beat

261

about the bush here, he told himself—fear. I'm afraid of that thing on the slab. It fits with nothing I've ever learned about the human body.

"If anything, my first guess would be catatonia. Or some drug-induced coma."

Electra moved closer to the body. He sensed her will-power; more than anything she wanted to rush screaming from the basement. But that iron will of hers held her there to watch every detail; to miss nothing. "Now," she said quietly, "watch what happens next." From the pocket of her jacket she took a compass of the kind used to draw circles in geometry. She pulled a cork from the needle then, before David could react, she stabbed it down hard into the arm of the corpse. Then she withdrew it with an effort; it was as if the skin of the corpse tried to hang on to the needle and hold it there in the body. As Electra pulled, the skin raised up into a pyramid. With a tug she yanked the needle free.

"Now. What do you see?"

David looked at the puncture wound caused by the compass needle. A clear fluid dribbled slowly out. Not blood, though, definitely not blood. It was a clear yellowish liquid, reminiscent of the body fluids of a fly when you crush it against a window pane. His medical training suggested that this might be blood plasma—only with the red and white cells removed, leaving the sticky amber liquid.

"There," Electra said in an awed hush. "There, we have a member of your vampire army, Dr. Leppington. You heard the legends. She is yours. So what are you going to do with her?"

Mouth dry, he bent down to look at the girl's face. It was relaxed, the eyelids were softly closed as if she slept. The eyelashes were long and luscious-looking. Eyebrows stood out darkly against white skin. That white skin smoothed firmly across high cheek bones; in turn the face was framed by the fluffy soft hair. There *was* a semblance of life. No escaping that.

He turned his attention back to the eyelids that were so lightly closed. Slowly he raised his fingers to the eyes; he'd ease back an eyelid and examine the pupil.

The second he touched the eyelid it swept back.

The eyelids were like great shutters shooting upward. The

eyes blazed up at him: the pupils had expanded enormously, so it was as if he looked down a well. Only a well set in a white surround that glistened and shone as brightly as pearl.

Those eyes were magnificent.

They held his eyes with a completeness that was hypnotic.

At that instant nothing else mattered. The rest of the world became indistinct; he had no worries; he experienced a complete and all-encompassing spiritual calm; he was a speck of dust floating, caught in a sunbeam; rose-colored lights burst gently inside his head, filling him with warmth; at that moment he'd never felt so wanted or so loved.

The eyes glowed up at him.

This was complete serenity; his self was dissolving in an ocean of total love; the pulse in his neck beat with a low bass rhythm; he sensed his rich, red blood squeezing thickly through the arteries.

Now the girl's eyes turned sleepy, and loving. Come-to-bed eyes.

"Oh, yes . . ." The words breathed sweetly from her beautiful lips. "Yes . . . I want to go to bed with you. I want you—"

The world exploded in a wash of hard light. Then his face smacked dully against something hard. He gasped with shock. His face was pressed to the cold, raw brick wall; the harsh light of the lamp glittered from crystals of saltpetre bleeding from the brickwork.

"You believe now, don't you?" Electra said quietly. "You believe in the vampire?"

Legs, arms, stomach shaking uncontrollably, he nodded; he was panting with shock. Now he realized Jack Black must have reached forward, grabbed hold of him, dragged him from the corpse and held him there against the wall, breaking the thing's hypnotic hold over him.

And behind him, there on the slab, beneath the brilliant glare of the halogen lamp, the dead thing twitched and grinned and giggled.

"Now you believe," Electra breathed the words into his ear, "the question is, are you going to run away like your father? Or are you going to stay here and fight them?"

In the basement she stood alone.

The shadows were alive; or at least it seemed that way to Bernice Mochardi. She flashed the torch from left to right, to the front of her, then behind her.

She wished they'd hurry up and finish gawping at the damned corpse in the basement storeroom and get the hell upstairs; there she could make the most of the afternoon daylight.

Christ, yes, she thought desperately, her heart beating fast, that's what I want: I want to wallow in sunlight; I want to stand in the open and feel fresh air and the sun warm on my face.

Shadows scuttled all around her feet.

The shadows were playing games with her. No matter how quickly she shone the torch they always slipped away to lurk in some corner waiting to dart out at her face and—

Shut up, she told herself; your imagination is running away with you.

Taking a deep breath she began to pace the barrel vault of raw brick.

As she neared the end of the vault, the torch light shining ahead, lighting piles of junk, the old lavatory seats on the shelf, the rusty parts of a bed leaning against a wall, she noticed the metal door again.

Noticed it? *No, it drew my eyes there.*

Gingerly she edged toward it, feet grating on the brick floor. The two new padlocks gleamed in the light of the torch.

She imagined that the steel door was glass.

What would she see there?

Did something have its ear pressed to the metal, listening?

And beyond the listener, what then?

Perhaps a tunnel ran deep under the town, under the river, then wormed deeply under the hill to where George Leppington's house stood like a fortress, awaiting the return of its lord and master?

She moved forward, drawn to the metal door.

Lightly, she rapped on the door. It shimmered with that chiming sound, reminding her of a tuning fork.

She tilted her head to one side.

What lay beyond the door?

A mystery.

A deep, unfathomable mystery full of purpling darkness. Pregnant with old magic.

Again, she raised her hand and lightly, oh so lightly, rapped on the door.

It was answered by a torrent of bangs. It sounded like a battering ram slammed against the door from the other side.

Clang . . . clang . . . clang . . . clang . . .

The thing could have been a monster bell that shook and boomed beneath a gigantic clapper.

She stared at the door, her eyes wide, painfully wide, the torchlight blazing on the quivering surface as something at the other side of the door pounded to be let in.

She turned and ran from the door, torchlight flashing madly from floor, roof, wall, bed springs, sacks, old newspapers . . .

A figure emerged from the wall.

"David?" she gasped.

He nodded. His eyes were as grim as hell. "Upstairs. Quickly."

She felt his hand grab her tightly just above the elbow. Seconds later both were clattering up the stairs.

4

Ninety seconds after that the four of them stood in the lobby just outside the basement door. Jack Black locked the door, his face expressionless as ever.

Now the silence was as palpable as the noise had been. Bernice's ears hummed; she felt incredibly cold; her chest was tight as if her ribs were closing in, imprisoning her lungs like one of those rooms from an old film, a room that gets smaller and smaller as the walls creep together to crush the occupants. She took a deep breath.

David looked at her. "Are you all right?"

"Yes." She inhaled deeply trying to get air into her lungs. "Yes, I think so. Are you?"

He nodded, face grim, but she noticed the navy sweater was smeared white with saltpetre and he had a dirty mark on one cheek.

Electra rubbed her face as if trying to restore the circulation. Her eyes glittered with sheer fright. "Showtime, folks," She gave a little laugh that bordered on the hysterical. "Now was that showtime or was that showtime?" She pulled a tissue from a box under the counter and dabbed the corner of her eyes. "Now . . . listen. I'm not going to open the bar this evening. There's no other guests, so . . . so, the hotel will be closed for tonight. Would you help me put up notices on the doors, Bernice?"

Bernice nodded, her teeth clicking as shivers rippled through her body.

After a moment David said, "Once you've done that we need to hold a council of war. We have to discuss what we're going to do next."

Black gave a grunt. "You're the boss."

David nodded. "Yes, I suppose I am."

He looked at the three faces as they watched him. They were depending on him now. Come what may, he had to come up with an answer to all this.

Chapter Twenty-eight

1

The late afternoon sun shone down on the town of Leppington.

It turned the brick flanks of the slaughterhouse the same color as the skin of an orange. A huge crow circled in the sky high above the town like some ancient omen of impending disaster. It glided with outstretched wings that were somehow crooked and when it turned its head to one side it resembled a black feathered swastika hanging there, borne up by cold airstreams.

The train that David and Bernice were supposed to board for an evening in Whitby pulled out of the station. It left without them, the wheels clacking hard against steel tracks that reflected the light of the sun. The train picked up speed quickly as if it knew that events as extraordinary as they were terrible would soon erupt in the town. Now it was eager to get out of the place before nightfall.

Maximilian, the Down's syndrome son of Sad Sam, the man who organized the poker parties in his house, walked slowly down Main Street, the Burger King crown hanging from his hand. A gang of youths had thrown stones at him as he'd crossed the park to buy beer for his dad's poker party tonight. Then they'd touched his ears with lighted cigarettes. After that they'd taken the beer money from him and walked away, calling him names.

He was used to all that now.

At the special school kids used to come to the railings and call him. "Come on, mate," they'd shout. "We want to be your friend. Come over here, we've got some chocolate for you." When he got close enough they'd spit at him.

Then they ran away, laughing.

Maximilian'd walk back to the classroom, his face, hair and clothes glistening with beads of gob that hung there like white pearls.

Outside the Station Hotel he paused. Beneath his feet was the heavy-duty iron grating of a storm-water drain. He looked down.

Something like white footballs bobbed through the darkness beneath his feet. They flowed from the direction of the slaughterhouse toward the hotel. He watched for a moment, almond-shaped eyes impassively taking in the white balls veined with purple lines. One ball stopped, then swiveled.

Maximilian gently swung his arm that held the cardboard Burger King crown. The white football had two eyes—they were dark and sunken. It had a thin nose; and a mouth that looked like it had been made by the wild slash of an axe. The teeth in the mouth were large.

And sharp.

Maximilian stepped forward, placing his feet on the iron grille two meters above the bobbing heads. The face was lowered beneath his feet. He saw only the top of the head as it moved with the others.

The wind blew. Papers and pop cartons skidded along the street. A beer can rolled by, reminding Maximilian he had to go home and face his father's rage.

*"You've lost the money? You've lost the money! I don't be-
lieve you could be so careless, you useless blood-sucking bastard . . ."*

For Maximilian Hart life was an unremitting waterfall of mysteries. He understood little of what people said to him, or why
they did things: why the trains clanked and rumbled out of the
station, or why they rolled in again, or why people came and
went and spat at him and stole his money. He knew none of the
devious strategies employed by those people with that all-
important one less chromosome.

That one less chromosome that, to him, endowed them with
dog-like faces with their prominent noses and thin-lidded eyes.

In a few short hours, in the dark watches of the night, Maximilian Hart would face the greatest challenge of his short life.
In the face of that coming danger the only weapon he would
have at his disposal was that same plodding stoicism with which
he'd faced past mysteries and endured past dangers.

With the cardboard crown swinging limply from his fingers
he plodded on down the street.

Sunday afternoon. The time was a little after five.

2

While Electra locked the revolving door at the main entrance,
Bernice taped up notices on the side doors that led into the
public bars. Written in black marker-pen on sheets of Station
Hotel letter-headed paper they read simply: *SUNDAY. HOTEL
AND BARS REGRETFULLY CLOSED TONIGHT DUE TO
TECHNICAL FAULT.*

Technical fault? Wasn't that an excuse-all?

A second cousin to a drunk excusing his actions by saying
he was tired and emotional.

The wind blew, flapping the paper in Bernice's hand as she
taped it to the door. Her hands were still shaking. The tape
preferred to stick to her fingers rather than to the paper.

Hell.

The thing lying down there in the cellar: she couldn't get it
out of her mind; it'd looked like a corpse; that white and ghastly
face; for heaven's sake, its nipples had been torn off. The sight

of the dead girl had scared her more than she could adequately describe.

Then Bernice had heard the thunderous pounding on the metal door.

Something had been on the other side of the door. One of those vampire creatures.

It had wanted to come inside, all right.

It wanted *you*, Bernice, she told herself. And right now I'm just supposed to walk calmly back into the hotel, am I?

Fear oozed through her; a cold fear that stained her soul blue with dread.

As she pressed pieces of tape to the corners of the notice she glanced out into the street. A Downs-syndrome man stood on the pavement gazing down into the drain. What looked like a cardboard crown dangled from his fingers.

She knew him by sight. If he looked up at her she'd nod and smile.

My God, so brain-washed are we by society that we still continue the social niceties. What she really wanted to do was scream and beat her forehead against that brick wall over there.

The man didn't look her way and continued to walk slowly away from the hotel.

Lucky man, she thought. Maybe I should do the same. Just walk away from it all. This isn't my battle.

But deep down she knew it was. Invisible threads bound her to this town, to this building, to these people. They could only be broken when . . .

She shivered, her arms goose bumping.

Those threads that bind me here will only be broken when all this madness has run its course.

With the poster taped in place she walked quickly back into the yard behind the hotel. Cloud scudded across the sky overhead, with little rents in it that sometimes allowed a beam of sunlight to come shafting through. It was so late in the afternoon that, by now, those rare shafts of sunlight shone at such an oblique angle they were almost horizontal, looking like golden pathways in the sky.

She liked the brightness of the light and the freshness of the air.

The hotel in comparison seemed like a prison holding the air captive until it became stale and, lately, almost unbreathable.

As she walked across the back yard she saw the gateway through to the river bank. The water gushing over the rocks sounded pleasantly soothing to her ears.

She crossed the yard to the gateway and stepped through onto the soft earth of the banking. A path led down to the water's edge just a dozen paces away. Overhanging the waters that foamed white around the rocks was a fringe of weeping-willow trees.

The idea of just sitting there for a while seemed so enticing. She could spend a moment or two just to refresh her scorched nerves, couldn't she? Heaven knew she'd earned it.

3

She stepped through the gateway. The path turned sandy as she followed it down to the water's edge. Rain had swollen the river and it swept along its channel like a living thing.

A beam of sunlight struck the river where it slipped across the water to play across her feet.

"Bernice, why did it take you so long to find me?"

With a startled gasp she looked up.

Before her eyes even locked onto the figure she knew who it would be.

She whispered, "You're Mike."

"I knew you'd remember me." The voice was pleasantly charming. Also, there was an intimacy there that conjured a thrilling tingle across the skin of her stomach.

For there, in the deep shadow, where the willow branches hung thickest, stood a man dressed in white. He seemed little more than a shadow himself. All she could make out was a pale wash of blond hair and the slivery twinkle of a pair of eyes shining from the gloom.

No more than ten paces separated them. She took a step back.

"I think it's time you and me had a talk, Bernice," came the gently accented American voice. A voice so soft and whispery it made her feel like she was falling into a gorgeously soft bed. "You will sit here and talk to me, won't you, Bernice?"

"Yes."

"Look, I've made a space for you on this branch next to me. We can sit here, swinging our legs, and talking until the cows come home, can't we?" The voice was good-humored, eager to be kind to her. "Sit down here, Bernice, where I can see you properly."

"How did you know my name?"

"Ah, Bernice Mochardi. Room 406."

"How do you know all that?"

Something hard and silvery glittered in the man's shadowy hand. "Even I haven't learned to walk through walls. I have a key to the hotel. Late at night when everyone's sound, sound asleep, I tiptoe in. Sometimes I look at the visitors' book. Sometimes I tiptoe upstairs. Do you know something, Bernice?"

"What?" She felt light-headed, drowsy, and so deliciously warm.

"You're staying in my old room. I once slept in your bed. I think that forges a bond between us, doesn't it?"

"I guess."

"And do you know something else?"

"No. What?"

"I'd really like to kiss you, Bernice."

In the hotel kitchen David talked to Electra. She'd tipped pasta shells into a pan of boiling water and was commenting, "An army marches on its stomach; even a titchy four-man army like ours." She stirred briskly. "Will you pass me the salt, please, David?"

At that moment Jack Black walked from the hotel lobby into the kitchen. His fists were clenched. Veins stood out on his scalp and in his neck. His eyes locked forward on the back door.

Suddenly, he ran at the door, charged it, swung it open with a crash, then ran across the yard, boots pounding the ground hard.

"Hell, what's he seen?" David asked. "Did you see the look on his face?"

"Something's wrong." Electra's face paled. "Where's Bernice?"

David ran for the door, too. In five seconds he was racing across the yard after Black. Cloud had settled low over the town, drawing down a premature dusk.

David saw Black running down a path to the edge of the river. There stood Bernice, staring trancelike into the shadows of the tree.

Black landed on the dirt shore of the river, his big feet hitting the ground hard. As David picked his way down the steep path he saw Black lunge into the shadows cast by the willow trees.

For a second David thought he'd caught hold of some huge wild cat.

There was a furious hissing snarl from the thing. It moved like oiled lightning, wrapping its limbs about Black's shoulders.

The big tattooed man twisted, throwing the thing so it landed at David's feet.

David took one look at the white bloodless face and knew what it was.

It bounded effortlessly to its feet again, snarling and hissing.

For an instant David thought the thing would spring at his face, its long fingernails clawing at his skin.

Instead it whirled around and launched itself at Bernice who looked as if she was just waking from a dream. The thing could rip out her throat in a second.

David dived forward like he was diving into a pool, both arms straight out.

With a bone-crunching concussion he hit the monster in the back. The momentum of his own body knocked it forward off balance.

A second later he was sprawling on the stones at the water's edge with the creature. It seemed all arms and hissing face. And it moved faster than David could actually see.

Now it was on top of him, its face just centimeters from his own; the mouth hissed; its eyes blazed with a mixture of fury and exultation.

"Leppington . . . LEPPINGTON!" The hissing became a bellow.

The monster's mouth opened wide, exposing strong white teeth.

For a second it seemed to David as if he saw through the creature's eyes. He saw his own thick artery pulsing with blood in his throat.

The concussion that came next winded him.

He looked up to see Black stamp in the middle of the creature's back. Black wore a grim expression on his face. He raised his boot again, then brought it down as if trying to crush some gigantic beetle.

The thing roared; its back arched; the head lifted; David felt the creature's hot breath on his face; *smelt* the breath—a dirty smell suggestive of neglected trash in summer.

Now Black reached down and tugged the creature from David. The creature swung an arm out, catching Black across the face. He staggered under the sheer force of the blow, but didn't fall.

With a huge effort Black pushed the creature as it spat and hissed.

Gritting his teeth and screwing shut his eyes with sheer effort, Black threw the monster backward into the river. The waters swallowed the thing with barely a splash.

Panting, David struggled up onto his knees. He stared at the foaming rapids, expecting to see a pair of white arms followed by that bloodless head breaking the surface.

Nothing did emerge.

There was only the headlong rush of water pouring down toward the sea.

"Thank God," David gasped at Black. "You've killed it."

"No such luck," Black grunted. "Bring Mochardi back to the hotel with you." With that terse instruction he turned around and stomped up the banking to where Electra stood watching them, her dark hair blowing out in the breeze.

For a moment David stood there, his legs as weak as water and his stomach trembling. He knew the shock of the encounter with that vampire, or monster, or whatever the hell it was, had started to bite.

He helped Bernice to her feet; her face was blank with shock, too.

At that moment he looked up to see a huge black crow hovering above the treetops. And he knew down to the pit of his stomach that the bird had observed it all. A second later the bird gave a screech that echoed across the town. Then it wheeled smoothly above them before flapping slowly away into the distance.

The bird's someone's lookout, David told himself with a kind of muted surprise at this insight.

Now it was going to report back to its master on what it had seen played out there on the river bank.

But what story would it relate?

And to whom?

Chapter Twenty-nine

1

"Well, that showed us," Electra said sourly as she poured three shots of brandy into tumblers. "I don't think we're going to be so lucky next time, are we?"

David sat heavily on the chair, feeling as energetic as a sack of potatoes; the events of the last twenty-four hours had left him feeling sapped. "Why don't these vampires play by the rules? Why don't they sleep in a coffin during the day, like they're supposed to?"

"Because they're not vampires, not exactly, anyway. As I told you, they are vampire-*like*." Electra handed him a glass. "Here. Drink this. Bernice . . ." She handed another glass to Bernice who sat with her elbows resting on the table top, her head in her hands.

With an effort Bernice lifted her head. Her eyes were dull with shock. "Thanks. Leave the bottle. I'm going to get blasted."

"Not a good idea," Electra said. "We need to stay clear-headed and wide awake tonight." She took a sip of brandy herself. "This is purely medicinal. So, what now? David?"

"We stick together as much as possible. If they don't shun daylight, there's no time of day when we can feel absolutely safe."

Bernice wiped her nose with a tissue. "I'm sure they try and avoid *strong* light. The man down by the river kept himself well in the shadows."

Electra said, "And I fitted the halogen lamp down in the basement this morning in the hope it would at least render Moberry inactive. My impression is that strong light, particularly daylight, does weaken them in some way."

"Light might give us one slender advantage, then," David allowed, "but how do we nail these bastards?"

Bernice and Electra shrugged; Black leaned against the kitchen wall and pulled on a cigarette. "They're strong, too," Black grunted. "If I hadn't got behind the thing and shoved it into the river it would have ripped our heads off."

"The main thing, at least for the time being," David said, "is to prevent them getting into the hotel. Now if I remember my old horror films right, vampires can fly in through a window, or even melt through a crack in the door. The question is, can these?"

"No. I'm pretty sure they can't." Bernice looked up, the glass held in both hands. "The one on the river bank was the American who stayed in the hotel. He's called Mike Stroud. He showed me a key to the hotel."

"Where on earth did he . . . *it* get a key?"

Electra shrugged. "He could have slipped in one evening when the lobby was deserted and stolen one from the desk. Easy enough to do. After all, you have an outside door key on the fob with your room key."

"Well, at least that's one more thing in our favor. We can lock them out; but that doesn't stop them breaking a window to get inside. Is the lift switched off still?"

Electra nodded. "I isolated it between floors again."

David looked out through the window. He couldn't avoid an involuntary shiver as he saw it was all but dark. Any second a white face might appear at the glass to stare in at them.

"Well, ladies and gentleman," his voice felt strained. "Night has now fallen."

2

At Electra's suggestion they retreated to her suite of rooms on the first floor. They took food and the bottle of brandy.

As Electra locked the door to her apartment behind her she told them, "Make yourselves comfortable. It might be a long night." She looked at David, then at Bernice. "Forgive me for sounding like your friendly neighborhood drug pusher, but I do have cocaine. It'll keep you wide awake, I guarantee it."

"My God," David said, shaking his head. "The tools of the modern vampire hunter—electric lights and cocaine."

3

At the same time as Electra was locking the door to her apartment within the hotel Dianne Moberry's two sisters, Chloë and Samantha, were clicking along the street in tall stilettos, microskirts and some pretty sassy tops that showed more than they covered. It was fully dark by this time. Street lights blazed. A couple of cars cruised by, catching the girls in the headlights. There were wolf-whistles.

The Moberry girls wore their make-up strong. Their lipsticks were a vivacious—some might say a predatory—red. They were glamorous-looking girls with broad hips, flat stomachs and they were as full-breasted as their big sister Dianne, who even now was swinging herself off the stone slab in the cellar storeroom. Her hungry eyes darted to the locked door. Her stomach blazed with hunger.

Meanwhile, a few dozen meters away, the two sisters crossed the street to the hotel, stiletto heels clicking busily against the pavement.

"Fucking wind," said one of the girls.

"I told you to keep off the baked beans, didn't I, Chloë?"

"Ha-fucking-ha, Samantha. Stupid wind's going to ruin my hair. I spent hours on the stupid thing."

"You should use hair spray, not mousse."

"You used all my hair spray, remember?"

"I did no such damn thing. Last time I saw it was on our Dianne's bedside table. She probably took it with her when— oh, crap."

"What's wrong?"

"Just look at that. SUNDAY. HOTEL AND BARS REGRETFULLY CLOSED TONIGHT DUE TO TECHNICAL FAULT." She pursed her pretty red lips. "Damn and crap."

They screwed their eyes up at the notice taped to the door.

The wind had caught one corner of it; it flapped with a tickering sound.

"Charnwood's only gone and shut the fucking bar."

"Shit. I was meeting Pete there tonight. Oh crap, I was on a promise, too."

"Who? Pete the poet?"

"Yeah."

"Jesus, you're getting weird tastes. I've never done it with a poet before. Does he talk in rhyme when he's on the job?"

"That's for me to know and you to wonder about. Come on, we'll go to Vines."

"Ladies."

They both turned and looked in the direction of the voice. Now, was this something special? An American accent? Here in godforsaken Leppington?

Emerging slowly from the darkness came a man all in white. They saw the glint of his blond hair, the flash of white teeth as he gave a broad grin.

"Ladies," he said in a voice as smooth as silk. "Ladies, I've been waiting for you."

Then he swept out of the darkness at them. He moved fluidly, like a wild cat. They didn't even have a chance to draw breath.

When it was done he said, softly, "Now, ladies. I would like you to bring something to me . . ."

4

Deep in the cellar beneath the hotel Dianne Moberry sensed her sisters were joining them; she sensed their ecstasy and fear and pain and excitement and joy.

She sensed their hearts beating faster and faster until orgasmic spasms shook their bodies, tingling from their thighs to their breasts.

Her sisters' hearts beat faster still.

Then stopped dead.

Presently they would begin to beat again. Only this time it would be to an altogether different rhythm.

Beating her fists against the locked door Dianne Moberry hissed and screamed with rage and hunger. Jealousy, too. She'd been invited to this blood party. She wanted to join in the fun. She wanted out.

5

In Electra's sitting room David sat in the leather armchair; Bernice and Electra had chosen the chesterfield sofa (Electra with her knees bent and feet up on the cushions as if she sat on a chaise longue). Black sat impassively by the window on a straight-backed dining-table chair.

The breeze blew against the window. The curtains were drawn, hiding the darkness beyond. Earlier, as David had drawn the curtains, he'd looked down into the deserted rear yard and the white strip of river beyond the yard wall. In the trees at the water's edge he fancied he'd glimpsed a lick of yellow.

His imagination had supplied the rest of the image. The creature that had once been the American, Mike Stroud, was hauling himself from the swollen river. He'd stand there for a moment, water dripping from his fingers onto the banking in big fat splotches, his blond hair plastered down across his forehead. On his face would be a smile of such evil. Because he knew it was only a matter of time before those people in the hotel were his. He'd take Bernice Mochardi first. His teeth would sink deep into her tender—

"David?"

"Sorry, yes." He snapped out of the reverie and looked at Electra who spoke to him in those tones of calm authority.

"I think it's time we had a council of war, don't you?"

"Definitely. I think we've only won ourselves a temporary refuge in here. It's only a matter or time before they break in and . . ." There was no need to finish the sentence.

Bernice nodded. She looked composed. Black stayed mute. But David knew the man was listening to every word.

Electra said: "The situation, broadly, is this: in the caves beneath the town are a collection of . . . of—well, we will call them vampires for want of a better word; they certainly have vampiric attributes. Agreed?"

David nodded; Bernice and Black followed suit.

"Good." Electra spoke crisply as if addressing a business

278

meeting. "For years, probably centuries, these vampires have enjoyed a close and relatively secret relationship with the Leppington family. It's clear to me now that the Leppingtons, formerly known as the Leppingsvalts, have acted as jailers to these vampires. For centuries the Leppingtons have provided these creatures with food."

"And that food is blood?" Bernice said in a small voice.

"Yes, blood—living, red blood, by the bucketful—the staple diet of mosquitoes, leeches and vampire bats." Electra lit a cigarette. "Excuse me, I don't normally; a filthy habit." She inhaled deeply before continuing. "The Leppington family assiduously cared for their charges who were locked safely underground out of the way. In the nineteenth century this care reached typical Victorian efficiency of industrial proportions when your great-great-grandfather, David, a Colonel Leppington, had the slaughterhouse built."

David nodded. "I take it that Colonel Leppington's motives for building the slaughterhouse weren't purely financial?"

"No, he decided to modernize the vampire-feeding operation by building a huge slaughterhouse where perhaps a hundred or more animals were killed a day. Their throats were cut and the blood gushed out onto the killing room floor where drains carried it to the vampires as they waited underground—no doubt hungrily licking their lips. Not a pretty picture, is it?"

"Then they weren't dependent on human blood?"

"No. Not entirely."

"But?"

"But I imagine for them human blood is the real McCoy. Animal blood is a substitute for the real thing—just as to a drug addict pethedine is only an inferior, weak-as-dishwater substitute for heroin."

David thought hard, nipping his bottom lip between finger and thumb. "Presumably these creatures have been satisfied with the blood of sheep and cattle for centuries. You can imagine my ancestors, hundreds of years ago, trudging into the caves with buckets of the stuff and pouring it into pig troughs for them. And for a long time this kept the monsters satiated. So what's disturbed the status quo? Why have they started feeding on people again?"

Electra blew out a cloud of cigarette smoke. "Perhaps some

inner biological clock is the trigger. You know, at some point in the Autumn geese know it's time to migrate. In the Spring buds suddenly start appearing on the trees . . ."

"No. You're wrong," Bernice said quietly. "I read the family history that David lent me this morning. You know how all this is supposed to have started, don't you?"

"Yes," Electra said, and tapped the ash off from her cigarette into the ashtray that was balanced on her knee. "That was the fairy story our grandparents told their children on dark and stormy nights like this. What would our politically correct child psychologists say about that?"

There was a look of concentration on Bernice's face. She'd been giving this some thought. Now she was reaching conclusions of her own. "In a nutshell, the story was this: A thousand years ago the Leppingtons were given a divine mission. To oust Christianity by killing the Christian kings and conquering all the Christian countries. To help them do this the Norse thunder god, Thor, gave the Leppingtons this army of the undead."

David nodded. "That's how the fairy story runs."

"But on the eve of battle," Bernice continued, speaking slowly, calmly, "disaster struck. The chief of the Leppingtons was in his palace along with his sister and his bride-to-be. The sister was ill with some unspecified disease and never ventured from the palace. The bride-to-be suffered a social handicap of her own. Originally she had been a harlot. The chief had saved her from what amounted to being the sex slave of a Christian warlord in the north. Also there with the chief was his right-hand man, the Goth warrior called Vurtzen."

David said softly, "For some reason the chief argued with his warrior friend, who was a wild beast-like man by all accounts. They drew their swords against each other, and fought in the palace all night."

"And during the battle a great wind blew open the doors of the palace. The candles and fires were put out in the gust. The two men carried on fighting in the dark, slashing at each other with their swords. So ferocious and full of hate were they for each other that unwittingly they killed the sister and the bride-to-be in the dark. Next morning, so the legend goes, both see what has happened. The Goth warrior Vurtzen is full of remorse and exiles himself in a land at the ends of the Earth. Chief

Leppingsvalt is so full of grief over the death of his sister and beloved fiancée that he burns down the temple to Thor and refuses to lead the invasion force of dead warriors on Christendom. Instead he seals the entrance to the cave."

Electra added, "And so the curse of the Leppingtons is wrought. Thor disfigures Chief Leppingsvalt and presumably commands the chief's descendants to continue to care for the undead—this army of vampires—until the time is ripe for the next invasion of the Christian nation."

"And the time has now come," Bernice said, quietly but firmly. "Don't you see what's happening?"

Electra shook her head, frowning. "No. What?"

"Somehow events have gone full circle," Bernice said, earnestly. "On Friday night, when we were all together in the kitchen—you, Electra, me and David and Jack. The wind pushed open the door and blew the serviettes into the air. At that moment I knew we'd been together before; the four of us. Now I know why." She looked from face to face. "You see now, don't you? We're the same people who were in *that* palace on *that* night, more than a thousand years ago." She stood up and paced the room. "You, David? That's easy; you're Chief of the Leppingsvalts, as they were known then. Electra is your sister. Jack Black here is the Goth warrior, Vurtzen. And I . . ."

Electra looked at her levelly. "And you are the bride-to-be."

For a moment there was absolute silence in the room. The wind blew hard against the glass. It swirled around the four towers of the hotel drawing forth a long, low moaning sound that sounded like a girl sobbing broken-hearted in the night.

David's mouth was dry. He sensed a gigantic mechanism that existed in some other world beyond this one beginning to turn its mighty wheels. That mechanism would drive the events in this world. It happened rarely, but it was happening now. Things beyond his comprehension would happen.

But despite this sensation that was so palpable he felt he could reach out into the air and grasp it, the rational side of his brain tried to put the brakes on the mechanism that was going to launch him on one hell of a nightmare roller-coaster ride.

"You're saying that something is going to force us to relive what happened to four people—four legendary people who might never have even existed in reality?"

Bernice nodded. "The legend in your book said that the gods would give the Leppingtons a second chance to complete the task that had been entrusted to them." She took a deep breath. "Now the four of us are together again."

"And tonight's the night," added Electra in a low voice as she tapped the ash from her cigarette.

David rubbed his face; it felt stiff; his ears were ringing. "And this is where I get a second chance to take command of my army of dead warriors and lead them into battle?"

Bernice nodded; Electra's face was as inscrutable as the Sphinx's.

"And if I don't take command of them . . ." David's mouth was dry. "They will run amok and kill everyone?" He shook his head, his palms moist with perspiration. "You expect me to believe that? I mean, would *you*?"

Electra spoke calmly. "Let's vote on it. Who believes what Bernice has just told us? Hands up, please."

David watched, with shivers running up his spine to tingle icily across his scalp. Bernice put her hand up straight away; her eyes, sober and serious, were fixed on David's. Then Electra slowly raised her hand.

David turned to look at the tattooed beast of a man sitting by the window. The scarred face remained stone-like; never a flicker revealed what he might be thinking. Surely Black wouldn't go along with this?

David held his breath. Slowly, without fuss, without a flicker of expression, Jack Black put the cigarette between his lips. Then he raised a hand as high as his shaven head.

"Three to one, David," Electra said softly.

David breathed deeply, closed his eyes. He thought of the thing on the slab downstairs, the attack by that creature on the river bank. Everything that had happened to him in the last forty-eight hours streamed through his head in a split second. And he thought about his own gut feelings that had told him the truth all along.

David opened his eyes and raised his hand, too.

Chapter Thirty

1

Sad Sam raved at his son.

"You lost the bloody money! How am I going to explain that you . . . you just threw away the beer kitty? How am I going to explain that to my friends!"

Maximilian Hart sat on the footstool in the corner of the living room while his father raved, red-faced and shirtless, his heavy belly wobbling with rage. His father had been in the middle of feeding the pair of cockatoos he kept caged in the room when Maximilian had broken the news, the Burger King cardboard crown dangling from one hand.

As was his father's habit the birds flew free when the seed bowls were set out.

"You stupid blood-sucking bastard! Where did you lose it?"

Maximilian gave a little shrug. It seemed better to pretend the money had been accidentally lost rather than admit that it had been stolen by the gang of youths.

"Stupid moron. Why your mother inflicted you on me I'll never know! You're a great bloody abortion, do you know that? A great bloody abortion!"

The two birds fluttered around the room, agitated by the angry voice; their wings struck the paper lightshade, bringing down feathers like falling snowflakes. One wing clipped a picture of Maximilian's dead mother, knocking it face down on the sideboard.

"A bloody abortion," his father raged. "Now! Give me that!" He snatched the cardboard crown from Maximilian's hand.

"Now, lad! This is something you really treasure, isn't it? You enjoy wearing this crown, like we enjoy drinking a can of beer. Understand? This . . ." he waved the crown in front of Maximilian's face, ". . . is precious to you. Well . . . you great fat fucking abortion, watch this."

He tore the cardboard crown into postage-stamp-sized pieces, then flung them in Maximilian's face.

And all the time the birds wheeled around and around the room, whistling shrilly. One darted in at Maximilian and pecked the tender skin beneath his right eye.

"Now," his father bellowed, "get *YOUR* money out of *YOUR* box and go and buy the beer. *All right?*"

Maximilian gave a small nod, pulled himself to his feet from where he sat on the footstool, and walked toward the living room door. His face was expressionless, but inside his heart was breaking.

"And get the beer from the mini-mart, not the off-license; it's too bloody expensive there. And I don't care if it is further to walk; and I don't care if it is dark; and I don't care if the bloody devil himself gets you and tears you another arse hole. Just get that beer back here by nine o'clock!"

A bead of blood swelled from the cut beneath Maximilian's eye. As he opened the door it rolled down his cheek, looking for all the world like a crimson tear.

2

In Electra's apartment they were restless. David had a sense that something was expected of them—well, of him particularly. But what?

What the hell could he do?

If he was confronted with someone who'd just been pulled unconscious and without a pulse from a river he'd know exactly what to do. Clear water from the stomach and air passages by placing them on their front, holding them by the waist and raising the lower back and tip the water from them, then start cardiopulmonary resuscitation. He was trained and trained well to do that and a host of other things, from using a hypodermic to cutting out a ruptured appendix on a kitchen table if need be.

But this?

The thoughts ran through his head as they made preparations; preparations for what they weren't exactly sure.

(But don't you bet some great slug-like vampire is going to come sliding in through that window?)

He closed off the more self-destructive thoughts and set out candles on a green-topped card table in Electra's living room. The lights had flickered a couple of times that evening. It might have just been the gales blasting around the power cables that ran up the valley but, you never knew, those things might have broken into a sub-station. They liked the dark. A power cut in the town would be just pure honey to them.

He watched as Bernice pushed the base of the candles into a motley collection of candle holders.

Her fingers were slender, gentle, the nails now unvarnished. He couldn't look at her oval face and her dark eyes now without feeling a kind of purring buzz inside of him. In a way he hoped her prophecy was right. The idea of Bernice Mochardi being his bride-to-be was strangely thrilling.

She looked up at him as she pushed a candle into a glass holder and gave him a small smile. And just for a moment the room seemed brighter; a warmth spread through his chest and arms.

And at that moment came the tap at the window.

3

Bernice shot him a startled look, her mouth frozen open in an "O" shape.

Electra entered the room. "What was that?"

David stared at the curtain covering the window. "It sounded like someone tapping at the window."

"We're on the first floor," Bernice said. "Surely they can't reach us up here?"

"Want to bet?" That was Black's gruff voice. He held a large hammer in one meaty hand and tapped it into the palm of the other hand as if assessing its ability to smash skulls.

The tap came again; just a single sharp rap.

David took a deep breath. "There's only one way to see what it is."

With that he swept back the curtain. He shivered from head to toe . . . *knowing . . . KNOWING that there would be a white*

285

and terrible face grinning in at them; eyes burning . . . hatred, hunger all locked in those burning eyes . . .

Beyond the glass pane, in the darkness, there was nothing.

He looked back at the others to double-check with them he was seeing nothing. Then he heard the sharp rap against the glass again.

"It's a stone," Black said. "He's throwing a stone at the window."

He?

David didn't need to ask who *he* was.

Gritting his teeth, he flipped the catch on the sash window and dragged it up on the runners.

Cautiously, he looked down into the courtyard below.

The night wind blew cold around his face, pressing his hair against his forehead then tugging it away again. The roar of the River Lepping in flood sounded loud, almost thunderous, with the window open.

"At last," came a steady voice from below. "I thought you would take all night to come to the window."

David looked down. There in the middle of the courtyard, dressed in white, was Mike Stroud. He smiled up at David; the vampire's bright eyes locked onto his.

Don't look into his eyes, David told himself, and with an effort dragged his gaze away, fixing it instead on the roof of an outbuilding.

"What do you want?" he shouted.

"What do I want?" the thing that had once been Mike Stroud echoed. "What do I want? I'd like to speak to you in a civilized way. Man to man over a drink in the bar."

"No."

"So you wish us to conduct this interview with myself down in this dismal courtyard? While you lean out yonder window like some shy damsel in a Shakespeare play?"

"Get on with it." David felt an oozing loathing at the sound of the thing's voice.

The creature chuckled—a wet sound, as if its lungs were full of pus. "Temper, temper, Mr. Leppington. Remember, we're on the same side. My friends beneath the town were sent to be of service to your ancestors."

"Well, tell them from me they can go to hell."

"Doctor Leppington, that's where they came from. You know that as well as I do." Again the wet chuckle. "Now to business."

"What business?" David was ready to shut the window and draw the curtains on the obscene thing below.

"Ouch, ouch. Why the hostility?"

"Because you are a monster."

"I am also your servant."

"You're nothing of the sort."

"I am. And I'm here to comply with my instructions."

David gripped the window frame so tightly his knuckles turned white. "What instructions?"

"Your army is nearly ready, Dr. Leppington. Just as the Leppingtons' legend describes. They are fed. They will soon be ready to march. By night, of course. All they need now is you to assume command of them."

"What if I tell them to march into the sea?"

"That's not the deal and you know it. Your ancestors were entrusted with a divine quest, remember? From a higher authority?"

David couldn't keep his eyes on the rooftops any longer; he looked down at the figure in the courtyard and locked his mortal eyes on the two monstrous eyes that looked up at him. David spat, "And what if I refuse?"

"You know the consequences, Doctor Leppington. You were told often enough on your uncle's knee when you were about so high."

"Go away," David hissed.

"I would also ask you to hand over the three people you have with you—the man who calls himself Jack Black, Electra Charnwood and Bernice Mochardi—they don't mean anything to you. They will be nothing more than impediments to your adventure."

David shook his head.

The vampire grinned. "Oh, David, how brave and noble, standing shoulder to shoulder with a little band of grubby strangers. You know Black would steal your wallet given half the chance, don't you? Electra Charnwood is diseased—and pretty little Bernice Mochardi has her own dark, dark secret."

"Go away."

"Don't take my word for it, David. Ask her, why don't you?"

David looked down at the eyes. It was like looking down into a pit blazing with fire.

The vampire laughed softly. "We would, of course, if you choose to accept leadership of the army, expect you to retain your human status. It would be so helpful to us."

"I bet it would."

"Take my word, David, soon you'll be more than eager to hand those three apologies for human beings over to us. As I said, between you and me, they'll just get in the way. Well, that wraps it up for now," he said suavely and broke eye contact with David.

David was suddenly aware of the breeze blowing cold against his face again, and the blocky shapes of the outbuildings lying down there in the darkness.

The creature held out his two arms; in the gloom he resembled some perverse approximation of a white crucifix.

David watched two teenage girls emerge from the darkness to stand at either side of the vampire; they could have been the two glamorous assistants to a stage magician.

They handed the white figure a bundle, wrapped in a sheet, the ends of which fluttered in the breeze.

A thin cry reached David's ears.

"My God," he breathed, "they've got a child."

David watched the vampire smile—a huge crocodile smile, exposing large white teeth that seemed to gleam with their own inner light. With a flourish Mike Stroud pulled back the sheet. A child of about two years old struggled, trying to escape Stroud's iron grip. The cries grew louder. A pair of bare, plump arms stretched up toward David as if the child was reaching out, imploringly, to its mother.

Stroud's mouth opened wider, then plunged downward at the child's face.

David looked away. Just in time. Before the sight of the monstrous became unendurable.

Chapter Thirty-one

1

David walked to the bathroom. The blood sang in his ears. The world seemed far away. For a moment he wondered if he would pass out before he reached the door.

Then he was in the bathroom, on his knees before the toilet and vomiting powerfully into the bowl.

It was another ten minutes before he made it back to the sitting room; his throat burning, his stomach aching and still spasming even though there was nothing more in there to retch out.

Electra held out a glass of brandy. Shaking his head, he picked up a coffee cup and drank half a cup full of the now cold liquid.

He took a deep breath, composed himself, then looked around at the other three. They looked back, their eyes grave. "You heard all that?" His voice rasped through his now sore throat. "We've just been issued with our ultimatum. And what he did to the baby . . . that was just to reinforce what he said in case we didn't take him seriously."

"The bastard," Bernice said in a low voice. "The complete and utter bastard."

"The thing is," David said, "how can he know so much about us?"

Electra looked up at David. "For me and you, he can uncover a good deal of information through the local people he's recruited, for want of a better word, into his vampire band."

"Electra. He said you were ill: is that true?"

"Ill? The word he used was 'diseased,' " she said. "Yes, I am diseased. I picked up a rather unpleasant virus a little while ago."

289

"Oh," David said in a low voice. He noticed the startled look Bernice shot Electra.

"Tests show I'm carrying a strain of the hepatitis virus."

"Hepatitis A?"

"No, the nastier one. Hepatitis B."

"But that is treatable," David said.

"It is, although there is a danger that the hepatitis will result in my developing cirrhosis, which, of course, is just a raunchier name for the early stages of cancer of the liver. And I shouldn't drink, but I damn well do. So, yes, the monster is completely and utterly right. I am diseased."

"But that's still a low grade risk when it comes to infectivity," David said. "It's highly unlikely any of us here will contract it from you."

"No," she agreed, "not through normal social contact, shaking hands or using the same hairbrush. But if you sleep with me or we share the same hypodermic then, I warn you, you do so at your own risk. Now I will have a small brandy; anyone care to join me?" Again, David saw Electra trying to make light of a truth that was unpalatably grim. Although one look at her face showed she was anything but good-humored. The muscles under the skin of her face were hard; her eyes had a bleak glassy quality to them. Inside, a little part of her had died tonight.

No one accepted Electra's offer of brandy. Black looked briefly out of the window without opening it, then closed the curtains with a brutal tug of his tattooed hands.

Bernice cleared her throat as if she'd been building up to saying something that was important to her. "Then all the pieces are still falling into place. I told you I thought that, basically, we're the same four people who were gathered together in Leppingsvalt's palace over a thousand years ago. For me, what Mike Stroud has told us bears this out. David here occupies the role of the chief and leader of the vampire army. His sister was ill: the legend suggests she had a leprous sore on her right hand. Electra has told us she is infected with the hepatitis virus. Vurtzen was a Goth, his exploits ransacking towns were already legendary. I am not being deliberately offensive here, but Jack Black fits that particular mold."

Black nodded, still stone-faced. He didn't dispute Bernice's theory.

Electra patted Bernice on the knee and said gently, "But in the legend Leppingsvalt's bride-to-be was a reformed harlot. I think even our friendly neighborhood vampire was wide of the mark there, my poppet. Especially as he was referring to you; butter wouldn't melt in your mouth."

Bernice gave a little shrug and spoke in a tight voice. "When I was fifteen I fell in love; Tony was my first real boy-friend. We'd had sex together a few times. Then he invited me to his bedsit. I got drunk. Before I knew it there were four men there—his friends, so he said. Anyway . . . cutting a long story short. I got really drunk—blind drunk. The four men all had sex with me. It was only later I found out that they'd each paid Tony twenty pounds for the privilege. That makes him a pimp. Now, what does that make me?"

Again there was a great silence—it seemed deeper than mere absence of sound. David could sense the meshing of gears in that supernatural engine in a world beyond this one. This was all part of some satanic machination.

Electra slid along the sofa and put her arm around Bernice and hugged her warmly. "Love, love. You were fifteen years old, a child, that's all. And they got you drunk. Don't blame yourself."

Bernice shook her head. "But I enjoyed it. There were all these men . . . and I was the center of their attention. That night I knew what it felt like to be a film star."

"You were drunk, love. No one can blame you for anything."

Bernice wasn't listening. "And do you want to hear a real coincidence? My name is Mochardi. I learned a few years ago that Mochardi is a Romany word. It means unclean woman. Bizarre, eh?"

She gave a rough little laugh. There was something dangerously careless about it. As if right now she couldn't care less if she opened the door and walked downstairs into the basement, threw open that steel door, bared her throat and said, "OK, boys, what you see is what you get—so come right here and get it while it's warm."

David sat down beside her on the sofa. "Bernice. Electra. Do you see what's happening? Stroud is being clever. He's trying to weaken us by demoralizing us. He's concentrating on our human frailties—your illness, Electra, and what Bernice sees as . . . as a sinful pleasure."

Bernice scowled. "What are you worrying for, David? You're safe from them. They told you. So why don't you hand us over?"

"No." David's voice hardened. "We've got to remember we're in this together; that we're on the same side."

"And are we?" Her eyes had grown large.

"Yes. And we're going to fight them together."

"But how?"

"That we have to find out."

"But they're indestructible," Bernice said. "Those things have been waiting in the cave for hundreds of years."

Electra sighed. "David's right. And we can't stay holed up in here. It'll only be a matter of time before they break into the hotel. And I'd bet a year's bar takings that a crucifix and a few cloves of garlic won't stop them."

Black slapped the head of the hammer against his open palm. "I'll go down there and take a crack at them."

David said, "I really would enjoy seeing you break their heads with that thing, but I think they're going to be tougher than that." He rubbed his jaw, thinking hard. "The real weapon to use against them is information. We need to learn more about them."

"We know they avoid bright lights."

"Particularly sunlight," Electra added. "And we know that the sunlight is comprised of more than visible light. The sun pumps out all kinds of radiation from the infrared to the ultraviolet. It's possible that some forms of radiation might be harmful, even lethal, to them."

"Good point." David felt a tingle of optimism. "Maybe we can nail these things after all." He stood up and reached for his jacket.

Electra looked aghast. "Where are you going?"

"To the hospital to see one George Alfred Leppington."

"You can't," Bernice protested. "Not in the dark."

David glanced at his watch. "It's eight o'clock. That means there's a good nine hours until daybreak. If we sit around here all night that's nine hours wasted."

"But your uncle might still be unconscious."

"I think he was unconscious last time we saw him. My belief is something else was speaking through him. I want to find out what that thing was. And I want to find out what's going to send those monsters screaming for their lives."

Electra stood up, her face a picture of horror. "You can't go out there. I won't let you. Jack, if he tries to leave the room knock him down."

Black moved to stand in front of the door. Trying to get past Black would be like trying to shove past a bull elephant.

"Please don't go, David," Bernice said in a small voice. "They'll be waiting downstairs."

"I know," he said grimly. "But I'm the only person in this town they need to remain mortal." He looked from Bernice to Electra to Black. "They need me like this—flesh and blood."

Electra said, "That's what they say, but do you believe them?"

"Well, shall we put it to the test?"

There was a long silence; David could hear the blood pumping through the veins in his neck up to his brain. For the first time in his life he had become so aware—so exquisitely aware—of the blood moving through his own body. There were tides in there and currents. After all, man is basically an aquatic animal—a creature of oceans—and he carries more than four litres of the equivalent of that ocean in the form of blood inside his body.

Electra gave a slow nod. "David's right. He's probably the only one of us, probably the only human anywhere on this planet, who won't be harmed by them."

"For the time being," Black grunted. "Until you tell them that you're not going to lead their maggot army."

Bernice asked, almost fearfully, "And you *will* tell them that, David, won't you?"

David gave a grim smile. "I see myself as staying a humble doctor, not a general, don't you?"

Electra returned the smile—albeit a ghost of one. "Jack, open the door, please."

"Electra, wait." Bernice stood up, her hands clenched by her side. "What if they're waiting outside the door?"

"I set the burglar alarm when we came up. Let's hope the infrared sensors would have detected any intruders—human or non-human."

"Right," David said, pulling on his leather gloves. "Wish me luck . . . oh, by the way, Electra, do you have anything that makes a very bright light?"

2

At the same time as David Leppington was zipping up his jacket in Electra's apartment in the Station Hotel, Maximilian Hart was walking through the night-time town, its lights flickering as the gales tugged at the power cables strung along the valley bottom. There was a storm coming. Much would break before the icy blast.

A trio of burly figures blocked Maximilian's way as he headed for the doorway of the mini-mart.

"Well, as I live and breathe," one said with a grin. "Aren't you going to say hello, Maxie boy?"

Maximilian stopped dead on the pavement; his face was as motionless as a rock; he became statue-like.

"Surely you remember us, Maxie?" said another one, taking a cigarette from his mouth. "You gave us money for cigarettes and a couple of bottles of grog. You come back with more of the old doh-rai-me for your pals?" He held the glowing tip of the cigarette close to Maximilian's earlobe.

They walked toward him in a line, their eyes glinting, their mouths grinning.

He moved backward from them; a slow, plodding step.

One step.

Pause.

Two steps.

Pause.

"What happened to your paper crown, Maxie?"

"Oh, he's not talking to us, are you, old buddy?"

"What's the matter?"

"Cat got your tongue?"

"Why you got slanty eyes, Maxie boy?"

"Mother get chased by a Chinaman?"

The three of them laughed roughly.

"Come on, Maxie boy, we know you've got some money."

"Yeah, hand it over."

"Or this time we'll kick your arse all over town."

Maximilian's face remained impassive. His oriental-shaped eyes that the Down's syndrome had endowed him with looked left and right. The pavement was deserted. The wind blew fish-and-chips trays down the street; a carrier bag, blown against his leg, briefly enclosed his calf and shin in a flimsy embrace before being taken by a gust of wind and blown high into the air.

One of the gang held a cigarette out under his chin. He felt the heat of the glowing tip against his skin, smelled the acrid tang of tobacco smoke. In front of him were three grinning faces that seemed so alien to him. So mysterious in their cravings and their speech.

Something thumped against his rump.

He glanced down; he'd backed up against a stretch of waist-high steel railings that separated pavement from road.

One of the youths looked at the other two. "Bad news, lads. Maxie doesn't want to cough up."

"Then we'll have to take it from him, won't we, boys?"

"OK, who's going to stick their hands into his filthy pockets?"

"You first, Jonno."

"You're kidding! I'm not playing hunt-the-hot-dog-sausage with that spasmo."

They all laughed.

The laughs turned to gasps of shock.

Maximilian watched as arms blurred past him at tremendous speed. Someone, standing behind him, had reached out to the three youths. The hands grabbed them by their jackets, then hauled them forward, turning them around as they did so.

It all happened so quickly, but Maximilian retained the images. One moment the three youths were standing there; then they were dragged forward, turned over so the backs of their necks lay across the horizontal bar of the fence, like they were prisoners being held down on the executioner's chopping block to await the fall of the axe. Only they were held there, facing upward at the darkened sky. Their throats bulged upward, naked and gleaming in the street lights.

They gurgled, struggled, eyes staring in sheer terror.

Maximilian saw heads dart down at the throats, then the heads twisted from side to side like dogs gnawing at a bone. When he next saw the three youths, their throats were torn; blood pumped

295

vibrantly out, squirting in jets as high as his shoulders. Then the heads came down again like pigs jostling for food at the trough. So many heads.

And the sound of hungry mouths eagerly feeding was loud in his ears.

He moved away from the fence, looking back at the cluster of people. Some he recognized—but only just, because their faces had altered. There were the Moberry sisters. And that one across there, joyously licking a thick smear of blood from his lips, that was Mr. Morrow who worked at the slaughterhouse.

The others were strangers.

He backed away.

He wasn't shocked. This was just another mystery. Like any one of the other mysteries that were paraded before his eyes each day. Like the man in black bringing white and brown envelopes to his house (*Bills, fucking bills*, his father would bellow). Or that time of year when people put trees, twinkling with lights, in their windows. Or when his father and his friends sat around a table, drinking that strange-tasting drink and staring at those pieces of card in their hands like they were the most important things in their lives. He turned his back on the scene and began to walk slowly away.

"Not so fast, my young scamp," came a low voice, "not when there's hungry mouths to feed." The yellow-haired man leaned forward, reached out a gleaming white hand and squeezed Maximilian's arm above the elbow. "Mmm . . . and such a juicy young chap as well."

The things that had been the town's men and women surged forward hungrily at Maximilian, their mouths open, showing the strings of spit in their mouths bloody from gorging so greedily on the three men.

"*No!*" Stroud held up his hand. "No. This one's for our friends underground." He smiled that crocodile smile again at Maximilian. "Walk this way with me, old buddy. We'll chat as we go."

Stroud took Maximilian's hand as if he was taking the hand of a child before crossing the road. "I think there's a fair old storm blowing up, don't you?" He smiled gently. "Say, how did you get that cut under your eye?" He lightly touched Maximilian's cheek, just below where the bird had pecked him earlier in the evening. It could almost have been a simple gesture of affection. "Mmm, it looks as if it could be quite sore. You know, I get the feeling you've had a tough time growing up here. I think people have ill-treated you for far too long. I was lucky, I suppose. I grew up pampered and probably more than a little spoilt." He spoke in a light, chatty way. "I was born in a little town in America. It was like one of those places you see on TV—although you Brits call it telly; such a wonderful invention it is, too. It should have made John Logie Baird a billionaire like Bill Gates—you know, the owner of Microsoft computer software? Windows? Never heard of him? No? Oh, well, not to worry. Anyway, I lived in a house made of white boards, with a porch and a rocking chair where my grandmother sat and scraped the skins of potatoes. I'm not walking too fast for you, am I? My parents were called Mark and Rebecca Stroud. They christened me Michael Luke—now there's a handsome brace of Bible names, aren't they?"

Hand in hand, they walked down the street in the near-dark. One figure blond-haired, tall, lean, almost willowy, light-footed as a dancer; the other short, dark, dumpy with a heavy plodding step.

Still talking in that gentle smooth-as-silk voice, a charming smile playing on his lips, Michael Stroud led Maximilian Hart up the hill to George Leppington's house. And to the cave that now yawned dark and wide like a hungry mouth waiting to be fed.

Chapter Thirty-two

1

By eight-thirty that evening David Leppington had left Electra's apartment on the first floor of the hotel. Jack Black went with him. The man's head—shaved, tattooed and Frankenstein-scarred—turned from left to right, alert to anyone—or anything—that might have entered the hotel undetected by the alarm system's infrared sensors mounted on the walls.

Black switched off the alarm system that had started its warning bleeps; both had triggered the sensors when they entered the lobby.

Black spoke in a low gruff voice, "I can come with you to the hospital if you want."

"No. I think you'd be safer here in the hotel with Electra and Bernice."

"But you still don't trust me, do you." This wasn't a question; it was a statement.

David stopped and looked at him sharply as a sudden realization pierced him through. "You can read my mind, can't you?"

Black nodded. "Sometimes."

"What am I thinking now?"

"You're shit-scared."

"That's an understatement."

"And there's a jumble of other stuff."

"Such as?"

"It's more feelings than words. You're scared for people— Electra, Bernice, the old man in the hospital. The people in the town."

"And there's something else?"

"Yes."

"What is it?"

"Bernice. You like her. You get a warm feeling when you think about her. And you think about her a lot."

"You think I love her?"

Black shrugged, his forehead wrinkling as he considered. "Don't know." He shrugged again. "Don't know what love is."

David paused and looked at the scarred man. "What am I thinking now?"

"That maybe you're starting to trust me. That you don't think I'm such a savage bastard after all." Black's ugly face split into a grin. "You still can't stand the look of my mush, though, can you?"

David found himself returning the smile. "Give me time. None of us are perfect."

"You're a good bloke," Black said. "That wouldn't have

stopped me wapping you one and taking your wallet. But you're a good bloke. But you're too hard on yourself, you know?"

"Believe me, Jack, I'm no saint."

"Damn' closest I've been to one. You care so much about people that sometimes it screws you up inside. Then it actually hurts you."

"Well, maybe that's a liability rather than an asset. Everyone should be a little self-centered at times. What do you say?"

Again came the grin, warming the ugly face. "Me? I always put me first. Had to. My mother dumped me when I was a couple of weeks old." For a moment a faraway look came into his deep-set eyes. David thought he was going to say something else about what must have been a miserable, godforsaken childhood. But suddenly he asked, "Who's Katrina West?"

David shot him a startled look. "Katrina West?" He shook his head, puzzled: surely he hadn't been thinking about her again? "She was an old friend. I went to school with her. Why? What's wrong?"

Black scowled. The faraway look stayed on his face. "Funny. It came like, y'know? Really loud." He looked at David. "She's thinking about you?"

"What is she thinking?"

"I don't know, but it's really strong like . . . powerful. Y'know?"

"Katrina West is hundreds of miles away in a hospital. You mean you can actually read her mind, too?"

"Just bits. It doesn't usually work to order. But sometimes I can sort of home in on one person, just sort of tune into their minds like it's a radio or something, y" know? Sometimes I think I can read every mind in a whole city and then there's just this great noise going boom, boom inside my head and I think my head's going to just bust in two . . ." His voice had risen in pitch and intensity. David saw the man swallow back down what must be a nightmarish experience. The blank expression returned to his face, reminding David of a concrete wall—hard, featureless, impenetrable.

They'd reached the kitchen. Ahead lay the back door of the hotel, locked and stoutly bolted. David checked the mobile phone, then slipped it back into his pocket. He'd asked for a light of some sorts and Black briefly vanished into a storeroom off from the kitchen. He returned carrying a big flashlight with a pistol grip and a glass lens as big as a saucer. It looked more like a quaint 1950s idea of a futuristic ray gun.

"A million candlepower," Black told him. "Electra said the batteries have been on charge all day so it should last you. Need anything else?" Black nodded at kitchen utensils hanging from a rack. "A knife?"

"No." David shook his head. "I'm more likely to damage myself rather than the . . . enemy, I imagine we should call them."

"Ready?"

David nodded. "As I ever will be."

"You really reckon that they won't touch you?"

"That's what I'm banking on. I think they need me as flesh and blood—at least for a little while."

"You're the boss."

David couldn't read minds. But at that moment he knew that was how Black saw him. The boss. Some kind of reincarnation of the long-dead Chief Leppingsvalt. He believed, too, Bernice's suggestion that they were those four people from the Leppingsvalt palace of a thousand years ago. On the eve of that great dark day of doom.

Black slipped back the bolts, then stood poised to turn the key in the lock as a prelude to opening the door.

David looked through the window into the courtyard. "Looks deserted," he said.

"I'll only open the door for a couple of seconds. Those things move bastard quick. OK?"

"OK. Do it."

It took just two seconds. Black opened the door, David slipped through into the night air, then the door was slammed shut behind him. The sound of the bolts being snapped home echoed from the buildings ringing the yard.

2

David zipped his jacket up toward his throat. Out there in the darkness his throat felt incredibly vulnerable; the skin unbearably sensitive; the breeze that swirled scraps of paper around the yard felt like cold fingers caressing the skin of his neck. Again he was acutely aware of the blood pulsing through his neck.

He glanced up.

Ragged pieces of cloud floated like ghostly rafts across the night sky. Here and there, clumps of stars pointed through with an icy clarity.

OK, David, he thought, here goes. First stop the hospital. Then find some way to rid this town of the nightmare plague of vampires.

Christ, sounds easy if you say it quickly enough, doesn't it?

He glanced back at the hotel. Black stood in the kitchen, looking through the window; he gave a single nod, which David guessed meant good luck.

And Christ, would he need it. He felt completely vulnerable. Now even the flimsy safety of the locked doors and windows of the hotel seemed preferable.

His hand tightened around the pistol grip of the flashlight.

For whatever use that would be.

These creatures didn't like light. But now the flashlight seemed about as potent a weapon as a handful of celery sticks.

The idea of pointing it at a vampire and saying "One more move and I'll let you have it" seemed ludicrously absurd.

David felt a darkly sour tide of laughter quivering up through his stomach. Go back to the hotel, David; take a full bottle of whiskey up to your room and get totally and gloriously and stupendously assholed. You're on a fool's errand. This won't work. You are going to die.

No, scratch that.

You're going to do worse than die. You will be undead like them. You will be Nosferatu. One of those bastard children of the night, howling for another fix of blood.

At that moment he thought of Bernice. Her large trusting eyes. The image brought with it a flood of warmth through his veins.

Do you want to see Bernice fall into the vampires' claws?

Do you want to see her like that thing locked in the basement?

Do you want to see her with her breasts gnawed raw and bloody?

Do you want that?

301

Do you?

He knew the answer. No. Did he, hell. He liked the girl. And Christ, yes, there was an emotional bond with the woman who was old before the two of them were even born.

In a past life she had been his bride-to-be.

And in that past life he'd failed her. She'd died bloodily.

So, now, David Leppington, he thought. Now's the time to correct the past mistakes. It's time to atone for the sins he'd committed in that previous existence.

Gritting his teeth, he held the pistol grip tight in his hands and rested his finger on the flashlight button, ready to switch it on if he saw anything.

He pulled the car keys from his pocket, then resolutely advanced across the courtyard.

The breeze blew more strongly; it made a fluting sound around the eaves of the outbuildings; the sounds merged with the deep roar of the River Lepping that lay beyond the courtyard.

The car lay in front of him, a sleek black form with silvery letters spelling out *Station Hotel* on the passenger door.

He thumbed the key button—the lights flashed as the doors unlocked and the alarm disabled itself.

Then he paused a dozen paces from the car.

A shape seemed to swell up from its roof.

He stared into the gloom, allowing his eyes to adjust to the dark.

He breathed deeply. He saw something that would be embedded in his mind forever. Suddenly his Adam's apple seemed too big for his throat; he swallowed the lump that grew there as hard as stone, while his eyes took in the nameless thing that was as heart-breakingly sad as it was monstrous.

A child stood on the roof of the car. David guessed it was little more than two years old. And clearly the same child that Stroud had used in his theatrical display earlier. The cot sheet patterned with teddy bears and stained with drying blood was gathered around the child's shoulders like a cloak. The child wore pyjama bottoms; it was bare-chested.

David couldn't stop his eyes traveling up the body, taking in every sickening detail.

There was very little blood considering there was a gaping

rip in the child's throat; it formed a three-cornered tear and a loose triangle of skin the size and shape of a slice of bread cut from corner to corner hung down on the child's chest.

The wound itself was (not surprisingly) bloodless and as white as paper. The windpipe was exposed; it looked like a piece of white plastic hose.

The child's hair was stuck up on end as if gelled there. It presented a cartoonish picture of someone being frightened by a ghost—the hair was vertical.

David realized with a shudder that the child had been licked clean of its blood. Every spurt, every trickle from the torn throat had been greedily tongued from the skin; the monsters had even licked the blood from the child's hair like dogs licking clean a feeding bowl. Now the creatures' saliva had dried, pasting the child's hair upright into that picture of cartoonish fright.

David moved slowly forward.

The child, standing there, cloaked in its teddy bear pram sheet, grinned and hissed. A tongue—an incredibly long dog-like tongue—flickered out through the lips. The two little eyes burned brightly in the gloom.

It did not blink.

The stare was that of a snake about to strike.

David moved toward the car, the flashlight gripped in one hand like a pistol.

The little creature watched him with those eyes that behind the glassy brilliance were dead and cold; the breeze fluttered the teddy bear-patterned sheet. David saw the ribs turning the little bare chest into a series of ridges. The chest itself heaved, palpitated as its undead heart furiously pumped whatever flowed through its veins.

David paused as the thing hissed loudly and bared its teeth.

"You know who I am," David said calmly, trying to avoid looking directly into its eyes. "You know I am Leppington. You can't touch me. I am—"

The toddler suddenly cocked its head to one side and said, "Inviolable." The voice was unnaturally guttural and dark.

David nodded, grim faced. "Inviolable," he agreed. "You know you must not touch me."

The little child pushed out its bottom lip as if it was about to cry. "Want a kiss—want a little kiss." The voice was sweet and childlike now.

David looked up as if he'd been slapped.

That was it!

These vampires weren't individuals. They were nothing more than ventriloquist's dummies worked by some dark implacable intelligence.

The child was dead after all. What he saw was a mere pretense of life. And whatever animated the child was now tormenting David by having it speak baby talk.

David blanked himself to the disgusting thing on the car roof.

He opened the door.

"Papa, papa—baby cold, baby hungry. Don't leave me up here, papa." The child sang the words in a tiny innocent voice while holding out two arms to be lifted off the car roof.

Quelling the paternal instinct that automatically welled up inside of him, David climbed into the car, expecting at any second that the tiny body would launch itself at him, jaws snapping hungrily at his throat.

As calmly, as deliberately as he could, he sat in the seat and closed the door. Don't let these things spook you.

They're playing mind games with you; they want to confuse you; disorientate you; they don't want you to think clearly or rationally.

He pushed the key home and turned the ignition.

The engine purred into life. He flicked the plastic stalk on the steering column and the lights flashed on, illuminating the brick walls of the outbuildings.

So far, so good.

As long as a vampire horde don't come charging across the courtyard and turn the car over.

Nice and easy does it.

"Papa, don't leave me up here," came the voice through the roof of the car, "I'm frightened. I'm frightened."

David engaged first gear.

At that moment the little toddler voice suddenly morphed into guttural laughter. The puppet master had changed its strategy.

The upside-down head of the child appeared on the other side of the windscreen. It grinned hugely. The eyes burned into his.

Then it began to beat its forehead at the glass.

The sound was heavy, somehow wet-sounding. Someone could have been slapping a big fish at the glass for the noise it made.

The guttural laughter continued as the child beat its forehead against the windscreen. Bruises appeared on the forehead, blossoming outward, filling the skin with dark shadows.

David wiped his mouth with the back of his hand.

It beat harder.

The skin split.

Now gobs of liquid—a mixture of clear and white bubbles appeared on the glass. The thing was bleeding but it didn't bother it one bit. It still chuckled and grinned rapaciously.

David accelerated, then braked hard. The tires screeched on the cobbles.

The child vampire slipped forward off the car roof, bounced down onto the bonnet, then slid off the end onto the ground. The sheet fluttered in the breeze.

Feeling sick to the pit of his stomach, David paused, his foot over the accelerator pedal.

Should I drive forward? Run the thing over? Crush it beneath the tires?

He took a deep breath, gripped the steering wheel hard in one hand, then threw the car into reverse.

He couldn't do it. He couldn't run one of the monsters down.

Savagely he reversed the car in a great sweeping circle across the yard, tires spinning, engine roaring. Then he slammed it into forward gear.

Seconds later, he was speeding the car along the deserted street in the direction of the hospital.

3

David drove through deserted streets. The breeze pushed at branches, making the trees shift restlessly. A sense of nervous anxiety had been transferred into everything.

The air was restless. The trees shuddered. Phantom rafts of cloud fled through the night sky.

He saw nothing on the way to the hospital. That was, he saw none of those foul creatures.

With the time only just approaching nine, lights shone from the houses; here and there he glimpsed the flicker of a reflected TV screen in the windows. For most people in Leppington it was just another Sunday night in early spring. They were content to settle down into armchairs and sofas, tickle the cat under the chin, microwave popcorn, open a bottle of wine, light another cigarette or any other of the myriad activities people indulge in on Sunday nights in front of the television.

The infection's only just begun, he thought. Perhaps no more than a dozen people out of a population of fifteen hundred are directly affected. If he acted quickly enough he could cut out the vampires like he could excise dead tissue from a wound.

Briefly, the idea of going to the police flitted through his mind. But that would be a non-starter; he knew he was the only one who could stop this now.

He pulled into the hospital car park and switched off the engine. It was long past visiting time; however, he'd been told he could visit his uncle whenever he wanted.

Now, that's always a bad sign, he told himself, as he climbed out of the car and shut the door after him. The old man was in a side ward, too. That meant the doctors were taking a pessimistic view of George Leppington's prospects of recovery.

David entered the hospital, passing quickly along the corridors painted that insipid mint-green that's the livery of many a municipal building.

He entered his uncle's room to find him lying on his back, his hand resting loosely on the blankets covering his chest. On the bedside cabinet was a cupful of what looked like pink lollipops. Instead of the boiled sweet that formed the head of a lollipop, these had little cubes of pink sponge; the nurses would moisten these with cold water and swab out the mouths of unconscious patients. If a mouth is allowed to become over-dry it's likely to fall prey to fungal infections like thrush. Soon the comatose patient's breath smells overripe, like a pedal bin left unemptied too long in the middle of summer.

George was breathing deeply, the rhythm steady and even. If it hadn't been for the bandage around the top of his head anyone would have thought the old man was merely asleep.

As David approached the bed he had an inkling what would happen.

It happened with all the suddenness of a switch being thrown.

The old man's eyes opened wide as if someone had reached down and dragged back his eyelids. The eyes were wide, staring; they could have belonged to a man who'd died of fright.

"David. You believe now, don't you?" The old man's voice was a soft whispery rasp.

"Yes, I believe." David sat on a chair beside the bed. "I've seen those creatures; I've talked to them, too."

The old man, still lying flat on the bed, his head on the pillow, nodded with the satisfaction of a man who knows when a prediction has come true. The eyes stared at the ceiling. Again David was struck by the notion he wasn't so much speaking to his uncle as to something that spoke *through* him.

Suddenly we're all damn puppets, he thought angrily. And there are two forces at work here. Evil is at work through the vampires. Evil speaks through their mouths. But what's this that speaks through the old man's mouth? Is it the voice of Good?

David shook his head as he looked down at his uncle. He just didn't know anymore. All he did know was that two opposing forces were meeting head-on in this little town. Two titanic forces—unimaginably powerful and enduring. And the town's people had become those forces' puppets to enact their will. *Go on! Pull the string. PULL THE STRING!*

The sudden rage that crackled through him left him grinding his teeth and clenching his fists.

"David," his uncle rasped, "you know what you must do now?"

David had to breathe deeply to quell the rage before he could speak. "I know what I'm supposed to do. But can you really expect me to somehow take control of this vampire army and march it against the rest of the world?"

"It's what you were born to do. I groomed you. You remember now? All the stories I told you? All the times I talked with you?"

"I remember. But I can't do it." He clenched his fists again. *"I won't do it."*

"Why not?"

"Because you're expecting me to lead a vampire army out and—and what? Topple governments? Create some kind of empire where everyone will worship dead gods?"

307

"Dead gods? No, gods that have been merely awaiting their return to pre-eminence."

David's mouth went dry. His mind spun. "You've dropped me in the deep end, haven't you, uncle? You blew up the steel fence in the cave to release them, didn't you?"

"Yes. There was a danger that if you were given the choice you might refuse to follow your destiny."

"That I might decide that it's crazy, so fucking crazy to lead these blood-sucking monsters out into the outside world?"

"Yes."

"And you're damn' right, too."

His uncle still stared at the ceiling, his eyes wide. "I did consider this eventuality. After all, your mother always fought against your destiny. That's why she took you away from the town."

"And thank God she did."

The old man smiled. "But I knew you would come back. And I knew I had to give you your chance to become king."

"But what now? What if I don't choose to take charge of this vampire army?"

"There will be bitter disappointment. In many more quarters than you know—or can even understand. But this eventuality has been prophesied."

"What? That this vampire army would rampage out of control across the country?"

"Yes. It was foretold many times." The old man smiled again, the dried traces of blood around the eyes cracked. "You're familiar with the word 'pyrrhic'?"

David nodded, his face stony.

"It is used in conjunction with the word victory," continued the old man. "And the phrase 'pyrrhic victory' comes from a certain King Epirus from ancient Greece who defeated the Romans at Asculum in 279 BC. Even though King Epirus—or Pyrrhus—won the battle, so many of his soldiers were killed that it rendered the victory valueless."

"So," David interrupted, sensing time was running short. "A pyrrhic victory means a victory not worth having. Why is this relevant?"

"Because the old gods will be content with a pyrrhic victory. They are, shall we say, philosophical about the idea that when the vampires are unleashed upon the world they personally will gain nothing; that they will see mankind perish."

"But what good is that to anyone?"

"Because even the gods have a limited lifespan. Even though it be tens of thousands of years. For centuries they have awaited Ragnarök, which is the day of doom when the gods will be destroyed and replaced by a new order of deities. Don't look so puzzled, nephew. We are the children of the old gods. When they die we die with them. The new gods will bring into being their own race of mortal beings on this Earth."

"So the vampires will be merely destroying the human race in order that it will be replaced with a different species?"

"If you like, nephew."

"But if I take charge of this army and lead them to create a new empire for these old Teutonic gods, then humankind will survive?"

"Yes. You realize the choice is yours."

"Christ. Out of the frying pan and into the fire."

The old man licked his lips; his mouth looked dry as paper. "But you would destroy your army of dead warriors if you could?"

"Lord, yes."

"But your destiny is already written. You only have two choices."

"I know. Take command of this filthy army, or leave it to run riot across the face of the planet, turning every man, woman and child into the same kind of abomination as them."

"What have you decided?"

"I've decided to destroy them."

"Impossible."

"Maybe. But I've got to try." He looked at the old man lying there, head swathed in bandages that were stained brown with dried blood. The eyes stared at the ceiling—they were wide and gleaming. "Uncle George," David said gently but firmly. "Will you tell me everything you know about these creatures?"

"I can. But it will do you no good. They have lived in the caves beneath the town for more than a thousand years. You can't kill them."

"Nevertheless, please tell me."

The old man ran the paper-dry tongue over his bloodless lips as he considered. A hospital porter pushed a trolley past the door. Outside the world went on as before. But already David sensed the world—the very fabric of the world that formed the chairs, beds, walls of the hospital, the soil outside, the rocks in the stream—he sensed all of this was holding its breath in a tense expectation of what would happen over the next few hours. The world was going to change soon. One Dr. David Leppington held the key to that change.

He looked down at the old man as he lay there in bed, the eyes staring fixedly at the ceiling; the lips moved quickly yet silently, as if George Leppington was discussing David's request with someone unseen but present in the room with them.

Then the lips stopped moving. The old man's breathing was deep, rhythmic.

"Well?" David asked at last. "Will you tell me about the creatures?"

The old man gave a nod. Then he began to speak.

"Be careful: they not only have the ability to reach out to you physically, they can reach out to you mentally; they can tamper with your mind." He gave a queer, slanting smile. "So beware, nephew." He continued talking in that whispery voice that was low, calm and strangely hypnotic. David leaned forward so as not to miss a single word.

4

Outside the wind rose, eliciting a long-drawn-out moan that ululated along the valley bottom to twitch at the power cables and shiver the trees so the roots strained against the earth that held them there. For all the world it looked as if the trees of Leppington longed to pull up their roots and flee the town. And all the danger and the dread that seethed through and below its darkened streets.

The cold wind blew harder. Power cables threaded between pylons swung back and forth, tree trunks bent with a dark, aching groan . . .

It was night. Eight hours of darkness remained until the sun would make its first hesitant appearance over the hills; it would come with all the trepidation of a woman returning home from work to find the front door open, a window smashed, blood dripping down the stairway banister rail. Like the woman, it would peep fearfully over the horizon, afraid what it would find there in the town, in the cool light of another day.

Chapter Thirty-three

1

Bernice felt safe. She felt secure.

The doors to the outside world are locked, she told herself. The lift has been switched off between floors. The alarms downstairs are set. Anyone breaking in—be they mortal or vampire—will set the alarms shrilling.

Bernice opened the door of Electra's apartment. The corridor on the first floor of the hotel was deserted. She felt very safe; very secure.

She stepped out into the hotel corridor. One bulb had blown in an overhead lamp. Otherwise, the lights were steady and bright.

The time was 9:15.

2

In the kitchen of Electra Charnwood's apartment Jack Black smoked a cigarette. A tattooed finger curled thickly around the slender white tube as he held it to his lips.

A sound no one could hear—the sound of the people of Leppington's thoughts—drummed rhythmically in his head. It was a low, muffled sound; like the beat of music coming through the walls of an adjoining house.

—put the cat out, Tommy; put it out while the adverts are on—

—no money in taxi driving, no money at all; there must be a

job on the buses; I'm not too old; might be worth writing to the bus company in Whitby; they might . . .

The voice faded to be replaced by another.

If I have sex with him tonight, he might take me into York tomorrow; those summer dresses won't be on the racks forever, girl; besides, it'd be nice to feel the weight of his body on me, and the heat of his chest against mine . . . I like that. That's nice . . .

Mum says I can watch another ten minutes of a wrestling video. I've still to see all of Wrestlemania, but I like the Undertaker's Greatest Hits.

If he picks his toenails in front of the television again I'll hit him; so help me I will . . .

The voices flowing into Black's shaved head beat gently on. They were like the roar of the river tonight; a continuous sound, only slightly altering now and again in volume and pitch. The sound was strangely relaxing for once. Sometimes it drove him crazy.

Tonight the voices were pleasant, somehow soothing.

He pulled on the cigarette and looked through the first-floor window. He saw only the darkened courtyard and the shadowy shapes of willows on the river bank beyond. A few stars pricked through the gaps between scudding clouds.

He yawned, relaxed.

He knew where everyone was.

Doc Leppington had gone to the hospital. He'd be back soon.

Charnwood read books on local folkore in her sitting room; her face set hard with concentration, a pencil lightly inserted between her lips. Every so often she'd make a note in an exercise book. She was trying to find out as much as possible about the Leppington legends. Maybe there'd be some information they could use to their advantage.

Bernice had offered to do her bit, too. She'd gone up to her room on the fourth floor to fetch the videotape she'd spoken about. Before she'd gone through the door he'd told her in his characteristically gruff voice, "If you see anything, or hear anything, just yell. I'll come running."

She'd given a grateful smile, then stepped out through the door.

He pulled on the cigarette, calmly blew a cloud of smoke into the air. The rising wind blew around the hotel.

Black heard the sound it made. Gentle musical notes, like those of a flute.

3

Bernice walked to the end of the corridor and out onto the landing. Down below, she could see the hotel lobby with the deserted reception desk complete with visitors' book and phones. The basement door was soundly locked. On the walls the infrared sensors silently scanned the air space for intruders. The lights on the lift control panel were dead. The lift was going nowhere tonight.

Bernice climbed upstairs, her sandalled feet making no noise on the carpet.

Outside, the breeze blew. As it passed across the ornate friezes, balustrading and Gothic stone carvings on the hotel's quad towers it made a flute-like sound: a gentle, lilting melody like some melancholy Irish ballad.

She climbed flight after flight of stairs, passing the second floor; the third . . .

I can hear the walls breathing, she thought, relaxing to the flute sounds coming from outside; it's a strange thought, but I can sense it, the bricks in the walls are breathing . . .

. . . in-out, in-out, in-out . . .

Oh, you're tired, Bernice. Your sleep has been disrupted. Wouldn't it be nice to choose one of the hotel rooms at random, then curl up on a bed as sleepy as a kitten and fall fast asleep until morning?

Those *things* outside the hotel seemed far away now. They couldn't get past the locked doors; they could not hurt her.

The breeze played the building like a musical instrument; soft lilting flute notes soared up to the ceilings before spiraling down the well of the staircase.

I'm safe, I'm sleepy, I'm ready for bed. Surely there's no real need to stay awake.

She remembered the times she'd pulled her chest of drawers across the room every evening to barricade the door, because of the silly notion that a ghost lurked outside on the landing.

The ghost of the suicide William Morrow—

—with no eyes and mossy graveyard lips and thick fingers to stroke the throats of vulnerable girls . . .

She smiled. Wasn't that a crazy idea?

This place is as safe as a castle.

Nothing can get in.

Even that thing in the basement with the torn breasts is locked securely away. It can harm no one.

In fact, it could probably not hurt a fly anyway.

Even if she walked straight downstairs, unlocked the basement door, then marched right down to that lock-up store, threw open the door and . . .

Oh, but I'm not going to do that, am I? she thought, feeling deliciously sexy and warm. She stretched and smiled and twirled on the stairs like a dancer.

No. I wouldn't do anything as wild and as carefree as that.

Would I, now?

4

The old man lay on the bed; he spoke in that dry whispery voice that was so hypnotic. David's eyes felt heavy. Still he listened to the words trickling smoothly from the pair of ancient lips.

"Always be on your guard, nephew. They are old and wily. In the past they have taken careless people. Remember, they are like fishermen; they can use their minds like baited hooks. They reach out, feel their way into your brain; then once you're hooked they reel you in—slowly but surely. The victim feels warm, secure; secure to the point of feeling completely indestructible and filled with a sense of utter well-being and peace. People have been induced to leave their homes in the middle of the night and walk up to the cave entrances. There they've pressed themselves to the fences—they were completely mesmerized; and there they waited until the vampires came, reached through the iron bars, and took what they wanted from whoever it was—man, woman or child . . ."

314

Bernice had reached the fourth floor. Now, impulsively, she wanted to spin and turn along the corridor like a princess dancing at a ball, twirling around and around, long skirt flaring out.

Everything felt so right now.

I'm in love with David Leppington, she thought with a sudden blush of pleasure; I'm in love with him. He's in love with me. She conjured his smile into her mind's eye and recalled his voice, and she felt like dancing again.

And she felt so sexy, so . . . *yes*! so downright erotic.

She longed to have her bare arms stroked and her back lightly scratched.

She reached the door of her hotel room and opened it. Her skin felt prickly. It was these old clothes. Why didn't she change into something nicer?

Why not the clothes in the cupboard? The forbidden clothes; the wicked clothes.

She giggled.

Yes, she loved the feel of Electra's satins and cool silks against her skin. Why not, Bernice? Looking good and sexy isn't a hanging offense, is it? She smiled. Not yet, anyway.

She whirled away out of her room and into the corridor again, toward the storeroom door where Electra's cache of exotic and ineffably erotic clothes lay hidden.

By ten o'clock she was nearly ready. Once more she wore the long gloves in black lace that came up above her elbows. She'd slipped deliciously into the long, black satin skirt; then eased her feet into the patent-leather boots that came up to her knee. These laced up the front along the line of her shin bone—they were exquisitely tight, too, holding her calf muscles firmly as if gripped by a man's large strong hands.

On her top she wore a loosely fitting blouse—very loosely fitting, bearing in mind it was cut for Electra's ample torso. This was of black lace, too; an incredibly fine lace that was transparent. The effect was wonderfully pleasing when she appraised herself in the mirror.

The lace was so sheer it looked as if her top half was clad in black mist; when she turned it seemed as if her body radiated an aura of black, just a centimeter or so beyond her pale skin.

Again she applied heavy make-up around her eyes. Lashings and lashings of deep, dark shadow. Then a jet black kohl around her eyes to form such a thick eye-liner it made her think of the faces of Egyptian princesses.

Then she applied the finishing touch. Red lipstick. A luscious, moist blood-red that stood out vividly from her white face. Perfect.

She looked into the mirror and glowed with pleasure. Again the effect was a clash of opposites—the funereal black of Victorian-style clothing meeting the smouldering-mistress look of man's most erotic fantasies. Her skin felt incredibly sensitive. She was aware of the different fabrics against her bare skin: the cool silkiness of the satin and silk; the slightly rougher texture of the black lace gloves that hugged her skin so close they could have grown there all by themselves.

Why am I doing this? she wondered. David isn't here to appreciate all this effort. Never mind. He'll see me later in all my dark, shimmering glory; perfectly adorned with shining come-to-bed eyes and voluptuous red lips.

Anyway, she'd show Electra. She could imagine Electra laughing in amazement and clapping her hands together. It would be a diversion—a bit of fun—on what would otherwise be a long, long night.

Humming lightly, she left her hotel room, sweeping along like the lady of the grand house. She paused, noticing something not quite right.

Well . . . something different.

What was it?

She looked back along the corridor.

Then she saw what it was and gave a light little laugh.

To her ears it sounded light-hearted and tinkling.

To other ears it might have sounded like the laugh of an inebriate or someone skirting dangerously close to the edge of madness.

She turned, looked and curtsied.

"Why, thank you," she said to thin air. "Thank you for sending the lift for me."

The lift doors were open. Inside it was brightly lit.

Light as a butterfly, skirts swishing, she stepped inside.

She raised a satin-clad finger to press the plastic button bearing a number 1—a worn and shiny number 1, at that.

But already the lift doors were closing before she had time to even touch it.

"Why, thank you," she said happily as the doors slid shut with a dry scraping sound.

The lift motor hummed, the walls and floor trembled. The lift had begun its descent, carrying her downward.

7

Electra Charnwood walked drowsily into the apartment kitchen, yawning, her hand over her mouth.

"I'm sorry . . . Uh, I'm so tired. I fell asleep on the books. Have you—Jack . . . *Jack*."

She looked at where he sat at the kitchen table. He appeared to be awake. His eyes were open, although the stare was glassy and fixed.

His hand rested on the table. Between his fingers a cigarette had burned right down to the fleshy web part between the first two fingers, leaving a little pillar of cold ash.

"Jack!" Her voice cracked like a whip. "Jack! Wake up!"

The eyes rolled blurrily, then snapped into focus.

"Uh . . . what is it?"

"Jack. Where's Bernice?"

"She went up to her room." He looked at the burnt-away cigarette between his fingers with a muted kind of surprise, as if he'd seen a mushroom sprout from the back of his hand. "Why?"

"When, for heaven's sake?"

Almost groggily he looked up at the kitchen clock on the wall. "Aw, fuck."

"When, Jack?"

"Over an hour ago."

Electra hissed, "Damn, damn, damn." A cold sensation licked

317

through her stomach and chest in long, ice-cold strokes. "Damn . . . just pray they haven't got her. Come on . . . best bring your hammer. We've got to try and find her."

They burst through the apartment door onto the first-floor landing. The first sound they heard was an electric hum.

"That's the lift," Electra cried. "Damn. I switched it off, it can't be working."

Black said in a flat voice, "It is now. Can you stop it?"

"We're going to have to." Fumbling for the key that would switch off the power to the lift, Electra ran for the first-floor lift doors.

She pushed the key into the keyhole beside the lift call button and looked up. The lift was coming; already the illuminated numeral set in the panel above the lift's doors was changing from four to three.

"Wait," Black grunted. "How do we know Mochardi's in the lift?"

"She must be. Who else can it be?"

"Might be one of them bastards. It might come straight out at us if you stop it on this floor. What could we do then?"

The lift counter showed floor two—just one floor above them. Electra could see in her mind's eye the dark coffin shape of the lift sliding down through the brick-lined shaft, the draft caused by its passing gently fluttering a hundred years' worth of cobwebs.

"What are you going to do?" Black prompted.

Electra stood poised with her hand ready to turn the key, her eyes anxiously looking up at the floor counter. If it was Bernice in there they had to stop the lift and get her out. The lift was, intuition told her, bound for the basement. And whatever might lurk down there.

But if the lift contained those monsters they'd fall upon the two of them the moment the doors opened.

Her mouth went dry. "I'll isolate the lift between floors. That way the doors will stay shut until we decide to open them."

"Better be quick—"

As the figure two winked out, leaving the counter blank, Electra knew the lift was now between floors. She twisted the key sharply.

She looked up, expecting the little screen to stay blank and to hear the muffled bump of the lift coming to rest.

Her mouth opened, her heart seemed to stop mid-beat. "No."

The figure one appeared.

"It's not working. They must have tampered with the electrics." She twisted the key backward and forward. Nothing happened.

Whatever cargo the lift carried within its pine-covered walls was, after all, going directly down to the basement.

Now, Electra knew for sure, Bernice was in the lift. She laid her palm flat against the lift door, felt the vibration tickle through the wood as the lift slipped by bearing its fragile mortal contents like a sacrificial offering en route to a dark and terrible god.

The panel showed a G. Ground floor.

Then a B.

Basement.

It had reached its destination.

8

She was outside the lift. She'd not been conscious of taking those three steps.

Nor conscious of her tightly booted feet touching the brick floor with tender little kissing sounds.

Nor the sound of her breathing.

Nor the pressure of the lacy material against the tips of her breasts.

But here I am, she thought, dazed, the walls of the basement seeming an immense distance away; as if she was viewing the world from another dimension.

She walked slowly forward—another three light steps, long skirts scraping against the brick floor.

She glanced back at the lift with its ornate cut-glass light covers and mirror, and plush piece of burgundy carpet that covered its floor.

Right now, the little lift seemed miles and miles away.

Her lips felt papery-dry when she licked them.

Her body had grown numb; that same feeling you get in your feet when you've knelt on the floor for too long.

She had no real compulsion to do so, but she found herself walking slowly forward. As if she was walking in a dream. After just a few paces she entered the main body of the basement. It was brightly lit. There were the shelves she'd seen before, bearing the weight of bundles of old sheets, boxes of nails, old wine bottles, a toilet seat.

She walked on.

To her left was the locked door of the basement storeroom.

Inside there she'd seen that corpse-like thing with the ruined breasts.

Now she sensed it in there, dragging its bare feet across the floor.

Bernice walked slowly on—a beautiful princess from a fairy tale walking in a marvelous land of make-believe, her blood-red lips slightly parted, her eyes, lined with black, bright in her face. She glanced to the left and to the right, as if expecting the amazing to present itself for her amusement.

She smiled. Her mind was distant and dreamy and happy: this was what she was born to do.

Then she turned a corner and looked along the basement as it narrowed down to the steel doorway.

Only it was different now.

The doorway was open.

She shivered.

The cold air suddenly had teeth to bite her with. It was so cold it was painful.

She drew in a stuttering breath; her teeth clicked together; her hands gave an involuntary clench as if a sadist had forced her to lick a dead man's open eye.

At that instant she came fully awake, snapping sharply from her trance.

She looked around the basement in horror; it was as if the walls had plunged at her in a rush. Where before they had seemed soft and warm and far away, now they were hard, brutally cold, and looked as if they'd clap together their brick palms and crush her, smashing her pulverized ribcage against her mangled heart.

Jesus Christ, why did I come down here, why did I come down here? Why did—

But the cold-hearted truth was that she *was* down here. They had lured her down here; as easily as her old boyfriend had got her drunk all those years ago, then sweet-talked her to his flat where the men had pawed the clothes from her back.

Only now there was the open steel door, the door that had once separated this basement from the passageway to—to hell, for all she knew.

She took two rapid steps forward. As if she needed to confirm that this was no illusion.

No.

The heavy steel door that had been padlocked for decades now gaped open.

The padlocks lay on the floor. They were, she saw, still locked. Someone, however, had done a thorough job of patiently sawing through the hasps.

She shivered. It was a long, painfully cold shiver. If she translated the ghastly feeling into a visual image that shiver would have been caused by a great thick-bodied slug, sliding across the bare skin of her stomach up toward her throat, leaving a slick trail of cold milky pus all across her breasts.

Get out of here, Bernice, get out!

As she turned to run, she glimpsed from the corner of her eye something pale moving from the shadows to stand in the opening left by the absence of the steel door.

She ran along the vaulted basement, past the door of the locked room that contained the creature.

Then she was inside the lift. It still contained the smell of the upper floors of the hotel. A clean dry smell, not like the cold stale air of the basement.

She hammered the buttons on the control panel.

In a second the doors would shut, the lift motor would hum, then she'd be riding back up to the safety of the upper floors (it didn't matter which upper floor, any would do).

With her lace-clad fist she pounded the buttons.

Any second . . . any second . . .

Then terrible things happened.

The lights went out in the basement.

With a cry she looked out from the illuminated box that was the lift.

Beyond the lift doorway stretched the brick floor, softly illuminated by the lift light.

Beyond that: the darkness of the basement, an intense darkness that seemed to bloom with violet blossom the more she stared into it.

As she stared, those violet blossoms became veined with dark red as her mind frantically tried to make sense of the random pattern of shadows and darkness.

Then came a slithering sound.

The sound of feet shuffling slowly across the floor.

Then, bobbing whitely from the darkness, came white balls.

Or so it seemed at first.

Then she saw those white balls were naked heads, devoid of hair. Eyes blazed from beneath dark, bristling eyebrows.

Noses were cruelly hooked. The mouths parted, exposing teeth that were as sharp as knives.

"Come on . . . come on!" she yelled as she pounded at the lift buttons.

Come on, please.

Any second now the lift doors would close. She'd be safe. The confined space of the lift, brightly lit, would seem wonderfully cozy and warm.

I promise I won't come down here again. I promise to be good. I promise to—

They fell on her from out of the darkness, a surge of white gleaming heads. Hands reached out; they were elongated, ghastly, pale.

Long fingers curled around her arms.

They pulled her from the lift.

She screamed.

9

In the hospital room the mobile telephone rang as the old man spoke in that whispery voice.

David quickly pulled the phone from his pocket and thumbed the receive button. "Yes?"

He heard Electra's voice. "David. I think they've taken Bernice."

For a moment he was unable to speak. Beyond the windows the wind blew harder; now it rose to a thin scream.

"David?" said Electra's voice in his ear.

"Yes. I'm still here."

"Are you coming back to the hotel?"

He realized that, absurdly, he was shaking his head as if she could see him there, sitting miserably hunched on the cheap plastic chair beside the old man. "No," he said at last. "There isn't enough time. I'm going up to my uncle's house."

"Why?"

"That's where there's an entrance to the cave."

He sat there for a moment. At last he was aware that Electra was still calling his name on the telephone. "David. David?"

He hung up and slipped the phone back into his pocket.

Deep down he knew he'd put off what he should have done a long, long time ago. More than a thousand years ago.

He felt the blood of his ancestors beating through his veins.

The time had come.

It was as simple and as inevitable as that.

Chapter Thirty-four

1

David left his uncle's bedside before midnight. His neck felt hot and gritty; his eyes were sore from staring at the old man's face as he hypnotically murmured out all he knew about the Leppingsvalt breed of vampire.

You can't stake them through the heart, nephew; garlic doesn't bother them; nor do fresh rose petals; holy water and crucifixes don't matter a fig to them. But they are disturbed by bright lights—disturbed to the point of confusion, even disorientation. They shun bright daylight. Sunlight is particularly repellent to them. Hurts their dark-adapted eyes, you see. But the ill effects of light will only be temporary . . .

And so on and on until the words rattled around David's brain like hot stones.

Right now he wanted to sit down with a hefty drink. Maybe vodka, or brandy mixed with port. Anything with a God-almighty kick.

But he knew he had work to do.

Oh, playing the Christ again, Dr. Leppington, wheedled the voice at the back of his brain. *Let the bastard town go hang itself. It's not your concern. Leave the shitty little place to the vampires. Let them suck out whatever blood's left in this crappy little hicksville.*

He shook his head as he walked across the car park. No. You don't walk away from this.

The wind blew hard now, screaming shrilly through the telephone wires; it rocked the trees until they groaned.

Empty crisp packets swept by him at head height. Above him ragged clouds sailed like life rafts desperately trying to escape this godforsaken piece of England.

As he unlocked the car door he was aware that eyes were watching him from the shadows; he knew whose they were. In a moment the vampires could have swept out at him, torn open his skin and sucked the blood from his flesh like a vulgar child sucking bathwater from a flannel.

He opened the car door.

No. They wouldn't attack him yet.

They still needed him mortal. A man who could function in the daylight while leading his vampire hordes to wage war on the outside world.

It occurred to him that it might be best for everyone if he allowed them to think he would do that. That he, David Leppington, would willingly accept the role assigned to him. That he would become the leader of these undead: he, the last of the Leppingtons, would become the Vampire King.

He gave a sour smile as the words came to him:

Some men are born great; some have greatness thrust upon them . . .

Hell, some inheritance.

He fired up the Volvo's two-litre engine, then swung the car out of the car park. The headlights cut a brilliant swathe through the night.

Within minutes he was pulling up outside his uncle's house. It looked bleak and forbidding in the dark. The trees in the garden seemed to be waving him away as the wind pulled the branches this way and that. They were gesturing that it was madness to go any further; that all he would find here would be pain and, ultimately, death.

He paused for a moment, breathing deeply and looking into the darkness beyond the windscreen.

There was no going back now.

They had taken Bernice. She must be one of them now.

He gritted his teeth, angrily. How could they have lost her so easily?

Even now she might be peering at him from the bushes across the road, licking her lips; her eyes burning with hunger at the thought of his blood pulsing richly through his veins.

Steeling himself, he grabbed the flashlight by its pistol grip. Then he climbed out of the car.

2

His head still buzzed with what his uncle had told him. He knew more, a hell of a lot more, about these creatures now but that knowledge didn't fill him with much optimism. He still didn't know how he could destroy them.

He'd come to his uncle's house in the vague hope that the steel fence in the cave might somehow still be miraculously intact; perhaps the dynamite his uncle had set hadn't been powerful enough to stave in all that solid steelwork; in that case, the vampires would still be imprisoned underground. Failing that, he had the idea—again vague and undefined—that he might be able to set more dynamite to bring the roof of the cave down. Maybe that was the answer—just seal the monsters underground forever.

He pushed open the timber gate—the wind pushed it back as though the forces of nature were conspiring to keep him out of harm's way.

But he knew this was the time of reckoning. He had to meet this danger head-on.

He walked along the path, shoulders hunched as the wind blasted down at him, screaming through the trees, howling across the roof of the house.

325

The house itself stood in darkness. The windows were blank as dead men's eyes.

He shivered.

Kept on walking.

No going back, he told himself. No going back.

First he went to the old man's workshop.

Maybe this was where the dynamite was stored.

But how the hell do you use dynamite? All he knew about dynamite was what he'd seen on television—probably from children's cartoons as much as anything. Tom was always shoving sticks of dynamite into Jerry's mousehole, lighting the fuse; then clever old Jerry the mouse would turn the tables, slotting the dynamite stick between the stupid cat's toes and—BOOM!

Hey presto. The cat was left blackened and furless, a look of pained surprise on his feline face.

But to actually use the real stuff. To plant the dynamite in the right place so it would bring down a cave roof. Then to judge how much fuse to use. And what about detonators? He realized he could easily end up blowing himself to kingdom come.

He switched on the electric light in the workshop.

The place was pretty much as he'd seen it before. Just two days ago. Christ, that seemed like half a lifetime ago, when he'd stood here drinking his uncle's industrial-strength tea.

The fires in the forge were long since out; there was now only a mound of brownish ash in the fire place. Every so often the wind caught the chimney and *throo-ooomed*; a strangely resonant sound.

As he looked around the place the wind-generated sound came like the call of some mournful spirit . . . *throom—throom*; the metal chimney canopy that came down like an inverted cone over the forge vibrated in sympathy.

He looked around the steel racks. Methylated spirits, iron-working tools, coils of rope, coils of electric cable, tin of Swarfega (that his uncle no doubt rubbed into his powerful hands to shift the dirt at the end of the day), steam iron that the old man must have been in the middle of repairing, boxes of nails, screws, washers, bolts (methodically sorted by size); a radio that he must have listened to while hammering to the rhythm of the music.

The place was meticulously tidy. It reflected his uncle's orderly mind.

Lying on a metal shelf above the work bench, by itself and almost reverently laid upon a piece of folded cloth, was the broadsword the old man had been working on.

Since David's first visit he must have put a good few more man-hours into it. It still wasn't finished but now the shape of the sword's blade was complete, long and tapering to a point. The handle was still bare metal, but the sword's pommel, a brass ball the size of a hen's egg, had been welded in place; also the sword guard had been fitted. The whole thing was reminiscent of King Arthur's Excalibur.

This was the Leppington version. What had his uncle called it? Helvetes. Yes, that was the name. Helvetes, meaning "bloody" or "blood-drenched."

Legend had it that it had been drawn from the belly of a fish that lived in a subterranean lake.

He touched the blade. The metal was still dull; the cutting edge hadn't been sharpened.

David ran his thumb along his fingertips the way people do when they're checking if a shelf or ornament is dusty. Only now David experienced a slight tingling in the ends of his fingers.

He touched the blade again. This time the tingle ran from the tip of his fingers to his wrist, then crackled up his forearm as if he'd touched the terminals of a heavy-duty battery.

Before he knew it he'd picked up the sword by its handle and was testing its weight and balance in his hands.

It felt right to be there. As if he'd owned the sword once before and only temporarily lost it.

He ran his fingers along its cutting edge. Too blunt. Much too blunt. It wouldn't even cut a cucumber.

Quickly he looked around the workshop. At the far side sat the electric bench grinder his uncle would use to resharpen tools.

His skin still tingled; he felt in gear now. Within moments he'd switched on the bench grinder; the abrasive grinding wheel began to spin.

He looked at it for a moment, frowning. He'd not touched one of these machines since he was fourteen, in metalwork classes at school.

Gingerly, he rested the blade against the white aluminium

oxide wheel that was already spinning at over 3,000 r.p.m. Sparks flew in a brilliant shower.

He nodded and smiled to himself. Those metalwork lessons were coming back to him. He applied the blade again. Sparks cascaded down to the floor; he carefully angled the blade so the abrasive edge of the wheel would grind the metal down to a thin cutting edge that would be scalpel-sharp.

With the wind vrooming across the forge chimney, he screwed his eyelids almost shut—an expression of sheer concentration as much as partially closing his eyes against the dazzling shower of sparks. Then he worked.

3

Within seconds of being dragged from the lift in the hotel basement, Bernice was hauled through the now gaping doorway into the tunnel beyond.

Shock strangled any attempts at more screams beyond her first terrified shriek. She could hardly breathe with fright, never mind yell the roof down.

Her feet were whisked from under her; she felt wiry arms around her body and legs as she was carried horizontally in the way men might carry a long roll of carpet.

The darkness was absolute.

She heard the rasp of their heavy breathing. How many there were of them she didn't know. Eight? Ten? Twenty?

The cold air of the tunnel chilled her face; fingers pressed tightly through the satin fabric of her dress to clamp against her legs.

Her mind spun; sparks shot behind her eyes; she struggled to gasp air down into her lungs; her heart drummed against her ribs.

As a child she'd watch those old adventure films where there was a car chase. What always preoccupied her was the part where the car crashes through the fence and plunges over the edge of the cliff. For a few seconds the driver of the car is there behind the steering wheel, staring out through the windscreen, as the car flies outward then downward in a long curving arc.

What goes through their minds? she'd wonder, wide-eyed,

hand on her lips, as the car fell. They know the car will smash into the rocks below; they know the car will immediately erupt into a fireball. (They always do when they crash in films, don't they?) They know they're going to die.

So what do they think about during the few seconds of freefall before that deadly impact?

Now she knew. A torrent of fear, shot through with fiery threads of terror, raced through her. She thought of everything and everyone. She thought how she could break out of those hands and run screaming to safety (but those hands are like steel, Bernice, no escape there); she thought about those dead lips touching her neck the second before they snapped their teeth down on her skin; she thought about dying . . .

Oh . . .

She writhed against their hands, her suddenly heightened senses registering the pressure of those black patent-leather boots against her shins; the clinging black stockings sheathing her thighs; the silky cool of the satin and silks against the skin of her stomach and her back; the faint prickling sensation of lace gloves encasing her hands, wrists, forearms and elbows.

And then there was the cold air against the bare skin of her face and throat, as if ice-cool panes of glass were being pressed there.

She was keenly aware, too, that she was being carried downward, through the filthy throat of the tunnel into the belly of the earth. There was nothing she could do to save herself now.

She was like that driver in the action flick, when his car's gone over the edge of the cliff . . .

. . . down it goes turning end over end over end . . .

Any second now it would hit rock bottom.

Any second now twenty-three-year-old Bernice Mochardi would meet her destiny with all the bone-shaking impact of that car hitting the quarry bottom.

Then she found her voice again; that was when, at last, she really began to scream.

Chapter Thirty-five

1

This is George Leppington's workshop at midnight. A torrent of cold air blasts up the valley, shaking the trees and rattling the workshop door as if it's terrified to be out alone on a night like this, and desperately wants to come inside.

The wind vroomed across the chimney pot, a moaning sound full of pain and despair. The metal hood that formed the inverted cone above the forge's fireplace shivered in harmony; it produced a sound like a malformed tuning fork, humming discordantly, madly. Cold air blasted down the chimney, stirring the dead ash of the fire until it looked like brown water being sloshed around a bowl.

David neither heard nor saw any of this.

His concentration was welded to the sword blade as he held it to the spinning grinding wheel. Sparks flew; the blade screamed as if in pain.

Every few moments he would run the ball of his thumb over the cutting edge of the sword.

Then he'd return to sharpening the steel. The sparks blazed with a scintillating brilliance. The effect was the same as leaning forward over a firework; he realized he should have worn protective goggles, but there was no time to break off even to do that. All he was aware of was the long steel blade and the endless flow of dazzling sparks that glittered with brilliant yellows, oranges and whites.

He checked the sword again, running the ball of his thumb along the cutting edge. Instantly he felt the tender skin snag as, at last, the blade parted his skin like a paring knife opening the skin of a tomato. Yet he was only distantly aware of the nettle-like sting on the ball of his thumb.

He stared wonderingly at the bead of blood painting a wet

line of crimson along the steel, marveling as it trickled down toward the sharpened tip of the sword.

The sight of it seemed so right. So incredibly *right*. As if he'd seen this happen a thousand times before: blood turning a sword blade wet and red.

Now the sword had been blooded.

Motionless, with the grinder still buzzing and the wind outside screaming like a lost soul, he stared at the blood—*his* blood—staining the metal blade. The bead of blood trickling down the blade stopped. Then a strange thing happened: it soaked into the tempered steel—as simple as that; it didn't dry there or roll off the tip of the blade. It just soaked right in like a drop of red wine being absorbed by a piece of kitchen roll.

The sword was ready.

2

Midnight. The Station Hotel.

Electra Charnwood and Jack Black sat in the living room of the apartment. The wind droned around the windows—a deep, soulful sound, full of heartache and loneliness. The two people sat in silence, without moving.

Electra spoke in a low, frightened voice. "We can't sit here until we rot."

"What do you suggest?"

"I don't know." She shivered a shiver that was more than a shiver: it was a great shudder that went deep into her muscles and her bones. "I don't know . . . I really don't know."

3

Deep under the town there was complete silence.

Utter darkness.

Bernice Mochardi had screamed until her throat felt as if it had been sandpapered raw. She couldn't breathe. The arms held her so tightly her body felt as if it was being crushed. Still they carried her down the dark tunnel. She heard a whisper of bare feet on rock. The sound of the creatures' breathing was a snake-like hiss.

Then above her she saw a light that was cut into oblong segments by a metal grille.

She realized she was looking up at a drain set in the street; briefly she saw the brick-lined walls of the drainage conduit running straight up like the walls of a well. A car rumbled across the grate, momentarily blocking street lights that seemed so far away they could have been stars in the night sky.

They're going to kill me, she thought, panting. They're going to tear holes in my skin and suck out the blood until I'm as dry as a sponge.

For one split second she saw with glittering clarity her sisters and mother standing by her coffin in the chapel of rest. They were crying and holding clots of damp tissue to their streaming eyes and noses. And she felt such sorrow, as if she'd let them down by dying young like this.

Soon she was being carried back into darkness again, leaving behind the splotch of yellow street light that fell down the well of the drain to the tunnel floor. She smelled the car's exhaust, then that too was gone, leaving the damp mushroom odors of the vampires that carried her.

There has to be some way out of this. The thought struck her by surprise. It hung there in her mind, turning like a glittering gem, hard and bright. There *had* to be a way. She knew there must be a way of escaping. No way was she going to surrender to fate like this. She couldn't let the vampires destroy her without a fight.

She opened her eyes as wide as she could and looked round. Still nothing but darkness.

All she could sense from the quality of the sounds made by the footfalls was that the tunnel was narrow; probably wide enough for two men to walk abreast and high enough for them to walk without stooping. It was probably hewn from solid rock. No light was admitted now that they were going deeper beneath the town.

And yet every so often she felt a whisper of fresher air against her skin as if they had passed the entrances to other tunnels branching off from this one.

No. She couldn't just curl up and die down here.

In any case, she told herself, you would become one of them—a blood addict craving your next fix.

She was still being carried horizontally, like a roll of carpet, by perhaps three of the creatures. An arm came down partly over her face but her eyes were exposed (not that she could see anything because of the total dark); and one arm was free.

But what could she do with that?

Hardly beat the monsters into submission with it.

They carried her on, the sound of their bare soles whispering across the stone floor, their breath coming in that same sinister snake hiss.

Soon they would arrive at their destination.

What then?

Chapter Thirty-six

1

Deep in the cave the gales roaring up the valley sounded distant.

David Leppington held the gas lamp high. The brilliant light cast by the hissing mantle showed him his uncle had done a thoroughly competent job of dynamiting the steel fence.

Just two days ago David had stood there with his uncle, looking through the metal bars into the deeper darkness that filled the throat of the tunnel as it disappeared into the hillside.

Now steel bars lay mangled at his feet. The tunnel was open to anyone who might choose to go deeper. Or it would freely allow anyone—or anything—to leave the tunnel's depths.

The old man had told David that the vampire army still waited down there, somewhere in the belly of the Earth.

Probably waiting for me to command them to follow me on the prophesied invasion of Christendom, thought David sourly. Well, they're going nowhere.

He hung the Calor gas lamp on the hook that had been screwed into the rock ceiling. In his other hand he carried the sword he'd sharpened in the workshop. The weapon felt right in his hand. As if it belonged there. As if he'd handled a sword a thousand times before.

If he saw any of those wretched blood-sucking creatures he'd use it on them. Whether it would be effective or not he didn't know; at least he'd try.

The cave floor underfoot was strewn with rubble and pieces of the metal fence. He had hoped that the fence hadn't been too badly damaged and that, somehow, he could have fixed it back in place. That would at least have held the vampire army down there, leaving only the ones on the surface to deal with. From what his uncle had told him, those creatures—Stroud, the film maker, the child he'd seen on the car roof, and the other recent recruits—were acting as procurers for the creatures in the caverns; they were supplying the older vampires with food in the shape of fresh victims still plump with fresh blood.

Sword in hand, he examined the rock walls of the cave; it was veined with another reddish-colored rock. He prodded it experimentally with the point of the sword. The rock was certainly solid enough.

What he needed to do now was to build a wall here where the tunnel was narrowest and the roof the lowest. That would imprison the vampire army. Then he could attempt to deal with the rest on the surface.

He looked down into the tunnel; the pale walls ran away into deeper and deeper shadow until he was peering into total darkness.

Were they there?

Watching him?

Did they recognize him as their leader?

For a second he imagined them rushing out of the darkness, their hairless heads gleaming in the light of the lamp, their dark lips parting to expose teeth that were white and hard and sharp.

He tightened the grip on the sword and waited.

Nothing stirred.

There was only the impenetrable dark of the tunnel. The longer he stared at it the more he became hypnotized by the darkness that seemed to bloom with deep crimsons and purples as his eyes struggled to make sense of that dark formless void.

His thumb began to throb from the cut he'd made with the

sword blade; his heart began to beat faster; any second they might come.

Flooding upward from the guts of the ground; a torrent of dead flesh kept alive by a warped and twisted evil and fed on the blood of innocents.

Behind him a stone rattled across the floor.

Damn. He'd let them creep up on him from behind as he'd stared into the cave, hypnotized.

With a cry he spun around and swung the sword.

"David!"

The figure in front of him ducked down; the sword struck the cave wall with a ringing sound; sparks flew where steel smote stone.

"Christ . . . Electra? Are you all right?"

"Fine." She breathed deeply while wiping her forehead with a trembling hand. She forced a weak smile. "But don't you prefer me with a head?"

"Jesus, I'm sorry, Electra. I thought you were one of the monsters."

"We could so easily have been. We had a hair-raising ride up here, didn't we, gang?"

Breathing deeply to steady her jangled nerves, she stood to one side. David saw four figures in the shadows. The identity of one was plain enough: Jack Black. The other three were strangers.

His first thought was: They've been taken too; they're vampires. He tightened the grip on the sword handle and took a step back, his feet grating on the chips of dynamited stone.

Electra looked up into his face and realized what he was thinking. "Don't worry, David. We're still clean. I guessed you might try and do something up here so we recruited a little help. These three gentlemen are Jack's friends. They've promised to help, haven't you, gentlemen?"

"Only if we get the money," replied one in a sulky voice. "You promised us."

"You'll get your money," Black grunted. "But you do as you're told first—OK?"

They nodded, sullenly.

"OK, David." Electra sounded businesslike. "What's the plan?"

335

"First we've got to block off this cave," David said. "I'd hoped to reuse what was left of the fence but my uncle used enough dynamite to reduce it to the size of lollipop sticks."

"Is there anymore dynamite?" Electra asked. "Perhaps we could explode more and bring the roof down?"

"I've searched all the outbuildings. I can't find any. Either he used the lot to blow the fence or he's hidden it somewhere else. I think our best bet now is to simply brick up the cave. There's cement out there in the store and a stack of stone blocks out by the garage. We can use what's left of the steel fence to reinforce the wall. Anyone mixed mortar before?"

One of the strangers nodded. But another didn't look happy. "What is all this? Why do you want us to brick this cave up in the middle of the night? What's down there?"

"I told you not to ask questions," Jack grunted thickly. "You're going to get paid, isn't that good enough for you? Or do you want me to do some more persuading?" He bunched his massive fists.

Electra moved in to smooth things over. "If we get the wall finished in the next two hours you'll get another two hundred each. What do you say?"

David saw the men's teeth shine in the lamplight as they grinned. One of them said, "I say, show us where the cement and the shovels are."

Within ten minutes David had cleared away enough rubble to form a clean strip where the wall would run from one side of the cave to the other. A few paces away, in the direction of the mouth of the tunnel, one of the men had begun to mix cement and sand; another tipped water onto the mound. Jack Black and the third man began wheelbarrowing the neatly cut cubes of sandstone into the cave.

In the confined space of the cave the scrape of the spade against the stone floor as they mixed the cement sounded frighteningly loud. David noticed that Electra, too, shot anxious glances into the darkness as if expecting to see ghastly figures lumbering toward them, hands outstretched, eyes blazing with hunger.

"Do you think they'll come?" she asked.

He shook his head. "My uncle said they're not ready yet to

face the outside world—but you can bet your life it won't be long before they are."

She looked at him, her blue-black hair framing her pale face. "That's exactly what we are gambling with, aren't we? Our lives?"

He nodded grimly as he shovelled a layer of cement onto the floor where the first course of stone blocks would run. "Bernice has already paid with her life; we're going to have to be vigilant or they're going to pick us off one by one."

"What did your uncle tell you at the hospital?"

David told her as briefly and as clearly as he could. That the vampire army still waited underground; but that the newly created vampires were moving about freely through the town, picking off innocent passersby either to slake their own thirst for blood or to feed the creatures in the caves.

She nodded, her sharp mind absorbing the information quickly, only interrupting to ask a pertinent question here and there. At last she said, "What you said earlier was right. Our greatest weapon against them is information. We've got to learn all we can about these monsters."

David stood back as one of Black's gang began to lay the first row of stones. He did a good job; he knew what he was doing.

David looked up at Electra and wiped the sweat from his brow. "But how do we learn more? George has told me what he knows. Where can we get more information? After all, you're hardly likely to be able to walk into a bookshop and ask for a How-to-Kill-a-Vampire manual, are you?"

"True, but I have plenty of folklore books at home. I started going through them after you'd left for the hospital."

"Any good?"

She tilted her head and raised her shoulders. "There might be some useful nuggets of information in there."

"But we need hard facts so we can nail these bastards once and for all, right?"

"Right," she agreed, "but did you know that in the thirteenth century a certain Sir William of Saxilby encountered what he called 'night faeries' just outside Whitby itself. These 'night faeries' had an appetite for human blood and had the rather

337

antisocial habit of stealing babies from their cots in the middle of the night."

David looked at her, interested. "You mean this Sir William might have encountered these vampire creatures seven hundred years ago?"

"David, I think he did just that. And being a fully paid-up knight of old, complete with armor, warhorse and trusty sword, he lay in wait for them one night, using his daughter as bait."

"His daughter? Chivalrous type, wasn't he?"

"But get this. These night faeries—our very own vampires, one might suppose, that had come from Leppington as far as Whitby—weren't indestructible."

David's interest increased. "What happened?"

"He trapped the three 'night faeries' in the room of the farmhouse where he'd laid the trap and cut off their heads with his sword."

David looked at his own sword, leaning against the cave wall. "You mean beheading's the answer?"

"Mmm, not quite."

"What, then?"

"When he beheaded the creatures there was a gush of clear liquid from the severed necks."

"That's what *we* saw when we punctured the skin of the vampire girl in your basement."

"Quite."

"Which suggests these creatures described as 'night faeries' are our vampires?"

"Absolutely. Anyway, Sir William cleaved off their heads with his sword. Apparently they then dropped dead on the spot, this watery fluid spurting from the severed veins."

"But?"

"But—and there is always a big 'but'," isn't there?" David nodded. Electra went on. "But the heads rolled back to the bodies—right back to the severed necks. There the two halves of the necks joined back together, the heads fused back to their bodies and—"

"And, hey presto, our monsters came back to life?" David said heavily.

"Got it in one. But our resourceful knight in shining armor cut off the heads again and quickly put them in a sack. He gave these to his squire with the instruction that they be buried on the far side of the River Esk, that's the river that flows through Whitby. The knight then had the headless bodies buried on this side of the river."

"Wait a minute. Isn't there something in folklore that says that ghosts, witches and whatever can't cross flowing water?"

Electra nodded, the beginnings of a smile reaching her face. "That's right. Apparently these night faeries did stay dead after being beheaded, once their bodies were kept well away from their heads."

"So we need to start cutting off heads, do we?" David mused. Both he and Electra looked at the huge sword standing against the wall.

"It's the only lead we've got," Electra said. "But if it worked for Sir William in the thirteenth century . . ."

David nodded, thoughtfully. "OK . . . after we've finished building the wall here we start hunting. Agreed?"

"Agreed."

"Meanwhile, can you go back to the hotel and start digging up any more information that might be useful? Anything about this Sir William or any other run-ins with these creatures over the last few hundred years, OK?"

"I'll get right onto it."

"Best take Black with you, you'll need a bodyguard."

Electra flashed him a grateful smile and turned to go. Then she paused and looked back at him, then at the sword gleaming there in the lamplight with a steely sheen. "Just one thing, David. You do realize that one of the creatures you're going to have to deal with will be Bernice Mochardi?"

David nodded grimly. "I know."

Chapter Thirty-seven

1

They're carrying me down to hell, Bernice thought. The tunnel seemed to run forever, like a great wormhole beneath the town. A cold, damp wormhole at that, and dark as the inside of Lucifer's heart.

I'm going to die alone down here.

Then I'll be reborn.

And then I'll go in search of fresh blood. Feeding, infecting, killing: the whole grim cycle will continue until the entire world is populated by these vampires. There will be no need for them to bear children as God intended because they will live forever. How long will it take for the population of the whole planet to turn vampiric? A decade? A century?

Probably not much more than that.

A high-school maths student could probably work out a mathematical formula on a cheap calculator. If one vampire bites two people in one night and those two become vampires and each bite two more people the following night, that means . . .

Her mind whirred on, strangely dislocated from reality. As the strong arms held her tightly she calculated the increase of the vampires: they would spread and multiply like an influenza virus until the greatest cities on Earth lay rotting, the ruins populated by these cadaverous creatures that lusted for nothing more than their next fix of blood. She could imagine them lying in their beds that were green with mold. Windows broken to admit the north wind and nesting birds, and buzzing bluebottles the size of a baby's fist. What do vampires dream about during the day? Probably they fantasize about their next conquest: picturing the next time they pin down a human being in the corner of an alley, tear at their clothes to bare their flesh, rip open the skin at the throat or wrist, then chew through an artery until they feel the blood hit the back of their throats in hot salty spurts.

As she lay there in their arms as they carried her, their bare feet dryly scraping the floor, she began to see the shape of the bricks that lined the tunnel.

Light, she thought in that distant, dazed kind of way. There's light again.

She tilted her head back so she could see along the tunnel. In front of her were more of the monsters, their backs to her as they filed their way into the heart of the earth beneath the town. Their around white heads gleamed like plastic footballs.

The light came from another drain set in the street high above her. The light was yellowish, obviously cast by street lights.

Lying there in the creatures' strong arms as if she was nothing more than a roll of carpet, she looked up as the drain came into view. It seemed a long way off, set at the top of a brick-lined shaft that stretched above her like the throat of a well.

At that moment she snapped out of her drowsy acceptance of her fate. She felt a prickle of near-exhilaration shoot through her arms and legs.

Hanging down the shaft was a length of chain composed of great rusty links. Spiders had spun a silky sheath along the chain.

The chain itself dangled so far down the shaft it almost brushed the bald heads of the vampires as they passed beneath it.

At that moment she knew this was it. This was her one God-given chance to escape from these monsters. And to escape whatever fate awaited her at the end of this subterranean journey.

2

With her free arm she reached up and grabbed the chain. The creatures carrying her carried on walking. The chain snapped tight and she felt a tremendous wrench at her shoulder as if her arm would be torn out by the roots.

She heard herself yelp with pain. But still she held on.

The vampires stopped pulling. She saw a face close to her own look around to see what had stopped their progress. In the dim glow of the street light funnelled down the shaft the creature's face gleamed with a sick yellow color; beneath a pair of black eyebrows that bristled thickly were a pair of deep-set eyes that glared with pure menace. (*Eyelashes—long and girlish— eyes that are hypnotic; eyes that are fascinating to look at.*)

Those vile eyes glared back at its companions. The creature appeared angry at being delayed.

He's probably hungry for me, thought Bernice, shivering. He's probably imagining tearing open an artery and longing for the spurt of warm blood in his mouth . . . but I'm not going to let go. I'm never letting go . . .

They'll have to rip my skin and drink me dry right here.

With a ponderous slowness, as if thought traveled at a sluggish pace through the neural pathways of whatever brains they possessed, the creatures looked at each other as if expecting one of their own kind to have the answer.

Bernice held on grimly to the chain that clinked inside its sheath of pure white spider web.

With ponderous slowness they released their grip on her body.

They obviously couldn't work out immediately why they could no longer make any progress along the tunnel.

Bernice looked up into the shaft above her. Iron loops had been set in the wall to form hand- and footholds that would have allowed workmen to climb down the shaft to inspect the ancient sewer, if that's what it was. The chain itself was fixed to a heavy balk of timber that ran across the top of the shaft, perhaps four meters above her head.

Still holding onto the chain, she tried to haul herself up, using the iron loops as footholds.

In twenty seconds she could reach the grating above her head Then, God willing, she could heave it open before hauling herself panting out into the street and the cold sweet night air.

The vampires had other ideas.

She'd barely put her feet on the iron hoops set in the tunnel wall when one of them grabbed her around the waist, his long bare arms, knotted with purple veins, wrapping tightly around her.

"Let go! Let go!" she screamed.

He pulled her downward. Her elbows and shoulders gave those cracking-knuckle sounds, only hugely amplified. She creamed in agony; it felt as if muscle would rip from bone.

But still she held onto the chain.

The creature pulled again.

It pulled in an implacable robotic way, no expression altering the cold stone face. The eyes gleamed like ice in the deep-set sockets.

At that moment she knew she couldn't keep her grip on the chain more than a few seconds. But there was nothing else she could do to save herself: this was her only escape route. She creamed and raged against losing it so easily.

She glanced round; more of the vampires tried to grab hold of her, their hands groping out toward her. Some of the hands were long and thin; others were rounded and pulpy—the fingers could have been white slugs sprouting from the fists.

Only they couldn't grip her properly because of the confines of the tunnel. There was only room for the one who held her to get a firm grip.

She smelled its breath; a stench reminiscent of unemptied rash in the heat of August, that stink of discarded cheese sweating hard, and of maggots and putrefaction.

It pulled again. A huge tendon-creaking pull that brought piercing screams from her mouth.

Then the chain went slack.

As simple as that.

It could have only lasted for a split second but a subjective eternity passed as she stared dumbfounded at the chain in her hand as it slackened and the links began to pour down over her arms.

Then she looked up.

The force of the creature's pull had brought down the supporting timber beam.

It plummeted down the shaft toward them.

Bernice balled her body in the creature's arms, tucking her head down as far as she could.

The sudden release threw the creature off balance so it bent at the waist; the top half of its body now covered Bernice.

And only just in time. The heavy chain pelted down across the creature's back followed by the debris of the timber and a dozen or more dislodged bricks. They came down with a full-blooded roar like a mini-avalanche, cascading down upon the

creature's broad back. More bricks smashed down onto the bal
skull.

One second later Bernice lay in the debris with the stunne
creature on top of her. It didn't groan or react to the pain in an
way but clearly it'd been dazed by the impact.

Bernice struggled out from under the body. Then she was o
her feet. The fall of debris had taken the other creatures b
surprise and they'd stepped back into the tunnel to avoid th
tumbling bricks.

Now Bernice's hands found the metal rungs set in the bric
wall. She'd already climbed out of reach by the time the vam
pires had gathered their dazed wits and rushed her.

Their outstretched hands clawed up at her, but all they di
was brush the soles of her feet as she climbed toward the glov
of the street light filtering down through the iron grate abov
her.

For one crazy moment she wanted to pause and laugh dow
at their dead white faces. To pour down a torrent of tormentin
insults. But she locked her attention on the grate above her an
climbed.

It wouldn't be long before they did recover from their surpris
and followed.

The iron hoops were slippery with moss; she forced hersel
to concentrate on gripping them tightly in her hands and placin
her feet carefully.

Whatever you do, girl, don't slip. If you fall into those ou
stretched arms they'll never let you go again.

Her heartbeat fast, adrenalin-fired exhilaration sizzlin
through her body to her fingertips.

Another five steps and she'd be at the grate set there abov
her head at ground level.

She reached the grate.

Heaved.

Heaved harder, pushing upward at the iron grille.

Damn. It was set there.

"Help! Let me out! Let me out!" She yelled until her throa
hurt but there was no sign of any passers-by.

As if there would be, she thought desperately. It must be thre
A.M. on a Monday morning.

She placed both feet firmly on the metal hoops, then pushe

again with both hands. Just one slip could send her tumbling down into those waiting hands.

She imagined their rough tongues greedily lapping the blood from her grazed skin.

She paused, listening hard, the pulse in her neck beating with a squelching, thumping sound; apart from that she heard only the moan of the wind blowing through the trees somewhere outside.

What now?

No way could she shift that iron grate above her head; probably years of road grit and windblown dirt had cemented it into its iron frame in the road.

She looked down.

The first of the creatures had begun to climb the shaft. Its eyes blazed beneath the thick lines of black eyebrows. The lips had parted into a grin. The panther teeth gleamed sharply in the streetlight.

It knows it can take me any time it wants, she thought bleakly.

Suddenly weak, she watched it climb the brick-lined shaft sluggishly, one hand deliberately reaching up to grab a metal rung; the whole movement, although slow, was smooth and snake-like. And why should it hurry? She was going nowhere.

She looked down the shaft, searching for a loose brick in the wall to hurl down into the smugly smiling face.

Then she saw a dark oblong set in the wall at the same level as her feet. Only this was behind her, so she hadn't noticed it as she'd climbed, hugging this wall.

She saw it was an aperture, no larger than a television screen, set in the wall of the shaft.

She shifted her position so she could get a better look.

Yes. It was a small tunnel leading off, possibly part of the drainage system beneath the town.

There was no time to lose.

She would have to climb down a meter or so to reach it.

And that thing was climbing steadily toward her. If she wasted another second it would be able to reach up and grab her feet.

Quickly she climbed down three rungs until she was level with the opening in the opposite wall. Then she turned, her feet firmly planted on the metal hoops.

345

It was risky but there was no alternative. She would have to allow herself to fall outward across the shaft so she could reach the opening.

Her breath roaring in her throat, her legs feeling weak and shaky from exertion and fear, she leaned forward, arms outstretched, and leaned the weight of her body on the opposite wall of the shaft.

Beneath her the creature had almost climbed within grabbing distance of her foot.

Along the narrow tunnel stretching in front of her was a series of pools of light admitted by what must have been drains set in the road.

With one last look at the vampire climbing inexorably toward her she squeezed through the tunnel opening, kicking her feet as she did so.

The entrance to the tunnel was a tight squeeze. Her long dress caught on the iron frame of the opening and she heard it tear more alarming was the sensation of fingers curling around her ankle. She kicked furiously.

With her hands supporting her weight as if she was exercising with press-ups she wormed her way into the tunnel.

After one last kick she freed herself from the hand.

Now she was fully inside the tunnel. It opened up sufficiently to allow her to move forward on her hands and knees, panting and grunting with the exertion. Her eyes blurred and her blood came in those great pumping squelches through the veins of her slender neck and into her head.

She moved forward into the tunnel perhaps a dozen paces before collapsing into a sitting position, her back to the wall.

Turning her head back, she stared in dazed fascination. There it was, the great white figure of the vampire framed by the entrance to her branch tunnel.

It reached in toward her, its thick arms stretching out, the fingers grasping, the burning eyes locked onto her face.

You can't reach me, she thought, drawing in huge lungful of air. You can't reach me and you're too big to climb through into my tunnel. I'm safe . . . I'm safe . . .

The words *I'm safe* played like a beautiful melody in her head. I'm safe . . . I'm safe . . .

Her heart seemed to expand outward in her chest; the sense of relief was enormous.

With the thing behind her, hissing in fury and struggling in vain to climb through the narrow aperture, Bernice once more rolled forward onto her hands and knees and began to move away from her former captors.

Now to find a way out of the tunnel.

Chapter Thirty-eight

1

It was dawn by the time Electra Charnwood and Jack Black climbed into the van for the short drive back to the hotel. David and the three men had made short work of building the wall in the cave and were now reinforcing it with a couple of hefty brick buttresses. By this time they were running out of raw materials so David was obtaining the bricks from ornamental garden walls that Black furiously demolished with an iron spike.

Gales shook the trees—with all the desperate viciousness of sentries trying to wake sleeping soldiers during a surprise attack. Water loosened from leaves by the blast rattled down onto the van. Above that sound was the soulful drone of the wind itself.

"Hell." Electra started the engine. "Some night." She looked at Black who stared impassively out through the van's windows. "See anything?"

He shook his head. "They don't like it when it gets daylight. They stay where it's dark."

Electra felt a buzz of astonishment. "Don't tell me you can read their minds?"

"Not read. I feel what they feel."

"You mean you can empathize with the vampires?"

"Empathize?

"You can tune into their emotions—know instinctively if they're unhappy, hungry, restless?"

"Sometimes. It comes and goes."

"What are they feeling now?"

"They don't like the light. So they'll find somewhere dark."

"Where?"

He shrugged. "Anywhere gloomy."

Electra slipped out the clutch and the van bumped off the grass verge and away down the hillside road toward town.

She shot Black a glance. His tattooed face was as inscrutable as ever. "Can you tell what I'm thinking now?"

He shrugged that enigmatic shrug. "Not really. It comes and goes."

"Jack, what's it like to read minds?"

"It's not a trick." He sounded defensive.

"I know. I just wondered what it feels like to be able to tune in to other people's thoughts."

"It doesn't work like that." He shot her a glance with his mean-looking eyes. "It's like this." He reached forward, switched on the van's radio and prodded the pre-sets at random. In a quick succession there were bursts of music, a DJ's voice, then a snatch of news, then a weather report, an advertisement for car insurance; it added up to a series of meaningless fragments of voices and music and static.

"There," he said, "that's the nearest I can show you what it's like."

"But sometimes you hear more?"

"Sometimes, not much. All I can get from you is a word here, a word there; then the thoughts come into my head of a guy down the road and he's thinking what he's going to eat for his dinner, or he's got an itch on the end of his cock and he's wondering if he's got the clap; then another voice comes just jolting in, you know, like interference on a radio, and you hear a girl thinking that her boyfriend's cheating on her, then I get your voice wishing you were in London working on that television programme, then that's all mixed up with my mother's voice when I was a few hours old and she's thinking 'the little bastard, why didn't I have you pulled out when I got the chance; I could have fucking aborted you myself with a fucking knitting needle,' and she's looking down at this baby in this cot in the hospital, and I know that baby's me, and I can hear my mother's voice going around and around in her head, 'I gotta have a fix,

I gotta do smack, I'm cracking up inside and all that fucking little bastard wants is to suck on my tit' and that's when she takes me out of the cot and throws me at the wall." He suddenly stopped talking and ran his finger along the scar that ran like a spectacle arm from the corner of his eye to his ear. "They believed her when she said she dropped me by accident. But I can see it all through her eyes and I can remember her thoughts and I can remember the way her stomach and her arms and her legs were going into cramps because she needed another shot of heroin. And then I see her boiling up a kettle of water and pouring it all over me." He gave a sudden grin that was savagely inappropriate. Only his eyes stayed icily cold. "The nurses saw that one, though. So that was the end of my loving mother—as far as I was concerned, anyway."

"So you've been a telepath ever since you were born?"

He nodded.

She shook her head wonderingly. "It's a wonder you haven't gone crazy!"

"I have." He shot her that huge, wild grin again. "Why do you think I look like this? Why do you think I've tattooed my face and my neck and my eyelids over and over and over . . ."

He broke off to stare out of the window as they drove along Main Street. His eyes glittered strangely. Electra reached out and rested the palm of her hand on his knee.

She thought he'd flinch away but he didn't move. She felt the heat of his body through the material of the jeans and the hard muscle above the knee. "Jack," she said softly, "I think we're both strangers in a strange land. Why don't we look after each other?"

She glanced at him as he gave a small nod, his head still turned so he stared out through the passenger window.

"And maybe," she continued in a small voice, "when this is all over we can stay friends. And perhaps you can stay on at the hotel?"

He said nothing, but she saw his Adam's apple bob slightly in his throat. That was his only concession to a display of emotion.

Ahead, she saw the brick bulk of the Station Hotel. Already people were on the streets—postmen, delivery personnel, a couple of train drivers ambling across the market square in the direction of the station, knapsacks on their shoulders containing Thermos flasks and packs of sandwiches.

It was six o'clock on a Monday morning.

Most people were waking now from their dreams—some from nightmares—but Electra knew her and her friends' nightmare was far from over.

Today, they would have to spend their daylight hours preparing for the next night when they would do battle with the vampire hordes that swarmed through their lair beneath the town.

She parked the van at the side of the road. After Jack Black's torrent of words he'd reverted to his usual stony silence.

The wind gusted around her as she climbed out of the van. She heard its drone as it rushed around the towers of the hotel. Again she could imagine she was listening to the groan of lost souls in the wind: the sound bleak, mournful, shot through and through with despair.

As Electra, with Black at her side, hurried toward the hotel, she felt her mind coming into focus. It was a sensation she hadn't properly experienced since her days working on the TV program when the minutes were ticking away to the deadline of the next broadcast: when all the material had to be pulled together into a single coherent script for the presenters. Oddly, for the first time in years, she felt fully in control of her life again. She knew what she had to do: apply her sharp analytical mind to mounds of scrappy information relating to local folklore, and then marshal those disparate facts into something they could use. David Leppington said that information would be their weapon against the monsters. He was right.

Feeling the rush of energy singing through her veins, she swung open the hotel door and marched across the foyer. It's time to go on the offensive, she thought, enjoying that buzz of exhilaration. No more hiding in locked rooms. This is where we fight back.

2

Bernice walked along the tunnel. By now daylight filtered through the grates set above her head. From time to time she heard cars pass by; then she'd glance up, seeing the undersides of their chassis, tires, exhaust pipes, the boxy shapes of fuel tanks. She'd shout but no one seemed to hear.

She did think about stopping and trying somehow to reach one of the grates—this would mean climbing the tunnel walls—but she was gripped by the urge to keep moving. If she stayed in one place too long she was afraid the vampires would track her down. In fact, with every few steps she took she would glance back, expecting to see the white naked heads come bobbing after her out of the shadows.

She moved quickly, her booted feet clicking against the brick floors that were sometimes bone-dry or sometimes covered with a thin skin of water that splashed up against the hem of her long satin skirt. Her heartbeat steadily, her breath showed a brilliant white in the pools of light beneath the iron grilles.

There's a chance I might find my way back to the hotel basement, she told herself hopefully. In a matter of seconds I'll be through that doorway and run across the basement floor to the safety of the lift. She could almost feel that warm dry air of the hotel and David's welcoming hug; she imagined Electra pouring a reviving brandy while excitedly asking what had happened to her.

These thoughts helped her. Especially when the drains above her ended and she had to plunge into the next section of tunnel in complete darkness without knowing just what might lurk there. Waiting.

3

With daylight creeping into the mouth of the cave David paused to wipe the sweat from his forehead. The three men Black had brought with him had worked without a break—they were an unsavory-looking bunch who could have been small-town crooks—which, he guessed, they were. They'd done what they'd been told to do, however. The wall was complete, blocking the cave from top to bottom. David now worked on the brick buttress that would reinforce the wall.

The wall looked solid enough. He was confident that the creatures couldn't force a way through. Although he decided to keep guard here for a few hours until the mortar between the stone blocks of the wall had begun to properly set.

There, gleaming in the light of the lanterns, was the sword his uncle had made. The cutting edge was sharp now; the throbbing in the ball of his thumb from the sword's cut was testament to that. But could the sword do any real damage to the vampires that were now probably sleeping beneath ground?

He hoped for all their sakes it would.

And it wouldn't be long before he put it to the test.

He wiped the sweat again from his eyes and returned to mixing more mortar for the bricks.

The time was 6:30 A.M.

4

Electra dissolved white powder into a glass of Coca-Cola.

I'm not doing this to get high, she told herself, just to keep awake. The effects of cocaine inhaled through the nose are almost instantaneous. Dissolved in liquid and ingested through the stomach lining the effect would be slower and less dramatic.

Taking occasional sips of the now scummy-looking Coca-Cola she set to work. For years she'd accumulated books on local folklore; she also had David's copy of *The Leppington Family: Fact and Legend* by Gertrude H. Leppington, which chronicled the family's mythical past from when they were known as Leppingsvalt to the latter-day Leppingtons when family interests centered around the slaughterhouse and cannery.

At the desk in her apartment, she flipped open the laptop computer and powered up. A glance at the window told her the sun had now made it above the hills that surrounded the town like the ramparts of a fortress. Shreds of cloud driven by the wind streamed across the sky. I'm already racing against the clock, she told herself; there were perhaps another dozen hours of daylight before dark. But, strangely, it was a good feeling—a very good feeling indeed.

She took another sip of the Coca-Cola.

"Need anything doing?" Jack Black asked, watching her from the doorway.

She shook her head. "I've posted new notices on the doors

telling the staff and any potential guests we're closed for today. Why don't you try and get some sleep?"

"No. I'm not tired. Want a coffee?"

She held up the glass of Coke. "I've something a little more potent than caffeine. Oh, there *is* something you could do for me." She looked across as he stood there flexing his massive fists as the tension began to cramp his muscles.

"Yeah?"

"You could sharpen the carving knives in the kitchen."

He nodded, his face stony. But she knew he'd realized this time that those knives wouldn't be used to prepare a meal.

She watched him go, then she returned to the books. As she twisted the swivel chair back, she caught the glass of Coke with her hand. Some slopped out onto a book.

"Hell . . . keep a cool head, Electra, old girl." There was a box of tissues on the desk and she tugged a couple out and began to mop the spilt drink from the title page of spinster Leppington's book.

She used the tissue to absorb the drops of Coke that stood in black beads just below the words *Fact and Legend*. Then she wiped the page at the bottom where the drink had dripped across the name and address of the company that had printed the book.

She read the name of the printer. It was a local firm—Archibald McClure & Sons Limited, Whitby (founded 1897).

Quickly, she binned the moist tissues and returned to the computer, opening a new file. As she began to type the word *VAMPIRE*, she suddenly stopped and looked back at the title page of the book.

The printer's name seemed to leap out at her in great black type:

ARCHIBALD MCCLURE & SONS LIMITED

She frowned for a moment, unsure why it had caught her attention. The skin on her arms tingled. Something was wrong, only she didn't know what.

Quickly she checked the publication date of the book. It was 1957.

Then she was on her feet, hurrying across the room to where a framed document hung on the wall. It was a menu printed specially for a Christmas dinner at the hotel in 1960. Her father had had it framed because a local girl had been guest of honor; she'd enjoyed a brief year or two of fame as a singer and Broadway actress. But she wasn't the reason that Electra scanned the menu so avidly. She was checking the name of the printer at the bottom.

When she found the name she read it twice, three times, then thoughtfully tapped her fingertips against her lips and whispered, "I'll be damned . . . you devious creature, you."

Five seconds later she strode into the hotel kitchen where Black was sharpening knives. In one hand she held David's book, the Leppington family history, in the other the keys to the van.

Black looked up. "What's wrong?"

"Nothing's wrong," she said, feeling her body blaze with excitement. "I've just smelled a rat—a big two-legged rat. Come on, we're going down to Whitby."

5

Bernice Mochardi felt her way through what seemed to be a stone archway. How deep underground she was she didn't know. The darkness was absolute. She groped her way blindly, using her fingertips to feel her way forward. Any second she expected to reach out and touch smooth, cold skin. A face perhaps. Or a hand.

Then the things would fall on her, biting.

She breathed deeply, trying to steady the mad fury of her heart that clamored inside her chest.

Fear heightened her sense of hearing, so that every rustle of her skirts or scrape of her heel against the stone floor sounded like thunder.

Now she sensed she was no longer in a tunnel. This was a confined space.

Perhaps a basement, she thought with a sudden surge of optimism. If it's a basement I can find my way up into the house. I'll be safe.

Her fingertips felt the rough brick walls; a nail or peg caught the palm of her hand. Then she could feel what seemed to be a line of stone shelves.

Breath coming in excited spurts, stomach trembling, she quickly groped her way through darkness to another wall.

Then rough brick gave way to smooth timber panels. It had to be a door.

She found the door handle and twisted it.

Damn. It wouldn't budge. Perhaps the mechanism had rusted solid.

She began to pound on the door. She wanted to yell: *Down here! I'm down here! Help! Help!* But she was trembling so much she could barely breathe, never mind cry for help.

She beat the door with her fists, sending the noise of her pounding echoing away into the darkness.

At that moment a hand rested on her shoulder. Now she found her voice.

She screamed.

6

"Why are we going to Whitby?" Black asked Electra as he drove the van out of town.

"We're going to visit a Mr. McClure of Archibald McClure and Sons. They're a firm of printers the hotel's used for years."

"So why are they important?"

Electra smiled at the brutish profile. Jack Black didn't waste energy on tact. "Archibald McClure and Sons are the same company that printed this book."

"The Leppington family history? So?"

"So, back at the hotel I noticed a discrepancy at the front of the book. It was supposedly printed in 1957, and the printer's name is given as Archibald McClure and Sons Limited."

"And that's meant to be important?"

"Enormously important. You see, there's a framed menu in my study for a formal dinner given by the mayor in 1960. There the printer's name is given as Archibald McClure and Sons— not Archibald McClure and Sons Limited. Do you see?"

Black accelerated to overtake a tractor. "Sure I see. They

missed off the word 'Limited' on the menu—why's that so crucial?"

"It is crucial," she said, "because this printing firm only became a limited company in the last few years. Exactly when I don't know. But when they printed the menu in 1960 they were still unincorporated, that means they didn't use the word 'Limited' in their name. But for some reason the word 'Limited' has been added to their name in a book printed three years earlier than that in 1957. You follow?"

"Do I hell. It's probably just a printing cock-up."

"Believe me, Jack, that's no cock-up."

"Then they stuck in the word 'Limited' to make the name sound better?"

"Nope. A company would be breaking the law to add the word 'Limited' when they've not been incorporated under the incorporation acts."

"What's that mean? In English this time?"

She smiled and lightly touched his knee. "It means that this," she held up the copy of *The Leppington Family: Fact and Legend*, "this, my dear Jack, is a fake and a forgery."

7

Bernice had screamed so loud it felt as if the lining of her throat would slough completely off like the skin of a snake.

And when the hands had closed around her flailing wrists she had clenched her teeth, inadvertently biting her own tongue.

She pulled back from the restraining hands, her eyes wide, but she saw nothing in the dark.

"Don't be frightened. Please don't be frightened," came a gentle voice from out of the darkness.

"Leave me alone, please leave me alone."

"But I want to help you."

"No . . . no, I don't need any help, get away from me . . . get away!"

"You're lost."

"Please don't hurt me."

"Why should I want to hurt you?"

She paused, hearing nothing but the rasp of her own frightened breathing. The hands that held her wrists were warm.

Living.

"Who are you?" she asked.

"Maximilian."

"You—you're not one of those things, are you?"

"What things?"

"The monsters . . . vampires."

"The people who live down here?"

"People?" She laughed; crimson veins of insanity shimmered through the sound. "People? Yes, if you can call them that."

"No. I'm Maximilian," he repeated in a calm voice. "Maximilian Hart. I live at 19 Ash Grove, Leppington, North Yorkshire."

Bernice took a deep breath; she was trembling so much she thought it would literally shake her apart.

"Give me your hand," came the gentle voice from the darkness.

"Why?" she asked suspiciously.

"So I can guide you out of here."

"Wait a minute," she said, still suspicious. "Did one of those things bite you?"

"Bite me?"

"Yes, if you've been bitten you will be infected. You will become one of them."

"No." The voice sounded puzzled now. "No. I haven't been bitten. They said I had bad blood. Why do you think they said that?"

"Bad blood?"

"Yes."

She let out a lungful of air. She was sure he wasn't one of the vampires. There was some quality to his voice that was indestructibly human. When she spoke again it was in a friendly way. "Here's my hand," she said. "Can you find it?"

"Yes . . . yes. Got it. It's a nice soft hand. You smell nice, too. What's your name?"

"Bernice."

"Bernice? That's a nice name. I like it."

With that she allowed herself to be led away into darkness.

Chapter Thirty-nine

1

Arnold McClure, the grandson of the founder of Archibald McClure printers (1897) was a shrewd sixty-year-old with short gray hair, a neatly clipped mustache and the most brilliant blue eyes: they looked as if they should be set into necklaces and worn by princesses.

Electra's father had always told her that Arnie McClure was so smart he could sell snow to the Eskimos. On that Monday morning Arnold McClure stood in the office of the printing firm and turned the book Electra had given him over and over in his hands as if handling a precious artefact just extracted from the ruins of a Greek temple. He ran his fingers reverently over the print on the title page.

"Feel that," he told Electra, holding out the book, "feel the impression of the typeface. You don't get that now with laser printers." Electra complied, feeling the minute depressions in the paper made by the metal letters of the printing press. The old man sighed, "Isn't there something almost affectionate and loving about the old-style printing process? There the metal dies that reproduced the text were brushed with ink, then pressed firmly but really quite gently, you know, against the paper. Now we have lasers that burn the letters onto the paper—that is so much harsher, don't you think?"

The sound of the tourists and shoppers moving along Whitby's Church Lane sounded far away. The printer's office occupied the top floor of a building that backed onto the quaintly named Arguments Yard. She'd left Black smoking outside on the steps. His tattooed and scarred face would, she thought, be too much of a distraction.

She knew Arnold McClure well; the hotel had had all its printing done here for donkey's years. Normally, she would enjoy a friendly chat with him, drink tea and share his biscuits from a big silver drum that sat on the filing cabinet. But now she was keen to zero in on her suspicions.

"Arnold. You recognize the book, don't you?"

"Oh, yes. One of ours, indisputably so."

"But Archibald McClure & Sons didn't become a limited liability company until comparatively recently?"

"That's perfectly correct. Let's see, it'll be, ahm, ten years ago this summer." He smiled good-naturedly. "Why all the interest in our company all of a sudden?"

"Well, I came across this book. And there appears to be something amiss with it."

"Amiss?" He raised his white eyebrows and smiled. "No typos, I hope? No misnumbered pages?"

"Oh no. Nothing like that. Only your logo at the front of the book describes you as a limited company."

"Which we are now. So why all the mystery?"

"The book was—it says on the title page—printed in 1957."

"And then we were just plain old Archibald McClure and Sons, not Archibald McClure and Sons Limited?"

"Precisely."

The old man held the book just under his nose and flicked through the pages as if to inhale the aroma exuded by the paper. "Mmm . . . still has a new-book smell, doesn't it?"

"That too. So why does a supposedly forty-year-old book appear to have actually been printed quite recently?"

"Where did you get this, Electra?" he asked, suddenly thoughtful. "You know, it's quite a rarity."

"It belongs to a friend of mine."

"A Leppington?"

"Yes."

"George Leppington?"

"No, he gave it to his nephew who's staying at my hotel."

"Ah, I thought it couldn't have fallen into your hands from a secondhand-book dealer."

"So, the book is a forgery?" Electra asked quickly.

"Well, no . . . I could hardly describe it as a forgery."

"But the book was printed when—two or three years ago?"

"Two years ago."

"And it bears a date stating it was printed more than forty years ago."

"The original print run was made in 1957. I was working in the print shop then—my father insisted I start at the bottom, learn the trade, even though it was my family's business."

"Oh . . ." She felt deflated. "This is just a reprint of the original, then?"

"George Leppington commissioned another print run two years ago. What's wrong, Electra? Are you feeling all right?"

"Yes, fine," she said wearily. "I just thought . . . oh, nothing really. It's not important."

"But important enough for you to hightail it down from Leppington to see me about it?"

She gave a weak smile. "I'd convinced myself the book was a forgery somehow. It never occurred to me that it was simply a reprint of an earlier edition."

"Electra." Arnold McClure sat down behind his desk and knitted his fingers together in front of him, his expression grave now. He looked at her levelly with his brilliant blue eyes. "I take it that it was important to you that the book is, shall we say, not as it appears to be?"

"Really, I'm sorry to have wasted your time, Arnold. I've been barking up the wrong tree."

"Wait, Electra, sit down . . . please. I've known you since you were so high. You're not the hysterical sort. And I'm long enough in the tooth to know when someone's in trouble . . . ah!" He held up a hand. "You don't have to tell me the ins and outs." He smiled sympathetically. "I might be turning into a bit of an old goat these days—I can give the lads on the shop floor a hard time if I catch them larking around—but I still think I'm intuitive enough to see fear in someone's eyes." He looked at her. "Do I see fear in your eyes, Electra?"

She nodded.

He stroked the side of his face, troubled. The light twinkled from his wedding ring. "OK. I think we need to exercise the old loyalties of what, after all, are two old family firms that go way back together."

"You mean there is something about the book—something more than meets the eye?"

He nodded. "Can I get you a drink? Coffee, tea, something stronger?"

"No. I'm pushed for time." She glanced out of the window. The sun, half hidden by scudding cloud, rode high in the sky by now. There were maybe another seven hours or so before dusk. The clock was ticking. "Thanks, anyway." She forced a smile.

"The truth is, Electra," he picked up the book from the desk, "this mystifies me somewhat. Oh, I know what it is: a family history of the Leppingtons. We've printed this kind of thing before for local families. We're typesetting one now for the Harkers from Ruswarp. Basically, we're happy to print anything as long as we're paid on time." He flicked through the book again. "Miss Gertrude Leppington commissioned us to print this book in 1957—three hundred copies, if I'm not mistaken. Good job we did, too, good-quality paper; the books were hand-stitched, not glued like you find today. This book will still have all its pages in a hundred years." He paused, considering. "And that was the end of the job. But two years ago George Leppington came into this very office, sits in that very chair where you're sitting, Electra, and asks me to reprint it. 'OK,' I reply. 'How many copies?' 'Two,' he replies. 'Oh, two hundred?' say I. He looks me right in the face and tells me, 'No, Arnold. Just two copies.' I pointed out to him that that's going to make for a couple of very expensive books. We still have the typefaces, but we have to set up the machines again—and, believe me, it costs a lot to set up the machines to print a whole book."

"Did he say why he wanted just two copies of the book?"

"No."

"And the books were to be exactly the same?"

"Well . . ." He knitted his fingers gravely together again. "Actually, no. He'd prepared alterations to the text. Not a great deal of difference. It was to one of the earlier chapters that describe the Leppingtons' past. He also wanted some kind of prophecy added to the chapter. He said he'd been researching the family history and needed to make a few additions."

"But that would mean typesetting part of the book again?"

The man nodded. "As well as renumbering the pages and altering the contents page to reflect the new page numbers of the chapters."

"That would have cost a small fortune, wouldn't it?"

"Indeed it did," he said. "And George was willing to pay. Not only that, he asked for it to be printed on 1950s paper, and for every other detail of the book to be the same so it would look identical to the original 1957 edition."

"But surely you wouldn't have paper that old in stock?"

"We do, as a matter of fact. Not very businesslike in this day and age, but we do carry stocks of paper that go back decades. We even have some high-quality vellum that dates back a hundred years—though the mercury content of the paper would probably be enough to make a toxicologist reach for the panic button." His blue eyes twinkled. "I'm going to print the invitations to my retirement party on that one."

"But what accounts for that new-book smell on the pages?"

"The inks. We had to use new inks, although we tried to match the shade as closely as possible to the original."

"If the new book was to be like the old edition in every detail—with the exception of George Leppington's amendments—why did you alter the name of the printer to include the word limited?"

"A matter of observing the laws of the land, Electra. If we were to omit the word indicating we are a limited-liability company we might be liable for prosecution by the Registrar of companies—the Companies Acts and all that. So well spotted, by the way. You'd have made quite a detective, Electra."

She acknowledged the compliment with a nod and a smile. "You don't remember exactly what changes were made to the book, do you, Arnold?"

"I can do one better than that. We keep copies of what we print—just in case there are any complaints from clients later—not that we receive many, I should add." He smiled, and picked up the telephone. "I'll just ring downstairs and get Judy to ferret out one of the original 1957 copies of the book for you. Then you can compare the two versions of the book and see the differences for yourself."

"Thank you, Arnold," she said gratefully. "You don't know how much this means to me."

"No, I don't," he said soberly as he stood and held out his hand. She shook it. "But there's a look in your eye that suggests that lives depend on what I told you today." He held on to her hand while resting his other hand on top of hers, then added gravely, "May God go with you, Electra, and keep you safe."

"Thank you," she said, touched.

Five minutes later she was striding through Whitby's busy streets in the direction of the car park. Jack Black walked alongside of her, his fierce expression enough to part the crowds.

"Got what you wanted?" he asked.

"And a whole lot more." They crossed the car park to where the van was parked. It overlooked the harbor where boats rocked on the wind-ruffled sea. She shot Jack Black a look as she pulled the mobile phone from her bag. "Do you believe in God, Jack?"

"Never have done. Load of bollocks."

"I shared your opinion. But we might have to revise our views."

"Why's that?"

She held up the two books. "Because I think one of our prayers has just been answered."

She tapped the keys on the mobile. Instantly it was answered. "Hello, David?" she said, pressing one hand over the other ear as the wind gusted, rattling the car park sign. "David, yes . . . it's Electra. David, listen. Have you finished at the cave? Good. You're back at the hotel? Stay there, I'll be back in twenty minutes. Yes . . . yes. I've acquired some information that you're going to find interesting. Also, get some rest while you can, because this afternoon we're going to conduct an experiment—a very important experiment."

After David rang off she slipped the phone back into her bag and looked up at the tiers of ancient houses climbing the side of the valley in row after row. The orange pantile roofs glowed warmly in the sunshine. Above the lines of houses, the church of St. Mary's stood on the hilltop. Behind that lay the ruins of the thousand-year-old abbey.

With a sense of surprise she found she was really fond of this little old town by the sea. It looked lovely. Utterly lovely. For much of her life she'd fostered a breezy indifference to the value of her life—and of actually being alive. But now she realized how much she would regret dying young. Well, God willing, that won't happen, she told herself firmly as she looked up at the houses. We won't be destroyed like poor Bernice. And, moreover, we will avenge her death.

Bernice Mochardi, very much alive but trapped beneath the town of Leppington, watched the stranger step into the little pool of daylight admitted by the iron grating above their heads.

"I've seen you before," she said, so grateful to be in the company of another human being she could have jumped up and down excitedly on the spot.

Maximilian Hart smiled beneath the gray wash of light. "And I've seen you, too. You live in the hotel?"

"That's right." She gripped his hand tightly. "But how did you get down here?"

"They brought me down into the tunnels. But none of the white people would touch me. They think I've got bad blood."

"They let you go?"

He shrugged and smiled, his almond-shaped Down's syndrome eyes twinkling. "I just walked away. They ignored me. You see, I've got bad blood," he added as if by way of explanation. "Why do you think I've got bad blood?"

"Well, I don't think you've got bad blood," she said with feeling. "As far as I'm concerned you're my knight in shining armor. A hero."

He smiled. "I wish I was a hero. I wish I could be brave."

"Believe me, Maximilian, you are," she said firmly, then looked along the tunnel that was intermittently lit by pools of daylight. "Maximilian, do you know a way out of here?"

He shook his head. "I've never been down here before."

Bernice kept a grip on his hand, reassuring herself with his physical presence. "I guess all we can do is keep looking. What do you say?"

"Keep looking. Yes, keep looking."

"As long as we don't bump into any of those creatures," Bernice added with a cold shudder. "Come on, sooner we're out of here the better."

Keeping her eyes locked onto the core of darkness that lay beyond the pools of daylight, she walked on, and wondered what Electra and David were doing now.

The time was just a moment past midday.

At half-past twelve Electra walked briskly into the hotel kitchen, followed by Jack Black. David leaned back against a worktop, chewing doggedly on a sandwich and drinking a syrup-thick black coffee. Quickly, Electra told David what she'd uncovered that morning.

He shook his head, puzzled. "You mean my uncle had two copies of a specially doctored version of my family's history printed?" He shrugged, perplexed. "What on earth for?"

"I think the reason can be summed up in one word," Electra replied. "Obsession."

"Obsession?"

She gave a confirming nod. "He must have been obsessed by your family's legendary past; he wanted more than anything else for it to be true, including the parts about the Leppingtons being blood descendants of Norse gods, and that the family were destined for some great and glorious future as empire builders."

David looked down at the copy of *The Leppington Family: Fact and Legend* that his uncle had given him. This was the newer, altered version. Electra had already hi-lighted the doctored text in fluorescent yellow. He shook his head. "But why go to all that trouble?"

"I think, originally, he produced the new version of the book purely for his own satisfaction."

"So he never intended anyone else to see it?"

"Absolutely. It would probably have been enough for him to sit alone in his house up there on the hillside rereading the version of your family history as he wanted it to be."

"Wait a minute, the original does describe our ancestors' dealings with the god, Thor, and the creation of the vampire army, doesn't it?"

"It does, yes. Although it makes no mention of the prophecy that the last of the Leppingtons—that's you, David—will return to the town to take control of the vampire army before marching it away to death and glory in the outside world."

David rubbed his jaw, his mind ticking over faster. "So what other changes have you identified?"

"It was all a rush job on the drive back up here. But it seems in the later version George Leppington cut all references to the folk tale of Sir William of Saxilby's battle with the vampires in the thirteenth century."

"So he was deleting all references to the vampires being destroyed?"

"Got it in one. He wanted to present a new version of the myth, that the Leppington breed of vampire was indestructible. That the long-lost son of the Leppingtons would return to lead them out to smite the old enemy. You see what's happened, don't you?"

David nodded. "He's sat down and rewritten the Leppington myth in a form he wanted to be true."

"But what he couldn't have foreseen was that you—the last in the blood-line of the Leppingtons—would actually return to the town."

"You think he's insane?"

"I think he was driven by this obsession to extraordinary lengths—in fact, ultimately, he believed in his own version of the Leppington myth, including the prophecy he'd concocted out of his own head that you'd returned to lead the monsters."

"But we've seen these creatures." David rubbed his forehead. "They're real, aren't they? I mean, we haven't imagined all this?"

"No," Electra said firmly. "We've not imagined those things. They are real, all right."

"So, we're still locked into this nightmare." He gave a bitter laugh. "I take it these monsters aren't going to evaporate into thin air if we all get a good night's sleep, are they?"

"No." Electra's eyes glittered with the beginnings of triumph. "But don't you see what this means, David?"

He shook his head. His mind was spinning dizzily. "No, I don't see what it means at all."

"Think about it, David. Your uncle deleted all references to the fact that these monsters can be destroyed."

"You mean by cutting off their heads?"

"Yes!"

David glanced at the sword he'd left on the kitchen work-top. "My God, Electra. You're telling me we should actually try and kill these creatures?"

"David, that's exactly what I'm saying!"

He rubbed his jaw. "But it's a hell of a risk."

"One we've got to take."

"But it means tracking these things through the caves, some-how cornering them, then hacking through their necks. How the hell do we do that? And how do we know beheading will ac-tually kill them?"

"Remember on the phone I told you we needed to conduct an experiment?"

He nodded, a cold-water sensation bubbling through his bow-els. He knew what she was going to say next. "The girl locked in the basement?"

Electra's eyes locked on his with an intensity that made him shiver. "That's right, David. What I'm proposing is that we put the theory to the test."

"Oh, Christ . . . you mean we cut off her head?"

Electra nodded. "And we do it now. While there's still plenty of daylight."

4

David watched Electra go to the door and call Black into the kitchen. He'd been sitting on a wall outside, smoking cigarettes with his three mates who'd helped with the building of the wall in the cave.

David sat there at the kitchen table, stunned by Electra's sug-gestion. She couldn't be serious, could she? To kill another hu-man being? He was a doctor, for Godsakes; hadn't he devoted all his working life to saving lives? Memories scooted through his head of his training on maternity wards, delivering babies; his time in A&E, stitching together flesh torn open in car ac-cidents, even holding together a child's raw wound with his bare hands. The arteries in one wrist had been cleanly sliced through after a fall onto broken glass. He'd nipped the cut closed with his fingers, stopping the blood squirting out in every direction until they'd got the child into surgery. Save lives. Dear God, that's what he believed he'd been put on this Earth to do.

Now Electra was calmly repeating to that tattooed monster Jack Black that they intended cutting off the head of a fellow human being. Jesus wept . . .

"Listen," David said, interrupting Electra. "This isn't as easy as you think, you know?"

"Why?" Black grunted.

"I see two obstacles to this."

"And they are?" Electra said evenly.

"One. Have we considered there maybe is a way of treating this girl's condition?"

"You mean cure her of being a vampire?"

"Yes."

"But David, we haven't got the time. It'll be dark in a matter of hours. Then those things might be pouring up from the sewers like rats. Do you know how we can stop them then?"

"For crying out loud, what if we're jumping the gun here? Locked down in that storeroom is a human being. Right?"

She shook her head. "Wrong, David. *Was* a human being. She *was* called Dianne Moberry. She *was* a pretty girl in her twenties."

"And now she's one of them bastards." Black crushed the cigarette under his massive boot. "Electra says we can kill these things. We can see if she's right by having a go at that thing in the basement."

David shook his head. "You mean you won't even give that girl a chance?"

"Would she—or her fellow vampires—give *us* half a chance if they got their hands on us? Have you forgotten what happened to Bernice?"

"Of course I haven't. But we could take the girl to hospital where—"

"Where they could conduct scientific tests on her forever and a day."

"The condition might be reversible."

"Might be." Electra nodded. "But how long would it take? Days? Weeks?"

"They could try."

"But we don't *have* the time. How long is it now until sunset? Six hours?"

"Electra, we could—"

"We're wasting time," Black grunted. "Come sunset those things will be after our blood. I don't want to be sitting here waiting for that to happen, do you?"

368

"Not me," Electra said. "I've got a bloody boring life, but it's the only one I've got and I'm hanging on to it with both hands. David?"

He stood up and walked across the kitchen to where the sword lay gleaming on the worktop. That morning he'd bound tape around the handle so he wouldn't be gripping bare metal. He ran his finger along the now shining blade. His thumb throbbed again from where he'd pricked it on the wickedly sharp point. It was almost as if his body responded in some kind of mystic harmony with the weapon.

David reached a decision. He turned around and looked at the pair of them. "I mentioned two objections."

"OK," Electra said calmly. "What's the second?"

"The second is a practical one. Do you have any idea how difficult it is to cut off the head of a human being?"

She shrugged. "Shouldn't be too difficult. There's some pretty sharp kitchen knives hanging up across there."

"Well, I have removed a human head from its body. At the university hospital med students are allocated a corpse—these are the bodies of men and women who donate their bodies to science. There I surgically removed the head of the corpse allocated to me. It was the body of a sixty-year-old man and, believe me, it was difficult—bloody difficult. The handles of the instruments get slippery from the moisture leaking from the body. So it's not at all easy to grip them properly. Remember that the thing—the creature—downstairs hasn't been drained of blood like the corpses used in the anatomy classes. There'll be bucketfuls of the stuff still in its veins. And the human body is a far tougher organism than most people appreciate. The windpipe's basically armor-plated with a hard shell of cartilage; the carotid and jugular arteries are incredibly tough, too, whatever you might have seen on television to the contrary. Then there is the spine that extends through the neck."

"We can do it, David," Electra said reassuringly. "We'll get whatever tools you need. There's even a power saw outside in the garage."

"Just one other thing," David said, looking at her. "Have you considered she might not submit to being decapitated?"

"You're worried she'll put up a fight?"

"Hell, Electra." He gave a dark laugh, edged with hysteria. "Wouldn't you?"

5

David Leppington had been a doctor for six years. He distanced himself—or at least tried to distance himself—from what he'd do fifteen minutes from now by concentrating on the necessary preparations. This was as much a ritual as you'd find in any religious service.

First he rolled up his sleeves before washing his hands. Then he took a large formica-topped serving tray with wooden handles. On this he laid three thick towels, one on top of the other. A little bird tells me we're going to need plenty of absorbent material, he told himself, as he worked there in the kitchen.

On the towels he laid out a selection of knives in order of size. There was no surgeon's scalpel, of course, so he chose a sharp paring knife, the kind kitchen staff would use to trim fat and gristle from meat. Then he laid out larger carving knives for cutting through the considerable slabs of muscle found in the neck that support and provide mobility to the brain, skull, teeth, muscle and skin that comprise the human head.

As he worked, checking the sharpness of the knives and the strength of the hacksaw blades, he ran through his other wants with Electra and Jack Black. Outside, the three men who'd helped earlier sat like vultures on the wall. The wind blew harder, drawing forth insane fluting sounds from the guttering and the eaves. As the wind dropped, these sounds, that seemed so mournful and despairing, deepened and softened into a breathy kind of sigh he'd once heard ooze from the throat of a man dying of lung cancer.

Again David forced himself to suppress the clamor of doubts. Speaking in a cool, dispassionate way, like a surgeon preparing for an operation, he said, "We'll need rubber gloves, and aprons. There will be body fluids. Probably copious quantities. Bring me as many towels as possible—preferably big bath towels, Electra; we'll drape them over the body as near as possible to where I make the cut. Also we'll need to carpet the floor with them. Prosaic as it sounds, it'll get slippery underfoot; we don't

370

want to hinder the operation by people falling. Jack, we'll need a bucket of some description."

"How big?"

David said grimly, "Big enough to put one of these in." He touched his own head. "After we've done, we'll have to wrap the body in plastic and bury it."

"Any ideas where?" asked Electra returning with armfuls of fluffy white bathtowels.

"I think tradition dictates either at a crossroads or next to flowing water. A river bank will be best. Then we have to make sure the head's buried on the side opposite to the body. I don't know if these folklore rules relating to the disposal of supernatural beings are all tosh, but we'd be fools not to observe them to the letter. You never know what might be vital. There . . ." Quickly he ran through the instruments. Paring knives, cleaving knives, hacksaws, touching each in turn as if conferring some kind of blessing on them. "That should do it."

Black asked, "Why don't you take the sword and swipe off the head in one go?"

"Because that would require the expertise of a skilled swordsman. And seeing as I'm not one, I'm going to have to resort to what I know best: surgical technique. Right, everyone ready?"

He looked at Black and Electra who nodded, their faces tight with tension.

"Good. Now, it's just coming up to three o'clock. We've got ample time to see if this works. If we can kill that thing in the basement we can then concoct a strategy that will wipe out the other vampires. OK?"

They nodded.

He picked up the tray set out with the knives and hacksaws. "All right. Let's do it."

Electra and Black picked up the armfuls of towels and the bucket. In the bucket were pairs of latex surgical gloves that the kitchen staff normally wore. Resting on top of the gloves was a roll of gaffer tape. This was a heavy-duty adhesive tape, something like Sellotape, only the tape itself was made of fabric and impregnated with a silvery plastic compound that resisted water—and any other liquids that might be split on it. The creature that had once been Dianne Moberry might not lie still when David cut into the throat. They'd use the tape to bind her limbs.

They crossed the hotel lobby. David glanced out through the windows of the locked doors. Beyond them the world outside still went about its day-to-day business. He saw buses rumbling by; people were shopping, a policeman looked at a map held out to him by a stranger to the town and scratched his head as he considered the best directions. Steam rose from a chimney that jutted from the slaughterhouse roof. A train pulled out of the station and David wished to high heaven he were on it.

When Jack Black unlocked the basement door the wish came again, with a pang so strong it hurt David all the way down to his stomach. What's that phrase? He'd give all the tea in China to be on that train, rattling down the track to Whitby and the sea. That's a lot of tea. A hell of a lot of tea. But worth it.

Only, right now, he had to go down those gloomy steps. Cold air welled up from the shadowed void below. He shivered. Then he took a deep breath and plunged down into a basement that could have been some terrifying anteroom to hell itself.

Chapter Forty

1

At three-thirty, exactly the same time David Leppington was taking that first step down into the basement, Bernice Mochardi and the Down's syndrome man walked beneath the town.

For all the world we might be walking through the intestine of some huge beast, she thought; an intestine of brick and stone. Every so often a surge of water came along the channel that ran in the center of the tunnel. Once soapy water had discharged with a roaring sound from a pipe at shoulder height, nearly drenching her.

She walked with her back to her wall, still holding the hand of Maximilian Hart. There was no doubt his presence was a comfort to her. Especially during the long—long to the point of seemingly neverending—walks through sections of tunnel that were blanketed in total darkness. If it hadn't been for the man's presence she felt she would have been reduced to a fit of lunatic screams as the darkness seemed to press into her eyes and mouth and throat like an inky black liquid that threatened to suffocate her sanity as much as her lungs.

Perhaps the dark does have a different quality down here, she thought. Like the air pressure varies from mountain tops to valley bottoms. Down here the darkness seems so much denser, almost liquid somehow. Shivering, she'd pushed on.

Now this section of the tunnel was marginally better. There was light from grates set in the ceiling high above her head. To people in the street, those grates would probably be no more than the everyday kind of drains inset between the kerb and roadway. Where the water poured down on rainy days, or where little children dropped their lollipop sticks.

But those little grilles of iron were a godsend. They admitted precious rays of gray light that lit their way. Now she could see the narrow path at either side of the drainage channel; the slick ribbon of water running through it; the herringbone pattern of bricks that formed the inner skin of the tunnel. It even lit downy webs spun by spiders over the decades, through which she had to push her hand, the sticky strands clinging coolly to her skin.

At that moment she sensed, rather than heard, a deep rumble. It tickled its way through the earth, then through the bricks and into the fingertips of one hand as she slid, back to wall, along the tunnel. That has to be a train, she thought, we're probably not far from the station. In that case the Station Hotel basement might not be more than a few dozen paces away. If only she knew *which* direction. And *which* one of the many branch tunnels she should take.

Still holding Maximilian by the hand, she branched off the tunnel from the one that she walked along. Yet this tunnel looked depressingly the same as the one she'd left. Same herring-bone pattern of brownish bricks. A channel cut deep into the stone beneath her feet. Same delicate fan shapes of spider webs spanning whole sections of tunnels. Here and there toadstool growths erupted from the walls; the same yellow as ripe bananas, they looked like pairs of clenched fists that had been somehow forced through the brickwork. On the far side of the tunnel a whole cluster of them had grotesquely fused together, forming the simulacrum of a tightly wound human foetus complete with eyes and ears and legs. Yet more feathery strands of spiders' web covered it lightly in a shroud that was gauzily see-through in the thin light.

She stepped forward, breaking yet another membrane of web with her free hand before stepping through. Much of the web clung to her black skirt. More of the web formed clots of dirty gray fluff on her black lace gloves.

Here she paused. The smell of the place was different. No longer cold and damp and earthy. The air was distinctly warmer; the air smelled coppery; yes, *yes*, she thought with a flutter of astonishment; there was definitely a tang of some altogether different odor staining the air.

Why was this tunnel so different from the rest?

It started without warning.

She looked up with a gasp.

There was a loud hiss like the sound of an ornamental waterfall. Seconds later liquid poured from drainage holes feeding down through the roof.

For a second she thought they were street drains that were being flushed through with water.

But then she saw the liquid was blood.

It gushed from dozens of outlets set along the spine of the ceiling. It poured thick and red and steaming down into the channel below. There it pooled, growing deeper and deeper. More blood joined the bloody stream. The hot blood heated the air in the tunnel until it became as warm as a greenhouse—a sticky, close warmth that pressed against her bare skin to fill her nose every time she breathed.

She saw it flow past her from right to left, carrying clumps of pink foam that floated on the surface.

She and Maximilian pressed themselves back against the wall to avoid being drenched by the crimson rainfall. Even so, drops of blood speckled the toes of her boots.

Now she knew what lay above. It must be the slaughterhouse, she thought; she looked again at the light filtering through the drains and now she saw it had the harder brilliance of electric lighting.

She thought: We must be just below the killing floor; they're slaughtering animals up there.

Blood would be gurgling around the boots of the slaughter-men before pouring thickly away into the drains.

Again she shouted for help. Although by now she knew that her voice must not be filtering through the grates to the outside world; or if it was, people who heard it didn't know where the distant cries were coming from. She imagined them looking round, curious about where the shouts originated. Then, when they saw nothing amiss, shrugging their shoulders and walking away along the pavements.

The sheer frustration of not being able to get anyone to hear was almost enough to make her weep.

She looked back along the tunnel they'd just traversed. Through the red spray of falling blood, she saw a cluster of white shapes come bobbing toward her; she glimpsed the deep-set eyes, the wide mouths with their dark lips and gleam of incredibly white teeth that were as sharp as a panther's.

"Oh, Christ," she whispered, a heavy weight settling on her heart. "Oh, my Christ. They've found us."

2

In the basement Electra had switched on all the lights, then shone the torch to the far end where the steel door was set.

"Dear God," she whispered.

"What's wrong?" asked David startled.

"Look." She nodded in the direction of the steel door. "They've somehow managed to open it."

"Christ, they might be down here already. Jack, can you see anything?"

As he pulled the hammer from his belt, Black's fierce eyes swept up and down the basement. "I see nothing." Nevertheless, he moved along the basement, ugly head swinging left and right like a bulldog looking for a rat. He checked every niche and cupboard where one of the creatures might be hiding.

"Still nothing?" called David.

"Nothing. They won't come out yet: it's still daylight."

"Yeah, but there's precious little light comes down here, though," Electra murmured in a low voice. Then, louder, she called, "All clear?" as Black walked slowly back, head still swinging from right to left, looking under racks of shelving.

"Nothing," he replied. "Like I said, they're waiting for sunset."

David looked at the gaping doorway. "That must be where they took Bernice." For a moment he wondered about seizing the torch and going in search of her.

Fat lot of good that would do, he told himself bitterly. The vampires would have opened her up and sucked out her blood hours ago. She would be one of them now. Pale-skinned, deep-set eyes, veins forming a purple lace design across throat and arms.

"Close it up," Electra said sharply. "Close it up, before they realize we're down here."

David said quickly, "Jack, push the door shut. I'll get the padlocks . . . wait . . . damn; someone's sawn through the hasps. They're useless."

"Here," said Black, tipping up a box that contained an assortment of bolts and hefty timber nails. "Shove these through the loops. They'll hold the door until we get more padlocks."

Black then heaved the massive steel door shut with a clang.

When the steel loops of the door overlapped the steel loops welded to the metal door frame David wedged through what bolts and nails would fit. Only when he'd finished did he sigh with relief. "That should do it for the time being." He wiped the rust stains off onto the legs of his jeans.

"Who do you think cut the padlocks?" Electra asked.

"My guess is that it was one of the vampires' new recruits. They had access to the basement through the trapdoor to the courtyard." He looked back at the doorway to the tunnel. Erupting into his head flared the image of the door bursting open and the vampires pouring through in a noxious flood of white heads, set with those dark staring eyes. Their jaws would crack open, revealing rows of glittering teeth that would snap down on the three humans' throats. He thought: Once they've torn open our bodies, they would lap at the bleeding wounds, like cats lapping from a bowl of milk. He fought the image back down. He could allow no more distractions. It was time to get back to the job in hand.

He took the storeroom key from his pocket, slotted it into the keyhole, turned it.

"OK," he said in low voice. "Here goes."

At the same time as David Leppington was unlocking the store-room in the basement of the Station Hotel, Bernice had frozen up tight with fear. She watched as the vampires swarmed into the tunnel.

The blood still fell in a waterfall. Rich and red, it cascaded down into the channel, frothing, splashing, steaming. The humidity soared, forming a pink mist that engulfed the tunnel, reducing visibility to a few paces.

They're going to attack us, she thought, unable to take her eyes from the bobbing white heads coming through the tunnel. Any second their eyes will lock onto us. And once they've seen us they'll come running this way.

Gripping Maximilian's hand, she shrank back against the wall until the brick pressed hard against her spine, as though if only she could press hard enough she could slip into the cracks between the bricks and hide there, safe and sound, until the monsters had gone.

"They don't want us," Maximilian whispered. "Look. They're thirsty."

The vampires continued to surge into this section of tunnel. Only they were taking no notice of Bernice or Maximilian. They were thirstily drinking the blood of slaughtered animals as it gushed down through the drains from above. Some of the vampires knelt on all fours, lapping furiously at the blood as it flowed along the stone channel. Their black tongues darted into the red liquid. Every so often a congealing lump of grue would float by, then they would ravenously scoop it up into their jaws and chomp, their eyes closing in bliss.

They look like animals drinking at a waterhole in Africa, she told herself. Animals that were brutally thirsty, drinking so fast they coughed and gipped. Yet more of the vampires walked beneath the bloody shower, soaking themselves in the gory liquid. They held up their hands to it, turned up their faces to it, revelled in it, as the purest gore splashed down onto their heads and shoulders and arms. They opened their mouths wide in a hideously abnormal yawn to catch the precious drops of the life-giving rain of blood.

"Come on," she whispered to Maximilian. "Let's get out of here before it stops."

Quickly, stealthily, they crept along the tunnel, taking care to keep their backs pressed against the wall to avoid the bloody waterfall. Even so a film of atomized blood settled on their faces and lips.

Bernice wiped the back of her gloved hand across her lips.

She grimaced. She could taste blood; a blend of salt and metallic flavors.

A few seconds later they reached the entrance to another tunnel.

Before she followed Maximilian into its gloomy throat, she glanced back at the vampires as they gorged themselves on the blood of the beasts. The blood absorbed their attention. Nothing else mattered to them. They coughed, spluttered, hawked, as they tried to swallow more than the bore of their throats could accommodate. Their bald white heads were smeared with blood; what tattered clothes they wore were soaked in it. And all the time their deep-set eyes fixed burningly on the blood stream as if it was the most wonderful thing in the world.

To them, it probably is, she thought. This daily deluge of blood was nothing less than *their* life blood. They'd wither away without it. She started to walk into the next tunnel. But then she paused, looked back at them again, staring hard at the feeding creatures.

An idea occurred to her with such a dazzling suddenness that her skin tingled from her scalp to her fingertips. She was still staring, deep in thought, when she felt Maximilian tug her hand to hurry her up.

At last she allowed herself to be led away by the hand, away from the tunnel of blood, but now she was thinking hard.

4

David recoiled from the brilliance of the halogen lamps in the storeroom. Squinting against the brightness, one hand raised level with his eyebrows to shield his eyes, he stepped into the room. The brick walls were a vivid orange in the vicious brilliance of the lights.

He paused, allowing his eyes to get used to the light. "Did you leave the lamps on all the time?" he whispered back to Electra.

"Yes. She only became active when we switched them off."

"Then hopefully she's still inactive now," he murmured as he stepped through the doorway into the storeroom. "Damn."

"What's wrong?" asked Electra alarmed.

"She's gone."

"She can't have, the door was locked all the time."

David, shielding his eyes, looked at the worktop. There, decades ago, kitchen staff must have butchered game, gutted fish, and carved joints from the carcasses of sheep and cows.

Now it was empty.

The blond girl that he'd seen stretched out there like a corpse had vanished.

He moved into the room, still dazzled by the brilliant wash of white light from the halogen lamps.

Suddenly he paused and looked into the corner where the raw brick walls met.

"It's OK," he said. "She's here. She must have tried to hide from the light."

The creature that had been pretty, blond-haired and blue-eyed Dianne Moberry had tried to worm her—*its*—way under the stone shelf to find some comfort in the cool shadow beneath.

Christ, anything to escape this pitiless light, David thought, as his own head began to ache from the brilliance. Who could blame the poor wretch?

Bending at the waist, he looked down at the naked figure. It appeared unconscious. As he bent further, hand outstretched, ready to give the bare foot an exploratory prod, Black moved past him.

"We can't pussyfoot around any longer," Black grunted brusquely. "We haven't got time."

With that he grabbed the creature by its feet and dragged the body across the concrete floor. It was naked, lying face down, one cheek resting against the concrete.

David winced at the thought of what it would feel like to be dragged naked across such an abrasive surface.

"Gently," he said. "We've got to do this as humanely as possible."

Black grunted back, his face like stone. "Five hours until sunset. Being humane's a luxury we can't afford . . . or do you want to administer a fucking anesthetic first?"

David glanced at Electra. She swallowed. Her eyes were fixed on the face of the girl whose features were as relaxed as those of someone asleep.

Black picked her up in his long arms. Her blond head lolled down over one arm, the hair swinging as he hefted her back onto the stone slab.

Her bare body made a slapping sound as he dropped her down onto it. He straightened the head, then lifted up an arm that had dropped to swing down from the side of the slab. With no sign of tenderness he pushed the arm across her breast.

"There you go, Doc. Do your stuff."

David swallowed. The girl looked like a corpse lying on a mortuary slab. Just get it into your head she *is* dead, he told himself firmly. She's dead, really a corpse. Nothing but a conglomeration of lifeless flesh, bone and internal organs. This is just a clinical dissection—nothing more.

Nothing more.

He wiped his lips—they were dry and hot. His heartbeat had increased, sweat had begun to creep out onto his neck.

Shit. Come on, David. Get this over and done with.

"OK," he said, briskly snapping on a latex surgical glove. "Everyone wearing their gloves? Good. Don't forget your aprons. This is going to get very wet, very messy. Electra, start by laying out the towels on the floor. Make sure they're at least three deep at this end near the head. Jack, bring me the gaffer tape, we'll bind her legs together; after that we're going to tape her arms to her torso."

"Gotcha, Doc." He went out into the basement where they'd left the tools for this grisly little job.

Electra lightly touched David's forearm. "Do you have to tie her up?"

"Yes."

"Do you think she will move? She *looks* dead."

"I think we're boldly going where no man's gone before," he said with a grim ghost of a smile. "I reckon we need to take as many precautions as possible, don't you?"

She nodded. "Christ, I hope she doesn't wake up and start screaming." She spoke with feeling.

"And Christ knows, I hope so, too," David murmured as he began to arrange the arms.

They worked well. David, helped by Black, taped the vampire's legs together. Then they folded her hands across her pale breasts with their scab nipples. While Black held her in a sitting position, one massive fist gripping her by the hair on the top of the head, David taped around the torso until the creature, as far as the neck anyway, looked like the makings of an Egyptian mummy. There the silver gaffer tape gleamed brightly beneath the halogen lamps.

So far, David hadn't noticed so much as a twitch or murmur from the creature. Perhaps if it is placed under a light that is bright enough it will render the creature so deeply unconscious it does appear to be dead, he thought.

A moment later, he cut the tape and put the spool by the creature's feet.

"Right. Bring in the tray and the bucket," he told them. "Let's get this over and done with."

Electra brought the tray and held it out to him, as if she was offering a plate of sandwiches so he could help himself. The line of knives and hacksaws neatly laid out on white towels gleamed beneath the light. The brass studs in the wooden handles shone like golden stars.

He chose a small paring knife first, with a blade that was as sharp as a scalpel.

"Right." He looked up at them. "Here goes. Jack, hold the head for me please."

Black did as he was told. In fact, he did it expertly and David couldn't help but wonder if he had done something like this before.

First, Black stood at the end of the stone slab. With one huge tattooed hand he gripped the vampire's hair and held the head firmly downward. After that, he cupped his other hand under the chin and pulled the head back so the throat was raised.

David looked down in a terrible fascination at that long bare throat. Jack Black's muscular pull stretched the neck while forcing the throat upward so it formed a smooth mound of naked skin, webbed faintly by fine veins. David swallowed.

A few hours ago men would have gladly kissed that living throat and thrilled to its smoothness and the scented warmth it would have exuded while the still-alive Dianne Moberry giggled and curled her long soft hair around her fingers.

"David?" He looked up at Electra's gentle prompt. Her blue eyes locked onto his while she gave a reassuring nod. "We're doing the right thing, David. Think of it as releasing her from suffering."

He rested the blade of the knife against that naked throat.

Electra is right, he told himself. This is a disease. A disease that's going to rot humanity like a filthy great necrotic cancer; he must cut it out.

Taking a deep breath to steady the shudders jolting through his stomach, he made the first incision.

The skin opened up under the blade like a pair of moist pink lips. He sawed at the soft tissue, quickly opening up the lips of the wound wider, until it looked as if a second mouth had appeared beneath the chin. A mouth with lips curling back into a snarl. Then he reached the gristly white tissue of the windpipe. He switched knives for a heavier carving knife. He cut.

Then the creature screamed. A great full-blooded ear-jarring scream. The sound beat back from the bricks; it was loud and terrible and full of rage and pain and disbelief.

"David! Keep cutting!" Electra shouted above the screams. "Don't stop now!"

The creature's eyelids slid back to expose the eyeballs. The eyes themselves were swollen and shining: they squinted shockingly from the sockets, staring up into David's own eyes.

"No . . . not this; oh, not like this . . . kiss me, kiss me, my love." This hissing voice was seductive, but those seductive, sexily sibilant words were punctuated by great braying screams as if two spirits inside the creature waged war for control of her voice.

"Shut up," Black snarled and pulled harder with the hand he'd cupped beneath her chin. So great was the force now that it raised her chest up from the slab, her back arched like a bow.

David sliced into the tough tissue of the trachea.

The screams came again, piercing his head, spiking his ears until he had to grit his teeth.

The body bucked on the slab. The movements, restricted by

the binding of tape, were limbless and maggot-like; but the hips still lifted impossibly high as the monster arched its back. Electra threw herself fully onto the girl-beast, struggling to hold down the body with the weight of her own. Electra's face was set with determination, her lips pressed tight together, her eyes glaring with concentration and her hair flying this way and that as she rode the bucking creature.

"Come on, damn you," David hissed to himself. Cut it through. You've done it before. Cut it through. Imagine it's a tracheotomy, imagine you're saving the poor wretch's life.

Gritting his teeth, he bore down as he sawed with the blade.

The screams stopped and the hissing voice came back as sexily as he'd ever heard in his life before: "Love me . . . kiss me. Oh, I want you to hold me. I want—*Oh!*"

At that instant the blade suddenly sliced downward, severing the windpipe. Instantly a great rush of air blasted up from the wound as the lungs found a shortcut now that they no longer needed mouth or nostrils to aspirate. Still no blood came from the wound.

The blast of air, as hot as that coming from an oven, was shocking. It hit David full in the eyes, forcing him to blink and move back. The force of it fluttered Electra's hair as if she was crouched over a fan.

The creature's eyes were wide, unblinking. The eyelashes seemed to mate with the dark eyebrows, forming a black crescent above each white staring eye. The mouth was pulled open into a great "O" shape. The sharp teeth clicked together, punching holes in the long tongue that darted snake-like from the mouth. He even saw the black well of her throat at the back of the mouth.

Cut. Cut. Cut!

Grimly, he sawed at the neck. His arm ached. His shoulder muscles twitched but he didn't stop now.

Cut. Cut. Cut.

Hot air blasted from the wound that was as gray as raw fish.

The cutting was easier now, like cutting through a loaf of bread.

Seconds later, he sliced into the arteries.

Liquid spurted. It wasn't blood. This was almost clear, with a yellow tint to it.

He didn't stop. Grimly, he sawed on with the carving knife. The creature's body fluids spurted out with enough force to spatter against the walls. Droplets sprayed over their heads.

The knife struck something hard.

Spine, he told himself.

He switched knife for hacksaw. Black pulled harder, parting the two sides of the wound so it looked like a valley stretching all the way down to the whitely gleaming bone. The valley walls—the two halves of the neck still bore that quality of raw fish.

Already the physiology of the creature must be changing. There was none of the redness associated with human muscle tissue. Only that bloodless gray.

Now the creature thrashed with one final effort to prevent its destruction. The gaffer tape began to snap. The creature's bare calves slapped the stone slab, its hands bunched into fists and flailed as Electra strove to hold the girl down.

Black braced one booted foot against the end of the slab and pulled the head by the chin and the hair.

The thing writhed and twitched, throwing Electra off it as if it was a bucking horse. Its feet kicked high, catching the arching wall, smashing its own toes to jelly. Its mouth snapped open and shut like that of a rabid dog; the sharp teeth ripped open its own lips and bit out its own black tongue. Foam and pus and that piss-yellow liquid erupted in gouts from the mouth and nostrils; the eyes bulged so hugely they looked as if they'd burst.

David pushed the hacksaw forward, then dragged it back, sawing with all his strength, trying not to let the thrashing creature dislodge the blade.

Snick!

The abrupt parting of head from body threw Black off balance. He fell backward, still clutching the head by the hair.

David blundered back from the writhing but now headless body. He watched it roll off the stone slab. It squirmed and wriggled there on the floor like some great pulpy maggot. Liquid gushed from the neck.

And, most shocking off all, air continued to flow from the windpipe with a wet blurting sound.

He looked to his left to see Black thrust the head into the bucket. It was still grimacing and chomping madly at the air.

The eyes stared from the head—they, too, were still very much alive, turning this way and that as they looked from Black to Electra to David with nothing less than vicious hatred.

It took a good five minutes for the violent movements in the body to subside. Even then the knees lifted spasmodically and great shudders ran through the torso. Air continued to sigh from the severed windpipe. It made a despairing groaning sound as if distraught at losing this monstrous travesty of a life that had animated it.

Electra pulled herself from the floor where she'd been thrown.

"Are you all right?" David helped steady her as she rocked back on her heels, dizzy.

"As I'll ever be," she said in a tiny voice. "Is it dead?"

"I think so."

Jack Black was the most composed of the three. Matter-of-factly he said, "I'll take this across the river and bury it." He put the bucket into a plastic sack. "That thing." He gave the headless corpse a careless prod with the toe of his boot. "That can wait down here tonight."

Chapter Forty-one

1

"How long until it gets dark?" asked David.

"About four hours," Electra replied.

They were washing their faces and hands in the kitchen. The towels—they were wet and heavy with body fluids—latex gloves, aprons, knives, hacksaws had been bundled into refuse sacks and stood lined up against the wall, ready for disposal. Black had already made quick work of burying the head, still in the bucket, on the far side of the river. Now he stood in the courtyard, smoking and watching the clouds scud over the sky. The sun had begun its fall to the hilltops.

"It worked," David said. "We now know we can kill them."

"But how do we repeat that process underground? They're not going to let us tie them up first, are they?"

He sloshed water up his forearms. "Well, it's going to be messier—but if we can lure them out into the basement one by one . . ." He vigorously dried himself with fistfuls of kitchen roll. "Maybe we can isolate them. The three of us can overpower them and then . . ."

He made a chopping motion at his throat with his fingertips.

It could easily have been a bloodthirsty gesture; but inside he felt cold—almost clinical. He told himself this was simply continuing that course of treatment they'd begun downstairs. These vampires were a disease that he was determined to cure.

Electra had dried herself. She lit a cigarette, leaned back against the worktop and regarded him coolly. "Lure them out of the tunnels one by one?" She blew smoke out into the air. "How do we do that?"

"Bait."

"Bait?" She knew what he meant but she wanted to hear it from his lips.

He nodded, grimly. "We bait the basement with what they want. When they come through that doorway from the tunnel that's when we spring the trap."

"And you're going to cut off all those heads with my titchy kitchen knives?"

He shook his head and dumped the wet tissue into the bin. "There was a question I meant to ask you." He looked up at her. "Where's the nearest place we can hire a chainsaw?"

2

While David went to the hire shop down the street to collect the chainsaws Electra paid off Black's three buddies. They were on their own again. The Three Musketeers.

She looked up at the sky through the kitchen window. The clouds scudded quickly across the sky. The shadows were growing long. Less than three hours until dusk.

She rubbed her arms and shivered.

David pulled the car up behind the hotel. Black was waiting there, ready to unload the chainsaws and the can of two-stroke fuel. They were wicked-looking machines with sharp teeth that could slice through tree trunks. Flesh and bone should be no obstacle to them.

Straightaway, David checked that the fuel tanks of the chainsaws were full, then he took them into the kitchen where he rested them on the floor.

"You can handle those?" Electra asked, stubbing her cigarette out into a saucer.

"Last summer I helped a friend clear a couple of acres of land he'd bought behind his house." David crouched down and patted the fuel tank of the chainsaw. "Doting man that he was, he'd bought his daughter a pony and needed to clear away a lot of bushes and dead wood; these babies did the job in no time."

"Hell, Doc," Black sounded impressed for the first time. "We're going to cut off the fuckers" heads with these?"

"It won't be pretty, but I can't see any other way of doing it in such a short time."

"And I take it I'm going to be the bait, am I?" Electra raised her eyebrows.

David nodded. "I can't think of any other way, can you?"

"No," she said, stoically gazing down at the wicked teeth of the chainsaws. "Well. Shall we take our two babies down into the basement?"

4

Bernice Mochardi, still holding the hand of Maximilian, made her way through the tunnel which grew increasingly gloomy. The sound of water running in the channel echoed from the walls.

"We can't be too far from the surface," she said in a whisper. "Can you hear the cars?"

"We're going down," Maximilian said. "The same way as the water."

"That means this tunnel might lead to the river. We might be able to get out there."

She certainly hoped so. Back in the tunnel of blood an idea had struck her that was as sudden as it was surprising. Now she needed to talk to David Leppington as soon as possible.

If only I don't bump into anything first, she thought bleakly, and walked faster into the gloom. The only thing we won't find down here are rats. Clearly the vampires had eaten them all years ago.

She glanced backward. She thought she'd heard another sound above the rush of water. She held her breath, listening hard. Maximilian stopped, too. She felt the pressure of his hand in hers.

It *is* a noise, she thought. I can hear footsteps. Lots of footsteps.

Gripping Maximilian's hand, she hurried on. The sound of footsteps grew louder. And she knew time was running out.

5

Electra asked: "Once we've lured one of those monsters into the basement, how can we isolate it from the rest?"

"Jack here's going to act as doorman." David nodded toward the steel door held shut by an assortment of bolts and nails. "He lets one in, then he slams the door shut in the face of the rest."

"The others in the tunnel will push to come in, have you thought of that?"

"They'll try. But I've got every faith in Jack. He's as strong as an ox."

"I'll crush their damn heads in the door if I have to," added Black with a hard grin. "The bastards won't get by me."

"Then we use the chainsaws, take them one by one," David told her as he set his chainsaw down on a shelf in the basement.

"You'd best use the big torch as well," Electra said, anxiously rubbing her forearm. "If the light's bright enough it seems to take at least some of the wind out of their sails."

"Where is it?"

"Up in the car, I'll get it."

David checked the starter cord of the chainsaw and familiarized himself with the feel of the hand grips and the throttle. Once they got the chainsaw motors started they'd have to keep them idling until they needed them. He wished the basement was better ventilated. The exhaust fumes would build up pretty quickly. Still, he could do nothing about that. They'd just have to grin and bear it.

Electra returned, holding the torch by its pistol grip. She also carried the sword.

"David. You'd better take Helvetes as well," she said. "I guess that completes your armory now."

"Thanks." He took the sword from her. Somehow the thing did feel reassuring. Comforting, like the surprise appearance of an old friend in a strange town. He took the sword and slipped it blade first through his belt.

The flat of the blade and part of the hilt pressed reassuringly against his hip. Its presence there made him feel more confident and somehow physically stronger.

"All right," David told them. "Let's talk strategy. How are we going to actually do this? Jack?"

Jack stood with the chainsaw in one hand. It dangled with the cutting blade pointing downward. In that massive tattooed paw of his it looked as though it weighed no more than a bamboo cane. The man's eyes gazed enigmatically at the steel door. For a moment David could have believed that to those man's eyes the steel had become as transparent as glass, that he could see right through into the tunnel beyond.

And what, exactly, did he see?

"Jack," Electra asked anxiously. "Jack? What's wrong?"

He didn't reply. His eyes remained fixed on the door. His face was cold as stone.

"Jack." She glanced at David then back at the big man. "Jack. What is it?"

Jack breathed in sharply as if he'd been touched by a piece of ice. "It's Bernice Mochardi," he said in low voice, head tilted as if listening to a faraway sound; a moment later he nodded with a grave certainty at the door. "She's through there."

David started, surprised. "She's alive?"

"I can hear her thoughts in here." Black touched his own head. "Going over and over fast. It's important."

"Is she alive?"

Black shook his head. "Don't know."

Electra spoke coolly. "Jack. What is she thinking?"

Again he shook his head. That slow, heavy shake. "I can't make out words. But she wants to find you." He looked at David. "She needs to find you badly."

"Why?"

Again that heavy shake of the head. "Can't tell," he said.

"Then she is alive?"

"Might be." Then he jerked his head back at the storeroom that contained the decapitated body. "Might have gone over to them."

David looked at the steel door, standing there mutely in the gloom. Then he reached a decision.

"I'm going to go find her."

"David," Electra's voice rose in protest. "You heard what he said. What if she's a vampire now?"

"What if she isn't?"

"David—"

"She'll need help. Perhaps we can get to her before those things do."

He picked up the chainsaw. The tip of the sword caught the wall with a scraping sound.

"David, you haven't thought this through. You can't just—"

"There's nothing to think through. I'm going in. Jack, open the door, please."

"I'm going too," Jack said. "I'm going to swat some of those bastards."

"Thanks." David nodded gratefully.

"And you'll need someone to light your way," Electra said with a weak smile and picked up the million candlepower torch.

"You don't have to do this."

"Believe me, I have to." Her smile broadened. "This is my destiny, David." She clicked the switch, lighting the torch. "I think we all know we were born to be right here, at this time, to do just this. Am I right, David? Don't you feel the truth of it all in your blood?"

David nodded, his face determined. "Jack? Get the door."

Jack slipped the bolts from the steel loops fixed to the door and pulled it open.

Beyond, the dark throat of the tunnel waited for them. Quickly they slipped through the doorway and into the cold—the shockingly cold—subterranean air beyond.

Chapter Forty-two

1

With a burning sense of urgency David hurried along the tunnel. Following him in single file were Jack, then Electra. She held the powerful torch high behind him; he was aware of its sun-like brilliance blazing somewhere above his shoulder.

It flooded the tunnel in front of him with light, illuminating the herringbone pattern of brick that was stained here and there with mold. Clusters of fungi like bunched fists grew out from the walls, webs patiently spun by generations of spiders rippled in the draft, and along the center of the tunnel a ribbon of water trickled through a stone channel.

And, huge and dark and somehow monstrous, there was his own shadow cast by the light from behind. The shadow surged eagerly ahead of him, as if in a desperate hurry to find the girl he'd only known for forty-eight hours. Yet already he found he cared for her with such a desperate passion he ached inside. Could the legends be true? Had he loved Bernice in a past life, then cruelly lost her?

"See anything?" Black asked from behind.

"They've been this way," David replied quickly, "I can see footprints in the dust. Jack, have you any idea which direction Bernice might be?"

"She's close, that's all I can tell."

David moved forward as quickly as he could. Here the tunnel was so narrow you could stand in its center and still touch both walls with your elbows. As he walked, the tip of the sword scraped against the wall to his left; the chainsaw was brutally heavy in his hands—already his arms and shoulders ached. Christ, this was madness. What if a vampire came at him from around the next corner? How could he start the chainsaw motor in time, then wield the lethal device in this confined space?

His mouth dried. His heartbeat faster. Sweat pricked through his forehead.

"Slow down," Electra warned in a whisper. "We're coming up to a bend in the tunnel."

Stealthily now, David approached the sharp bend. Breathing deeply, he inched his way forward and looked around it.

"It's clear," he whispered. "Come on, the tunnel's beginning to widen out."

Now the tunnel ran beneath a road. Grates set in the roof high above his head showed the undersides of cars and trucks as they rumbled by. A chocolate wrapper slipped through the bars of the grate and drifted down like a single large snowflake.

He stopped.

"What's wrong?" whispered Electra.

"Nothing yet. But it's only a matter of time before these creatures find us down here. I think we should fire up the motors of the chainsaws before they do."

"But the noise?"

"My guess is that they know we're already here. The sound of the motors won't alter the situation. Agreed?"

"Suits me," Black grunted.

Electra gave a grim nod. "OK."

David turned on the fuel tap and tugged at the line that would snap the motor to life. His started first time. A thin blue jet of smoke shot from the exhaust tube. Jack Black's chainsaw fired up at the second pull of the cord.

Instantly the racket was deafening. There could be no whispers now; they had to shout above the clatter of the motors.

"Electra," he shouted. "Save the torch batteries." He pointed up at the grates that admitted rays of slanting sunlight. "It'll be bright enough for the time being!"

Electra switched off the light.

With the chainsaw throbbing in his hands, he walked quickly forward, eyes straining ahead, looking for the first sign of the creatures.

For all the world he looked like a dragon-slaying warrior of old, with the chainsaw held high like a great sword before him.

Now came a series of tunnels branching off. Bernice might be in any one of those. With luck the sound of the chainsaws might bring her to them.

But what if she was now one of the monsters?

He'd have to use the chainsaw on her, and sweep her lovely head from her shoulders. He gritted his teeth and hurried on, this time moving in a crouching run like a soldier crossing no man's land.

"David!"

Electra's warning shout punched through the air like a bullet.

He turned to see a mass of white heads bobbing out from one of the side tunnels; the deep-set eyes blazed with fury.

They reached out their thin naked arms, hands hooked like claws. One seized Electra by the hair and pulled her back.

Jack Black raised the chainsaw above his head, wielding it like a battleaxe The engine screamed, blue smoke churned through the air, then he brought the chainsaw down, slicing through the arms of the creature that held Electra.

The severed arms dropped from her to lie twitching on the ground.

The vampire jerked back, furiously waving the raw stumps of its arms.

Jack shoulder-charged the creature, knocking it back into the column of sunlight shafting down through the grate. It screamed thinly, the bald head twisted to avoid the light as if the creature had been caught beneath a shower of sulfuric acid.

Mewling and whining like a scalded cat it fled into the gloom of another tunnel.

One moment there had been half a dozen of the vampires pouring from the tunnel, now there were none. David watched them scurry back into the depths of the tunnel, bald white heads bobbing in the gloom.

An object moved on the periphery of his vision. Damn, now they were coming from another tunnel. This time behind him.

He turned around and twisted the throttle of the chainsaw so that the sound morphed from a metallic ticking to a full-blooded scream. The teeth on the saw blurred.

The creatures attacked from the shadows, black-lipped

mouths open, exposing teeth that were panther-sharp. Their arms stretched out toward him as the fingers became talons ready to rip out his eyes.

He saw Electra move to his side. She held the torch out like she was aiming a pistol, then thumbed on the switch. A million candlepower light blasted into their faces. The deep-set eyes screwed shut.

The vampires recoiled, dazed by the torch's brilliance.

For a moment David hoped the light alone would be enough to push them back into retreat. But after cringing back from the light they began to edge forward, holding up their claw hands to shield their eyes and hissing fiercely.

Now that the tunnel was wide enough, Black moved up to David's side. He pushed the chainsaw blade forward in a series of stabbing movements. One of the creatures lunged at Black.

David seized the chance and, raising the screaming chainsaw, swept the blade in a flat arc from left to right.

The buzzing blade caught the creature at the side of the neck.

David felt the chainsaw buck in his hands as the whirling teeth bit into the vampire's flesh; the pitch of the motor changed as the blade made the first cut. He watched in a mixture of fascination and horror as the blade slashed into the monster's neck in a spray of body fluids and diced flesh that spat outward, showering the creatures behind and hitting the tunnel's walls.

Just one swipe. That was all it took.

One second later the chainsaw had buzzed its way completely through the monster's neck, severing head from body. The body dropped, twitching, while the head bounced down at David's feet.

Instantly, Black kicked the head—that still grimaced and snapped with its powerful jaws—sending it cannoning along the tunnel like a football, away into the shadows.

Once more the creatures melted away into the side tunnels.

"Do you think we've got them on the run?" Electra called above the racket of the chainsaws.

"I don't think so yet," David called. "So watch your backs."

Electra switched off the light. Hesitantly they moved forward again, carefully looking around bends in the tunnels, or watching the shadowy corners for any sign of a lurking vampire that might suddenly lunge at them.

They passed beneath columns of sunlight that shone down like stage lights from the drains above. And all the time they glimpsed the feet of passers-by walking over the grates or saw the undersides of cars, buses, trucks. Once, David saw a child of about three peer down through the grate at him, its eyes steady and unperturbed as if it had looked down through the street grates a hundred times before to watch these life-and-death battles taking place underground.

The child smiled and posted a chocolate button down through the iron grille. It fell with a tiny splash into the stream of water. A hand appeared and seized the child's arm—an irate mother, he supposed, in that strange, dislocated way that comes with extreme emotional pressure. The child was pulled away, no doubt noisily complaining, into yet another shop.

So. Just a few meters above his head life went on as it always had done in this little town in the hills. The people went about their everyday business, oblivious to the war being waged beneath their feet. God Almighty, if only they knew . . . if only someone could help . . .

David swallowed a bitter taste rising in his mouth. He shifted the chainsaw into one hand. The weight of it was tremendous; the vibrations of the motor jolted through the bones of his hand and his arm to rattle the teeth in his head. The cut on his thumb he'd made with the sword tingled in some mystic harmony with the chainsaw.

He felt a slap on his arm; he glanced back at Electra. She jerked her head toward the mouth of another tunnel.

"Watch out," she shouted. "Here they come again!"

A dozen or more vampires were moving down the tunnel toward them at a shuffling run. David couldn't take his eyes off the heads that were as around and as white as bobbing footballs in the near-darkness.

David revved the chainsaw, and prepared himself for the onslaught.

2

"Maximilian?"

"Yes?"

"What's making that noise?"

"Sounds like a motorbike."

"But it seems so close."

"Coming down through the grates?" he suggested.

Bernice looked back at the pale oval of his face in the near-darkness. "But it sounds different from the traffic. It sounds more like a power tool."

He shrugged.

"Perhaps some workmen have come down into the tunnel?" she said hopefully. "If only we can find them they'll get us out of here."

"It sounds to be coming from down that tunnel there." He gazed up at her with his almond-shaped eyes. "We could look?"

She nodded. "I don't think we've got much of a choice, do you? OK, follow me, watch out for the stream; it's deeper here. I think if we can keep right back against the brick wall we should be—*Look out!*"

A white figure ran from out of the darkness. It came at them at what seemed a tremendous speed. Instinctively, she pushed herself back against the tunnel wall. Simultaneously she stretched her arm out against Maximilian's chest and pushed him back, too.

From the gloom came a white face. The expression on it was shocking. The mouth was wide open; it emitted a thin piercing cry, so high it almost sounded like a whistle. The deep-set eyes were as wide as the skin surrounding the sockets would allow.

Bernice held her breath, her heart thudding furiously.

The vampire ran toward them, making that fantastic whistling scream that bored right through her skull.

Then it came out of the darkness into the half-light; it waved its arms.

Or what was left of its arms.

Bernice realized, with a shock that left her breathless, that the creature's arms had been severed above the elbows.

She glimpsed the white bone in the center of the thing's muscle, the slashed arteries pumping liquid out in forceful squirts that jetted against the walls as it ran.

Then it passed her.

She turned her head to watch it run by, its feet slapping at the floor, the open-ended arm stumps flailing at the air. A moment later it had gone back into darkness. The scream faded.

Now she could hear the sound of the motors again, rising and falling; they reminded her of angry dogs snarling at intruders.

Now she knew who was responsible for the sounds she was hearing, and for the injuries to the creature.

"Come on!" She grabbed hold of Maximilian's hand and set off at a run.

"Where are we going?"

"My friends are down here. We've got to find them—now!"

3

David and Jack stood back to back with Electra sandwiched between them. The air filled with exhaust fumes and the deafening snarl of the chainsaw motors.

The creatures lunged out of darkness from either side, eyes blazing hatred, mouths open as they screamed their high-pitched screams; their pointed teeth flashed in the light of Electra's torch.

Severed limbs twitched in a growing pile around their feet.

A creature lunged low at David's legs. He brought the blade of the chainsaw down like a club.

Damn . . .

He missed the back of its neck.

Instead, the spinning saw bits slammed into the back of the thing's bald head; instantly the screaming saw stripped the skin from the skull, leaving denuded gray bone.

David bore down, like he was cutting through a felled tree trunk.

Grey pieces of bone flew in every direction. The creature fell to its hands and knees.

He leaned forward, pressing the blade down. It sliced easily through the creature's head, hacking through the skull in a line from the back of the head to exit at the bridge of its nose. The top half of the head came away in one neat piece.

There was a gush of yellow fluid and the creature lay at his feet, arms and legs jerking in post-mortem spasms.

Behind him, Jack Black fought with near-superhuman strength; he used the chainsaw like a gardener uses a scythe to fell stinging nettles. He swept the chainsaw from side to side, beheading the vampires with almost balletic grace. Bodies dropped to the floor.

Meanwhile, Electra used the torch like a weapon, flashing the brilliant light into the vampires' deep-set eyes, dazzling them and distracting them from their attack.

A head rolled under David's feet; he saw the raw end of the cut-through neck rest against a severed arm. Instantly arteries and nerves sprang from the raw mouths of the wounds to connect. The veins contracted, drawing the severed head to the open wound of the arm.

Hell, the things are fusing together, he thought in disgust. If he left the head there it would join to the arm.

He tore his fascinated gaze from the process and stooped to cut through the arm with the chainsaw. At that moment the chainsaw coughed and stopped.

He opened up the throttle and pulled the starter cord. It spluttered.

Didn't fire.

He tried again.

And again.

Shit!

He threw the useless machine to one side. More of the vampires were surging toward him, while all the time the head was fusing to the severed arm. He glanced down to see the head suddenly twitch back to life: eyelids flicked back; the eyes stared up at him; the mouth opened and shut goldfish-like, then suddenly it bared its teeth and snapped at his ankle.

David stepped back, dragged the sword from his belt and, gripping the handle firmly in both hands, swung down the blade, cleaving the head from the arm.

He kicked the head away into the stream where the force of the current rolled it away.

Now he slashed the sword at the faces of the vampires.

And yet still they jostled forward.

One darted at him. With a huge effort he drove the sword forward so the point of the blade stabbed the creature in the center of its chest. The point punched through the rags it wore. David pushed harder, driving the sword inward, as if he was pinning a butterfly to a board. He could even hear the blade grating against the ribs.

The creature tried to claw at his face.

Using the sword to hold it at beyond striking distance he called out: "Jack! Jack!"

Then Jack was at his side, swinging his chainsaw in a smooth horizontal arc that neatly decapitated the creature.

It fell limp, the weight of the thing pulling the sword downward with it. David planted his foot on the creature's chest to withdraw the sword.

He looked along the tunnel.

Dazed, he thought: *Oh, Christ Almighty, there's dozens of them.*

They surged in at the three people in their single-minded fury. The destruction of their own kind didn't matter. As long as the creatures destroyed the three humans.

David's arms and shoulders ached from wielding the sword. Sweat streamed from his face. His clothes were soaked with the blood—if you could call it blood—of these monsters. The handle of the sword was slippery.

Another figure dashed at him from a side tunnel. He raised the sword; the metal blade seemed to tremble as if it had a life of its own; he tensed his muscles ready for the downward swing.

"David!"

His eyes focused on the face in front of him.

"David! Stop! It's me!"

"Bernice?"

She looked up at him, eyes wide, her light hair fluffed into a golden halo in the light of Electra's torch.

He paused; she might have been bitten by one of those things. She might be a vampire, too. A voice in his head pleaded with him not to take the risk, but to bring the sword down against the side of her neck.

"David," she said breathlessly, her eyes huge and trusting. "It really is me. I'm fine. Look." She reached up and slid her thumb against the sword's keen edge. Then she held her thumb up at David.

He saw a bead of blood well out from the nick. It was red, a dark living red, a human red. Not the piss-like yellow liquid that sprang from the vampire's veins.

Black's chainsaw buzzed furiously against his ear as a vampire leapt at him. Head and body separated, it bounced down at his feet; yellow body fluids gushed incontinently from the severed neck.

"Get behind me," he shouted to Bernice. "Get between me and the wall." She did so, but she pulled at his arm.

"David," she cried. "Stop fighting them, stop it!"

"Are you crazy? They'll tear us apart!"

"No, you don't understand," Bernice shouted. "They're as afraid of you as you are of them!"

"What?"

"It's true! They don't want to fight us; they've been forced to do it," she shouted. "Listen, David! It's not their fault."

David paused. The creatures had stopped attacking for the moment. They watched from the shadows of the tunnels, deepset eyes boring at them.

Black throttled down the chainsaw until it ticked over. The reduction in noise seemed almost painful in comparison with the sound and fury of the last five minutes. The vampire dead lay strewn like giant stalks of obscene white celery across the stone floor.

Electra, panting, looked at Bernice. "Did I hear you right? You're saying these things aren't dangerous?"

Bernice looked shaken and had to force herself to speak clearly. "They're only dangerous because they're being controlled by the others."

"What others?"

"Stroud and the rest. I've seen these vampires down here. I've seen how they live. They drink blood that comes down the drains from the slaughterhouse. I don't think that normally they behave much differently to cattle themselves. Maximilian? Max. Come out here, it's OK, these are my friends." David watched her beckon a Down's syndrome man into the tunnel. "We watched them," Bernice continued. "They seem to be responding to some outside force. It takes control of them."

Electra looked back at Jack. "This dark light you were speaking about. You said how powerful it was. Do you think that's been controlling these creatures?"

Before he could answer they heard a light cough, as if someone was politely trying to catch their attention.

"She's quite right, of course."

David spun round. Standing there in the tunnel, dressed in white, his bare feet slightly apart on the stone floor, was Mike Stroud. His hair glinted blond in the torchlight.

"Good afternoon," Stroud said pleasantly. "Or should that be good evening?"

He gestured to the iron grates above his head. No sunlight fell through them now. Beyond the brilliant light of Electra's torch the shadows had crept in to engulf the tunnels in utter darkness.

Stroud was cool, relaxed, as if nothing on earth could faze him.

He glanced back at the other vampires standing hunched in the shadows, bald heads showing as white discs. "These, my children of the night, are nothing more than our humblest foot soldiers, my dear David. They are nothing more than the cannon fodder of war. The same miserable kind of low-quality troops that generals send into no man's land to help absorb the bullets and artillery shells of the enemy before the real attack begins."

David froze there, but his hand tightened around the handle of the sword. If he steps just a little closer, he thought, I can take a swing at the monster's neck.

Stroud did take a step forward, yet it was only to kick one of the severed heads toward David. It was a gentle kick; like a pass at football. The head rolled toward him, then stopped against the wall. It was the head David'd cut through level with the bridge of the nose.

"These are poor, atrophied creatures, David," Stroud said with a smile. "See for yourself. Look at the size of its brain. It's withered to little more than the size of a peach—a dried and shrunken peach at that. That's right, these things have the mental abilities of little children. They can't think for themselves. So I do the thinking for them. And in a little while I'm going to put a little mental picture in here." He touched his golden temple and smiled. "And that little mental picture will be of these pathetic little creatures rushing in to finish you once and for all. Oh, you'll kill a dozen or so more. Mr. Black operates that chainsaw with quite some aplomb. And you, David, well, I believe some ancestral memory carried in your genes is guiding your hand when you wield Helvetes."

Electra said under her breath to Jack, "This black light you told me about. Does it come from him?"

"No . . . no," he shook his head, puzzled. "It's coming from up there somewhere." He raised his eyes to the tunnel roof. "I can see it like a great black lightning, flashing through the clouds. It's filling the sky. It's running through the whole fucking town."

"Speak up, Mr. Black," Stroud's voice rose to a boom as if addressing a mischievous child at the back of the class. "I'm sure we'll find what you have to say most fascinating." He smiled. "What's wrong? Afraid to speak in front of our little gathering? Fair enough. I warrant you have little of interest to say after all. Well, perhaps, I could say my own little piece. And it is simply this: David Leppington, you inherited this army, as you inherited the divine quest to conquer the world. However, you chose to reject your inheritance; a very foolish choice, if I might add my own opinion. Therefore, I have stepped into your role as leader of these poor, benighted creatures. And yes, Electra, my dear, I am in charge now. I have the power of life and death over you all. And, David, your uncle's power too is now at my disposal."

David's scalp prickled. "So that's the answer, then," he said, shaking his head. "You're controlling all this. But it is my uncle who is providing the power. He is the source of the black lightning!"

"What do you mean?" asked Bernice, bewildered. "Who brought all these creatures to life?"

David spoke with a bitter satisfaction as the realization struck him. "My uncle. He did it through the force of his own obsession, through the power of his own twisted mind. Somehow old George Leppington, without him even knowing it, tapped into some ancient power source. But Stroud here has now hijacked that power for his own evil purposes. To satisfy his own warped ambitions. Isn't that right, Stroud?"

"Oh, no, David." Stroud gave that affable yet superior smile. He was like a millionaire condescending to speak to someone living homeless in the street. "That's not correct and you know it, my dear David. I am merely stepping into your shoes after you abandoned your God-given quest. I am to continue your divine mission to reinstate the true deities of old: Othin, the father. Loki, lord of mischief. Heimdall, the guardian god of the eighth hall. Ull, god of justice, and, of course, your blood ancestor, Leppington—mighty Thor, the thunder god, who even now lies in his timbered hall awaiting Ragnarök. Yes, Electra, Ragnarök is the day of doom. The day the world ends."

"The old gods are dead, Stroud."

"Not dead. Merely waiting."

"They're dead." David spoke in a low, controlled way. "It's just your sick obsession that's driving this show now. It's time to realize that there never will be a great flowering of Nordic culture, or a great new empire devoted to Thor or Othin or any of the others. They've had their day. Humankind retired them centuries ago."

"Oh, David, please," Stroud chuckled. "You know what goes around comes around. It's time for the old gods to make their great comeback."

"Stroud—"

"Don't waste my time, Leppington." Stroud's voice was suddenly angry. "You scorned your inheritance. You scorned me. And now I have this." He slapped his chest. "I have the power to do exactly as I wish. I am immortal. And I am more than content for you to remain with the sick, miserable group of people you call your friends. In any case, you will become one of these." Grinning triumphantly, he jerked a thumb at the white-headed creatures in the shadows.

"We're not giving up without a fight," David told the grinning vampire. "You'll have to come and take us."

"To fight to the bitter end is your prerogative," the creature acknowledged with a tilt of the head. "But I think we shall conduct the final scene under a veil of complete darkness, don't you?"

David didn't have a chance to realize what Stroud meant until something flashed out of the shadows: it was a girl, or had been a girl. Like lightning it shot out a hand and snatched the torch from Electra. The light bobbed away down the tunnel, lighting swathes of brick; then the light jerked sharply. There was a crash. The light went out.

The torch, David knew, had been dashed against the wall.

The darkness was total.

The man's voice floated out of the darkness. Inescapably, now the voice had all the cadence and rhythm and phrasing of someone in total control.

"So, this is how it ends for you, Leppington," Stroud boomed. "If I were you I wouldn't struggle. It will be much easier and less painful and stressful if you submit now to that final bite." David could imagine those lips still wearing a complacent smile. "Because now I'm implanting the image of you five people in the heads of these creatures that surround you. I'm imagining that they advance slowly on you, their bare feet slopping through the little stream in the middle of the tunnel; I'm imagining them coming closer, their arms extended toward you, their mouths open, their tongues wet with drool as they anticipate the taste of your blood—your fresh, hot blood, sweet as honey on their tongues. Now . . . now . . . can you hear them moving toward you? Can you hear their excited breathing? Can you hear them grunt with hunger? I've planted that image in their heads. They are my puppets and I'm pulling all the strings. Oh, and believe me, they have a dark-adapted eye. They see you perfectly as you cower there against the wall. Electra with her hands over her mouth trying not to scream. Jack Black holding the chainsaw above his head, why, as if it was the hammer of Thor itself. David there, the sword Helvetes gripped in both his hands while the blood of his ancestors—divine blood at that!—thunders through his traitor's veins. Fool that he is, he's prepared to die nobly to protect his friends. And there we have Maximilian Hart wringing his hands together, scared half to death he is, poor devil. And last of all, chin held high, defiant to the end, we have little Bernice Mochardi, my very own dear *bloofer lady*. David? Do you think she'll live long enough to curse the first time she clapped eyes on a town called Leppington? Don't fret, my dears, soon you will be joining us."

David strained his eyes into the darkness. He saw nothing. Beyond his eyes there was only a wall of black.

But he heard, though. Rustling. The sound of feet lightly splashing through water. Excited breathing. Then a rising hissing that rose in fury as the creatures prepared to strike.

Chapter Forty-three

1

David heard a voice in his ear—a great full-blooded roaring voice—driven by fury and defiance. "I'll kill the bastards!"

It was Jack Black.

The man's voice roared again. "Get down as low as you can! Crouch down! Electra, you too! Get down on your hands and knees!"

David crouched, tucking his head down until his chin bumped against his knees. He heard the sound of the chainsaw motor being revved until it became a rasping scream; the exhaust smoke bit into the back of his throat, making him cough. But he didn't raise his head so much as a centimeter, because he knew what Black was going to do.

Even though it was so dark he couldn't see a thing, he could picture it all in his mind's eye. Black would stand there, with Electra, Bernice, Maximilian and David clustered at his feet. Then he would scythe the chainsaw from right to left in continuous sweeps as the monsters attacked.

No sooner had the image hardened into crystal clarity in his head than he heard the sound of the chainsaw's wicked teeth ripping into flesh.

David screwed his eyes shut. Fluid sprayed onto the back of his neck. A piece of some material that felt like a piece of raw steak landed on the back of his hand.

Black was felling the vampires like stalks of corn as they pressed forward their attack.

"Run!" Black yelled. "I'll hold them here. Go on! Run! Run!"

David felt a concussion in his rump; the pain that followed felt like a piece of red-hot wire being driven up the length of his spine, and he realized Black had kicked him.

"Run!" Black yelled again.

And again came a kick. Black wasn't pussyfooting around with the people he was protecting, either. "Get into the tunnel behind me," he roared at them.

The chainsaw howled. The monsters shrieked in an inhuman harmony with the machine as the spinning steel teeth of the saw shredded flesh, slashed through bone.

David shuffled backward on all fours into the tunnel that branched off behind them. When he put a hand down to the ground to steady himself his palm rested on a severed head. He could feel the face still twitching, a tongue curled around his thumb. He pulled his hand away sharply and moved back fast.

Still there was total darkness. Without being able to see they'd be split up from each other in seconds. Once separated, the vampires would pick off the fragile human beings one by one in the dark.

Still gripping the sword, he held out his free hand. "Get hold of my hand!" he shouted. "Everyone get hold of someone's hand. Bernice? Electra? Hold out your hands." He grasped someone's fingers and grabbed tight. "Who's this?"

"Bernice," came her voice from the darkness, "I'm holding Maximilian's hand."

Electra's voice came above the howl of the chainsaw. "I've got a hand, too. Come on. Run!"

David ran first. He was running into that utter darkness; his eyes strained into it until he was seeing the darkness bloom with phantom purples and crimsons.

Christ, he thought, here we are, running to God knows where, all holding hands like some kind of human paper chain: him first, then Bernice, then Maximilian, then Electra bringing up the rear.

The sound of the chainsaw receded, and he realized that Black must be staying to hold the vampires at bay for as long as possible. He saw him there in his mind's eye, standing so as to block the mouth of the tunnel. A tattooed warrior, roaring obscenities at the monsters while sweeping the chainsaw from left to right; the creatures would press forward only to have their heads sliced from their shoulders.

David still held the sword in his free hand, pointing with it as he ran, partly using it like a blind person uses a stick, tapping the point against the wall, and partly as a weapon: if there was one of those things ahead it would be impaled on the sword before it could reach him.

Behind him Maximilian was shouting, he couldn't make out what exactly: the sound of the chainsaw motor echoing along the tunnel drowned out everything.

They could only keep running. God willing, they'd find a way out soon.

2

Hell, Electra thought, as they ran. This is madness. They couldn't run through the dark forever. Any second now a pit might yawn open there right in front of them; they'd plunge down into a well of raw, stinking sewage. Or someone would slip on the slimy stones and break a leg. What could they do then? Just what the hell could they do? Crawl whimpering across all this oozing shit like wounded animals, waiting for their throats to be ripped open by the vampires?

Her mind whirled: she was as disorientated as if she'd just downed a tumbler full of vodka; she was dizzy and sick and confused by this lunatic dash through the tunnel—this endless tunnel choked with darkness and this dirty, sour air that hurt the back of her throat.

And for pity's sake, the Down's syndrome boy was gripping her hand so hard she was sure the bones would give way with a sudden cracking crunch, as if they were nothing more than a bunch of dry sticks. She could hardly breathe. Her head spun. Her chest felt so tight with exertion and a sheer terror that held her in its hard blue fist.

Her elbow caught the wall as she ran. Pain flashed up into her neck like crimson lightning.

"Slow down," she shouted over the clatter of the chainsaw. "Slow down. Someone's going to fall . . . *please*, slow down. Let me get my breath!"

Then, just a little way ahead, came a misty pool of light. It was the gray light of dusk, empty of any magnitude. Nevertheless, it was light, and thank God for that, Electra thought with feeling.

"Look, there's light," she panted, relieved. "Slow down. And for pity's sake don't hold my hand so hard."

Suddenly they ran into the light. Electra looked down at the hand gripping hers. It was a woman's. She looked up at the face in shock. And screamed.

Instantly she wrenched her hand free, then backed away until her back hit the wall of the tunnel and she could go no further

"Remember me, Electra," hissed the girl, smiling through the most voluptuously red lips Electra had ever seen. "You once invited me to your birthday party."

Electra stood trembling, seeing the creature in the thin gray light.

My God, I held hands with THAT?

"I'm Samantha Moberry. You do remember me, don't you?"

Electra stared. Her breath came in sobbing pulls. Her strength leaked from her body; she didn't feel as if she could take a single step, never mind fight this monster if it attacked.

"You do remember me." The creature smiled. The full red lips slid back, exposing teeth as sharp as a panther's. The eyes glittered diamond-bright. "I'm Samantha Moberry, Dianne's sister. I'm eighteen years old. I sang on the karaoke for you? Remember, Electra?"

The voice dropped to a whisper.

"You know how the song goes: *It's my party and I'll cry if I want to, cry if I want to . . .*" She sang the words in a low breathy voice that was dry as a husk.

"Cry if I want to . . ."

Dry as a husk: that's what this creature was. A husk. A shell. A simulacrum of a human being. A phony. A counterfeit person. Electra pushed the words through her head, trying not to allow herself to be mesmerized by the diamond-bright eyes that fixed on hers, or the seductive sound of the whispery voice, singing to her.

"I'm in a tunnel. I'm going to die," Electra spoke slowly, deliberately, struggling to control the panic rising inside herself. "But I'm sure as hell not going to listen to you."

"But I'm singing this song for you, Electra. *It's my party . . . cry if I want to . . . cry if I want to . . .* I always thought the song could have been written for you. You've always been unhappy, haven't you? Even on your birthdays? I saw the sadness in your

408

yes, and I just wanted to hug you, and whisper nice things to you. You'll let me do that now, won't you, Electra?"

"You are not Samantha Moberry. Samantha Moberry's dead."

"Some of my friends told me that you prefer girls to boys, or that you have no preference either way. Is that true, Electra?"

"Samantha Moberry is dead . . . *dead!*"

"But you can see me in front of you, can't you? Here . . . take my hand again. You can feel my fingers, can't you?"

"No."

"Here. Electra . . . Electra. Feel how sharp my fingernails have become? Aren't they the longest fingernails you've ever seen?"

Electra kept her hands balled into fists. "I don't care what you look like. Samantha Moberry is dead. You're a monster. You're a vampire."

"And I desire nothing more than to drink your blood?"

"Yes."

"But I do have other needs, Electra, my love. I'm not quite a corpse yet, you know?"

"Go away . . ."

"Does this look like dead flesh?"

"Leave me alone."

"Look at me, Electra. Don't I still look . . . *nice*?"

Despite herself, Electra felt compelled to look. She watched the vampire smile as it unbuttoned the silk blouse it wore; it unbuttoned slowly as if to please and titillate. With its long fingers it pulled open the blouse, then straightened its arms and allowed the blouse to slip off the arms to the floor of the tunnel. Then it stood there in the light filtering down from the grate above. It turned round, still smiling, still maintaining eye contact, as if to allow Electra to admire its slim waist, its flat stomach, its small firm breasts cupped by the black lace of its bra.

"See, my darling Electra, aren't I perfect?" The vampire Samantha smiled; the teeth glinted. "What do you think to my breasts?" It unhooked the bra, letting it fall. "Sometimes I wonder if they're too small. But they're a nice shape, aren't they? Can you believe how pointed they are?"

"Stop this."

"And look how dark the nipples are?"

"Please . . ."

It twirled provocatively again, arching its back and lifting its luxuriant chestnut hair in both hands. "I used to worry about my hair—it was dry, like straw. But see how rich and healthy it looks now."

Electra saw the gash in the side of the vampire's neck. That must have been how she'd been brought over to the other side. How she'd been converted from human to vampire. With a single tearing bite in the neck. Now, yellow, urine-like fluid—not real rich blood as red as a Valentine's rose—flowed through the neck.

"Beautiful, aren't I?" it whispered. The smile grew more hungry—but this was an erotic hunger; a craving for sexual gratification. Not a craving for blood—at least, not yet. The creature that had been Samantha Moberry held out its hands to Electra.

"Oh, I want you to touch me, Electra, darling. Won't you kiss me? I want to feel your mouth here." It ran its long finger down its breast from chest to nipple. Then it pinched the nipple lightly between finger and thumb. Electra stared, fascinated by the undead girl's long red fingernails, how they lightly scraped her own nipple; how it toyed with the dark tip of skin. And all the time the girl talked in that breathy, husky way that sent thrills prickling up and down the length of Electra's legs and back. Those eyes held hers. They shone. Perhaps it was the darkness of the skin surrounding them that set them off; but there was a jewel-like brilliance. They were gray—a pale, pale gray; somehow cold and fiery, both at the same time.

And in those eyes there came a collision of other opposites too.

I want to pull away, Electra thought dizzily, I want to run and run until my shoes wear away to nothing and I'm running on the bare skin of my soles right down to the center of the Earth. Somewhere I'll never be found. Somewhere where I'll be safe forever.

And yet she longed to get closer to this fascinating creature. Her heart thudded hard as a sheer sexual energy crackled through her hips and stomach.

I want to touch her lips. I want to marvel at the size of those great white teeth beneath the lips. And they are beautiful lips. Oh . . . just to touch them wouldn't do any harm, would it? And if I'm going to touch them with my fingertips, then I might as

410

well kiss them, too. And close my lips around the dark tips of her breasts. Then I might as well slide to my knees, kissing all the time; then run my fingers up her bare thighs, and then breathe the warm scent of her—

The howl nearly split her head in two.

Electra jerked back, slapping both palms against the wall.

She gasped.

At that moment the erotic smile on the vampire girl's face changed to one of fury . . . then agony. The eyes bulged.

Electra threw her hands up to protect her own face as a glittering piece of steel swung out of the darkness. The howl came again: the throaty howl of the chainsaw.

Steel teeth bit.

The vampire's chin jerked up; the claw-like hands clenched in pain; a thin screech pierced the lips.

Simultaneously, the chainsaw spat minced flesh.

Electra watched in horror as the head came clean off and bounced down, actually striking the toes of her left foot with a force bruising enough to make her clench her teeth.

For a second the body of the girl stood straight, the arms straight out in a crucifixion pose, fists clenched. Fluid spurted up from the yawning hole between the shoulders to splash against the ceiling. Bare breasts quivered.

Then the body fell down with a slapping sound.

"Where are the others?" Black stepped out of the gloom, the chainsaw in one hand, his tattooed face wreathed in the blue smoke from the motor. "Electra. Listen. Where are the others?"

She shook her head, she was trembling. "I don't know . . ." She nodded down at the headless vampire. "She—it tricked me. It grabbed my hand in the dark . . . I thought it was one of us. Dear God, I really thought it was one of us."

Black jerked his head. "Walk in front of me. I'll watch your back. The bastards are swarming up here like rats."

"Your arm! What happened?"

Black looked down at his arm as if Electra had mentioned nothing more important than a piece of fluff on his sleeve. He didn't seem to notice that the arm had been smashed so that a piece of bone jutted through the flesh of his forearm and blood dripped from a mangled set of fingers.

"Those things have bitten you, haven't they?"

411

"I'll be all right. Now move. I can hear them."

Electra moved along the tunnel. Black walked sideways, repeatedly glancing back the way he'd come. He held the chainsaw in one massive paw; the engine ticked over, sounding harshly metallic in the confined space.

Electra set her eyes grimly ahead into the black throat of the tunnel and walked purposefully on.

3

David Leppington walked quickly beneath the town that bore his name. They'd reached a grating set in the roof. The little light filtering through showed they were, for the time being, free of the vampires. And that Electra was gone.

"We can't go back for her," he told Bernice. "We'd probably run back into the arms of those monsters. Just pray she managed to get away in the dark."

Bernice nodded, grim-faced, and glanced back at Maximilian. He looked impassively back at her. "Are you OK?"

"I'm OK, thank you," he acknowledged politely. "But I would like to eat some pizza."

"Pizza?" David nearly guffawed, and if he did laugh it would, he knew, border on the hysterical. "Pizza. You like pizza?"

"No," Maximilian said calmly. "Not much. But anything's better than being down here with those white people."

"Christ, you can say that again." David smiled at the man, feeling a sudden powerful kinship with him. They were all in this together, made comrades-in-arms through fear.

Bernice walked on a few steps. She rubbed her forearm, her teeth chattering but not with cold. David noticed for the first time the clothes she was wearing. The long black lace gloves, the black satin skirt, black leather boots that were so tightly laced they looked as if they were part of her legs; her lips were thickly reddened with a blood-red lipstick; her eyes were outlined with kohl and shaded with a black that gave them a darkly erotic look. She could have played the part of the vampire bride with consummate ease.

With the sword still in his hand, he looked back along the tunnel. It lay in utter darkness. He could see none of the vampires, but he didn't doubt that they would not be far behind.

"Any sign of Jack?" asked Bernice.

"None."

"Do you think the monsters have him now?"

"I don't know." He shook his head grimly. "I really don't know." He took a deep breath. "The question is, which way now?" He pointed with the sword at half a dozen tunnels branching off in front of them.

Bernice shook her head.

Maximilian said, "Eenie, meenie, minie, mo."

David forced a grim smile. "It's as good a way of choosing as any, I suppose. OK. We take mo here, on the right. Stick close. Damn . . . we're going into the dark again. Everybody hold hands."

Once more that black-as-hell darkness consumed them in its deathly grip.

4

Electra stopped dead. She couldn't believe her eyes. There, directly in front of her, was a circle of amber light. "Thank God for that." She moved quickly forward. Now there was a faint roaring sound. "Do you hear that, Jack?"

"What is it?"

"That, my dear love, is the sound of the river. The bloody lovely River Lepping. This must be one of the culverted streams that runs out from the river bank. Damn. There's a grille. We can't get out."

"We'll get out all right," Black grunted. "Stand back. I'll kick the damn thing down."

The grille was made of welded iron bars. A couple of hefty padlocks held it shut.

Christ, thought Electra, feeling something like a giddy rush. So near, yet so far. There was the outside world just three short steps away. Beyond that was the river. She could see the moon through rags of cloud streaming through a windy sky. She could see the willow branches swaying. She could see a street light on the far bank casting the amber light that now fell on her hands.

413

Black held the chainsaw in one hand—it still ticked over, blowing out puffs of blue smoke; in that no-nonsense way of his he walked forward and kicked the grille. It shook beneath the force of the blow. He kicked again. The padlocks rattled.

Black's ferocious gaze swept over the railing, searching for a weak spot. He shifted his position and kicked to one side of the grille near the hinges. Electra saw these were misshapen with years of rust. He kicked hard; a great clanging sound went ringing away down the tunnel—for all the world it sounded like the tolling of a cracked bell of monstrous dimensions.

Electra shot anxious glances into the darkness, expecting figures to come racing down upon them.

When he kicked his mangled arm flailed limply as if it was a sleeve filled with nothing more than rags; blood flicked against the wall.

He aimed a massive kick at the grille. *"Uph! Got you, you bastard!"* The top hinge had snapped. He lifted his foot. This time he didn't kick, he pushed. The grille sagged outward with a screeching sound.

Sweat glistening on his tattooed forehead, he grunted. "Think you can get through that gap?"

"I think so."

"Best do it, then. We've got company."

He lifted the motor end of the chainsaw to his mouth and, using his teeth, twisted the throttle. Instantly the motor raced to a chattering roar.

Electra quickly squeezed through the gap between the grille and the stone frame of the tunnel's mouth. She found herself on the dirt banking. She turned back to help Jack through the grille.

Instead of following her out of the tunnel, she saw him rest the chainsaw down on the ground, then one-handedly pull the grille back from the inside, sealing the tunnel.

"Jack!"

He picked up the chainsaw and jerked his head, indicating she should go.

"Jack! Get yourself out here, right now!"

He mouthed the word NO and jerked his head again for her to leave.

"Jack. I'm not going without you."

414

"No! Get back to the hotel. Lock the doors."

"Listen to me, you idiot. I'm not leaving you."

Shaking his head, he turned his back on her; the chainsaw buzzed noisily in one hand, blue exhaust fumes filling the air.

"Jack. Get out of there!"

He ignored her.

"Jack." Tears streamed down her face. "For crying out loud, I love you! Don't you dare leave me like this! Don't you dare!"

He kept his back to her.

"Did you hear me, Jack Black? I love you! *I love you!*"

For a moment she thought he hadn't heard. Then he turned slowly to face her. She looked him in the eyes. They'd always been cold, hard. Now for the first time, they softened. "Electra—"

The sudden screech that exploded in the air like a high-explosive shell came with a blur of movement. Black swung the chainsaw; there was an eruption of shredded skin. The headless body of a vampire flopped down behind the grille.

"Jack—Jack!"

Electra screamed his name; almost as if that alone would empower him somehow. But from the black heart of the earth the vampires fell on him in a screaming, ravening hoard.

He retreated until his back was pressed against the grille.

On the other side of the grille, separated from the man she now loved by those cold iron bars, Electra could only stand and watch the battle.

The chainsaw screamed; Jack roared in fury and sheer bloodlust. The creatures swarmed all over him, biting, clawing. He shrugged them off; scythed at them with the chainsaw, severing heads, even bisecting one at the waist so a torso fell one way, twitching and kicking, the legs another.

Then the attack ended as quickly as it'd begun.

At that instant, the chainsaw coughed and died.

The sudden silence was stunning. Electra found herself struggling to breathe—she must have held her breath, not daring to breathe until the attack was over.

Black turned back to face her through the grille.

Surely he'd leave the tunnel now?

He looked at her, fixing her with his eyes. He moved his lips. No words came.

Then she saw a tide of red—a wet, living red, creeping down his white T-shirt. Her eyes swept up to his throat. There she saw a deep gash: blood pumped freely from the wound. She could see—even in this shit-awful light—the blood swell, bubble, then pour down his throat and down his chest, soaking the T-shirt red.

"Oh, Christ," she breathed, her hand to her mouth. "Oh, dear Christ." She reached through the bars of the grille as he slumped forward. She tried to hold him up on his feet but the weight of him sliding down face first against the grille dragged her down to her knees.

He slumped down on his side. Then, still looking into her eyes, he gave a slow blink. Which she guessed meant *It's OK, don't worry*.

But it wasn't OK. She gave a cry which sounded like a ridiculous, a damn' ridiculous hiccup in her throat.

Then the tears came. "Don't leave me, Jack. Don't . . . please don't . . . I need you."

His eyes dulled and she knew he was gone.

"Jack. I love you. I love you."

Pushing her arm through the bars she stroked his forehead; it was smooth, cool as marble. Tears streamed down her face. "Oh God, you were my knight in shining armor after all; you were, you were. Only I was too stupid to see it."

A white ball lunged out of the darkness of the tunnel.

She saw glaring eyes; an open mouth; pointed teeth.

She threw herself back, tugging her arm free of the bars as it crashed face first into the grille.

The eyes glared out at her. They were malevolent, laced with hatred.

And oh so hungry.

She saw the vampire straighten and reach up to grasp the bars of the grille. She knew then what it would do. Tear down the bars. Then take her, too.

Behind it more of the figures came stealthily as panthers from the darkness.

The only barrier between her and them was this flimsy piece of old ironmongery.

Then there was a scuffling motion, followed by a sharp hissing.

"Oh, my God," she breathed. "The bastards are fighting over his body." In horror, she saw them crouching down over the fallen man. They were lapping at the wound at the throat. Another creature sucked at a torn finger; another battened itself onto the wound in the arm.

The vampire that was about to tear down the grille saw it would lose its share of the kill. With an angry snarl it let go of the bars and fell down on top of the dead man's body; soon it too was feeding.

Electra shook her head; she wanted nothing more than to vomit.

With a wrench she turned away from the unspeakable scene.

In front of her the river roared over the boulders in licks of white foam. The wind blew hard, cooling her burning face and tugging her hair.

It was precisely at that moment that she knew what she must do.

Chapter Forty-four

1

Electra focused her mind. You've got intellect. Use it!

She ran up the banking from the river. The towers of the hotel loomed in front of her. Behind them the sky was spattered with stars. Clouds raced across them like animals fleeing from a catastrophe.

OK, she told herself, this is where you put this lunatic drama to bed once and for all.

Emotions, thoughts, memories clamored inside her head: Jack standing there, soaked in blood . . . the way he folded up like a rag doll, knees and forehead thumping against the grille . . . the vampires feeding on his blood; is he one of those things now? Vampiric? No, close off those thoughts. Concentrate on one idea. Imagine that idea is a single star in the sky. A great shining star. Think clearly. You've only got a matter of minutes before those creatures smash through the gate.

Now she felt herself grow calm, clear-headed.

She hurried to the hotel, unlocked the door, grabbed her leather bag from the peg, then returned to the car.

The time was a little after eight.

The wind blew harder, drawing fluting sounds that were soulful—and as dark as the blood at the heart's core.

She looked about her constantly, expecting to see the bobbing white heads pouring from out of the darkness.

Even though her limbs shook, she moved purposefully, without a hint of panic. Her coordination was machine-like as she unlocked the car and climbed in, dropping her bag on the passenger seat beside her.

She started the engine and pulled out of the car park, murmuring softly, "All right, Jack. This is for you."

2

In the tunnel David looked up. A watery yellow light from a street lamp filtered down through a grate high above. He reached out and touched the wall in front of him, hoping it wasn't really there; that it would just be a cruel illusion.

It wasn't.

"I'm sorry," he murmured to the other two. "We've reached a dead end."

"What now?" asked Bernice.

"We'll have to go back the way we came and try another tunnel."

She nodded. Her face was expressionless; she could feel no more emotion; at least, not yet. All feeling—fear, hatred, disgust—had been milked from her; she was dry as paper, her heart empty.

Slowly they began to retrace their steps. David took the lead again, the sword held out in his hand.

Electra drove to the hospital.

The lights burned brightly. It was visiting time; the car park was full.

She parked the car in the space reserved for a Dr. Perrault (so the sign told her). Then, taking her bag, she climbed out of the car and headed coolly and purposefully for the hospital entrance.

Her mind ranged on ahead, as if reconnoitring the route.

She knew the name of the ward; and that George Leppington had been put in a side ward off from that.

The corridors would be busy. No one would notice her.

But they'll notice the blood on your hand, she thought. Jack's blood from when you tried to catch him as he fell dying, his throat ripped open.

She quickly retraced her steps to the car, took the coat from the back seat and hung it over the bloodstained hand. There, that should hide it. Then she slipped the strap of her bag over her shoulder and headed for the hospital once more.

People milled in the foyer. They were mainly visitors, either coming or going, or buying drinks or snacks from the vending machines. There were a couple of nurses. They were hurrying, busy on errands of their own.

Still cool, unflustered, Electra walked quickly up the stairs, then took one of the mint-green corridors toward the general wards. The lights seemed hideously harsh to her after she'd been so long in the gloomy tunnels. The brilliance itself was like a pair of thumbs pressing down into her eyeballs.

No, she told herself, allow no distractions. Stay calm. Stay focused.

This is it.

She stepped into the side ward. There was one bed. On the bed lay an old man. She recognized him immediately. George Leppington. He'd been a fixture of the town all her life.

He lay flat on his back. The bandages around his head were brilliantly white. So bright that again she felt the pressure on her eyes. A thin pain ran from each retina back through the eyeball, along the optic nerve to deep inside her head.

She blinked.

The pain stayed.

Never mind.

She swiftly closed the door behind her. Again she made no fuss; her body language was that of a member of the man's family who just wanted a few minutes alone with him.

She approached the bed.

An IV tube ran from a bag of saline solution on a stand down to the man's forearm.

He appeared to be deeply asleep. But she saw his pale lips moving as if he was holding a conversation with someone she could not see. Perhaps, in another dimension beyond this one, she thought, he spoke to the old Viking god, Thor. Perhaps he explained, trembling in awe, that his nephew, David Leppington, had abdicated as successor to the Leppingsvalt legacy. Perhaps the old man begged for more power to be diverted to those creatures that no doubt even now surged in revolting waves through the tunnels beneath her feet. Electra shivered. How would Thor reply? Did his voice sound of thunder? Was he content with how the ambitious new prince of darkness, Mike Stroud, was running the divine mission?

She looked down at the face with the closed eyes, the strong nose that resembled David's so much, the thick white eyebrows and strong lashes that lay against the cheek.

Inside, Electra felt cool, in control; she knew she'd not flinch from what she must do next. Nor would she experience guilt.

Quickly she opened the cupboard beside the bed. There were coils of IV tube, pink mouth wipes in plastic bags, a box of tissues, and a tube of skin moisturizing cream to help prevent bed sores.

Her eyes absorbed what she saw.

Yes, everything was there for what she needed to do next.

4

"David? David. My goodness, I didn't even have to search for you, did I? You came back all of your own accord."

David froze in the tunnel. Bernice and Maximilian stopped behind him.

He raised the sword. Stroud tut-tutted and smiled. He was

flanked by twenty or more of the white-headed vampires.

"The tunnel came to a dead end, I take it?" Stroud smiled. "A dead end. Isn't that a perfect metaphor for your present plight?" The smile widened. "So, where do you run to now?"

"We'll run right over you if we have to," David said, pointing the sword at Mike's throat.

"Go on, David," said Stroud, grinning. "Hack off my head, why don't you?"

"I think I just might do that."

"With my devoted bodyguard standing right here? I don't think you'd get within half a dozen paces of me."

"Stroud. What the hell are you going to achieve?" David asked bitterly. "Why keep all this hatred alive?"

"You know full well. The outside world has destroyed the Leppington family. Destroyed them economically and as a family unit. Your uncle's hatred—his passionate hatred—for all those who are responsible for those crimes against your family has given us . . ." His gesture embraced the vampires. "Has given us a new lease of life. And not only life, but a glorious purpose."

"So you intend to launch an attack on the outside world, using this vampire army?"

"Of course. You know the plan by now. Your uncle told you it often enough as you sat on his knee as a toddler."

"But what would it gain?"

"The destruction of Christendom."

"But you wouldn't *gain* anything. You've heard the phrase pyrrhic victory. It means a victory so costly it's not worth having. That's all you could have. You could never achieve anything of value, you could never create a new empire. You and your monsters can only destroy. You'll inherit a world full of ruins inhabited by vampires. It would be soulless. A dead world."

Mike smiled, but it was a cold, hating smile. "What wonderful rhetoric. See, you could have become emperor. Instead, you've abdicated your responsibility. You could—"

David swung the sword. Another pace nearer and he could have slashed off the head. As it was the sword missed.

"Poor try, David." Stroud smiled. "Ah, but look here. I see we have a new recruit. A strapping young buck, hmm?"

He stood to one side.

"Jack. My God, are ..." David's voice trailed away. Behind him Bernice gasped.

Black stood there. The light in his eyes had changed. It was darker now. Evil.

David glanced down, seeing the gashed throat and bloodied T-shirt.

"That's right, David. Mr. Black here is one of us now. Just as you two will be—Bernice, David. I'm afraid Maximilian must be rejected. You see, his genes just don't fit." He laughed at his own joke. "Therefore, when he dies in a few moments from now, he stays dead. Now ..." he glanced around at the other vampires before turning to look back at David and Bernice. "Shall we at last bring this phase of your lives to an end?"

5

In the hospital, Electra quickly took a plastic bag full of the mouth wipes from the bedside cupboard. Outside in the corridor there were voices. She paused, tense, expecting any second to see the door open and a nurse to enter. The voices grew louder. Then receded.

Letting out a huge sigh, Electra tipped the mouth wipes out onto the bedside table.

Then, carefully, she opened up the plastic bag. It was made of transparent polythene; quite tough, really.

Certainly tough enough.

Hands moving with a calm dexterity, she raised the old man's head with one hand. He still muttered on, conversing with someone, or something, she could not see. With her free hand she pulled the plastic bag over the old man's head.

Once she'd done that she gathered the opening of the bag in her fingers so it pulled tight around his neck and throat; she pulled it tighter, confident it now formed an airtight cuff around the neck.

Instantly the bag around the old man's head inflated as he exhaled. The wrinkles smoothed from the bag as it tightened with a crackling sound.

When he inhaled the bag deflated. The plastic clung to the

contours of the old man's face; the effect was of a head vacuum-packed in plastic. Hideous, but Electra did not flinch.

George Leppington exhaled. This time the bag misted up, so the unconscious man's features became blurred.

She stayed there, hands firmly holding the bag around the old man's throat, listening to the bag crackle with every inhalation or exhalation.

Now the pace of the respiration quickened as carbon dioxide replaced the oxygen inside the bag.

Beneath her hands, she felt the neck tremble.

She looked through the misted plastic.

Dear God. A pair of blue eyes gazed back at her.

The expression was ferocious.

Dear God. Dear God, don't wake up . . . please don't wake up.

Even though the eyes were open he didn't appear to be conscious.

Dear God. Don't wake up. Please don't wake up.

The muttering from the man's mouth increased in volume. The body's tremblings turned into convulsions. She glanced down as the big hands bunched into fists.

Still she didn't release her grip on the bag.

Let the air turn poisonous. Let him choke. Let the bastard choke, she thought with such a white-hot fury that tears sprang to her eyes.

The man's body shook now with enough force to rattle the bed against the wall. And even though unconscious the old man panted breathlessly.

Dear God, someone will hear; they'll come in.

They'd stop her.

Then there would be nothing else she could do.

She gritted her teeth and held the bag around his neck. Saliva bubbled through his lips; the nose turned a brilliant red, then as quickly paled until it became as white as the pillowcase he lay on.

The chest heaved. But all that did was recirculate the now poisonous air in the bag.

And from the chest she heard a deep gurgling that grew louder, louder. LOUDER.

Then stopped.

It was over as suddenly as that.

The build-up of carbon dioxide had killed the old man's heart.

The body relaxed with a hollow-sounding sigh.

Come on, it's not over yet, she whispered to herself. After checking his pulse to make sure that life had departed that eighty-four-year-old body she tugged off the plastic bag, then carefully scooped the mouth wipes back into it. She placed the bag full of wipes back into the cupboard, exactly in the position she had found it.

Damn.

A trickle of blood ran from the old man's nose. A tell-tale sign of asphyxiation.

Hell, it wasn't over yet—far from it.

She tipped her bag out onto the bed.

Car keys, three tampons, pencil, fountain pen, nail scissors, couple of lipsticks.

Moving with near-superhuman speed she snatched a tissue from the box in the cupboard, wiped away the blood from the nostril. Then she snipped one tampon in two with the nail scissors. After that, she inserted one half of the tampon into each nostril. Deftly, she picked up the pencil and pushed the tampon halves up as far as she could into the nostrils. She pushed so hard that the pencil snapped.

Quickly, she substituted pen for pencil. Seconds later, the tampon halves had been pushed so far up the nostrils they were out of sight. There they'd swell on contact with the blood oozing up from the man's oxygen-starved lungs. With luck they'd block any flow of blood entirely.

Then she opened the dead man's jaws, tilted his head back and stuffed the other two tampons into the back of his mouth. This time she used her middle finger to shove them deep down into the throat, far enough down so they wouldn't be noticed by a busy doctor as he certified the old man dead. With the airways sealed there'd be no tell-tale flow of blood to arouse a doctor's suspicions and suggest that the old man might have died of asphyxiation. As far as that (hopefully rushed-off-his-feet) doctor was concerned, he would determine that the man had simply died of heart failure, brought on by sheer old age and exacerbated by the dynamite explosion.

The old man lay still now. His mouth was silent; his eyes

stared up at the ceiling. They saw nothing. They'd never see anything again.

After she'd cleaned up every trace of her visit, Electra slipped the strap of her bag over her shoulder, folded the coat over her arm, then walked out of the room.

Chapter Forty-five

In the tunnel they heard a rushing sound. It came up from the tunnels, like the sound of a coming storm.

David felt Bernice grip his arm. He glanced at her, saw her eyes were wide with fear.

The sound grew louder.

Then he realized what it was.

A great sigh. All around him the white-headed vampires were letting out an enormous sigh. At the same time they pressed their hands to their ears and shook their heads as if struck by a grief that was as intolerable as it was sudden.

Black moved forward into the pool of light cast down through the grates from the street lamps. He looked round, a puzzled expression appearing on his tattooed face.

David now looked back at Stroud; he, too, appeared bewildered. He was shaking his head as if gripped by a sudden dizziness.

"What is it?" Bernice whispered. "What's happening to them?"

"I don't know. But now's our chance. Run!"

They got no further than a few paces. As they tried to run by Stroud he lunged out and grabbed Bernice by the wrist. He still shook his head, his lips twisting in pain, but he held on tight to her.

"You're not going anywhere!" he roared. "You are mine!"

All around them the white-headed vampires wailed; it was like a bereaved family mourning the passing of a father.

The creatures clamped their hands to the sides of their heads, twisted their bodies from side to side, and wailed so loud that the sound that reverberated from the walls was nothing less than agonizing.

"David . . ." Bernice cried, trying to escape Mike Stroud's grasp. Stroud still shook his head as if suddenly disorientated.

Black looked around at the wailing vampires, obviously in a state of confusion himself.

David gripped the sword handle in both hands and moved toward Stroud who held Bernice as easily as if she was a little child.

At that moment Maximilian lunged at Stroud, shouting, "Leave her alone . . . let go of her. You're hurting—"

In a blur of movement Stroud dumped Bernice brutally on the floor and grabbed hold of Maximilian as he flailed his fists. Then the vampire clamped his mouth on Maximilian's throat.

David watched in horror, seeing the vampire's lower jaw move as he chewed.

A second later Stroud threw Maximilian to one side, as though he was discarding a piece of rubbish. Stroud looked up at David, his eyes blazing. Blood slicked his chin red. He grinned and spat something out at his feet. David recognized a bloody piece of human trachea. The vampire had bitten out Maximilian's Adam's apple.

"There!" Stroud spat, disgusted by the taste. "What did I tell you? Bad blood."

"You bastard," David screamed. "You miserable bastard!"

Stroud's grin of pure evil broadened; the teeth were stained red. "You can watch if you like, dear boy." He bent down and grabbed Bernice by the hair.

Then all of a sudden Stroud grunted, "Ah. Let go of me, you rodent."

Maximilian wasn't dead yet. With blood spurting from the hole in his throat he gripped Stroud's leg with one hand.

Stroud bent down to bat the arm away from him.

David seized the moment.

As Stroud bent forward at the waist David swung the sword downward; the blade came down in a great flashing arc.

It struck the vampire at the nape of the neck. The still razor-sharp blade went clean through, severing spinal cord, muscle, arteries, then windpipe.

Severed, the head bounced down onto the brick floor; the body jerked upright and for one brief moment stood there, its arms jerking spasmodically. Fluid gushed from the open wound.

A second later the body dropped down into a heap of twitching limbs.

David didn't hesitate now.

He swung the sword like it was a scythe, cleanly decapitating the thing that had been Jason Morrow.

He had expected the white-headed vampires to attack but they seemed too wrapped up in their own misery. They clutched their heads in their long-fingered hands and wailed, rocking backward and forward as if all the miseries of hell had been heaped upon them.

Now Black appeared in front of him. The man's eyes were dull, dazed-looking. Although Black had made the physical transition from human to vampire he had yet to make the mental transition.

David realized what was happening. The vampire mind was still taking root in that dead brain, feeling its way into his arms and legs and fingers like a driver climbing into the seat of an unfamiliar car.

David raised the sword high above his head. This time he brought it straight down as if chopping firewood. Something else must have strengthened his arm, and guided the blow; something that shone with light and pure good.

For the sword blade hit the top of Jack Black's shaven head with more force than David alone could ever have mustered.

As if it was all happening in slow motion, David watched the sharp blade cut down through the scalp, down through the forehead, down the center of the nose like a sharp knife cutting a melon in two.

The eyes suddenly blazed into David's with such unimaginable ravening fury.

The creature that had once been Jack Black raised its hands, ready to smash David's skull.

But nothing could stop the blade now: it was as if the angel Gabriel himself guided that final blow in one clean, unstoppable cut.

Before the sword hit the upper lip, a blast of air came from

427

the creature's mouth. It shaped one final word: "LEPPING-TON . . ."

The sword passed through the center of the lips.

David no longer used any force. The sword continued of its own volition, slicing smoothly down through the center line of the throat, following the windpipe, cleaving down through the collarbone, down through the ribs and stomach, then exiting between the legs at the groin.

At that moment the body fell into two halves, cut perfectly down the center.

The wailing of the white-headed creatures became a whistle-like shriek.

A hand clutched his elbow. "David!"

He saw Bernice's face in the gloom. "David, come on. Leave them!"

Before they could take a single step the piercing scream stopped as if a button had been pressed.

At that moment the vampires dissolved. As simply as that.

They collapsed into billowing clouds of dust that turned amber in the light of the street lamps filtering down through the grating above.

Here and there, ribs, femurs, jawbones jutted up through the mounds of powder.

The sudden silence was all but overwhelming.

David looked up, his head still echoing to the sound of the creatures' mournful cries as they slowly became fainter, more attenuated, as the reverberations faded away into the tunnels to die somewhere under the town.

Perhaps they cried for a future that now would never be. A future where the vampire inherited the Earth. All that was lost to them now. The vampires had failed.

He shook his head, mouth gritty with the airborne dust of those dead things" bodies. That dust settled on his lips in a noxious layer; it grated against his teeth.

Slowly, wearily—achingly wearily—he looked up. Bernice stood, holding out her hand. He took it.

There was no need to run now.

At their feet lay the body of Maximilian Hart; his eyes were closed as if in sleep. Probably the man would never have a headstone, David thought; but if there was any justice in this sometimes lonely and often unfair world, Maximilian Hart *would* have his headstone: a huge one carved from granite that stood higher than all the rest. And beneath the name MAXI-MILIAN HART should be a word so deeply carved that it would never be faded by time, nor cracked by frost, nor worn away by storms. And that word should be:

HERO

Then, tightly gripping Bernice's hand, David walked away.

It Ends In Darkness

1. One Year Later

A year to the day after George Leppington's funeral, the three of them—Bernice Mochardi, David Leppington, Electra Charn-wood—gathered for dinner at the Station Hotel.

Spring had already pushed winter into its northward retreat for another few seasons. The leaves of hawthorn and willow on the river banking were unfurling with a fresh, newborn greenery. There were starling chicks, speckled and somehow scintillat-ingly fresh-looking, chirruping noisily in their nests. A big mother cat padded across the hotel courtyard followed by four kittens that were a plump and fluffy ginger.

The sun had slipped down to rest on the hilltop; it turned the mackerel sky a golden color; the air grew still. A sense of peace and tranquillity was settling over the old town of Leppington as it wound down after another day. In the market square men in fluorescent yellow nylon waistcoats swept up the debris—knots of string, cabbage leaves, paper bags, newspapers. One sweeper noticed a camcorder tape lying in the bottom of a bin. The tape had been pulled so it had unspooled in a long tangle of shiny black. Whistling cheerfully, he tossed it into a skip with the rest of the rubbish. There was a label on the tape that bore the hand-written words: *VIDEO DIARY—ROUGH EDIT*.

2. Song For A Dead Hero

No one knows Jack Black's real name. No one knows where he came from, or who his mother and father were. And, with the exception of three people, no one knows that, like Maximilian Hart, Black died a hero.

Or that he died vampiric.

But now, with the two halves of his head buried separately from the two halves of the body, the remains are mortal enough; they rot in the earth like any man's. Although it should be said that those mortal remains don't lie in hallowed ground. Instead, the body lies on a windy hillside far away from town.

The head lies on the river bank, downstream from the Station Hotel, beneath a clump of weeping willow.

Sometimes Electra Charnwood visits the spot on the river bank where the head is buried. She watches the water foaming white around the boulders, feels the wind tug at her blue-black hair and envelop her body, and she wonders if this is nature's way of reaching out to embrace her.

Later, she'll sit on a fallen tree and gaze at the patch of soil that holds Jack's head. She cries freely now. Once in a while she'll scatter a handful of white petals on the river bank there. For in some parts of the world white flowers are a symbol of mourning.

Electra still wakes in the middle of the night, with the moonlight streaming in through the windows; often she senses a presence moving through the hotel. It moves with great speed, fluidly sweeping up the stairs to race along the corridor to her room. Then she'll sense it pacing beyond her locked door. Back and forth, back and forth, bare feet pressing down on that old red carpet.

She pretends that the presence is Jack Black. And that like an angel—a dark and somehow monstrous angel—he watches protectively over her, keeping her safe.

What she imagines may be an illusion; yet she holds the image of that dark and powerful guardian angel close to her and will never let it go.

And with that image in her head, of the presence walking back and forth forevermore beyond her bedroom door, she'll go contentedly to sleep, to dream, perhaps, of a night-borne lover who will never abandon her.

3. Unfinished Business

Bernice, Electra and David dined alone in the restaurant as they had done a year before. Then one of the kitchen staff had interrupted the meal to tell them there was a stranger at the back door. That stranger had been the tattooed and shaven-headed Jack Black.

This time they ate uninterrupted.

Electra sipped mineral water. When David offered her wine she shook her head and smiled. "No, thank you. The specialist at the hospital tells me that, against all odds, my liver is really in good shape." Her smile broadened. "I'm trying hard to be virtuous now." She poured a little more mineral water into the glass. "So, Bernice. You're not tempted to return to our blessed leech farm? I hear there's a vacancy."

Bernice shook her head; she smiled but there was a hint of sadness. "No, the job in London's permanent. I'm going to start looking for a flat of my own."

"A flat in London?" Electra gave a quiet laugh. "They must be paying you too much." She raised her glass. "Anyway, my dear. Here's to you. You deserve it." She turned to look at David. "And Dr. David Leppington. What about that post of general practitioner in our town? You will take it, won't you? Then you can come into the bar, recklessly disregard doctor-patient confidentiality and tell me all the really juicy gossip."

He smiled, then shook his head. "No. I'm taking a leaf from Bernice's book. I'm being lured away to the bright lights of London. There's a teaching post at the university hospital that really caught my eye."

She sighed. "It would have been nice to have the pair of you around. You know, last year, I'd grown accustomed to your faces." She paused, then the smile broadened. "Now, now . . .

both of you working in London? Have I missed something of significance here? David? Bernice?"

Bernice didn't answer. Her hands were shaking as she laid her knife and fork down across the uneaten food. "I came back here today for two reasons. One: did that *thing* really happen last year? Because sometimes I wake up and think I imagined it. And, two; is it really all over? Will they come back?"

David set his own fork down and looked back at her, his face serious. "Yes. It really did happen. I came into town yesterday and found I had to go back down into the tunnels. There's nothing down there, at least no trace of those things. And, no, I'm sure they never will come back."

Bernice relaxed with a sigh. "I just needed to find out. It had begun to prey on my mind. You know, sometimes I thought that we made this happen; that by coming together we created a kind of conjunction of personalities that somehow caused a shift in the status quo."

Electra nodded. "I'll go along with that. But I think it was our destiny. There was no escaping that the four of us would come together, and that those events would be played out; now I sense an inevitability—" she smiled "—a cosmic inevitability, if that doesn't sound too New Age, that we would become part of the drama; perhaps we are only chess pieces of the Gods after all. More wine, David?"

She refilled his glass. "So, if you're not taking that job as country doctor here, why have you returned to Leppington?"

He smiled. "Because you asked me, Electra."

"True; in my best copperplate writing, too, if I recall. But I think there was another reason for you coming. Apart from satisfying yourself that the tunnels under the town are deserted now."

"A recurring dream." He wiped his mouth on the napkin. "That's what brought me back here."

"A dream?"

"In this dream I saw myself taking the sword my uncle had made. I stood on the river bank and threw the sword into the water."

"And?"

David shrugged. "And what, Electra?"

She smiled. "No arm emerged from the water clad in white samite to catch the sword?"

He smiled back. "No. Nothing like that. Perhaps it's just a stupid dream after all."

Electra looked at him, her face becoming serious. "No, David. No dreams are stupid or ridiculous. What was it that Freud said? Dreams are the royal road to the unconscious? Clearly your unconscious is telling you that you've unfinished business here, David."

"Perhaps. I really don't know."

"Bernice," Electra said, dabbing her lips on the napkin. "The sword is on the top shelf in the Dead Box. Would you show David where it is, please?" Then, standing, she added, "And I just need to find something of my own."

4. Envoi

The sun was slipping toward the horizon when they gathered on the river bank behind the hotel. Already the crescent of the moon gleamed nickel-bright in the sky.

A large black bird, possibly a rook or a crow, circled high above them, as if watching what the three people down there by the river would do next.

David unwrapped the sword from the bed sheet. It was clean now. Electra must have washed it after he'd left on the day of his uncle's funeral.

Electra gazed down at the water as it cascaded over the boulders. "I'm a great believer in ceremonies, too." She held up a white envelope. "These were my return train tickets to London all those years ago. I never used them. But I kept them safe. They were my talisman to reassure me that one day I'd leave that big old pile." She glanced back at the hotel with its four solid towers standing against the sky. "That I'd go back to work in television." She gave a little smile. "I know that'll never happen now. I know my future lies here. That I'll grow old and die in Leppington." With that she threw the envelope into the water.

The current caught it and quickly bore it away in the direction of the sea that lay twenty or more miles from here.

David gazed at the sword. Although he told himself it must be the speed of his pulse in his thumb and wrist carrying the vibrations to the tip of the blade, it seemed to hum in his hand.

"Well . . ." he said, not sure whether or not he should make a speech. "I guess, for me anyway, this wraps it up."

With that he flung the sword into the middle of the river.

It seemed to hang there for a moment, as if suspended by an invisible thread above the water, the sharp tip of the sword pointing straight downward, so that the weapon formed an elongated cross. The blade reflected the dying rays of the sun.

Then, at last, the sword fell straight down into the water.

The splash must have disturbed a fish, a big fish at that, because David saw something long and silver dart just below the surface of the river. It sped upstream like a torpedo.

For a moment he allowed himself the illusion it was really the sword. And that, just below the surface of the water, the sword would fly along the course of the river, up through the town, up the hillside, smoothly weaving around rocks with the speed and grace of a salmon.

Eventually, the sword would slip silently up through the stream in his dead uncle's garden where it would vanish into the cave from where the waters of the source of the River Lepping tumbled. From there, the sword would speed down into darkness, into the very heart of the mountain.

And after that, it would pass from this world and into eternal mystery.

The black bird called out across the town, a long echoing cry that seemed to shimmer on the evening air. Then it wheeled high above them and glided across the hills and out of sight.

Electra stood on his left, Bernice on his right. With an unspoken harmony of feeling they linked arms with him.

There they stood and watched the sun slip down between a cleft in the mountain. For all the world it looked as if it was being swallowed by the jaws of a great wolf.

With the vanishing of the sun, the night, at long last, came to rest softly upon Leppington town.

SIMON CLARK
DARKER

Richard Young is looking forward to a quiet week with his wife and their little daughter. Firing up the barbecue should be the most stressful task he'll face. He has no idea of the hell that awaits him, the nightmare that will begin with an insistent pounding at his door.

The stranger begging to be let in is being hunted. Not by a man or an animal, but by something that cannot be seen or heard, yet which has the power to crush and destroy anything in its path. It is a relentless, pounding force that has existed for centuries and has now been unleashed to terrify, to ravage . . . to kill.

SIMON CLARK

Darkness Demands

Life looks good for John Newton. He lives in the quiet village of Skelbrooke with his family. He has a new home and a successful career writing true crime books. He never gives a thought to the vast nearby cemetery known as the Necropolis. He never wonders what might lurk there.

Then the letters begin to arrive in the dead of night demanding trivial offerings—chocolate, beer, toys. At first John dismisses the notes as a prank. But he soon learns the hard way that they're not. For there is an ancient entity that resides beneath the Necropolis that has the power to demand things. And the power to punish those foolish enough to refuse.

___ 4898-1 $5.99 US/$6.99 CAN

Dorchester Publishing Co., Inc.
P.O. Box 6640
Wayne, PA 19087-8640

Please add $1.75 for shipping and handling for the first book and $.50 for each book thereafter. NY, NYC, and PA residents, please add appropriate sales tax. No cash, stamps, or C.O.D.s. All orders shipped within 6 weeks via postal service book rate. Canadian orders require $2.00 extra postage and must be paid in U.S. dollars through a U.S. banking facility.

Name————————————————————————
Address—————————————————————————
City———————————— State———— Zip—————
I have enclosed $ ————— in payment for the checked book(s).
Payment must accompany all orders. ❏ Please send a free catalog.
CHECK OUT OUR WEBSITE! *www.dorchesterpub.com*

SIMON CLARK

Blood Crazy

Saturday is a normal day. People go shopping. To the movies. Everything is just as it should be. But not for long. By Sunday, civilization is in ruins. Adults have become murderously insane. One by one they become infected with a crazed, uncontrollable urge to slaughter the young—even their own children. Especially their own children.

Will this be the way the world ends, in waves of madness and carnage? What will be left of our world as we know it? And who, if anyone, will survive? Terror follows terror in this apocalyptic nightmare vision by one of the most powerful talents in modern horror fiction. Prepare yourself for mankind's final days of fear.

__4825-6 $5.99 US/$6.99 CAN

MOON
ON THE
WATER
MORT CASTLE

It's a strange world—one filled with the unexpected, the chilling. It's our world, but with an ominous twist. This is the world revealed by Mort Castle in the brilliant stories collected here—our everyday lives seen in a new and shattering light. These stories show us the horror that may be waiting for us around the next corner or lurking in our own homes. Through these disquieting tales you will discover a world you thought you knew . . . and a darker one you'll never forget.

RED

JACK KETCHUM

Fans and critics alike hailed Jack Ketchum's previous novel, *The Lost*, for its power, its thrills and its gripping style, and recognized Ketchum as a master of suspense. Now Jack Ketchum is back to frighten us again with . . . *Red*!

It all starts with a simple act of brutality. Three boys shoot and kill an old man's dog. No reason, just plain meanness. But the dog was the best thing in the old man's world, and he isn't about to let the incident pass. He wants justice, and he'll make sure the kids pay for what they did. They picked the wrong old man to mess with. And as the fury and violence escalate, they're about to learn that . . . the hard way.

SECOND CHANCE
CHET WILLIAMSON

You are invited to a party. A reunion of old college friends who haven't seen each other since the late 1960s. It should be a blast, with great music and fond memories. But be forewarned, it won't all be good. Two of the friends at the party weren't invited. In fact, they died back in college. But once they show up, the nostalgia will turn to a dark reality as all the guests find themselves hurled back to the '60s. And when they return to the present, it's a different world than the one they left. History has changed and the long-dead friends are still alive—including one intent on destroying them all.

FREE BOOK GIVEAWAY!

As a special thank you from Dorchester Publishing for purchasing *Vampyrrhic*, we'd like to give you a free copy of *Nailed by the Heart* by Simon Clark.

The Stainforth family believes the ancient sea-fort in a nice little coastal town is the perfect place to begin a new life, to start fresh. But they have no way of knowing that they've moved into what was once a sacred site of an old religion. And that the old god is not dead—only waiting. Soon the dead no longer stay dead and a nightmare is brought forth that can end only with the ultimate sacrifice.

PLEASE NOTE
You must submit proof of purchase for *Vampyrrhic*.
U.S. residents:
Please include $2.50 for shipping and handling.
All non-U.S. residents:
Please include $5.00 USD for shipping and handling.

Please mail all materials to:
Dorchester Publishing Co., Inc.
Department SC
276 Fifth Avenue, Suite 1008
New York, NY 10001

NAME: _____

ADDRESS: _____

_____

_____

PHONE: _____

E-MAIL: _____

Offer good while supplies last.